THE
Painted
DAISIES

Green
JEWEL

WRITER'S DIGEST AWARD WINNING AUTHOR
LJ EVANS

The Painted Daisies, Book II

Green Jewel

L J Evans

This book is a work of fiction. While reference might be made to actual historical events or existing people and locations, the events, names, characters, places, and incidents are either the product of the author's imagination or are used fictitiously, and any resemblance to actual persons, living or dead, business establishments, events, or locales is entirely coincidental.

GREEN JEWEL © 2022 by LJ Evans

LJ EVANS BOOKS

www.ljevansbooks.com

Cover Design: © Emily Wittig
Cover Images: © Unsplash | weston m, Deposit Photos | VadimVasenin and Dekues, iStock| Punnarong, and Shutterstock | Alex Manders
Chapter Image: © iStock Vidok
Content & Line Editor: Evans Editing
Copy Editor: Jenn Lockwood Editing Services
Proofing: Karen Hrdlicka
Sensitivity Editor: Evans Editing, Kathryn Nolan

ISBN: 978-1-962499-12-5

Library of Congress Cataloging in process.

Playlist

https://spoti.fi/3fylO6M

Green JEWEL PLAYLIST

PROLOGUE NO BODY, NO CRIME BY TAYLOR SWIFT
CHP ONE THAT DAY BY NATALIE IMBRUGLIA
CHP TWO EVERYBODY'S A FOOL BY EVANESCENCE
CHP THREE THE LONGING BY IMELDA MAY
CHP FOUR IT'S TIME BY IMAGINE DRAGONS
CHP FIVE GLASS HOUSES BY STEEL MAGNOLIA
CHP SIX I WON'T LET GO BY THE BROTHERS BRIGHT
CHP SEVEN SHALLOW BY BRADLEY COOPER AND LADY GAGA
CHP EIGHT WICKED BY LEE ANN WOMACK
CHP NINE DARK SIDE BY BISHOP BRIGGS
CHP TEN WHAT'S IT GONNA TAKE BY SARAH MCLACHLAN
CHP ELEVEN FALLING SLOWLY BY GLEN HANSARD
& MARKETA IRGLOVA
CHP TWELVE THE DARK OF YOU BY BREAKING BENJAMIN
CHP THIRTEEN THIS IS NOT YOUR LOVE SONG BY SCARS ON 45
CHP FOURTEEN TRAIN WRECK BY SARAH MCLACHLAN
CHP FIFTEEN FADING BRIGHT EYES DARK BY SCARS ON 45
CHP SIXTEEN BROKEN BY SEETHER W/ AMY LEE
CHP SEVENTEEN FEVER BY PEGGY LEE
CHP EIGHTEEN CHANGE MY NEEDS BY SCARS ON 45
CHP NINETEEN WITHOUT YOU HERE BY THE GOO GOO DOLLS
CHP TWENTY CRAZY FOR YOU BY SCARS ON 45
CHP TWENTY-ONE BELIEVE IN LOVE BY SCORPIONS
CHP TWENTY-TWO DON'T LET ME STAND ON MY OWN BY
IMELDA MAY & NIALL MCNAMEE
CHP TWENTY-THREE LULLABYE (GOODNIGHT, MY ANGEL) BY BILLY
JOEL CHP TWENTY-FOUR DON'T LET GO BY BRYAN ADAMS
W/ SARAH MCLACHLAN
CHP TWENTY-FIVE HELP ME MAKE IT THROUGH THE NIGHT
BY BRYAN ADAMS
CHP TWENTY-SIX AIN'T NO GRAVE BY CROOKED STILL
W/ AOIFE O'DONOVAN
CHP TWENTY-SEVEN BLOOD ON MY NAME
BY THE BROTHERS BRIGHT
CHP TWENTY-EIGHT LOVE BESIDE ME BY SARAH MCLACHLAN
CHP TWENTY-NINE BARTHOLOMEW BY THE SILENT COMEDY
CHP THIRTY BEAUTY'S WILD RUNNING WILD BY SCARS ON 45
CHP THIRTY-ONE –TWICE BY CHRISTINA AGUILERA
CHP THIRTY-TWO ME AND MINE BY THE BROTHERS BRIGHT
CHP THIRTY-THREE LOVE IS ALIVE BY LEA MICHELE
CHP THIRTY-FOUR YOURS ALONE BY THE BROTHERS BRIGHT
W/ VALERIE MILLER
EPILOGUE LOVING YOU IS EASY BY SARAH MCLACHLAN

Dedication

For those brave enough to show the world who they really are,
and the families who hold them up in the light.

Prologue

NO BODY, NO CRIME
Performed by Taylor Swift

EIGHTEEN MONTHS BEFORE

> *FIADH: I hired you three weeks ago. What do you have for me?*
>
> *ANGEL: Patience.*
>
> *FIADH: You came to me. You offered to do this.*
>
> *ANGEL: Do you want the truth, or do you want conspiracy theories?*
>
> *FIADH: The truth.*
>
> *ANGEL: Then, patience.*

FIFTEEN MONTHS BEFORE

> *ANGEL: A money trail started around the time of Landry's murder. It's passed through several shell corporations. He's hiding something.*
>
> *FIADH: He actually paid someone…to…God, I can't even type it.*
>
> *ANGEL: This isn't a one-time payment. It's the*

same amount every month.

FIADH: To the baby momma, maybe?

ANGEL: There's no trace of her either since a year after the birth.

FIADH: So, you're telling me something happened to yet another woman he knew?

ANGEL: I'm saying she dropped out of view.

FIADH: Find her.

TEN MONTHS BEFORE

ANGEL: The ex's mother disowned her over a decade ago, and they've had no contact since. Former friends haven't heard from her in a few years, but they said she had an opioid problem. She could be anywhere now, which may be why there's no trail.

FIADH: What about the money in the shell corporations?

ANGEL: It disappeared. Some interested parties in the U.S. government are looking into it, but I'll find something before them.

FIADH: This is ridiculous. He's not a spy or some exclusive hacker. He's a businessman. A very rich businessman.

ANGEL: Money can buy you anything. Remember that. I don't say it often, but I think I'm wrong about him. I think we both are.

FIADH: *I know what I heard that night. He said, "It's done."*

ANGEL: *Which could have meant anything.*

FIADH: *You didn't see the look he gave me. All the looks that night. I'm not wrong.*

FOUR MONTHS BEFORE

ANGEL: *You won't be hearing from me again.*

FIADH: *What? Why?*

ANGEL: *You've turned this into a witch hunt.*

FIADH: *Fine. I'll start over with someone else.*

ANGEL: *No one will be able to do more than I did. I wanted this to be our guy. It was important to me as well.*

FIADH: *Why is that? You never told me why you even approached me.*

ANGEL: *It doesn't matter now. He's not the one.*

FIADH: *He was up to something! You never found the money trail or the kid's mother. If you're so good at your job, why didn't you find where they went?*

ANGEL: *I'm not going to hang a man without proof. I told you all along we'd do this one way. My way.*

FIADH: *Fine. I'll get the information myself.*

ANGEL: Exactly how do you plan on doing that?

FIADH: It's not your problem anymore.

FOURTEEN DAYS BEFORE

ANGEL: I might have found something.

FIADH: You said we were done. Why are you even still looking?

ANGEL: Because I encouraged you to start this, and I can't let you get hurt doing something stupid.

FIADH: I will find out the truth. I will find out who killed her, and if it's him, I'll bury him with my own shovel and hand it over to the cops when they come looking.

ANGEL: Wait to hear from me.

FIADH: In five days, I'm going with Plan B.

Chapter One

Fiadh

THAT DAY
Performed by Natalie Imbruglia

NINE DAYS BEFORE

Fiadh ran down the hotel hallway with her heart pounding as loud as her feet in her clunky Doc Martens. Fear, anger, and guilt blended together into a swell of emotions so large they compressed the air in her lungs until she was gasping.

Her bodyguard was on her heels. He'd barely said the awful words before she'd fled the room, desperate for one thing—to get to Paisley. Standing outside in the muggy air left over from the storm, she cursed the amount of time it took the detail to bring her a car. Once she was safely inside, nausea took over, making her wish she was anywhere but the back seat. Fee's body shook until it felt like it would implode, or explode, or some version of bursting.

God...I'm so sorry, Lan, Fiadh whispered silently to her dead friend. *I'm so sorry I couldn't keep your sister safe any more than I kept you.*

"How the hell did you all miss this?" Fiadh growled at the two men up front.

Chin shot his almost-black eyes in her direction and rubbed a hand over his shaved head. He was square and muscled and wore dark cargo pants and a black T-shirt that was the uniform for Reinard Security.

"There was no indication the stalker was anyone other than Artie Mason," he said, but Fee heard the frustration in his tone. She imagined they felt as pissed as she was. As sick to their stomachs.

Fee no longer had faith in any of them.

Landry had been killed while their last security company, the FBI, and the U.S. Secret Service hovered around them. And now...now Paisley had almost been kidnapped...attacked...

Her stomach churned again, bile burning its way up into her throat.

The only reason she wasn't at the same hotel as Paisley was because the people protecting them had sworn splitting them up would make it more difficult for the stalker to find them. What a joke. All it had really done was leave her friend—her sister—alone. Damn it, where had the rest of their detail been?

The SUV had barely rolled to a stop when Fee shoved open the door without waiting for her bodyguard. A cacophony of press burst into life outside the hotel as soon as her feet hit the sidewalk. A wall of questions was thrust at her. "Is it true there was another attack on the Daisies?" "Is Paisley Kim alive?" "Are you canceling the tour?"

The questions only made her chest tighten more. What were Paisley's parents going to say? The Kims had been through so much already. They'd been adamantly opposed to Paisley coming back on tour.

Chin jogged forward, shielding Fee from the bulk of the shouting and flashing lights as he guided her into the hotel lobby. Two men in dark suits stood in front of one of the elevators, and as soon as they saw Fee running toward them, they pushed the button, and the doors popped open.

Inside, out of breath, heart stammering, Fiadh caught her image in the reflection in the shiny metal door. She looked pale, the shadows of her hangover clinging to her. Her mahogany hair layered in lavender was a rat's nest of curls because Chin had woken her in order to tell her about the attack.

She was a mess—inside and out. Almost as bad as their manager. He'd been drunk or high almost twenty-four seven since Landry's death. Last night, Fee had allowed herself to get lost in alcohol as well because their first concert without Landry had been a brutal reminder of the gaping hole she'd left behind, ratcheting up the loneliness clinging to Fiadh even though she was back with the band. Heartache and sorrow hung over her so deep it bled through every vein.

Lan...

Fee bit her lip and clenched her jaw in an effort not to cry.

The elevator dinged open, and she saw the other bandmembers were already there, hovering outside the doors to the penthouse where Paisley and Jonas had been staying. They turned toward her, expressions as dark and worried as hers, as she sprinted down the hall to them. She pulled them in for a group hug, the emotions wafting through them so strong they almost vibrated in the air. Fear. Regret. Relief. Sadness.

"What are we doing out here? Where's Paisley?" Fiadh demanded as they broke apart. Adria, Leya, and Nikki were all tall and dark-haired, but it suddenly struck her how different they looked these days, whereas before, the band had played up their similarities.

Adria turned her gaze to the two bodyguards at the door. "They told us we couldn't see her until the FBI had debriefed her."

Rage spiked through Fee.

"Feck that," she said, her Irish accent coming out when normally she hid it well. She moved to face off with the men. "Let me in, or plan on getting a different job."

The two guards eyeballed each other, eyes shifting toward Chin and the other security team members standing behind the Daisies. It was the Secret Service agent assigned to Leya, due to her dad being the Vice President of the United

States, who broke the silence. "Let them in."

Fee barely had time to shoot him a grateful look before they all burst into the penthouse, calling Paisley's name.

They found her, locked in Jonas Riccoli's warm embrace, in the bedroom. He stepped away from her reluctantly, letting them surround Paisley with their love while he watched. Paisley was crying softly, her body shaking, and it brought another wave of tears to Fiadh's eyes that she barely held back. Leya let out a strangled sob, and Adria and Nikki were right there with her. Waterworks all around. When Fiadh's eyes met Jonas's, he started to step even farther away, but she caught him, pulling him into their circle.

He was one of them now. Not only because he and his friend had been the ones to storm the hotel room where Paisley had been held captive, but because he loved Paisley with all his heart. They were a family. Mixed-up, battered, and bruised, but together.

Relief and gratitude flew through Fee.

"Thank you for saving Little Bit," she told him.

He shook his head, causing his shaggy, dark-blond hair to fall into his vivid, green eyes.

"You need to start calling her Little Warrior instead of Little Bit because I guess she was already saving herself before we even got there." His deep voice was full of awe and adoration.

Paisley snorted from deep within their circle, her tiny frame dwarfed by the group. She was a good eight inches shorter than the rest of them and more than a foot shorter than Jonas.

Adria chuckled. "Little Warrior. It's perfect."

They all stood there, hanging on to each other for what felt like a lifetime.

Eventually, Fee stepped back with reluctance, and the bundle of limbs and love they'd become loosened. She assessed Paisley from head to toe for the first time, watching as she lifted an ice pack to a bump on her temple turning a ghastly shade of purple. Other than that, she looked okay. Her long black hair, straight and soft, swung around her face, drawing attention to her round eyes with lashes so thick they almost looked fake. Her skin, normally the palest of whites, was even more so, emphasizing the star-shaped birthmark by her eye she used to hide with a press of a finger.

Sometimes, it was difficult to look at Paisley without being stabbed in the heart, because she could almost be Landry's twin. A mirage that wavered until she spoke, breaking it. The band and the Kims had lost so much already. What would they have done if they'd lost Paisley too? The ache deep inside her grew.

"What happened?" Leya asked, and Paisley shivered.

Before she could answer, the door to the suite opened, and a pile of men and women in suits and various uniforms entered.

"You'll need to leave while we get statements from Paisley and Jonas," a man in a FBI windbreaker said, shooting a glance at Fee and her bandmates. "Where's Trevor?"

"I'm here," the blond-haired giant stormed into the room with his pale-blue eyes snapping unhappily. Fee's heart flipped with a mix of relief and anger. So many of the people in this room had failed them time and time again. But Trevor hadn't. He may not have saved Landry, but he'd saved Paisley. It wasn't quite redemption, but it was more than any of the others had accomplished.

Fee squeezed Paisley's hand as Jonas stepped up to link their pinkies together on her other side. "Are you going to be okay to do this now?" Fiadh asked her.

Paisley's chin came up, the soft and shy little girl she'd been when she'd joined the band at eleven years old disappearing behind a fierce façade that had once belonged to her sister. It simultaneously made Fee proud and sad. She wondered what Landry would think of the change.

"I'm okay, Fee. I just want to get this over with."

Fiadh shot a look over Paisley's head at Jonas, and he met her gaze with a steely one. He wouldn't let any of the idiots upset her more than she already was. No longer just the co-manager of their tour, Jonas was now Paisley's partner. Whenever they were in the same room, they gravitated to each other like magnets rejoining, snapping together as if their opposite poles had been built just for each other.

She hugged Paisley one more time and then followed the rest of the band and Leya's USSS agent out of the room and into another penthouse across the hall. Like the room they'd just left, the expensive suite was decorated as if it were a chateau in France instead of a hotel in New York. Antique furniture, gold filigree, and luxurious silks draped everywhere.

Adria leaned up against the French doors leading onto a balcony, her fingers steepling nervously. She didn't have her drumsticks in her hands, and those, more than anything, were what she used to stay calm at times like this.

"Ads, you okay?" Fee asked, perching on the arm of a couch.

This had to have brought back painful memories for Adria of that awful day when everything had gone to hell for the band. The same day Landry had died, Adria's sister had been kidnapped, and twenty months later, she was still missing.

Adria turned her bright-blue eyes back to Fee. She was the only one of the group who had eyes any color but a variation of brown. Her black hair was as straight as Paisley's and Leya's, but she'd added some choppy layers to it, so strands swung around her chin. While the layers suited her, Fee was certain she'd done it simply to reduce the chance of another mistaken identity ending with one of them dead.

Acid burned through Fiadh's stomach as memories of the night Landry had died assaulted her. The body bag...Paisley's raw sobs. Things she saw and heard repeatedly in her nightmares.

"I'm glad they caught him..." Adria trailed off.

"But?" Leya's black brows scrunched together.

"Landry's killer is still out there," Nikki finished for her. Her voice was heavy with a host of emotions. She pulled back the mass of onyx corkscrews that had settled around her face, glancing away as, for a moment, remorse settled over her features before it disappeared again.

Adria looked back at the bright sunshine beyond the windows. The sky was the complete opposite of the mood in the room. It should have been gray and shadowed just like them.

"There's no chance it's still Artie?" Leya asked, her eyes darting from one friend to the other and then over to the door where Special Agent Kent stood.

"They've cleared Arthur Mason," Kent said. With his light-brown hair, blue eyes, and wide shoulders, he looked like the epitome of the stereotypical captain of the football team. All American. All hero. "He has an alibi for the time of Landry's death."

Another thing the authorities had gotten wrong. Disgust filled her. Left to their own devices, she doubted any of them would ever solve Landry's murder. While they all agreed the murderer's skill in slashing Landry's and her bodyguard's throats in mere seconds was more assassin-like than hate-filled stalker, there'd been no movement on the case. Not a single suspect remained.

Except, Fee had one. A man she hated as she'd never hated another. The man who'd stood by coldly while the band had come apart. The man who'd spoken quietly and calmly into a phone, saying, "It's done," while his icy blue gaze had settled on Fee with disgust and contempt.

Asher Riggs had barely arrived in Grand Orchard on the day Landry had died. As the new owner of their label, he'd spouted nonsense about making the band smaller, eliminating some of them. Eliminating Fiadh. And then, it had been Landry who'd been gone.

"Whose room is this?" Fiadh asked as a sudden foreboding shifted over her spine. Her gaze met Kent's, knowing what he'd say before he spoke.

"Mr. Riggs's," Kent replied.

"Where is he?" she demanded.

"He and Tommy are handling the press," Nikki answered. "Don't start on Asher, Fee. We don't need it right now."

"Asshole-Asher, that's his name, remember," Fee groused.

No one responded. They couldn't because they all knew the truth. He was an asshole. He'd threatened to sue them mere weeks after Landry had been killed if they didn't finish the album and get the tour back on track. It was only after some intense negotiating that he'd agreed to wait this long. Twenty months... God, Landry had been gone for twenty months already.

Fee's throat bobbed as she tried to keep back her tears.

She looked around the room, focusing on the hatred that burned through her instead of the loss. None of her friends knew the deep, dark secrets Asher kept. And as ridiculous as it might have been to think the co-owner and president of Ridgeway Media Industries would hire a hitman to take out a band member, she knew to the very bottom of her soul he was guilty of something. Something that could have ended with Landry's death.

All she had to do was prove it. She had to move on to Plan B. She couldn't count on Angel any more than she could count on the failed authorities around them. Fee rose, heading toward the bedroom.

"Fee," Nikki's voice was pure warning, and her friend didn't even know what she had planned. She probably just thought Fiadh would swap his toothpaste for shaving cream.

The door of the suite swung open to reveal the asshole himself, along with their manager. Asher's gaze immediately landed on Fee, eyes narrowing, and she glared back, her body acutely aware of every move he made. His dark-brown hair was shaved slightly on the sides and longer on the top. Not one lock was out of place, as if even his hair was afraid to move and disappoint its owner. There was a hint of gray at his temples that seemed more pronounced these days. Like always, he wore an impeccably tailored suit cut to fit his wide chest and shoulders. The steel-gray made his cobalt-colored eyes stand out even more than they usually did.

His jaw ticked as they continued their stare-down. The chiseled lines, hard as stone, made him appear exactly like what she thought he was—a heartless, soulless creature. A mere statue of a human being.

"No one talks. Is that clear?" he commanded, eyes finally releasing her to take in the entire band. All his demand made Fee want to do was run out and find the nearest reporter just to spite him.

His gaze returned to her, scowling as if he could read her mind and daring her to challenge him. She crossed her arms over her chest and met his glower with one of her own. His eyes fell, taking her in, inch by inch, resting briefly on her diamond-studded nose ring before scrolling languidly downward. He scrutinized each tattoo wrapped around her arms and shoulders before returning to linger on the lines written across her chest just above her slouched black T-shirt. The neckline had shifted to reveal the swell of her breasts and edge of her black lace bra.

She hated the way her body burned everywhere his eyes landed almost as much as she hated the idea of him completely. Why him? Why did her body react to this damn man? Electricity flew between them like a live wire whenever they were in the same room together. Attraction she had no power to stop but refused to give in to either.

Asher Riggs was only thirty, but there was an aura around him that screamed dominance and submission. As if he was the male lion who'd easily win the battle for the pride, casting aside the former king with a mere flick of a paw. But she wasn't going to just stand by and let him take over. She wasn't one of his lionesses, ready to fall at his feet and do his bidding. She'd continue to do what she'd been doing since Landry's death—fighting to uncover the information she needed to bring him to his knees. She'd die before she stopped.

She dragged her eyes away from him and back to their manager, who'd made his way over to the bar in the hotel room. Tommy looked as he always did—as if he was an aging rock star instead of a music manager. His black hair was gelled into perfect spikes, and his sleeves of tattoos were on display under an artfully torn shirt layered with several pounds of gold chains dripping down to the ripped jeans he had on instead of his almost ubiquitous leather pants.

She frowned as Tommy tossed back one drink and poured himself a second with shaking hands. There'd been a few nights in the first weeks after Landry's death that Tommy and Fee had drowned their sorrows together. But she'd pulled herself together after that, determined to be there for Paisley and the Kims—the people who'd helped her get on her feet when her own family had abandoned her. But their manager... He'd just continued to derail.

"That's enough, Tommy," Asher growled.

Tommy looked over, startled by Asher's rebuke, and an awkward silence settled down in the room. Fee bit her lip. Normally, she would have snapped at Asher to mind his own damn business, but today, she held her tongue. Not only because she was worried about Tommy, but because of the plan she needed to enact.

There was a timer counting down above her now. She had until the end of the tour to discover the truth about him. After that, the band would be asked to re-sign with Lost Heart Records and Ridgeway Media Industries, and she had to have a solid reason to give her friends for why they shouldn't. Something more than Asher being the ultimate jerk.

She needed the truth. She needed to uncover all his dark secrets.

She'd tried Angel's way. She'd waited patiently.

There was only one thing left to do. It made bile rise in her throat and yet, perversely, filled her with excitement at the same time. Regardless, she had no other choice left.

She had to seduce her enemy.

Chapter Two

Fiadh

EVERYBODY'S A FOOL
Performed by Evanescence

Fiadh swiped another layer of liner on with shaking hands, determined to hide the dark shadows below her eyes with heavy makeup. She pulled her hair up, hiding it under a knit beanie while doubts flickered through her. After everything that had happened today, staying in was the better call.

A quiver of residual fear traveled through her just like it had all day whenever she'd thought about what Paisley had gone through. She'd almost fecking died.

And where had Fee been?

Passed out in her room. Hungover from the after-party and the emotional toll the concert had taken on them. She was sick and tired of doing nothing. Of leaving their fate in the hands of people who seemed unable to protect them from even one of their own.

If Landry's murder was going to be solved, Fee had to take matters into her own hands.

Which meant she had to go out tonight.

She was following the enemy.

She shimmied into tight black jeans and a sleeveless, black, lace top before pulling on her flare-heeled boots with oversized silver eyelets and buckles. It was a normal outfit for her, but she skipped the leather jacket with her green jewel daisy emblazoned on it to go with a simple jean one instead. It wasn't much of a disguise, but with her hair covered, she might be able to skip past all but the most rabid fans.

She shoved her I.D. and some cash in the pocket of her jacket and then stared down at her phone. She jotted off one last text.

> *FIADH: How are you feeling?*

> *PAISLEY: Tired, sore, relieved, and frustrated. All at the same time.*

Fee's chest was so tight she wasn't sure she could breathe. Maybe she should go over there and leave her plan for another night? But then she remembered Paisley had Jonas at her side. She didn't need Fee. So, instead, she tossed back a line that would hopefully make Paisley laugh or at least smile.

> *FIADH: Good thing you've got sex god Jonas there with you to pound out all those emotions.*

> *PAISLEY: *** eye-roll GIF ****

> *FIADH: Really, Little Bit, are you okay?*

> *PAISLEY: I will be. I wish it had been him, Fee. I wish I'd faced Landry's killer and watched him get arrested.*

The semi-permanent lump in Fiadh's throat grew to an almost painful level.

> *FIADH: We'll find him, Paise. I promise you.*

> *PAISLEY: What are you doing tonight?*

She hated lying to any of them, but if she told them the truth, they'd think she was off her rocker. And maybe she was.

FIADH: Watching old Benatar videos and deciding how to incorporate her look into my wardrobe.

PAISLEY: Funny you mention her. I've been playing around with some chords that make me think of her sound.

FIADH: Go make love to the sex god, Paise, and forget about the band and music for a night. Just revel in being here with us. With him.

PAISLEY: I love you.

Fee's throat bobbed again. Her bandmates were the only ones left in her life who said those words to her. She didn't truly belong to anyone anymore. Not even the Kims. They'd helped her get settled into her own apartment when her parents had walked away from her, but they hadn't taken her in and loved her as one of their own.

In some ways, Asshole-Asher had been right the day he'd insinuated the band didn't need her. No one really did.

Landry does.

The thought rang through her brain like a bell going off. Landry needed justice, and Fee wanted to find it for her. To bring peace to all of them.

Asher hadn't seemed surprised that Paisley's attacker hadn't been Landry's killer. Other than commanding the Daisies to keep their mouths shut, heads down, and out of the media's sights, he hadn't seemed perturbed by what had gone down on his watch at all.

He'd moved right on to business as usual, getting them to Boston for their first official concert stop and making sure this didn't give the band another excuse to derail his plans.

In fact, he'd been so unconcerned with what had happened that he'd arranged to go see another band tonight with Tommy. A group he was interested in signing under the Lost Heart Records label.

Cold-hearted bastard.

She brought up the CarShare app on her phone, ordered a ride, and then looked at herself in the mirror over the dresser one last time. She inhaled deeply before grabbing the vodka leftover from last night and walking out of the room. Chin stood by her door with his arms crossed and eyes alert.

"Going out, Ms. Kane? Shall I call for a car?"

Fiadh shook her head, plastered on the saucy smile everyone knew her best for, and swung the bottle in his direction. "No, just going down to Leya's room."

She'd been moved from her hotel to the bed-and-breakfast where Leya had been staying after the paparazzi had discovered her room number and flooded the hallway, waiting for her.

Chin started to follow her, but she waved him off. "After everything today, could you just stay and make sure the room is secure? Leya has Special Agent Kent with her, so I'll be good."

He looked uncertain.

"You can watch me walk down the stairs, how's that?" she asked, winking at him.

She was almost certain he flushed, and she sort of felt bad. He was new to the detail, and if he'd been around longer, he probably would have known not to let her escape.

She headed for the bed and breakfast's main stairwell, waving to Chin one last time before disappearing out of sight. She continued past the second-floor landing where Leya's room was, not even looking down the hallway for fear of making eye contact with any security. Instead, she kept a nonchalant, nothing-to-see-here look on her face until she hit the ground floor. Two guards stood outside the front door with their black outfits visible through the beveled glass. She ignored the entrance, easing her way toward the kitchen instead.

When the owners had shown her around earlier, she'd paid extra attention to the bathroom near the kitchen with a huge window overlooking the owner's quaint herb garden. She beelined for the room now, locking herself inside and sliding the window open. She pushed out the screen and stuck her head out. No sign of security on this side of the house. She knew they patrolled the perimeter, so she'd be lucky if she had a minute or two before a guard appeared. She slithered over the wood casing and landed with a thump amongst the plants.

She held her breath, waiting for someone to come running, and when they didn't, she slipped along in the shadows. This was the tricky part—getting out of the backyard and onto the street without someone seeing her. She ducked behind a tree just as a dark figure rounded the corner, his earpiece squawking. The voices sounded panicked. *Shit.* She'd already been missed.

The bodyguard headed away from her, and she quietly and swiftly pulled herself up over the low fence into the neighbor's yard. There, she eased out the gate. On the street, she ducked her head and walked quickly along the sidewalk, but not so fast as to draw eyes. She rounded another corner with a sigh of relief, watching as the car she'd ordered got closer.

A smile, real this time, lit up her face as she slid into the back seat.

She hadn't had that much fun ducking out since she and Landry had done it as teens. While the Kims' quiet home in a gated community had made it almost impossible to escape unnoticed, it had been easy to leave hers. Her parents were always too busy with the chaos of her younger siblings to realize they were gone. She and Landry had seen a whole host of live shows before her parents had caught on and put a kibosh on it.

"That was for you, Lan," Fee whispered and felt a calm come over her that she'd been missing ever since finding out Paisley had been attacked.

A few minutes later, the driver stopped outside a club on a street busy enough to allow her to feel safe but not so busy it would increase her chances of being identified. The bar's neon-pink sign blazed down, spreading a dream-like hue onto the small line of people waiting to get in.

She kept her face averted, nose buried in her phone, until she'd reached the front. Thankfully, the bouncer hardly glanced at her I.D. before waving her inside. The lights were low, a country anthem blared from the band onstage, and the tables buzzed with energy. The dance floor was packed with people line dancing, clapping and tapping to the beat.

With an internal eye roll, she realized there was no way she'd blend in here. Her purple-and-red hair, black Docs, and tattoos stood out in the mass of jeans, plaid shirts, and cowboy boots.

She scanned the tables, looking for Tommy and the Asshole, but couldn't find their manager's spiked hair anywhere. Her chest tightened, hoping he hadn't done something stupid that had sent both men back to their hotels early.

The song came to an end, and a round of applause broke out. The band thanked the crowd, taking a quick break before diving into another song. The sea of people on the dance floor parted, and that was when she saw him. Her stomach gave a delicious little flutter she shoved back into the dark recesses of her soul.

He was in a booth at the back, glass in front of him, and his phone in his hand. Every time the Asshole had ever looked in her direction, there'd been a frown on his face that took his full lips and flattened them out, so it was a surprise to see a soft smile curving them upward as he looked at the screen. The quiver in her belly grew, pulse hammering. The grin transformed him from a stonelike statue into an approachable human being. It took him from handsome to beautiful. If Jonas was a sex god, then Asher was a titan. A deity above the rest. Even hating him, she could acknowledge how perfect he was. She was sure it was what had allowed his misdeeds to go unnoticed by others. A disguise, almost like the one she wore every day.

Unwanted curiosity filled her. What could possibly have made the grumpy, cold-hearted bastard smile like that? She pushed aside the thought, heart skipping several beats as she eased her way not to his booth but to the bar. She wanted him to think he'd seen her first. Wanted him to hunt her down so he believed he was in charge—just the way he liked it.

She elbowed her way to the front and caught the eye of a blue-haired bartender with vivid pink lips. She asked for a lemon martini, and the bartender squinted at Fee as if trying to place her. Fiadh looked away, hoping she'd maintain her cover for a few more minutes.

When the woman came back with her drink, Fee slid some cash her way, saying, "Keep the change."

As she started to leave, the bartender stopped her with a flirtatious smile. "This might not be your scene, but there's a bar down the street called Kay Jay's. I'll be there in an hour. There's a punk-rock band playing tonight."

The woman was pretty and confident, which was normally Fee's catnip. But tonight, a lion was calling to her. A lion she had no desire to lose herself to but had every intention to seduce. If she got close enough, she could get into his room, his phone, and his life. She could find out the truth. She would do it. For Landry.

"Thanks," Fee said, returning the woman's wink with a large smile. "I'll think about it."

Fiadh headed toward the dance floor, and she knew the minute the Asshole spotted her because she felt the ripple of his gaze like a touch. It scorched her from head to toe, just like it did every single time he looked her way.

She ignored it, pulling off the beanie, and stuffing it into a pocket of her jacket that she tied around her waist. She dragged her finger through her curls and swallowed her drink in a couple of gulps. The band broke into a slow song. It was sensual and sexy and just the right thing to torment one Asher-fucking-Riggs. She turned to the man standing next to her. He screamed cowboy from the huge gold buckle at his waist to the boots on his feet and the pearlescent buttons on his shirt.

Fee touched his shoulder gently and gave him her very best come-home-with-me smile. "Wanna dance?"

The man's eyes widened a little, taking in the spirals of burgundy, her shoulders and chest on display, and the tattoos wrapped around her body before landing back on her face.

"Sure, darlin'," he said.

She put her hand in his and led him onto the floor. They moved together slowly, legs tangling, hips sliding against each other's. His hands found her ass and pushed her against him tighter. It was overly friendly, but she'd known what she was getting into when she'd asked him onto the floor, just like she'd known she wasn't his type. She wasn't someone he'd bring home to Mama, but she was someone he'd fuck.

She tried not to look in the Asshole's direction, pretending she didn't know he was here. But once they'd spun around, her eyes flitted to his booth only to find it empty. Her partner had just slid his palm underneath the hem of her top at the back when a large hand landed on his shoulder.

"Remove your meat hook," Asher's deep voice was low and threatening. It sent unwanted tingles through Fee.

"Excuse me?" the man asked, feet stalling as he took in Asher's frown and wide stance. Fee hadn't noticed when he was at the table, but he wasn't in a suit or any of the business apparel she'd come to associate with him. Instead, he was in jeans and a T-shirt, blending into the country bar twenty million times better than Fee. Only the Salvatore Ferragamo dress shoes on his feet didn't fit.

Asher ignored the man as his cold gaze landed on hers, holding it. Anger simmered in the depths.

"Where's your detail?" he demanded.

Her dance partner quickly caught up to the fact that there was more going on than just some random guy interrupting them, and he took a step back. "Sorry, darlin', I have no desire to get into a fight tonight, but thanks for the dance."

Then, he practically ran.

"What a jerk," Fee breathed out.

Asher's eyes narrowed. He grabbed Fee's wrist and all but hauled her off the floor. If this hadn't been what she wanted, Fiadh would have put up a fight. She would have dragged her booted heels and even made a scene. But this—Asher pissed and coming after her—it was exactly what she needed. Maybe even craved in some sick way. Not only because her body seemed to love his touch but because she wanted to expose him, and making him lose his control was the only way she could think to do it.

He all but tossed her into the booth he'd been at, sliding in next to her and blocking the exit. He stabbed at his phone and barked into it, "Tommy, what the hell is Fiadh doing at a bar without her detail?"

The growl of her name pronounced so perfectly, just as it was supposed to be—like Thea with an F—and with a hint of an accent only her family had ever done, made her chest ache. Made her miss her mom, her siblings, and even her dad in a way she hadn't allowed herself to do in a long time.

Whatever Tommy's answer was, Asher didn't like it.

"I'll bring her back, and then I want the person at her door fired."

"You can't fire Chin!" Fee exclaimed, anger finally filtering through the lust, longing, and loneliness. "You have no right. Our security detail has nothing to do with you."

He hung up on Tommy and turned his arctic gaze to her.

"I have every right. I'm the person footing the bill."

"Not for the detail. That's personal."

He laughed, and it was cold and disdainful. The anger she'd seen in his eyes on the dance floor had been carefully tucked away. "Who told you that?"

She crossed her arms over her chest and said, "The bill I get every month told me, Asshole."

His eyebrows lifted, but his gaze flitted to her breasts before returning to her face.

"That's only half of their actual cost. Do you even read the contracts you sign? The label has been picking up fifty percent since before The Red Guitar Tour." Condescension dripped from his voice.

His arrogance shouldn't turn her on any more than his manhandling had. And yet...she was turned on. Suddenly, she felt in over her head, as if she might drown, and it caused a wave of panic to flow through her. She shoved at him, trying to push him out of the booth so she could get out, but he didn't budge. His large shoulders and muscular frame made him exactly the statue she'd imagined him to be.

"I came here to dance, not be some wallflower like you. Let me up," she insisted, trying to keep the quiver out of her voice.

He scoffed. "I don't think you can call a man a wallflower."

His look flickered over her again, the blaze returning, but it wasn't anger she saw as his eyes narrowed in on her mouth. The heated gaze made her chest spin and her pulse leap. At least she knew the stupid attraction was mutual. She could use it to get what she wanted. What she needed. What Landry needed.

She pushed aside her panic and pasted on her smartass smile.

"Wall." Fee pointed to the wood paneling she was tucked up against. "Sitting." She pointed to the booth and then to him. "Not dancing. Isn't that the epitome of a wallflower?"

"I'm not here to dance."

"You're here to check out the band," she said, and his eyes squinted. She held her breath. *Crap.* She'd wanted it to have been some random coincidence that they'd met up. "Where'd Tommy go, anyway? I thought he'd be here?"

She played it off with a toss of her curls.

"Because Tommy would dance with you?" he asked, expression turning impossibly colder as disapproval radiated from him. "He's old enough to be your father."

"I wouldn't be screwing him. I'd be dancing with him. One doesn't always lead to the other."

He looked back out at the dance floor where the cowboy she'd been with had found another partner. The way the couple was shimmying and shifting made it clear how their night would end.

"Your partner disagrees," he said dryly.

Asher's thigh was tight against hers from when she'd tried to push herself out of the booth, and the heat of it bled into her. The scent of him, something earthy and yet citrusy, was a sensual combination filling her senses. Every synapse in her body was on alert, leaning toward him, wanting to taste him. Wanting him to taste her. It made what she was here to do easier and harder because she couldn't afford to let her natural attraction make her forget the truth.

He was the enemy.

Chapter Three

Asher

THE LONGING
Performed by Imelda May

Asher felt every single millimeter of where her body was pressed against his. The heat was almost ungodly. Devilish. Which was exactly what she was, tempting him as he hadn't been tempted in years. He wanted to devour her, peel back every tough layer and saucy look and find the real Fiadh beneath it. The one he'd seen backstage in Korea.

He'd agreed to the concert after closing a deal with his Korean distributor. They'd practically begged him to go, and Asher had expected to hate every moment of it. But watching the band—her—had put the idea in his head to expand RMI into the music industry. When his business partners had used their backstage passes to meet The Painted Daisies, he'd stepped away and watched from the shadows, eyes drawn immediately to Fiadh and the glow that seemed to emanate from her.

She'd taken a call, and her face had turned soft, eyes crinkling and lips quirking. One side of her mouth had gone up slightly higher than the other, completely fascinating him in a way that screamed danger. Observing her, he'd been overwhelmed with the same feeling he'd had the day Wren had been placed in his arms. Like his life had shifted.

Then, one of the crew had called her name, and everything soft and sweet had disappeared from her face, returning to the fiery flame the world knew as Fiadh Kane. Her smile had grown larger, the sides evening out. He'd known then, and every time he saw her smile since, that her large one was her fake one. That night, not even knowing her, he'd ached to have the small one back.

To this day, he'd never seen it again. Not a single time.

It definitely wasn't there now as she sat, arms crossed, next to him, pushing the swell of her breasts up over the top of her indecently see-through top. She wasn't smiling, but she still knew exactly what she was doing—how her body was sending coded messages to his. She was using it to get her way. What she didn't realize was he knew every game women played and had become immune to them long ago.

Liar, his brain screamed as the feel of her body lined up against his threatened the control he prided himself on.

"I'm finishing my drink, and then I'm taking you back to the hotel. The hotel you should never have left after today's events," he told her calmly. It was a challenge to keep every ounce of growl and snarl out of his voice. But he was practiced at showing an unemotional face to the world while his insides churned. He had to be. Otherwise, it only aggravated the other temptress in his life.

"Maybe that's exactly why I need to be here," she said. "To forget what happened. To silence the constant loop in my brain screaming how I almost lost Paisley too." Her voice cracked at the end, and damn if that didn't flip his insides more. He gritted his teeth, determined not to let her emotions affect him.

He'd long ago learned exactly what tears could do. They broke down your shield, allowing the person inside, where they festered and grew until they stabbed at all your weak spots and left you bleeding. Every man in the history of the Riggs family was familiar with it. But Fiadh would never get inside him. She'd never earn the right to his feelings.

"Fucking your way through your grief won't help you feel any better in the morning," he replied dryly. He knew this for a fact because he'd watched the failed attempts of others as they tried to do just that.

A flare of knowledge hit her eyes, making him regret the words that had revealed something even as he'd tried to hold back. She'd slid past his defense with her cherrywood scent and curls he ached to touch.

"Is that what you think?" she asked. "That I'm denying my grief just because I'm not hiding it in cold stoicism like you?" When he didn't respond, she kept going. "The cruel reality of grief is that it's unique to each person. A solitary journey. Some people demand to be cocooned in warm embraces, while others rant and rave and storm. Some people try to solve all the issues and control the death. Some people retreat into an apathetic void where they grieve internally and privately. Others lose themselves in their daily routine, keeping going as if nothing has changed. And then, there are those who need to be alone, and if you touch them, they'll break and shatter and not be able to be put back together again."

She inhaled sharply, as if debating whether to go on, and then, in typical impetuous Fee way, continued. "That doesn't mean any of those people aren't grieving properly. The doers. The stoppers. The criers. The ranters. The loners. The extroverts. They're all mourning. They're all fighting to figure out how to keep the last remnants of the precious thing they've lost. Don't judge me for how I grieve, or the person who is making twenty meals, or someone staring out at the sunshine, wondering why it's not raining. We all have to process and heal in our own way."

She reached for his drink and took a sip, leaving her mark on the glass, and he felt it low in his groin and high in his chest, as if her mouth had landed on him.

"That stupid saying that time heals all wounds may be true," she said. "But in the meantime, we hide behind scabs and scars and layers of cotton gauze until we find our way back to breathing again."

Asher watched as her eyes flashed. Watched as the fiery shell that was Fiadh Kane cracked just a bit and gave him a glimpse of the soft underbelly she hid from the world. He suddenly found himself wanting to know what had happened to make her retreat just like he had. His shell was a cold, heartless bastard. Hers was a passionate, saucy dynamo.

What would they look like without their layers? Without the scabs and cotton gauze?

Fee took another deep breath, this one pushing the swell of her breasts upward and making his entire body rock hard in two seconds. It wasn't just from the way she looked or the way she smelled. It was because she'd shared a little piece of herself. A piece he couldn't afford.

She looked down at his glass of scotch she'd taken a sip from, picked it up, and downed it. Then, she met his gaze with a hard one, her walls back up, and said, "I need to dance."

She pushed against him again, and he almost caved. He almost let her up so she could find a way out from underneath her grief by dancing and screwing and forgetting the weight of her anguish for even two seconds. Then, he glanced at the crowd and the men making their moves, and he knew there was no way he could sit here and watch her while she was wrapped in someone else's arms. Not if he wanted to walk away from tonight without hitting someone. Without losing the cool he prided himself on. That not even Nova was able to break. Not anymore.

"No," he grunted out.

Her face contorted into fury. "It's what we do best, right? Us women rock stars? Shake our pretty little asses. It's what you told us to do when you demanded we hold this 'practice' concert before we were ready."

His eyebrow arched, remembering the words he'd tossed at her in the bar in Grand Orchard as they'd celebrated finishing the album. He'd been watching her and Leya as they'd moved their bodies sensually together on the crowded floor. It had made him hard and uncomfortable, just like now, which had made him angry at himself for the damn electric current drifting between them. He'd tossed the words out, knowing they'd piss her off and that her reaction would then turn him off.

Except, it hadn't. Just like all of her emotions tonight were doing nothing except making him want her more.

He didn't respond nor did he move, and she pushed at his arm again.

"You ass. You don't get to control what I do. Either you let me find a dance partner or take me out there yourself."

Her eyes widened as if she couldn't believe the suggestion had slipped from her mouth. And hell if it wasn't tempting, but he knew better. In his current state, if he had his arms wrapped around Fiadh, it would become obscene in two seconds. He'd have her hips slammed against his, his fingers in those damn curls, and his lips would devour every inch of her.

As if she'd read his mind, her gaze drifted to his mouth. She whispered breathlessly, "I think we should dance."

He didn't even bother replying. He wasn't dancing with her. Couldn't.

Asher's fingertips dug into his thighs with the effort of not touching her.

"Maybe if we did, we'd stop hating each other," she offered with a small shrug, and it was clear she was talking about more than dancing.

He dragged his gaze from hers, searched the room for the waitress, and raised his chin in her direction. The waitress scrambled over.

"Can I get you another?" she asked.

"Just the check," he said.

The waitress looked at Fiadh, eyes widening slightly, and then she scurried off to the POS system. As she typed in his order, she kept glancing back at the booth while jabbering at another waitress. When the second woman turned in their direction, he knew they were screwed.

Asher turned to Fiadh and growled, "Put the damn beanie back on."

"Excuse me?"

"You've been recognized. Put it on." He stood up, took a wad of cash from his wallet that was triple what his scotch cost, and threw it on the table.

She still hadn't moved.

"Fiadh, get your ass up, put the beanie on, and help me get you out of here before we have a mob at the table."

Fee glanced at the waitress and the little crowd forming around the computer screen. She swallowed hard, fished out her beanie, and attempted to tuck her waves away. He leaned in, pushing some of the escaped curls underneath the edge. Electricity zipped along his fingers, the tendrils softer than he'd ever imagined, her skin a satiny embrace. Her lips parted, their eyes locked, and something in his chest let go, bursting into an inferno that was more than desire. Every tormented emotion he'd ever felt and kept hidden seemed to swell through him. His thumb landed on her lower lip, brushing it, the sensation of the velvety plushness going straight to his balls.

Goddamn. He'd never wanted someone like this—as if not having her would be the thing that destroyed him rather than if he did.

She nipped at his thumb, and it sent a shock wave down him.

"They're coming," she said, head tilting toward the waitresses.

Asher searched for an escape route. The back hallway to the bathrooms had a neon emergency exit sign glowing at the end.

He gripped her arm, all but yanking her from the booth, and pushed her in front of him down the darkened corridor smelling of beer and sweat and urine. He didn't slow down, not even when they reached the door almost simultaneously and his body engulfed hers. When he shoved it open, the back of her brushed against his aching front, and she stumbled as if realizing exactly what she'd felt.

Asher ignored the hard-on, urging her forward again until they were both in a back alley that smelled worse than the hallway. He wrapped his hand around her wrist and hauled her toward the street and the bright lights. The noise of the city burst around them—car engines and drunken laughter.

Fiadh ducked her head, looking down and shifting closer to him as if she'd suddenly realized what would happen if even one of the intoxicated revelers recognized her. It pissed him off, sending the waves of lust spiraling into the background. She'd been stupid to come here by herself. To duck her security. And for what? A drink? A dance? A fuck? Tommy?

The last thought filled him with a sudden desire to fire the man.

He was already on Asher's shit list because every time he saw him, he was inebriated or as high as a kite. Tommy Barbados had once been one of the most desired music managers in the industry, but now he needed rehab.

When they reached the midnight-silver Tesla Roadster he'd driven up from Boston, he pressed a button, opened the passenger door, and all but tossed Fee inside, much like he'd flung her into the booth. Just like inside, she let out a surprised huff that he ignored.

He stormed around to the other side, got in, turned the car on, and zipped out into the traffic. Horns honked around him, but he didn't give a shit. He needed to get her back to the hotel and out of his space before he did something he'd regret. Kill her. Kiss her. Kill her by kissing her.

"So, you're an asshole in everything you do, including driving?" she said.

"I'm the asshole?" He risked looking at her and saw the beanie had fallen back, sending her purple and mahogany curls dancing around her face.

She looked offended. "Are you implying I'm an asshole in some way?"

He snorted. "You tell me. You're the one who ditched your security to go dancing in some random bar on the same night your friend was attacked and nearly murdered. Seems like a selfish, asshole move to me."

It wounded her. He could tell because she flinched. But better he wound her than let her get under his skin. She looked away from him, out the window, as the streets went by in a blur.

"Paisley didn't need me tonight. She had Jonas," she said quietly.

His jaw clenched. He would not feel sorry for her. He would not let the little wounded ache he heard in her tone squeeze inside his cracks.

"What about your other friends? This had to have brought back pretty strong memories for Adria. You ever think maybe one of the others might need you? Of course you didn't, because all you were doing was thinking about yourself."

"You don't know shit about my motives for going out tonight," she stormed, facing him again instead of the window.

"Your little rant at the bar told me everything. You wanted to grieve—your way."

"What I was doing tonight had nothing to do with me and everything to do with Landry!" Her voice broke again, and when he glanced over at her, she looked frazzled, as if she'd said one too many things.

Asher's eyes narrowed, goosebumps going over his skin as something skittered at the edges of his mind. "What does that mean?"

He could feel her gaze on him as he navigated the streets.

Her voice was suddenly calm and cool and almost deadly with promise as she said, "I will find out who killed her. I will find them and make them pay if it's the last thing I do. That's what I can do for Paisley. For the band."

He frowned. "You thought he was there? Tonight? Or were you baiting him? To come after you?"

She didn't respond, and he couldn't tell if it was anger

or fear threatening to burst from him. He thanked God when the bed-and-breakfast finally came into view. He skidded to a stop in front of it, slammed the car into park, and turned to face her.

"You're not serious right now, are you? Paisley almost died today! The last thing this band—this label—needs is another dead Daisy. What the hell were you thinking?"

"Like you care," she sneered. "There were too many of us in the band anyway, right? We're down to five. One more dead Daisy means you're at four. Would that be the perfect number for you?"

"What the fuck are you talking about?" he growled.

Her eyes narrowed. "That night we met in Grand Orchard, you told me six women leads were too many."

Asher's chest tightened as he tried to recall his words. Six women were too many. For him. For his life where women had done nothing but stab and steal and tear enormous holes in his soul. But had he said that to her about the band? He'd thought it, wondering if they really needed all the members or if some were just coasting on the talented coattails of the others. Now, after having watched them in the studio and onstage multiple times, he could see they each had a unique role, a unique sound they brought to the band. The space Landry had left behind hadn't been filled completely. Nikki had taken up the slack, picking up Landry's vocals and lead guitar, and the bassist they'd hired had backfilled her, but it wasn't the same. The band was incredible, maybe even better than before, but there was still an element missing without Landry there. It had proven that none of them could be lost without affecting the whole.

Fiadh, with her fiery looks, tantalizing Irish accent, and range of instruments would be the hardest shoes to fill after Paisley. And that was only because Paisley wrote their songs. Adria was one of the best woman drummers on the planet, so she'd be difficult to replace, but not impossible. The Indian instruments Leya played would take some serious luck to try and replenish. Out of everyone, Nikki's talent on the guitar would be the easiest to find. But getting someone with the husky tone she had—that Landry had once had as well—still wouldn't be a picnic.

The band was refreshing and successful because of how they came together.

Asher didn't remember saying the words, but if he had, it would have been for the same reason he'd snarled about her shaking her ass onstage. As retaliation for the way she'd assaulted him by just being in the same room. He'd been personal when he never was. Seeing Fiadh knocked him for a loop every damn time, just like it had the first time in Korea. She shredded his self-control, filled him with a desire that burned away at his insides until there was nothing left but flames.

So, he was an asshole instead.

Fee's bodyguard approached the car, looking as pissed as Asher felt.

Asher closed his eyes and gripped the steering wheel so he wouldn't be tempted to yank her to him and soothe away her anger and hurt and grief just like she'd been wanting someone to do tonight. It would be better if she thought he was unfeeling and cruel. Just like it would be better if he kept thinking she was a selfish woman, because the alternative was a disaster.

"Get some sleep, Fiadh. And don't dodge your security again, or so help me God, I'll strangle you myself."

She jerked open the door and stomped out. Then, she ducked her head back in and said, "You're not my dad, my manager, or my friend. You don't get to tell me how to live my life. You're the money. That's it. And after this tour is up, you won't even be that."

She slammed the door, and his heart raced.

They weren't going to sign with Lost Heart Records again?

Fuck.

If he lost them, the label would crumble. There'd just be Brady O'Neil left as the big ticket, and he was pretty sure

O'Neil felt the same damn way about him as Fiadh did. Asher's dad and the RMI board were ready to wash their hands of the two music labels after the clusterfuck they'd both been since bringing them onboard. They'd almost lost millions in the lawsuit with Ziggy and the Serpents. They couldn't afford for Lost Heart Records' two largest artists to walk away.

Asher couldn't fail. Not now. Not only because he never failed, not only because he was determined to see the company his great-great grandfather had started survive into the next century, but because he wanted his dad to hand him the chief operating officer position he'd earned. He'd do anything to make sure he got the labels back on track, even if he had to manage The Painted Daisies' every move himself.

An idea hit him as he watched Fiadh sway her way inside the front door. It was smart and foolish all at the same time because it meant Fiadh Kane would be too close, but it might just save everything. He hit the gas pedal, barreling out onto the quiet street and heading for Tommy's hotel.

Chapter Four

Fiadh

IT'S TIME
Performed by Imagine Dragons

EIGHT DAYS BEFORE

It was the first time they'd been on their tour bus in over two years—since their Red Guitar Tour. As Fee climbed onboard, memories of Landry assaulted her everywhere she looked. It felt as if Lan's presence hovered at the edges of her peripheral vision. Maybe it was. Maybe she was sitting, disapproving and grouchy, beside Jonas and Paisley who were huddled together. Or maybe she was sneaking a peek at Paisley's phone full of lyrics they were both staring at. Or maybe she was goofing off by dancing on the bed in the back in a rare lighthearted moment.

Fee swallowed hard, forcing a smile on her face. "Did you get any sleep, Little Bit? Or did the sex god keep you busy?"

Paisley turned a deep shade of pink, and Jonas's ears turned red. It made Fee chuckle.

"You're one to talk," Leya said from where she was sprawled on the couch next to the lovebirds, her feet almost touching Paisley. "Isn't that why you snuck out last night? For some nookie?"

"What?" Paisley's head jerked up, dark-brown eyes meeting Fee's. "You ditched your security?"

There was a tone to Paisley's voice that was all Landry these days. Strength. Leadership. As if the youngest member of their band, by a good five years, had suddenly become the oldest. She ignored Paisley's question, latching on to Leya's comment in order to keep the mood light.

"Nookie, Leya? Really? Your sexual self really is twelve years old. What happened with the guy you were supposedly going to marry? How the hell is it you haven't gotten down and dirty with him?"

Leya grimaced, and Fee noticed how tired she looked. Exhaustion had layered itself over all of them like a second skin. "Vodka at its worst. I should never have told you the stripper in Vegas was the first time I'd seen a man's junk," Leya pouted.

Fee forced a laugh as worry for all of them grew inside her. "You're avoiding my question."

Leya gave a half-smile. "I still plan on marrying him. But it's never been that way between us."

It was impossible to keep her grin as the truth of Leya's words hit her. "Why would you agree to marry someone if you didn't have those kinds of feelings for him?"

"Respect, tradition, family, and lust doesn't mean…forever," Leya said, but she shot an eye in Paisley and Jonas's direction, holding back everything she really wanted to say. Leya didn't believe love started with a pile of passion and sin. She thought you built it over time. Her family was a model for arranged marriages with her parents' marriage having survived the scrutiny of her father's political campaigns and three genius-level kids.

But Fiadh had born witness to great love and passion. She'd grown up watching her mom and dad's adoration for each other. It was so strong you could almost see it shimmering in the air around them. And sure, they'd fought as hard as they loved, but the only time they'd ever thought of ending their relationship was when they'd argued over Fee. She'd almost broken them, which was why she would never regret walking away so they could stay together. Her heart tightened at the little lie she'd almost convinced herself into believing.

Adria and Tommy climbed into the bus, and it took Fee's concern for Leya and wiped it away with a bigger one. Tommy had dark sunglasses on and looked worse than any of them. Worse than even the day before. God, he really needed help. She needed to say something to him privately, and if that didn't work, she'd have the band stage an intervention.

Fee sat down in one of the swivel chairs by a small folding table she'd spent an incalculable number of hours at on the last tour. Instead of Landry joining her in the chair opposite, their manager did. She tried to get his attention, but he purposefully avoided her gaze.

Adria sank onto a love seat, one drumstick already twirling through her fingers like a baton, the other tucked down the back of her tank top like a sword in a scabbard.

"How's your head, Paise?" Adria asked.

"I'm not going to lie. It hurts. But as Jonas and Ronan have similar bumps, I won't whine about it," Paisley said, worried eyes flitting to the man at her side.

Jonas had fought with the stalker after he'd shot at Paisley the day before he'd attacked her in the bathroom. He'd lost the man in a struggle and had a large knot on his head to show for it. Poor Ronan Hawk, who was just trying to finish his documentary on the Daisies, had been taken by surprise when the assailant had held him hostage in order to get to Paisley.

"Anyone hear from Ronan? Is he okay?" Adria asked. The true concern in her voice took Fee by surprise because Adria hated the film maker almost as much as Fee hated Asher. Fiadh just didn't know why. Another puzzle to unwrap, but it would have to wait because she could only handle one mystery at a time, and finding Landry's killer had to take precedence.

"Careful, Ads, someone might think you actually care for him," Fiadh taunted.

Any softness in Adria's face disappeared, and she snorted as she flung her long, jean-clad legs across the arm of the love seat. "Not hardly. It'll be a relief to not have the Hollywood Player Prince's ugly mug hanging around." When Tommy shot Paisley a look, Adria groaned. "No. Tell me it isn't so."

Tommy tugged at the chains around his neck. "Ronan went home to LA briefly, but he's meeting us in Chicago. He seems more determined than ever to finish the documentary."

"*Dios*," Adria said, her sapphire-blue eyes flashing in displeasure.

"He was pretty shaken, though. I heard Nikki give him the contact information for the ex-Green Beret friend of her family's that worked out with you Paisley," Leya said.

"Just what we need, an even beefier Player," Adria glowered.

"What exactly is the reason you hate him again?" Leya asked.

Adria's drumstick picked up pace, but she didn't respond, and Fee's worry for her friend grew.

"I think we'll see less of him than ever before because he's also working on a sequel to the film he made for RMI," Tommy said.

Fee's stomach clenched at the mention of Asshole-Asher's company. Everything that had happened at the bar last night...the words...the desire...bubbled back up, and she was suddenly angry all over again. He hadn't denied being an asshole. He hadn't denied wanting to get rid of one of them, if not more. He was as callous and cruel as she'd always known him to be.

Then she remembered the look he'd given her as his thumb had slid over her lip, and her lungs forgot to breathe. Both motions, tucking her hair in and the soft caress, had almost been tender. It was difficult to pull both images of him together in her mind. It was like he was two different people.

Thankfully, Nikki bustled in, distracting Fee from her thoughts. Their guitarist was out of breath with her hair tied up in two loose top knots that seemed about to slide off her head. While Adria was the actual former beauty queen of the bunch, Fiadh had always thought it was Nikki who would someday grace the cover of a magazine as one of the world's most beautiful people. Her high cheekbones, full lips that naturally curved upward, and perfectly arched eyebrows were a painting of perfection, like ancient royalty on display in a museum.

"Sorry I'm late. I was waiting for Zia to get back with my prescription," Nikki said.

"You have a migraine?" Fee asked.

"No, but I ran out and didn't want to be unprepared."

Nikki's headaches were severe enough they'd actually stopped her from performing a couple of nights on The Red Guitar tour. They were debilitating in a way Fee could only imagine.

"Where is Zia?" Adria asked.

"I'm here!" Zia said, bouncing into the bus and somehow making the entire thing shake even though she was barely the size of an elf. Tiny, bubbly, and with curls as big as Nikki's, she managed her hair by wearing a wide assortment of wildly patterned headbands every day.

Zia climbed up front where their driver already had the bus idling and waiting to go. She looked back at them with a wide smile you couldn't help returning. "Everyone ready to get this show on the road?"

As co-tour manager with Jonas, Zia was responsible for making sure the band, their gear, and everything they needed for each concert showed up at the venue on time.

"Not yet," Fee said, and she went to the kitchen and started opening cabinets.

"What are you looking for?" Paisley asked.

"Something to toast with," Fee said.

"What are we toasting?" Leya asked, frowning at her.

Fiadh found a bottle of champagne at the back of one of the cabinets, wondered if it was any good, and then didn't care. They'd just have a sip. She found some plastic cups and worked on popping the top.

She shot her friends a grin she hoped looked real as the cork went flying. "First, we had an amazing concert, showing Asshole-Asher and every hater in the world that we are more than a bunch of teen has-beens. Second, we're finally together and on tour again, and I fucking missed you all!"

She poured the champagne, and Adria came to help her pass them out. Her friend squeezed her arm as if to apologize for not being there in the months since Landry had died, but Fee didn't blame her. Her family had definitely had more than their fair share to deal with.

"Third," Fee continued. "We're alive, and we all know how precarious that can be. Fourth, and finally, we're toasting Little Bit, who is now Little Warrior. Thanks for figuring out exactly what we needed, saving yourself…and saving all of us." Fee's voice cracked, but she pushed the emotions down and gave them all her widest smile—the one that was renowned for fooling everyone.

"To albums, concerts, and our Little Warrior," Adria said, raising her cup and giving everyone her signature wink that the majority of the world drooled over.

Everyone joined in while Paisley blushed, and Jonas kissed the side of her head.

Fee looked at Zia. "Okay, I think we're ready now."

"Boston, here we come," Nikki said, sinking onto the couch next to Adria and resting her head on her shoulder.

The bus shifted into gear, and they were on their way.

Tommy futzed with his cup and then got up to throw it away. Fee wasn't sure he'd even taken one sip. Maybe he'd be okay. Maybe they all would.

It was just a three-hour journey to Boston, but as Fee watched Albany disappear, it felt like they were leaving yet another chapter of The Daisies behind them. Another ending that had been forced on them, stained and etched like a tattoo. She wondered how many more they could take before there was no skin left to mark.

Chapter Five

Asher

GLASS HOUSES
Performed by Steel Magnolia

Asher swallowed the finger of scotch in one gulp instead of savoring it as he usually did. He needed to settle his nerves as quickly as possible—the ones crawling up his spine and sending spirals of goosebumps over his body. She was getting worse. Something was going to have to be done…again. His stomach clenched along with almost every other muscle in his body. He hated this part of his life, and yet he wouldn't change it. It was a screwed-up dichotomy.

He ran a hand through his hair, trying to tame it back into neat layers. His fingers landed on the rough patch of gray at his temple. He was pretty sure she was the reason for it. He'd grayed earlier than anyone he knew. He was barely thirty, for fuck's sake.

The door of his study opened, and he lifted his eyes from the cut crystal to watch his father saunter in.

"Rough one, eh?" his dad said, rubbing a hand through his thick brown waves in much the same way Asher just had. His dad's hair had hardly any more gray at double the age.

Wrapped in a deep-burgundy robe over silk, striped pajamas that made him look like a Hugh Hefner wannabe, Kellan Riggs was actually one of the straightest arrows you could ever meet. The man rarely drank, hadn't had a female companion in years, and ran their family's company with an integrity no one could question—unlike his son, whose integrity had been thrashed around multiple times and even taunted on the witness stand. It made Asher's already tight stomach rebel further. The scotch wasn't going to cut it. Asher was going to be up all night, which meant he'd be cranky as shit by the time he made it to The Painted Daisies' rehearsal.

He shouldn't have come home, even for one night. He should have gone straight to the hotel and checked himself in. Even though it was barely twenty minutes from his family's estate to Boston, he needed to be onsite with the band as much as possible right now. He'd felt that way even before he'd made the deal with Tommy.

"We need to talk," his dad said, and Asher's jaw clenched. They did. His dad didn't even know the half of it. He watched as his father fixed himself a rare glass of scotch from the heavy crystal decanters lined along the sideboard and then sat down across the desk from him.

It wasn't good if his dad was drinking.

He escaped his father's stare, moving across the old morning room to the wall of windows behind him. Unlike his father's office—embedded in the enormous library with its twenty-foot ceilings stacked with black-and-gold gilded bookcases, rare novels, and expensive expressionist art— Asher had renovated this room until it looked nothing like the rest of the family's dark, Georgian mansion.

It was lighter and more modern even if it lacked color as much as the library. Here, silver and white linens drenched the space from the wingback chairs to the couch in the corner. Wrought-iron and glass bookcases matched the huge desk sitting kitty-corner between two walls of floor-to-ceiling windows. The only hint of color in the room was the navy-blue wallpaper that, in the nighttime, looked black. Even the original Ansel Adams prints on the walls were black-and-white.

Perched as the mansion was above the rocky shoreline with the Atlantic Ocean crashing below it, the windows in his office made it feel like you were actually floating above the waves. When they were open, like tonight, the sound of the surf normally soothed him. It wasn't just the rhythm of the sea that was peaceful. It was the knowledge that, even after the centuries of pounding by the waves, the land was still there. It might have been dented and smoothed, forced into a slightly different shape than when it had first broken away from Pangaea, but it still existed. Like him and his father. They'd survived the waves—the women—who'd thrown their worst at them.

He'd eventually survive Nova too. He already had. He just had to continue to stick it out.

He looked down at the long scratch on his forearm just below the rolled-up sleeves of his dress shirt. It was deeper than he'd originally thought, still dripping blood. He stalked over to the side table and pulled a white cloth napkin from the stack by the array of decanters and pressed it onto the cut.

He could feel his father watching him as Asher was forced to heal, once again, from the biggest mistake he'd ever made. One that continued to haunt them.

When he sat back down, his father's brows were drawn tight.

Instead of asking about the gash or the screams that had torn through the night, his dad directed their conversation to RMI. It was what they were good at—avoiding the personal problems to focus on business. A tradition passed down for over a century as each Riggs ancestor dealt with their own blows from the women they'd tied themselves to, as if they were cursed—even if you didn't believe in that sort of thing.

"Is this thing with the Daisies going to be yet another nightmare?" his dad asked.

Asher's jaw clenched, but he didn't respond. Instead, he tried to figure out how to tell his father the plan he'd come up with. One that seemed way too impulsive in the light of day but couldn't be taken back. Just like all his mistakes.

"No successful businessman is perfect, Asher. We've all had deals go bad," his dad continued. "You shouldn't be ashamed, but we do need to fix it before it sours completely."

Asher's eyes closed, and he leaned back in the ergonomically correct, leather chair that had cost more than a dozen custom suits and laced his hands behind his head, elbows spread wide. "The labels aren't a mistake."

"We were a breath away from losing a hundred million dollars fighting Ziggy on behalf of Wide Underground, and The Painted Daisies went to hell in a handbasket as soon as we bought Lost Heart Records. With this latest attack, the drama doesn't seem to be ending anytime soon. The labels are practically bleeding us money."

Asher opened his eyes just as his dad's settled on the bloody napkin setting on his desk. He almost laughed at the symbolism. Both his mistakes oozed like infections, but he still believed in what he was trying to accomplish with the labels.

"If we'd stayed with the status quo, we risked losing more than a hundred million. We risked becoming obsolete." Asher couldn't help the growl of defensiveness that snuck into his voice.

His dad didn't argue his point. Ridgeway Media Industries had been founded almost a century and a half ago by his great-great grandfather who'd invested in newspapers and print. His father had spread their wings into radio and news stations. But technology was eating away at all those industries. Streaming services and music had been his contribution to the company's portfolio.

"I agree. Taking informed risks into the future is an absolute must if we want to keep RMI profitable and growing," his dad said. "But every new venture comes with an inherent risk of failure. What saved me—and will save you and RMI in the long run—is knowing when to cut our losses. The first radio network I brought onboard was a shitshow. We divested of it as soon as we could. I licked my wounds, moved on, and brought in a hell of a lot more profitable businesses. It happens. I'm not upset about this. The board isn't upset, either. But we do need to decide if it's time to wash our hands of the labels and turn our eyes in a different direction."

"Such as?" Asher asked, trying not to be belligerent but also not ready to just let go of the idea yet. He wasn't sure exactly why. But then, mahogany curls layered with purple and brown eyes rimmed in black ink danced in his mind, taunting him with the truth. He ground his teeth together. He wasn't doing this for her. Never again would he make a decision based on a woman.

"The streaming service has done even better than projected," his dad continued. "It was smart bringing Ronan onboard and producing our own shows immediately. What's he working on now? How can we expand more in that direction?"

"Ronan's finishing up the documentary on The Painted Daisies he started before Landry Kim died. Then, he's playing around with a new script from the same screenwriter who created *The Secrets Inside Us*. We're debating whether to make it into a series or just another movie."

His dad was already nodding as if this idea was the solution to everything.

His gut churned. A part of him knew his father was right. Cutting the labels that had cost them a boatload in lawyer's fees and him personally a chunk of his inheritance, should have been on the table. But there was more to Wide Underground and Lost Heart Records than just two troubled bands. And even with the storm circling The Painted Daisies again, the band could turn the label into something huge if he could just make sure there was no more drama. The band needed to keep their image squeaky clean, take advantage of the fans' sympathy, and execute a flawless tour.

He intended to make sure it happened.

"Give me six months," he told his dad. "If I can't turn it around by then, I'll agree to sell them."

"What's your plan?"

"I'm going on tour with the Daisies."

His dad choked on his drink. "What?"

Asher smirked. "Just for a few weeks. I worked out a deal with their manager where I don't fire his alcoholic ass while he's in rehab, and I get my hands a little dirty. It'll give me a better understanding of the business."

His father gave him a look from under a raised brow, as if he smelled something fishy. He purposefully pushed back the flash of colorful hair that threatened once again. She may have been the reason he'd gone in this direction to begin with, but he'd never admit it to his father—not when he all but refused to admit it to himself.

"We can hardly afford for our president of mergers and acquisitions to just disappear for weeks," his dad said.

"I'm not disappearing. I'll continue working from the road. I'm rarely in the office as it is. If I have to step away from the tour here and there for a business trip, I will."

More silence from his father. "I appreciate you're going all in, Ash. I really do. But a schedule like that will leave you home even less."

Asher's heart clenched tightly again, this time with regret. His eyes fell on the silver frame on his desk with his black-haired, pale-skinned girl smiling up at him. She looked nothing like him except for her blue eyes and arched eyebrows. She already tended to be flighty and forgetful like her mother in a way that made his stomach turn, but he loved her like nothing else in his life. She was the only woman who would ever get that emotion from him again.

Unfortunately, unlike the music labels, which he knew he could turn around, he had no idea how to fix the strained relationship with his daughter. She saw her grandfather and her nanny more than she ever saw him, which meant she remained polite and shy when he was with her. What would his constant trips and semi-permanent absence in her life do to her? Would the scars be as deep as the ones his mother had left behind with her departure?

His dad finished his drink, got up, and set the glass on the tray where one of the daytime staff Jozef managed would find it, clean it, and return it without either his dad or Asher seeing them.

His father turned back at the door. "I wasn't a very good

father or husband. I wasn't here for either of you." When Asher tried to disagree, his father waved his hand and continued. "No. I own my mistakes just like you do. I taught you that much. I'd just hate for us to repeat them with Wren."

Then, he left, and Asher's chest squeezed until he wasn't sure he could breathe.

A scream filled the air, and he groaned, glancing down at the wound that had barely stopped bleeding. He should have gone to the hotel. As soon as he thought it, he regretted it. He wasn't a coward, and yet he continued to run from this house. From Nova and Wren. From his past and his failures.

He'd fix it. As soon as he got the record labels sorted and the chief operating officer job in hand, he'd have time to figure out what the hell he needed to do with them both.

Chapter Six

Fiadh

I WON'T LET GO
Performed by The Brothers Bright

They were still forty minutes away from arriving in Boston when the bus stuttered to a stop. Fee was in the bedroom, cleaning her instruments, and she lifted her eyes from her Uilleann pipes to see what looked to be a large cabin-like resort outside the windows. She left her things on the bed and headed for the front of the bus, glancing around at the others who were either sleeping, listening to music, or lost in their phones.

"Where are we at?" she asked, a frown on her face.

Everyone looked up from their devices and their slumber to take in the sprawling wooden building, the absurdly small parking lot, and the wall of trees surrounding the place. They were clearly not in Boston.

Tommy cleared his throat, tugged on his chains, and then leaned forward so his elbows were on his knees, hands clasped tightly. "It's a rehab clinic."

Fee met his gaze while everyone else's darted away. A part of her was dancing joyfully, happy because it was exactly what he needed. But another part of her flickered with a wave of panic. More loss. What would they do? He'd been there every step of the way since first signing them in LA almost nine years ago. They hadn't even graduated high school when he'd taken them under his wing. He was more than a manager. He was like a favorite uncle or a much older cousin. He was the reason they'd found Nick and Lost Heart Records and had been handed the spotlight of fortune and fame.

The tension in the air grew thick until it was almost palpable. Fiadh and the other band members exchanged looks, but it was Paisley who spoke first.

"We're glad you're getting help, Tommy," her voice cracked a little, and Fee's eyes filled.

Fiadh moved toward him, resting a hand on his shoulder. "I'm sorry I didn't say anything even though I saw you were out of control."

Tommy's throat bobbed, his hand landing on top of Fee's.

"My job is to look after you girls, not the other way around. And a piss-poor job I've been doing of it. Look at what happened to..." His voice faded away. He lifted his hand away from Fee's, and she suddenly realized how clammy his was. "Asher pointed out to me that it was damn selfish to continue like this. That I was only hurting you more."

Fee snorted at the mention of Asshole-Asher. As if he should have been the one to point out to anyone they were being selfish. His words about her last night were still burning holes inside her.

"No, Fee," Tommy said, shaking his head. "He's right. I want to get better. I want to get better so I can be the manager you hired and the person you deserve at your backs."

"We want you better. We want you with us," Leya said.

There was a heavy knock on the door, and then it was opened by Special Agent Kent.

"We good?" he asked, his gaze landing on Tommy.

Leya grumbled under her breath, something about Captain Annoying keeping things from her.

Tommy stood and cleared his throat again. "I hope to

rejoin the tour in a couple of months."

His eyes darted to Zia who nodded encouragingly. She'd obviously been in on the news as well. The band circled Tommy in a hug they usually saved for before and after their performances.

"Take your time, Tommy," Fee said. "Be better. Be healthy."

His shoulders shook, and then he pushed out of their embrace to take them all in. "You'll be in good hands while I'm gone. Someone just as vested in The Daisies' success as I am." At their confused expression, he continued, "Asher's decided to step in for me."

Fee's heart froze, unsure she'd heard him right. She shook her head, wanting to scream from the top of her lungs that she wasn't letting that man close to any of them. Not until she could prove what he'd done. Not while she wasn't sure any of them were safe if he was around, but the words got stuck in her throat.

Tommy gave her a wry smile. "He won't be quite as hands-on as I am because he still has his day job at RMI, but between his connections, Zia and Jonas here, and the rest of your crew. You'll be okay."

"No," she finally breathed out, and everyone's eyes swung toward her.

Tommy grimaced. "He and I had a long talk last night, Fee. He's determined to learn the business and make sure you succeed. He has a lot riding on all of you after the shitstorm with Ziggy and the Serpents."

Fee and the others frowned, more confusion shuffling over their faces. Everyone in the industry was aware of the ugly lawsuit Ziggy had filed against the band's label, Wide Underground. He'd sued for a hundred million dollars when they'd let him go after he'd been arrested on assault charges in Berlin, breaching the morality clause in his contract. The criminal case had been thrown out on a technicality, but Wide Underground had refused to continue working with him anyway.

"What does that have to do with Asher?" Leya asked.

Tommy looked at them as if he couldn't believe they didn't know. "RMI owns Wide Underground. Bought the European label months before they bought Lost Heart Records. You didn't know?"

None of them had. But then, they'd been barely muddling by after Landry's murder at the time RMI had come onboard.

Suddenly, Asher's anger at the media sensation they'd become, at Tommy's drinking, at any hint of impropriety on their part suddenly made more sense. He'd gotten burned buying a label with a sleazy artist at the top of its charts. She'd once met Ziggy when she'd gone to a party with her ex, Lars Ritter, and every single one of her red flags had been raised. She'd given him a wide berth that night.

In some strange part of her brain, she actually felt sorry for Asher. But then she pushed it aside. If he'd bought the label not knowing the truth about Ziggy, then he hadn't done his due diligence.

"How does he think he can just step in and manage a band?" Fee pushed.

"He has my phone, all my contacts, and the schedule Zia and I worked out with the press junkets at each stop. Alice is handling the record release from Oakland. Jonas has the tour crew in check. Asher will most likely be needed for urgent situations only. And the truth is, managing a band has to be a lot easier than managing mergers and acquisitions for a corporation the size of RMI."

"It's completely ridiculous," Fiadh continued to grouse.

Tommy looked at Special Agent Kent, Zia, Jonas, and their driver. "Can you give me a minute alone with the band, please?"

Jonas didn't look like he wanted to go, but Paisley squeezed his hand and nodded. Once everyone had left, Tommy said, "I think he's being pressured to sell. I think between what happened with Ziggy, then Landry, and now this, he's been asked to drop us all like hot potatoes."

"Good!" Fee said, but along with the feeling of relief crashing through her, a warped sense of sadness flared, as if she'd missed something big. Like Christmas.

Tommy tugged a chain. "I know you don't care for the man, Fiadh, but I'm telling you, we could be in a lot worse hands than Asher and RMI. Machine Music was crawling all over Nick to buy Lost Hearts before Asher picked it up, and you know what a fucking mess we'd be in if that pig was in charge."

He let his words settle in, and they did nothing to ease the waves of nausea floating through Fee. It was like having to choose whether you were going to be eaten by a boa constrictor or a lion. Either way, there'd still be nothing left but the bones they'd picked clean.

"RMI hasn't interfered with your creativity." He shot a look at Paisley. "They've let you decide how you ran your tour and your brand. Sure…they were kind of dicky about getting the record done and hitting the tour trail after—"

"They threatened to sue us," Adria said. "The week after Landry died."

Her eyes met Adria's. Fee was glad she wasn't the only one who remembered just how awful Asher had been to them. The demands he'd made.

"Tough love," Tommy said.

"I can't believe you're even supporting this," Fiadh stormed.

"Look. I'm not sure how, but he got wind you were considering not signing with him again."

Fee's heart thudded to a stop again as the words she'd thrown at him the night before came back to her. *Shit.*

"I think he wants to do a little groveling. I think he wants to prove that you can both be happy in this relationship. I've known Nick Jackson for almost twenty years, and I believe, in my heart, he would not have sold the label he bled for to RMI and Asher if he legitimately thought it was going to be bad for any of his artists. We got off on a rocky footing. Asher being more involved can go a long way to smoothing it out."

"Or dropping us off a cliff," Fiadh grumbled.

"Maybe Tommy's right, Fee," Paisley said. "Maybe...maybe we all deserve a do-over."

Paisley shot a glance out the window to where Jonas was standing on the curb, arms crossed over his enormous chest, worry shaping his brows. Paisley and Jonas had lost their way when she'd forced him from her life after Landry's death. Coming back to Grand Orchard, the couple had found each other again, so of course Paisley would think second chances were good for everyone.

But none of the band knew what Fee did—about what Asher had said that awful night, the threats he'd made to get rid of one or more of them, the money Angel had followed, the mother of his child who'd disappeared. If she told them about having investigated him now, they'd think she'd lost her mind. They'd want her to join Tommy in rehab.

So, she bit her lip and said nothing.

"We vote," Paisley said, looking around at them. "It's the way we've always done it. It's what Landry would've wanted us to do."

"I'm with Fee," Adria said. "I don't trust the guy farther than I could toss him, and with his size and muscles, that wouldn't be far."

Nikki and Leya looked at each other and then back at the rest of us.

"We already agreed to finish with RMI and see where we stood after the tour ended. I don't see how this changes any of it. Let's just get it done," Nikki said. She rubbed her temples, the stress a perfect trigger for her migraines, making Fee's anxiety increase. More things to worry about. More people who she could lose if she didn't keep her arms around them all.

Leya grimaced. "I hate being the tie-breaker."

"Don't go all politician on us, Ley," Adria said. "Suck it up, and tell us what you really think."

"I think if Asher is willing to take the time out of his day job to manage a band under some tiny label he bought, it means we're important to him," she said softly, and Fee shot her a betrayed glare.

Tommy sighed as if a huge weight had been lifted off his shoulders, and it made Fiadh feel guilty for making him worry about them when all he should have been doing was concentrating on getting better. She hugged him, and he squeezed back tight, whispering in her ear, "Take care of them."

She swallowed hard. It wasn't exactly her role anymore. Back in high school, it had been Fee and Landry who'd created The Painted Daisies, even coming up with the name in art class and designing their original blood-orange-colored logo. The two of them had done everything together to get the band started, including recruiting Adria, Nikki, and Leya. But when everything had spun out of control with Fee's parents, she'd barely been able to function. Landry had taken over and stayed in charge until she'd been killed. And now Paisley had stepped into her sister's shoes.

It left Fee barely pulling the strings in the background, watching from the shadows. But one thing was certain. This news did nothing but fuel her determination to find out the truth about Asher. Maybe having him hanging around meant she'd get another stab at her plan to seduce him and uncover his secrets. Either way, she vowed to get to the real man behind the shell, come hell or high water.

Chapter Seven

Asher

SHALLOW

Performed by Lady Gaga and Bradley Cooper

THREE DAYS BEFORE

The Daisies were on their last song in a sold-out stadium with not a dry eye in the place. The bubbles and fireworks along with the video of Landry and the song Paisley had written for her sister were enough to make even a cold-hearted bastard like him feel a prick at the back of his eyes.

Tonight, he was surer than ever that the labels were a smart business move. This group was the stuff legends were made of. If they kept their shit together, stayed alive, and stayed sober, then The Painted Daisies would be in the record books. They were unique, stunning to watch, and talented beyond belief. It didn't hurt that every single one of them was as gorgeous as their music. The blend of ethnicities and sounds was addicting, making them accessible to people around the globe. Their audience right now was on the younger side, teens and twenties, but he could easily see how the band and their fans would mature. This new album, *The Legacy*, was already a step in that direction, pulling from a deep well of loss and dreams remade that even the most cynical of adults could relate to.

The Daisies exited the stage to a thunder of applause and

screams begging them to come back on. But this tour would have no encore. He wasn't sure they could manage one even if they tried. Ending each concert with the tribute to their dead friend and sister left them emotionally drained. As they came off the stage, they all brushed at the tears littering their faces. Paisley flew into Jonas's arms, and the band moved forward to surround the duo in a tight circle, celebrating and comforting all at the same time.

Asher's jaw ticked at the display. He knew just how feelings could be manipulated in order to get what someone wanted from another person. As much as he didn't care for Jonas Riccoli, he pitied him being at the center of all those heightened emotions.

After Landry's murder, Asher had ordered Jonas to be investigated just like he'd had every single person in the band's entourage. The kid had a past and anger issues. Asher had seen it up close, live and in person, just a few nights ago when Jonas had almost hit Ronan at the after-party in Albany. And while God only knew how many times he'd been tempted to hit Ronan himself, it didn't excuse Jonas's actions or make Asher prone to trust him. Unfortunately, the bond between Jonas and Paisley was painfully clear. A love story that made his gut twist and turn. Something he'd never want for himself again. But pulling the couple apart would do nothing for Asher in his attempt to gain the band's trust, and he needed it so they'd re-sign with RMI.

The group broke apart, heading for the dressing rooms to change before returning to the hotel for the after-party where a handful of press waited. Asher had kept the numbers small, paring the list down even more from what Tommy had left for him. He wasn't sure any of the Daisies were ready for more discussion about what had happened in Albany. The press who'd been invited were under strict orders not to ask about it because the entire event was still under investigation.

As the crew began to break the stage down, expertly stowing equipment and getting it ready to load in the semi-trucks and buses that would leave in the morning for Chicago, his eyes landed on Fiadh. She hadn't walked away like the rest of the group. Instead, she was glaring in his direction. His body tightened from head to toe, fighting the visceral reaction he had to her. She wore a tight black leather skirt, a halter top that showed off her creamy skin, and fishnet stockings that ended in mid-calf Doc Marten's decked out in metal grommets and buckles. Her curls were sweaty and sticking to her face, neck, and chest from the performance.

His mind flashed with images of her sweaty and breathless for other reasons. Moving beneath him, over him, next to him. It wasn't healthy. It was the last thing he needed—this damn lust he felt for her and couldn't seem to escape.

She swept her thick mane of hair over one shoulder and stalked toward him, and he swore he could see a fire blazing behind her amber lights.

"Why are you really doing this?" she demanded, hands on her hips.

He clenched his fists so he wouldn't reach for her waist and the tempting strip of flesh she had on display there.

"Doing what? Managing my investment? Making sure nothing else happens to the millions I've already sunk into it?"

"That daddy has sunk into it, don't you mean? It's not your company. It's your father's company, right?"

He didn't know if he wanted to laugh or growl at her jab. He arched a brow at her, surprised she'd done even that much research on him. "It's my family's company. Been ours since the turn of the twentieth century. We're not publicly held, so it's mine as much as my father's."

"I won't let you break us apart," she said as she stepped closer, stabbing him in the chest with a finger.

Even through the layers of his suit jacket, he could feel the heat of her. It zapped through his veins with a simple touch of her fingertip. What would it feel like if they were joined more? Limbs and hips and chests.

He snagged her hand, and the touch burned his palm, causing him to drop it. He knew what it looked like to her, as if he was disgusted with her touch when, really, he was disgusted with himself. She crossed her arms over her chest in response, pushing those damn full breasts up in the halter top just like she'd done at the bar in Albany.

"I have no intention of breaking the band apart, Fiadh," he responded, keeping his voice even.

She squinted at him as if she didn't believe him before whirling around and storming off. Her scent remained—a barely-there hint of cherrywood and musk that made his entire body ache. An ache that would do nothing but leave a brand he didn't want. A brand he'd sworn to himself he'd never allow again.

So, he walked away, running through the checklist of items to be done before the end of the night, and determined to keep Fiadh Kane at more than an arm's length.

But several hours later, watching her from across the hotel suite, his body was still aching to pull her to him. She'd had three drinks while none of the other band members had indulged in more than one. Instead, they'd focused on food, water, and recovering from the exhausting performance as they mingled with the handful of VIPs in the room. As the reporters had been instructed, their questions had remained about the record releasing later in the week, the song inspiration, and the tour rather than the events in Albany.

Asher wished he'd limited the press even more, because it wasn't just the three drinks Fiadh had indulged in that was eating at him. It was the way she was flirting with the lone TV reporter in the room. It brought back memories and feelings Asher hated. The desperation and anger he'd felt every time Nova had flirted with Ronan or any of his other friends. At first, he'd told himself Nova didn't even know she was doing it—accidentally encouraging their attention with her whimsical charm. But then later...later he'd realized she'd known exactly what she was doing. She'd done it purposefully, needing the attention and the high it gave almost as much as she'd needed her drugs.

Once only the TV reporter and her cameraman were left with the band, Fiadh downed her last drink and put her hand on the reporter's arm, making contact for the first time. She looked up from under thick lashes into the reporter's gray eyes and smiled a breathtaking smile. It still wasn't her real one—the soft, half-tilted one—but it was damn stunning. Before he realized what he was doing, he strode over and pulled Fiadh away.

He looked down at the reporter. "I think you've gotten what you needed tonight, don't you?"

The reporter's red lips turned down in a pout, and she shot a regretful look in Fiadh's direction. "I guess."

Fiadh tried to jerk her arm free, but he only held on tighter, taking a step backward and bringing her with him.

"Then, it's time you leave," Asher said to the sulking reporter.

When the silence turned awkward, the reporter looked over at her cameraman. "Let's go, T."

The two left, and Asher felt relief wash over him until he looked down into Fiadh's pissed-off face. She jerked her arm again, and this time, he was forced to let go even though the snarling animal inside him was telling him to hold on. He stayed in her space, glaring down at her, keeping his voice low so he wouldn't disturb the other members of the band spread out around the suite. "Should I have put you in rehab with Tommy?"

Her eyes flared with surprise and anger.

"No!"

"You're drunk."

"I've had three drinks. That's hardly drunk."

"Isn't it? You're slurring your words, and you would have taken that woman to bed."

Her cheeks turned pink, and he itched to run his fingers along the color. "Who I take to bed has nothing to do with you."

"Right now, the band's image is under enormous scrutiny, so you can't sleep with someone at every stop. You can't be the epitome of a rock star—drunk, drugged, and sexed."

"Because I'm a woman? If I were a male rock star, everyone would expect it. They'd chuckle and laugh and pat me on the back, right? But because I happen to have boobs, I'm supposed to be some Virgin Mary?"

He laughed, dry and sarcastic. "Trust me, Fiadh, everyone knows you're not a virgin."

She stepped to the side to go around him, and he blocked her path.

"Let me by."

Even though he knew he should just let her go, let the entire conversation slide, he was overwhelmed with a jealousy he hadn't felt in years and was fighting to control it as he growled out, "Not until you promise you'll curtail your activities until we get the band's image back intact."

While it was the most important reason, he also wasn't sure he could make it through concert after concert watching her take someone to her hotel room. Not without losing it. Not without pulling her to him and proving exactly what *he* could do in her bed.

"There's nothing wrong with our damn image," she tossed back. "We've been victims of assholes who objectify us. Who try to pick us off because they think we're weak. We're not."

"Go to bed, Fiadh. Sleep it off. Alone."

"Hey, Fee," Leya called out, making her way over from the couch, eyes darting back and forth between Asher and Fiadh. "You strike out?"

Asher took two steps back. It felt like it cost him a bit of his soul to do so, but Jesus, what had he been thinking? His grip had been so tight it could have left a bruise. And then he'd followed her around the room like a dog with his teeth bared, ready to take another bite. This wasn't him. He was never the one to leave a mark. The deep scratch on his arm that hadn't quite healed screamed at him. Even then, he hadn't left a mark in return. He never had.

He bit the inside of his cheek.

Fiadh shot him a glare and then flounced closer to Leya. "I guess my dry spell is going to last a little longer."

Leya put her arm through her friend's. "Don't worry. Your droughts always end in a torrential storm."

God, did that eat at him. Gut curling with disgust at himself and at her because a torrential storm of Fiadh Kane was what his body was craving.

His phone buzzed, and he looked down at a message from his assistant.

> *TORRANCE: Someone has put a sniffer on the money you're sending to her.*

His stomach jerked. This was the last thing he needed at the moment—another damn woman to be worried about.

> *ASHER: Have Eduardo piggyback onto it and see where it's coming from.*

> *TORRANCE: Already did.*

> *ASHER: Did you check on our friend too?*

Torrance would easily understand the sarcasm in the simple words.

> *TORRANCE: He's in the U.S.*

Asher's chest tightened. He didn't want to be on the same continent with the man.

> *ASHER: Trying to find a new label?*

> *TORRANCE: I think he has a meeting with Machine Records.*

Figured. Swamp rats would always find their own kind.

He had a long night ahead of him. He glanced at the clock and saw it was almost one in the morning. When he looked back at the band, Fiadh was still glaring at him, and all it did was make him want to show her all the ways he could turn that glare into a smile. Not the one she was renowned for—the saucy, don't-give-a-shit one she'd been shooting at the reporter—but her real one. The soft and charming one.

"We've got to be at the airport by nine o'clock, ladies," he said. "Perhaps we should call it a night."

It wasn't really a question. It was a command, and it only deepened Fiadh's scowl. She looked like she wanted to flip him off, but the others didn't argue. They just rose and headed for the door.

He watched as Jonas and Paisley drifted off toward the suite's bedroom with their bodies practically entwined. He wasn't sure if their hands had left one another all night—even if it was the barest of pinkies. Compared to Fiadh's casual hookup at each location, the sweet romance between Paisley and Jonas was something the fans were eating up. The way they'd known each other for years. The way they'd lost each other and come back together. Even their damn, opposite-sides-of-the-track trope was like the theme of a perfect love story.

The perfect story on paper, at least. But it was a temporary story because Asher had never witnessed a love that had been perfect or lasting. He wasn't sure it existed beyond a figment of imagination that chemistry-filled lust created in the human mind. Like the lust demanding he touch every single part of Fiadh.

Maybe if he had her just once, he could burn the desire out of his system enough to regain control of his body. But he couldn't afford to let even one night happen. Not just because he was managing them. Not just because he owned their label. But because he was afraid he'd realize Fiadh Kane wasn't the type of woman you ever forgot.

As he watched her hips sway their way down the hotel hallway toward her door, he wondered if being on tour with them was just another colossal mistake. Maybe he should do what his father suggested and wash his hands of the labels and focus on things that didn't make him feel out of control and on edge. He desperately craved stability and structure in his work because it allowed him to forget the chaos of his personal life. But right now, one sexy rock star was making it all but impossible to have either.

Chapter Eight

Fiadh

WICKED
Written by Lee Ann Womack

TWO DAYS BEFORE

The last thing on Fee's mind when she went to bed was the first thing on her mind when she woke after tossing and turning for a couple of hours—Asher-fucking-Riggs. She groaned, her arm still burning from the imprint of his hand. She hated how her body had flared to life under his commanding hold. Hated how she wanted to touch him, taste him, and be consumed by the flame he ignited every time he simply looked at her.

She'd needed to burn off some sexual energy last night, but even if he hadn't interrupted her flirtation with the reporter, she probably wouldn't have brought the woman to her room. Fee's words to Leya had been the truth. She'd been in a dry spell since Landry's death. She'd started to think grief had cut the emotions of desire and lust out of her body until Asher had proven otherwise. When he was near, every vein and nerve jumped to attention, craving him, wanting him to fill her up.

Why did it have to be him? The one person she couldn't trust. The man who'd cost them Landry…

Her subconscious screamed at her to stop being fanciful. But her stubbornness knew there were things he was hiding.

As if reading her mind, her phone buzzed with a text from the one man she'd thought would help her but had failed, just like the rest of the authorities and bodyguards.

ANGEL: I need to see you before you leave.

He was in Boston? An uneasy feeling settled over her. He'd been the one to approach her after Landry's funeral in LA. He'd convinced the doorman he lived in her building and then joined her in the elevator while her bodyguard eyeballed him. He'd slipped a note to her behind her detail's back, reading, *I can find him for you.*

Those words were all she'd needed to hire him because finding Landry's killer had been smoldering in her breast ever since they'd gotten back to California. She'd hidden her anger and grief behind her smile while helping Paisley and her parents. She'd tried to be there for them whenever she could, practically living at their house, stepping up as Paisley faded away, for weeks. But during every moment, her body had pulsed with the need to find who had done this to her friend...her sister...her family.

Fee glanced at the alarm clock on the bedside table. It was seven thirty in the morning, and the band was due at a private jet terminal by nine, which meant they needed to be in the cars by eight thirty. If she hurried, she could give him thirty minutes.

FIADH: I can meet you, but it has to be somewhere close and soon.

ANGEL: There's a park four blocks over from your hotel. I'll be there in thirty minutes.

Fiadh didn't know how she felt about him always knowing where she was at, especially after everything that had just happened with Paisley. Was this another leak in their security? A hole to plug? But then, the press found them all the time too. Maybe it was just a process of elimination, finding the hotels the band was most likely to be at and marking them off one by one.

Fee threw back the covers, dressed in a pair of jeans, a thick, long-sleeved sweater that clung to her thin frame, an oversized hoodie, and her Docs. She tucked her hair beneath the same beanie she'd used the other night, and her fingers stalled, thinking of the gentleness with which Asher had helped her hide the curls. It was a complete contrast to the cruelty of his grip last night. She shook off the images, pulling the hood of the sweatshirt up over the beanie and shoving a pair of dark sunglasses on.

She assembled her luggage, leaving it by the hotel room door where Zia or Jonas would have someone pick it up. Then, she grabbed her phone and her wallet and slipped out the door.

It wasn't Chin, but Lake, one of the few women bodyguards they had, who stood there. Chin hadn't been fired like Asher had threatened, and she was glad. She hadn't wanted her sneaking out to cost anyone their job, even if she had serious doubts about any of their team's ability to actually keep them safe.

The tall, blonde bodyguard was dressed in black from head to toe. The windbreaker she had on held the Reinard Security logo, just like the polo shirt underneath. Her black cargo pants ended in military-grade boots that had a knife tucked into them somewhere. She had a gun hidden beneath the jacket at her back and a two-way mic in her ear.

"I need to meet up with someone," Fiadh told her with a wink as if she was going to have a quickie somewhere. It was what most people believed of her anyway. It was what Asher had believed last night. She'd had plenty of hookups in her lifetime, but not nearly the amount she was credited with.

Most of her casual one-nighters had stopped when she'd first started seeing Lars. And after Lars, she'd been more hurt than she'd ever thought she'd be. Maybe if Landry hadn't died, she would have been able to get past it with her friend's help. Maybe she would have gotten back on the horse before now. Instead, she'd gone from the loss of a relationship to the loss of her sister, and no one had tempted her to try again—

no one she would allow herself to have, at any rate.

"We're supposed to be leaving for the airport in an hour," Lake said hesitantly.

Fee nodded. "I know. We'll make it. I just need you to give the white-sock-on-the-doorknob signal for a few minutes."

Lake's lips twitched. "That's not what we call it."

Fee laughed softly and started for the elevator. Lake followed, talking quietly into her earpiece. Fiadh felt a twinge of something that wasn't embarrassment but close, but screw it. Let them all think she was meeting up with someone for a quickie. And it would be even better if it got back to Asher, because it would piss him off after the way he'd acted the night before.

Once they were outside the hotel, Fee headed toward the park she'd looked up after Angel had given her the name. Lake didn't say a word, just tagged along quietly.

The air was frigid. Not simply cold, but downright frozen. The sky was so dark you could barely tell it was daylight. The wind howled down the streets, sending chills through every bone in Fee's body. Boston was supposed to be nice in April, but instead, there were soft flakes already falling. She hadn't checked the weather before she'd left, and neither she nor Lake was really dressed for a storm. She needed to make this fast and get them the hell back to the hotel before they became popsicles.

The early hour and the weather meant the streets were empty. A strange hush had fallen over the normally busy city. When they reached the park on the shoreline, it was practically desolate, the gray skies blending in with the frenzied waves, white caps blooming before crashing to the shore. Lake gave Fiadh a questioning glance. It was hardly the place for a romantic hookup. What were they going to do, bare their butts and do it on a cold metal bench with the snow already falling? Even the thought made Fee chuckle softly to herself.

Then, she saw the shadow that was Angel, leaning on a

lamppost near the water, and her smile slipped away. The entire scene felt off. Risky. Otherworldly.

"I need you to stay here," Fee said. "You'll be able to see me, but I need to talk to him alone."

Lake frowned, unhappy now that she realized something else was going down other than sex.

"Ms. Kane—"

"I promise he's safe, and I'll be fine."

The bodyguard still looked doubtful, but Fee didn't give her more time to argue. She put her sunglasses in her pocket, tucked her chin to her chest against the headwind, and started along the path toward Angel. When she eased up next to him, he didn't even acknowledge her, and irritation flew through her. She'd come out in this miserable cold because he'd said he needed to see her in person, and now he acted like he didn't even care if she was there.

"What was so desperately important you had to tell me in person?" Fee demanded.

He finally looked up. Midnight-blue eyes so dark they were nearly black hit her from beneath the edge of his hoodie, and she almost flinched when they met hers. It was only the second time she'd met Angel Carter in person after the elevator ride, and she was struck with the same overarching impression of him she'd had before. He was dangerous.

He had a straight, aristocratic nose over full lips with a cruel twist to them and a scar on his chin hidden below a couple of days' worth of dark stubble. The black hoodie he wore under a black coat hid the sleeves of tattoos Fee remembered taking up both muscular arms. The man was at least six foot five because he towered over her when she wasn't short, especially not in her heeled Docs. His shoulders were so broad she wasn't sure he'd fit through a regular door without turning sideways. And despite his height and the deep well of muscles rippling when he moved, she had the impression he'd be as fast as a panther. Just like any wild cat, he was on high alert right now, even when he appeared to be lounging lazily.

"Someone backdoored my trace. I think he's onto us," Angel said. His voice was as ominous as his looks.

Sometimes, Fee wondered what the hell had possessed her to hire him. Sure, he'd sought her out, but he didn't look like someone you should trust with your secrets. And he'd failed at every turn, uncovering enough to keep her interested but not enough to give her answers.

"You don't appear to be as good at your job as you insist you are," she said and felt her voice catch as he shot her a glare that could have incinerated her.

The wind picked up, causing the snow to fall faster, swirling around them and making it difficult to see him even when he was right next to her.

"Ms. Kane?" Lake's voice called out.

"I'll be right there," she hollered back.

Angel tossed a look in her bodyguard's direction. "She's the one who isn't good at her job. I could have killed you by now."

Fee's heart hammered in her chest, but she didn't let it show.

"Just tell me what you know so we can get out of this fecking storm," she growled.

"The money trail led to someone in a German witness protection program. Whoever followed me out likely planted a worm no one could have seen, not even me. Means someone is spending a lot of money to keep whomever this person is out of sight."

"Is it his ex?" Fee asked.

He tapped the snow from his hood but gave the barest of head shakes.

"I don't think so. I ran across a prescription for her. Clozapine gets filled regularly in her name at a pharmacy here in Boston. It was easy to find once I had access to the state's prescription drug monitoring program."

Fee thought about what he'd just admitted. He'd hacked a secure website full of personal data about millions of people. Something not just any private investigator could do, and she wondered again, just who Angel was, why he was helping her, and what he got out of it.

"What's clozapine?"

"One of the heaviest antipsychotic drugs on the market."

A chill went up Fee's back that had nothing to do with the wind and snow circling her like an eagle hunting its prey.

"He's drugging her?" Somehow, it seemed ridiculous. Like something you'd only hear about in a movie or a book.

"I don't know where she's at, who's administering it, or even if it's being administered. Besides what you've seen, I am one of the best in the world at this, and if I can't find anything, it means it stinks. It means it's ugly in ways you won't want to know. I think you should stop sniffing around. I think you should tell your band to cut ties as soon as they can with Riggs and RMI."

"I didn't hire you for your opinion."

"You didn't hire me at all," he grunted back.

And it only increased the chills up her spine. "Don't call me again."

Fee went to leave, and he reached out as quick as lightning to stop her. His gloved hand retreated almost as soon as he'd touched her. Not like a certain man the night before who'd held on as if he'd never let her go.

"You've got wolves circling the henhouse, Fiadh. That stalker up in Albany…he was nothing. He was a pissant with a wacked idea of female sexuality," Angel said, the warning in his tone taking his already deep voice even lower.

Her stomach flipped not only at his words but because no one except the feds and their security team were supposed to know the details of what had been said to Paisley in the confines of the hotel room in Albany. And yet, this private investigator knew. Her unease grew, chest pounding, blood pumping loudly through her ears as fear started to creep in.

"How did you get my information, Angel? How did you know I wanted someone outside of the authorities to find the asshole who killed Landry?" Fiadh asked.

He backed away, ducking into the wild flurry until she could no longer make him out.

"I won't contact you again," his disembodied voice said. She blinked and swiped at the snow on her cheeks as the glacial wind cut through her. "Do me a favor and stay aware. Stay alive."

"Angel?" she said after there was nothing but silence.

"Ms. Kane?!" Lake's voice was panicked now, and Fee turned toward what she thought was the entrance of the park where she'd left the bodyguard. There was nothing but a swirl of white and looming black shadows that might have been the trees.

"Lake?" she hollered. "I can't see shit. Where are you?"

"Follow my voice. I don't want to leave the street, otherwise I'll lose sight of it."

They kept talking, and Fee picked her way through the snow until she reached her. Their black outfits were hidden beneath a layer of white, and Fee was shaking from head to toe. The sweater and sweatshirt were no match for the blizzard-like conditions. Even tucked into her pockets, her fingers were like ice.

Lake turned in the direction of the street and said, "Grab my jacket, and don't let go."

Fee latched on to the dark windbreaker, hoping her frozen hand could remain clutched to the material as they inched their way along. Lake kept looking at her phone, but the storm was messing with the signal, and Fee wasn't sure if they were even going in the right direction. The bodyguard attempted to contact the team over her mic, but all she got back was static. They proceeded at their snail's pace. There was no way they were going to make it back to the hotel by eight-thirty. But Fee wasn't sure it mattered. No one would be flying out in this. They were stuck in Boston.

Chapter Nine

Asher

DARK SIDE
Performed by Bishop Briggs

𝒜*sher had gotten the nor'easter alert* on his phone only two hours after falling into bed in the hotel room, and he'd jumped into action, waking Zia and putting them both to work. She'd immediately gotten the semi-trucks and band's bus on the road while he'd arranged for a couple of four-wheel-drive vehicles to take the Daisies to a private airport farther inland. They had to get the band out of Boston in the next few minutes, or they'd be stuck here for days while the storm of the century settled over the Atlantic Coast from Massachusetts to Maine.

He was glad he'd decided to stay the night at the hotel instead of heading the few minutes north to his family's estate. It allowed him to start pounding on doors at six thirty. While the equipment had made it out before the first flake had hit the ground, he'd made the wrong decision to let the Daisies sleep. The weather maps had shown the storm holding off longer than it had, and now it was a scramble he didn't like.

The elevators dinged, and the band members poured into the lobby, looking even more exhausted than they had several hours before.

"We need to get out now," Asher said as Paisley and Jonas approached him, waiting at the hotel entrance.

"There's no way we're flying out in this," Jonas said, jerking his chin toward the snow that was falling fast and steady.

"I have SUVs taking us inland to Springfield where a plane is waiting for us, but if we don't leave soon, we won't be able to take off from there either."

The security detail hustled the group toward the doors.

His heart skipped a beat when he realized one band member still hadn't shown up. "Where's Fiadh?"

God, just saying her name was torture.

Leya and Adria exchanged a worried glance. It was Special Agent Kent who spoke up. "We got a do-not-disturb call for her about thirty minutes ago."

"What the fuck is a do-not-disturb call?" Asher asked.

The detail all shuffled awkwardly.

"You know…when they shouldn't be interrupted," one of the bodyguards spoke up.

The knowledge hit him in the gut like a fist. She was screwing someone. She was out doing the one thing he'd told her not to do, at seven in the morning, when her band—her supposed friends—needed her to be there.

His jaw clenched as anger and disappointment filled his veins in equal measures. "Go. I'll find her, and we'll be right behind you."

Nikki hung back, clearly not liking his tone. "Maybe I should stay with you."

He shook his head. "No. There's no use risking more of you because of one stupid decision."

"I don't think you should be the one to go after her," Leya said, and he wanted to shake Fee even more for abandoning her friends while they were still trying to protect her.

"I'm exactly who should go after her. Tommy would do it if he were here, right?"

They all started talking at once. It became clear that not

only was the band well aware of Fiadh hating him, but they worried if he went after her, it might end with one or both of them seriously injured. He wasn't sure it wouldn't. But someone needed to call her out on the shit she was pulling, and he was pretty sure none of her friends would.

A loud whistle from Zia brought silence—the sound completely contrary to her size. Zia was small enough that even tiny seemed like a generous description, not unlike Paisley. But whereas Paisley was all serious, slow motions, Zia was a lightning bug bouncing from one landing spot to the next.

"Asher's right," she said. "You need to leave, or you'll all be stuck. I'll stay."

That seemed to ease everyone's concerns except Asher's. He wasn't leaving. Not until he'd found Little Miss Sneak and told her a thing or two about what he thought of her irresponsible behavior.

The four bandmembers, Jonas, and two bodyguards got into the large Escalade up front and took off. The rest of the bodyguards, Asher, and Zia loaded the luggage into the second SUV, and just before it was going to take off, Asher looked at Zia and said, "Get in."

She shook her head. "No, I said I'd wait for her."

"Look, I don't know enough about your job and the tour to be able to do it without you. If you get stuck, they'll be screwed. If I get stuck, it means nothing."

"They have Jonas," Zia said, uncertainty in her eyes.

"They do, but they need both of you. They don't need me."

"You and Fee…" Zia trailed off.

Asher's jaw clenched. "I know. But I promise I'll be on my best behavior."

Zia laughed. "Do you even have a behavior other than asshole?"

If he wasn't so angry, he would have laughed. This little creature was damn good at her job and saw exactly what she needed to in the people surrounding the band. It inched up his respect for her.

"I'll try to be less of an asshole, how's that?"

She still seemed wary, but the snow coming down in buckets and the wind spiraling about them increased the urgency to get out.

"Just go," he said.

She climbed in, and he turned to one of the bodyguards climbing in after her. "Give me a mic."

The man shifted his feet, uncomfortable.

"Give it to me or find another job."

The man pulled his two-way mic out of his ear and handed it over to Asher before saying, "I've been trying to get a hold of Lake—that's the bodyguard who's with her—but it's just static. I think the storm is messing with it until they get close enough."

Asher nodded, and then the man joined the others in the vehicle. It took off down the street, disappearing in the blanket of churning snow before it had gone more than a few feet.

There was one SUV left parked at the curb. The vehicle belonged to his family just like the driver behind the wheel. Reggie was ex-special forces and had been hired by his father back when Asher was a kid. He had bright-red hair and a dark-brown beard that seemed at odds with each other. If it wasn't for the suit the man wore, it would be easy to see him behind a sawmill, pushing wood as his father had before him.

"We're not getting out," Reggie said matter-of-factly, leaning down to speak to him through the window.

Asher sighed. He'd known it as soon as he'd sent Zia on her way. The band would be lucky to make it to Springfield and the flight themselves. Even five minutes more would have made it impossible.

"I know. Think we can make it back to Taran Ridge?"

If he was going to be stuck in Boston in the middle of a nor'easter, he'd rather be at his home where there was a generator, food, and staff.

Reggie eyed the snow piling up. "If we leave in the next twenty minutes, I'll make sure we do."

Asher headed back inside, shaking the snow off his jacket and stomping his boots. He blew on his hands and took in the empty lobby. No one was stupid enough to be leaving the hotel. Everyone had holed up in their rooms.

He wiped the mic and put it in his ear. "Lake?"

Nothing but static returned.

Below the anger, Asher started to feel a prick of anxiety.

Why couldn't she have had her little fling in the safety of the hotel? Why did she have to go out somewhere with one damn bodyguard and nothing else to protect her? In the middle of a fucking storm.

It was stupid. Rash. Flighty.

It was something he'd expect of Nova or, almost as bad, his mom. Memories fought their way to the surface. Being left alone at a museum because Mom had disappeared. Nova slipping away at a party to come back high, eyes glossy. He was cursed, like every male member of the Riggs family, when it came to relationships. A cycle on repeat he was damn sure he didn't want to repeat again.

Beneath the static, a voice came through. "This is Lake to command. We're almost back. What's our status?"

The brief flicker of fear he'd felt for Fee disappeared, and only anger remained. "Your status is fired. Fiadh's status is yet to be decided. The band's status is departed."

"Mr. Riggs?" Lake said over the mic.

"Yes."

He didn't wait for them in the lobby. Instead, he stepped out on the sidewalk, glancing in both directions as a gust of wind nearly knocked him over. The air blew so strong it actually made a screeching sound along the corridor between the buildings. This was not a quiet, beautiful snowfall. It was a blizzard-like squall.

His jaw was ticking, and his stomach was clenched tight

by the time a distorted shadow shifted into the shape of the two women. The bodyguard was up front, plowing through the chaotic flurry, and Fiadh was tucked behind her, grasping her jacket like it was a lifeline, which in the goddamn limited visibility, it was.

They'd barely reached him when Asher opened the door of the Escalade and growled at Fiadh, "Get in."

She didn't even argue. She just scrambled into the back. He slammed the door behind her and turned to Lake. "You're fired."

Her chin went up. "You can't fire me."

"I can. I'm paying the bills, and I just did."

Lake went to sidestep him and climb into the front passenger seat, but he blocked her path. "Go back into the hotel, call your boss, tell him what you did, and I can guarantee he'll agree with me."

Asher opened the front passenger door, slid in, and shut it before Lake could respond.

Reggie was already driving away as Asher reached for his seat belt.

"Wh-where's L-lake?" Fiadh asked from the back. Her voice was shaking, teeth chattering, and when he looked at her, he realized she was in nothing more than a goddamn sweatshirt and jeans.

"Turn up the heat, Reg," Asher said, but he didn't respond to her. He couldn't, not without breaking the promise he'd made Zia.

When he risked glancing at her again, she was shivering uncontrollably. His teeth clamped together with a harsh crack that rattled up through his temple. Good. She deserved a consequence for ducking out in the middle of a storm at all hours of the morning to sleep with some nobody. Some schlump she'd never see again. He couldn't remember the last time he'd felt this angry. This out of control.

"Wh-where are we g-going?" Fee asked. He watched as she tugged at her wet boots, pulling them off and then curling her knees to her chest and surrounding her toes with her hands. "N-no one is g-going to fl-fly out in this."

"Your band is driving out to Springfield where they'll be catching a flight. If you'd been where you were supposed to be, you would be with them and not stuck in a goddamn storm in Boston."

Her eyes widened.

She was shaking so bad her feet kept slipping off the back seat. Her fingers looked almost purple, and her nose was bright red. She'd flung her hood back, and the beanie underneath was drenched, loose tendrils of hair stuck to her face that was decidedly pale beneath the windburn.

He wanted to climb into the back, wrap her in his arms, and warm her up. To make her teeth stop chattering. To drag the wet clothes off of her and show her that whoever she'd been with hadn't done even half of what he could do to her. It pissed him off even more, that a large part of the fury he felt was from the simple knowledge of her having spent the morning draped in someone else.

He had no claim to her. For Pete's sake, he didn't even want to claim her impulsive, selfish self. And now he was stuck with her while the storm blew through. Bringing her to Taran Ridge was going to be, at a minimum, awkward as hell and, at the worst, another enormous mistake.

The reality zapped him in the chest.

He was going to have them both under the same roof.

It was worse than a mistake. It was a disaster of epic proportions. One that risked everything. Risked his secrets and his truths.

All because of Fiadh-damn-Kane.

Chapter Ten

Fiadh

WHAT'S IT GONNA TAKE
Performed by Sarah McLachlan

Fiadh couldn't feel her toes or her fingers as she gripped her feet in her hands. It was like they were disembodied parts barely flickering with warmth as they collided, scarcely putting a dent in the ice filling her veins. She tugged at her sopping wet sweatshirt, fumbling to get it off and hoping, in removing it, she could dry out at least the sweater underneath.

The men upfront were silent. The driver had a death grip on the wheel as he inched through the flakes whipping in all directions. Gusts were hitting the SUV so hard she thought it might tip over.

Asher kept glancing back at her, and every time he did, his jaw seemed to get tighter. She'd be surprised if he didn't have a set of broken teeth by the time they arrived at wherever they were going. The way her teeth were banging and clanging as she shivered, she might end up with the same result.

Asher unzipped his coat, shrugged out of it, and tossed it in her direction. The heat of it surged over her cold hands and feet, and she almost cried with relief, but she didn't. Instead, she handed it back.

"I-I don't want your c-coat," she said, trying to sound sure.

"I can't afford for you to get sick, Fiadh. Just put on the goddamn coat."

Money. This was about money.

"One less p-person to pay," she shot back.

But the warmth was too tempting. She pulled the jacket to her, shoving it on backward over her shoulders and curling her entire being up inside its downy softness. The heat of him was dissipating from it fast as her wet, icy body soaked it up, but it still smelled like him. That heady combination of earth and citrus.

"How many times do I have to tell you, I'm not looking to lose any of you," he growled.

She didn't respond. She just buried her face in the coat, trying to let it warm her.

As her body started to thaw, her brain kicked back into gear. Angel's warnings about the wolves circling came back to her.

What had he meant?

He'd told her they needed to drop Asher and RMI. Had he known more than he was telling her? Where was the drugged-up ex? Who had followed Angel's electronic trail?

She closed her eyes, exhaustion hitting her. Not just from the jaunt in the snow and the fretful few hours of sleep but from nearly two years of worry. Twenty months of trying to put on a happy face for Paisley, Landry's parents, and the band while wallowing through a pool of grief chest high all alone. Fee had thought she'd always have the band at her side. But the truth was, when the worse had hit, they'd all gone off in separate directions until Paisley had pulled them back together. If the Daisies ever broke up for good, would they even remain friends?

It tortured her. The thought of being completely by herself in this world.

Paisley and the Kims wouldn't let her slip into nothing, would they?

The thought clogged her throat, tears hitting her eyes

that she barely held back.

She couldn't cry here, in the back of the car, with Asher up front, waiting for a sign of weakness.

She pulled her head out of the jacket and met a frowning blue gaze.

He swiveled around as soon as she caught him staring. She turned to look out the window at the sea of white and the flashes of shadows. It was like watching an expressionist painting come to life—a blurred vision of buildings and trees and roads. She wasn't sure where they were going, and that thought should have bothered her more than it did.

She pulled out her phone from where it had been tucked in her pocket to find she had no signal in the storm. She couldn't respond to the dozen calls and twenty texts from the band sitting there waiting for her. Knowing she'd worried them made her stomach clench even more.

It felt like three hours but was less than one by the time they rolled up to enormous gates set in a stone wall towering over the road. Perched on pillars on either side of the black wrought iron were marble griffins standing on their hind legs with their tails curled around them and wings spread wide as the snow piled on their shoulders. They were terrifying and beautiful all at the same time.

Just like Asher.

She pushed the thought away as the gates swung open, and the SUV continued down a long and meandering drive. Trees on either side reached over the road, blending together and making the dreary day even darker.

Fee's heart pounded in her chest.

"Where are we?"

"Taran Ridge," the driver said just as Asher said, "My family's estate."

The pounding of her heart picked up to an almost frenzied pace.

She was stranded in Boston with Asher. At his home.

Angel's warning sounded in her brain again before she

shook it off. This was what she wanted, right? To have access to Asher. To find out his secrets. What better way than in the one place he was sure to let his guard down?

A large, gloomy shape loomed in front of them, and the snow eased just enough for her to catch a glimpse of the house. Dozens of gabled and stained-glass windows glimmered like the multi-faceted eyes of a dragon reflecting the storm. A façade made of huge black slabs offset with white limestone shone like the dragon's scales, and statues hanging off the ornate scrollwork along the roofline became the dragon's talons. Tall spirals of half a dozen chimneys gave the impression of spikes stabbing at the gray sky.

She shook her head at the vivid picture she'd conjured. In reality, the mansion was a wild mix of a French château and a Georgian manor set down on an estate outside Boston. She swallowed hard, remembering everything Angel had discovered about Asher's ex, and found her eyes darting to the upper windows, wondering if this was where the woman was being held. Maybe Fee would join her, or maybe they'd both be locked in a dank cellar instead of an attic room. Lord knew there was plenty of space in a place like this to lose two women.

Lost in her ominous thoughts, she hadn't realized they'd stopped in front of the ornate portico until her car door was practically ripped open. Asher reached in, undid her seat belt, and pulled her into his arms. He strode toward the swirl of beveled glass and wrought-iron vines making up the front door like a groom carrying his bride.

"What are you doing?" she asked, voice quivering as the warmth of him blended in with her disturbed thoughts.

"Should I have let you walk through the snow piles in nothing but socks?" he demanded without once looking down at her.

His body was almost rigid as he carried her, but everywhere they touched, she was being zapped with heat, prickles that had nothing to do with her skin defrosting and everything to do with the chemistry that wafted between them.

84

He'd barely stepped inside before he all but dropped her. She wobbled on feet that were still practically numb. He grabbed her waist to steady her, and more waves of awareness swept through her. He jerked his hand back, face settling into a mask that fit the dark mood of the house.

Fee let Asher's coat slide away as her gaze swept around the circular entrance. The gloominess of the exterior trailed inside like a smoky haze from the dragon's nose. Black marble floors led to black wainscoting that bled into etched white wallpaper shimmering like diamonds under the light of a car-sized chandelier dripping with crystals. Above a grand, spiraling staircase that was as black as the rest of the house, intricately carved strapwork crisscrossed the ceiling.

In the center of the entrance, a white marble table with black, clawed feet held a gigantic vase holding at least four dozen red roses. They were the only color in the entire room. It filled Fee's mind with blood and gloom and vampires, and when she looked at Asher's face, jaw still tight and anger brewing in his eyes, she couldn't help but laugh. He was the perfect Gothic hero.

Once she started laughing, she couldn't stop. She put a shaky hand up to her eyes to brush at the tears forming from the humor bubbling out of her.

"There's not one thing funny about this entire fucked-up morning, Fiadh," he snarled.

This only set her off more because, of course, the Gothic hero would never see anything as funny. Ever. Except, Asher wasn't a hero. He might even be the villain.

That had her laughter dying away. His eyes drifted down her body, taking in her wet jeans and damp sweater and the socks that were leaving marks on the marble floor.

His jaw ticked again. "Let's find you some dry clothes."

He headed up the staircase. He was up several steps before he realized she hadn't followed. He looked down and said, "Do I have to carry you up the stairs too?"

She could have sworn there was a hint of tease in his tone that wasn't visible in his face. It did nothing to reassure her that going with him into the bowels of the beautiful but menacing house was wise.

It was only her desire to feel warm again that eventually pushed her to go with him.

As they spiraled around the staircase, she caught glimpses of long hallways filled with more black wainscoting, glittering white wallpaper, and blood-red flowers on marble tables. On the third floor, he led her down a corridor lined with mirrors in delicate silver frames, making the hallway feel endless.

Asher strode through a set of double doors. At the entrance, her feet faltered. The contrast of the room to the rest of the house was like emerging from a plane traveling through night skies onto a sunshine-filled beach on a Caribbean island. A gigantic sleigh bed made of white oak was perched upon pale wooden floors while linens and curtains of heavy brocade embroidered in vivid teal patterns added to the feel of sand and sea.

Asher stalked over to a set of engraved doors, threw them open, and disappeared inside. She could see a row of shirt sleeves peeking out, and her curiosity had her trailing after him. The closet was a perfectly arranged walk-in. Men's shoes were aligned in straight rows on the shelves, suits sat at the exact same distance apart on the rods, and all the drawers were closed, hiding what she instinctively knew would be sharply folded garments.

Asher opened and shut several drawers before coming toward her with a small stack.

"They'll be huge, but they'll be dry." He held the clothing out to her.

She took them, and their hands skipped across each other, shooting her with another round of awareness that curled low through her belly.

"You're not screaming," she said finally.

One brow arched as he stared down at her.

"Why aren't you yelling?" she asked.

His jaw ticked, but he didn't answer. Instead, he put his hands on her shoulders and spun her around, directing her back into the bedroom and through another set of doors that led to a bathroom as bright as his room, even on this gloomy day.

"Change. Then, maybe I'll yell," he said, slamming the door behind her and making her jump.

Her body felt stiff and numb from the cold, and when she caught a glance of herself in the mirror, she groaned. She looked like a wet dog. She eyed the shower, wishing she could step inside and melt away the ice in her veins, but she didn't want to spend more time in what was obviously Asher's room than she needed to. Not without a plan.

Instead, she fought to get her clinging, wet clothes off her body and pulled on the sweats, T-shirt, and Columbia University sweatshirt he'd handed her. The socks were the softest pair she'd ever felt in her life, and she almost groaned as she wiggled her toes into them. Everything smelled like Asher, and it did something to her chest she didn't like—an ache for something she couldn't name flitting at the back of her mind and then away.

She rolled the waistband of the sweats over several times to keep them up and thanked heaven she wasn't as tiny as Paisley, who would have been lost in them. She grabbed a towel from the stack of them on an open shelf and dried her hair as best she could. She missed having her makeup as it served as armor she felt desperately in need of at the moment.

But she had nothing. Not her band. Not her clothes.

Not even a working phone.

She took a deep breath, threw back her shoulders, and opened the door.

Asher was waiting, and his gaze trailed lazily over her in his clothes, the look a caress that had her veins humming. It screamed danger and seduction. Things she was no longer sure she could handle when simply touching him was already sending her senses into overdrive, tapping at the edges of her achingly lonely soul. But maybe she wouldn't have to seduce him. Maybe just being stranded in his house would allow her to get the information she needed. She ignored the disappointment that thought sent trickling through her.

It was better this way, wasn't it?

She swallowed hard, stepping toward him just as the lights flickered before going out completely. She couldn't help the startled yip that escaped her. Asher chuckled, and the sound was almost worse than his touch. It ran through her veins like the burn of vodka.

"The generator will kick in. Give it a moment," he said.

And sure enough, the lights sprang back on barely a minute later.

He was at the door, having moved in the darkness, and her mind filled with images of gothic vampires again. Asher would make a phenomenal one.

"Let's get you something hot to drink," he said, opening the door and waving her through.

She slid past him, knowing with a sudden sense of clarity that she was in over her head. She wanted to run, and she wanted to stay. She wanted to pull his mouth down and kiss him, and she wanted to keep him at a distance. She wanted the truth, and she wanted to remain in the dark, because if she found out he'd been responsible for Landry in even the slightest way, she'd be forced to bring him down, and there was an ever-growing part of her that found the idea deplorable.

Chapter Eleven

Asher

FALLING SLOWLY
Performed by Glen Hansard and Markéta Irglová

Seeing Fiadh in his clothes made Asher want to quickly divest her of them and toss her onto his bed where he could explore the dusting of freckles he knew would twine over her entire body. He'd ravish them one by one, memorizing them, playing them like she played her instruments, recording the notes in his mind.

But it was the last thing that could happen.

So, he opened the door and ushered her out into the hall, taking the back stairway down to the kitchen. His family took most of their meals there unless it was a holiday and Jozef decided to pull out the china in the formal dining room. The kitchen was as full of black and white as the rest of the house, but the bright colors Jozef had tossed into every corner made it feel more like home.

To Asher's surprise, the rectangular table with huge, clawed feet was laid out with breakfast. The hours spent getting things ready for The Daisies' escape, the harrowing minutes he'd waited for Fiadh, and the gripping ride back to the estate made it feel like it should have been the afternoon instead of morning.

Jozef bustled about the kitchen in slacks and a button-down shirt that would have had him fitting in at a bank instead of at a stove. But Asher couldn't remember seeing the slim, dark-haired man in anything else for as long as he'd been at Taran Ridge.

"Ash, I'm glad to see you made it back," Jozef scolded. "But I'll skin you alive and roast you with my next dish if you ever make Reggie drive in weather like that again."

Jozef came around the large island, wiping his hands on a towel he carried and then sticking one out toward Fiadh. The scowl on his face turned into a smile, blurring the wrinkles just starting to age him.

"Ms. Kane, it's a pleasure to meet you in person. Can I say, your new single, 'Riding the Green,' has quickly become a favorite? The way you play the harp in it"—he did a little chef kiss—"it's perfection."

Fiadh seemed thrown off-kilter by Jozef's joy, as if it was a piece that didn't fit in the puzzle that was Asher's life. But she eventually stuck out her hand to shake the one he'd offered. "Thank you."

"This is Jozef," Asher told her. "His official title is chef and housekeeper, but he's more like the estate's dictator."

Jozef laughed, eyes crinkling at the corners.

"Which is why both Ash and his father depart from my kingdom whenever possible. They don't like to be told what to do in their own home, but I'm afraid it's my fate in life to make others toe the line. This is why I could never have worked as anyone's sous chef and have been working for the Riggs family my entire career."

"She doesn't need your life history," Asher said, making his way to the table and sitting down. Jozef had come to Taran Ridge when Asher had been younger than Wren at a time when his mother had still been there. A knot formed in his throat he couldn't quite clear at the thought of his mom. When Asher glanced over at Fiadh, he realized she didn't just remind him of Nova but also the woman who'd given birth to him.

Her eyes bounced around the kitchen from Jozef to him and back before she made her way to the table, choosing a chair as far away from Asher as she could get. He was relieved and pissed off by the action all at the same time.

Jozef went back to the stove and returned with a kettle. He hovered the water over Fiadh's cup. "Tea?"

"Is there any chance of getting a coffee?"

Jozef pulled back.

"Thank God. I finally have someone else to share my love of the bean with. I like you already. Cappuccino work?" Jozef asked, and she nodded fervently.

Jozef tipped water into Asher's cup where a tea infuser dangled. Then, he buzzed back into the kitchen and went to work at his favorite machine, making it come to life with hisses and clanks.

"I wouldn't have pegged you as a tea drinker," Fiadh said, glancing at Asher before looking away again. She was uneasy, waiting for him to rant and rave about the stupidity of her going out in a storm to sleep with some stranger, and he'd get there. But he had every intention of being calm when he did so. The drive from Boston, which had taken more than double the normal time, had given him plenty of time to strategize.

Yelling at her would only increase their animosity and risk sending her off into more flights of fancy. Hadn't every scar he had on his body left by another woman taught him the same thing? No, he wouldn't make the same mistake with Fiadh. He'd already made too many.

Having her here was the perfect opportunity to win her over, to make her realize that being with RMI was what was best for her—the band. Then, he'd do the same with each of the members until they were all in agreement.

"Is there some tea-person code I don't know about?" he asked, pulling the strainer out before cupping the mug and letting the warmth ease through him.

"It's just…you're way too wound up. Like you pump caffeine intravenously."

Jozef snorted from the kitchen before all but twirling back to the table and presenting Fee with a perfectly crafted cappuccino.

"I beg to disagree. I'm rarely wound up," Asher said.

It was Fiadh's turn to snort, but any further response was cut short by a soft voice that had everyone glancing toward the carved trefoil archway.

"Good morning, Father."

His heart caught in his throat as he took in his daughter—small and fragile just like the red-backed, fairywren she'd been named after. Her skin was so pale you could see the veins in places, but her eyes were full of life belied by her quiet movements.

He caught Fiadh staring as his daughter made her way over to him, but he didn't let it change how he greeted her with a warm hug and a kiss on the cheek. "Morning, Birdie."

Wren slid into the chair next to him. She pushed her shiny black hair behind her and reached for the toast with graceful, slow movements that made her seem like a dancer when his daughter had no interest in anything so vigorous.

She was dressed as she always was, in a long dress that looked like it should have been thrown away after the 1970s had come and gone. Flowers and layers of ruffles. She had dozens of similar dresses in different colors and patterns. In the spring, when the grass was littered with wildflowers and she lay amongst them with her books, she looked like she belonged to that era. She looked like Nova...

Wren's hand stilled in the process of reaching for the jam as she finally realized there was someone else at the table. "Oh, hello." She tilted her head as if trying to determine where she'd seen Fiadh before.

"Wren, this is Fiadh. She got stranded in the storm and will be staying with us until it passes."

Wren took in Fiadh's hair that was curling upward as it dried, the clothes that were clearly his, and the tattoos peeking out from the sleeves of his sweatshirt.

"You are wearing Father's clothes," she said softly.

"Everything I own was drenched through, and my

luggage is somewhere across the state," Fiadh said, recovering herself and surprising Asher by sending a stunning, soft smile toward Wren. It was Fiadh's real, slightly crooked smile. A smile he'd spent years longing to see again while hating himself for wanting it. And now, in mere seconds, one had been directed at his daughter. It had his throat closing around the tea until he was coughing, drawing everyone's glance as he attempted to pull himself back together.

"Are you okay, Father?" Wren asked. He nodded, trying not to notice the way Fiadh's eyes squinted at Wren's calm politeness. He knew what she was thinking. Knew she'd assume the "Father" and the well-mannered demeanor was his doing…his requirement. As if he'd forced his daughter into this perfect, quiet mold.

And in some ways, he had. By his absence. By his inability to look at her and not see her mother, even though he loved her with a fierceness he couldn't explain. But what Fiadh would never know was how much he longed to hear Wren call him Dad, make a mess in the kitchen, and destroy his best suit with paint. The knot in his throat didn't lessen, and he put the tea down while he tried to ease the pain that had lodged itself there.

After Wren had layered her toast with a thick pile of Jozef's homemade strawberry jam, she looked at Fiadh and said, "You do not have to wear Father's clothes. There are boxes and dressers full of clothes in the attic. If you would like, I could show them to you later."

Fiadh shot Asher a glare as if he'd purposefully put her in his clothes, and he had, because there'd been no way he'd been willing to take her up to the attic. Half of it was a storage room, and half of it was a room he chose not to go into unless he had to, unless it was the only way to stop the screams. No, his clothes would do the trick until the storm passed—a day or so at most, as long as it didn't settle in and stick around.

"You're not supposed to go to the attic," he reminded Wren with a small frown.

"I never go alone. Jay goes with me."

He could practically hear the wheels turning in Fiadh's head. This was exactly the disaster he'd expected it to be. Not even an hour in, and all his secrets were about to come tumbling out.

"Where *is* Jay?" Asher asked.

"Here! I'm here!" Jay said, sauntering in and pushing aside the floppy brown bangs that made Asher's teeth grind. Jay had been with them for two years, but the man still appeared more college sophomore than grad student with multiple degrees in education and child psychology. His jeans, sweatshirt, and sock-clad feet only added to the laid-back, collegiate look. "Morning, everyone."

He didn't stop at the table. Instead, he rushed to the espresso maker. He was the only person Jozef let touch the machine, and that had been after months of tutelage. It took until Jay was carrying the drink back to the table for him to notice Fiadh was there. His feet stalled, and he almost dropped the cup.

"Holy sh—shish kebabs. You're Fiadh Kane," his voice was awed.

Fiadh smiled, but it was no longer her real one. It was the one she put on for the fans.

"In the flesh," she teased, and Jay turned a thousand shades of red.

"I mean. I knew Asher was off running around the country with you…but…you're here."

"Stop drooling, Jay, and take a seat before everything gets cold," Jozef said, sitting down next to Fiadh.

Jay made his way over to the chair next to Wren.

"Is Dad here or in New York?" Asher asked.

"Here, but you know how he feels about breakfast," Jozef said with an exasperated noise.

A door slammed in the distance, and moments later, Reggie appeared. His cheeks were red and his hair wild from the wind with layers of snow still embedded in it. He made his way over, kissed Jozef on the cheek, and sat in the chair on Jozef's other side while Jozef brushed the flakes away.

Jozef took the opportunity to formally introduce Fiadh to his husband while Asher dished himself eggs, sausage, and toast before sending the bowls around. As everyone fixed their plates, a silence settled down that was normally easy but today felt awkward because there was a guest they'd never had. Not in nine years. For the entire length of Wren's existence, the enormous house had held only the handful of people at the table and a silent, disappearing cleaning crew.

"What are your plans for your snowy Saturday?" Asher asked Wren.

She tilted her head while she thought. "*The Mystery at the Ski Jump* seems appropriate. What do you think, Jay?"

"If the storm lets up, we can build a snowman," Jay told her, and Wren shivered.

"Outside? In the cold?" She was already shaking her head, and Asher had to hold back a chuckle.

"I don't think the storm is letting up anytime soon," Reggie said. "The news said it's likely to settle down over us for at least a day, if not longer."

Asher groaned internally.

"Thank goodness we have the generator and plenty of fuel to run it. We could be weeks without electricity again, like the time the hurricane hit us," Jozef said.

Asher's heart thudded wildly as the memories of that horrible night assaulted him. Nova had proven just how far gone she was. He'd thought he'd lost Wren... Thank God, his daughter didn't remember it, not in any real way.

He barely registered the soft chatter between his staff and Fiadh as he tried to calm the panic flooding his veins. Wren was here. She was fine. It was Wren kissing him on the cheek as she left the table that finally grounded him.

He tapped her nose softly, and she slipped out of the room in her soundless way, saying she'd be in the library. Knowing Wren, she wouldn't make it there. She'd be found hours from now, sitting in a hallway on the floor with a

Nancy Drew book in her hand.

Asher glanced over at Fiadh's plate to see the single piece of toast she'd nibbled at was mostly gone. She'd not touched any of the other food, but she had drunk her coffee and asked for a second. It turned Asher's stomach, filling in painful memories of Nova doing the same...barely eating but overindulging in other areas.

He'd been home mere minutes and was already tired of the way thoughts of Nova and his mother had taken over his mind. Having lost his appetite, he pushed himself away from the table, grabbed his mug, and headed for the arched doorway.

"Are you coming?" he asked Fiadh. It really wasn't a question. It was a command she bristled at, but she looked around at the others and clearly didn't want to say what was on her mind in the midst of people she didn't know, so she stood.

"Thank you for breakfast," she told Jozef, and he grinned.

"Ms. Kane, what you ate could hardly be called breakfast, but I'll see what I can do to convince you it's the best meal of the day before you leave us."

Her lips twitched, and Asher found himself jealous of the fact that Jozef had earned it. Just like he'd been jealous of the real smile she'd sent his daughter. The one he wanted for himself and couldn't have.

"It's Fiadh, please," she said with a saucy wink.

Jozef's smile grew. "Fiadh it is."

She brought her coffee with her and followed him down the hall and out through another carved archway to his study. He flicked on the light and went directly to the huge wall of windows that normally soothed him with visions of the sea. Today, they revealed only a blanket of snow drenched in the gloomy light of the storm. The wind howled, pushing the icy piles against the glass.

When he turned around, Fiadh was examining the room with a surprised expression.

"What?" he asked.

"What, what?" she asked, finding her way to one of the white-and-silver wingbacks across from his desk and curling her feet underneath her as she sat.

"You looked surprised."

"Both of your rooms are a complete contrast to the rest of the house," she said.

"I don't like the dark," he found himself saying before he thought better of it.

She tilted her head in a way that wasn't unlike Wren's, and his heart tugged.

Silence settled between them, full of expectations, but half of them were ones he could never fulfill.

"Go ahead," she said.

"Go ahead? As in tell you what a selfish, stupid, ridiculous thing it was to go out in the middle of a storm to bang some person you'll never see again? Is that what you want me to say?" he asked calmly. It cost him a layer of skin on his cheek in order to hold back from saying the things he really wanted to say—the demands and commands he wanted to lay down.

"That wasn't why I left," Fiadh said, and his eyes narrowed disbelievingly. "I wasn't out screwing someone. You ruined my chance at that last night."

He scoffed. "What? You had important business to attend to at seven thirty in the morning?"

"Yes."

"What?" he demanded.

She shook her head. "You don't get that answer. Not yet. Maybe never. You have to earn trust, Asher, and you have done nothing to earn mine."

He hated how right she was. "Trust goes both ways, Fiadh. You've hardly built a reputation that instills it. I've bailed you out twice from sneaking away from the safety of your detail. You put your entire band at risk every time you do so." When she started to talk, he held up his hand. "And don't even start with that bull about me being happy if something happened to you."

His voice lowered on the last few words. The thought of something happening to the bright, shiny fire that was Fiadh Kane left him almost breathless. Hit him in the solar plexus like a fist. Except…in some ways, something already had. The fierce woman he'd first watched backstage in Korea had been slowly disappearing under the weight of what had transpired with the Kims. He wanted to see her at full steam again—a torrential wildfire instead of a flickering flame.

She looked away, uncoiled herself from the chair, and wandered over to a side table laden with pictures in an array of silver frames. It put his life on display for her in a way he wasn't sure he was comfortable with. But she was here, and if she was going to be stuck for a couple of days, she was going to find out some of it. It would be impossible for her not to.

"Contrary to what you believe, my actions were actually all about the band," she said, shooting him a glance as she picked up a frame and glanced down at it.

"Yet you give me no proof."

"It's all I can give you until we trust each other," she said, studying the image. "Do you think that will ever be possible?"

No, his mind screamed, but his body was saying something entirely different. It was his body that had him journeying across the white marbled floor to stand next to her.

"It looks like we'll have a day or two to find out," he said as he took the frame from her hand. His fingers skated over hers, fire leaping up over his wrist and into his blood, lighting him up in a way that could melt the snow. When he looked down at the picture she'd been perusing, his throat closed again as it had in the kitchen.

It was him and Ronan with Nova between them. She had her arms around each of their waists, but her head was leaning on Asher's shoulder, a dreamy smile there. The smile she'd worn more often than not. Still wore, even when evil and violence appeared behind it many times now. The similarity between her and Wren was almost painful. Pale skin and black hair, but Wren had his blue eyes instead of Nova's gray ones.

"I didn't know you knew Ronan personally," Fiadh said, a question in her voice.

"We met at Columbia, both trying to fight our family names while simultaneously trying to find a way to live up to them." He'd only intended to give her the facts, but somehow, he'd ended up giving her more—a piece of himself he hadn't given anyone in years.

"I don't understand," Fiadh said, gaze resting on him.

Asher put the frame down and stepped back, putting space between them. She smelled like herself, but she also smelled slightly of him now with his clothes on, and every single cell in his body yearned to imprint more than just that faint scent of him—to cover her with it until nothing else remained.

"Ronan is from Hollywood royalty. I'm from business royalty. It's hard to just be yourself or find others who like you for you. And yet, if you love what your family does, you're also fighting to find a way to be worthy of it. To find a role that fits you."

She was still watching him, and he finally met her glance with his own.

She swallowed hard, as if he'd just told her his darkest secret about love and loss.

He'd had plenty of both, and unlike time healing him, as Fiadh had insisted it would at the bar in Albany, his scars and scabs were torn back open every single time he walked through the door of Taran Ridge. There was absolutely no escape for him.

Chapter Twelve

Fiadh

THE DARK OF YOU
Performed by Breaking Benjamin

Fee had expected him to rant and rave. Instead, he'd been calm and collected. She'd almost rather the ranting because at least then she'd know there was a soul inside him. Passion she could reach. The emotionless Asher was like the man behind the curtain, one you'd never see pulling all your strings, and that was more terrifying.

Everything about him since arriving at his home had tilted her image of him in some way. His attempt to carve a light space for himself in the midst of all this dark, the tender expression on his face when he'd kissed his little girl, and the warmth in his voice when he talked to Jozef all spoke to layers she hadn't wanted to admit existed in the statue-like man. The way he'd sat down to a meal with his staff as if they were family instead of employees might have surprised her the most. The entire morning—the entire house and the people inside it—made her feel like she was living in a dream she would eventually wake from.

The door to his office opened, and a man who looked exactly like Asher, only older, came into the room. He had on an expensive, custom-tailored suit, much as Asher normally did, and his blue eyes were just as piercing. His face held more wrinkles, but his hair was just as thick and dark. Even the gray at his temples matched. He was fit with wide shoulders and a trim waist. They could have been brothers if

Fiadh hadn't known that Asher was an only child.

"Fiadh Kane, lovely to meet you. Kellan Riggs," his father said, sticking out his hand. "I'm sorry it's the weather that's forced you here instead of something more entertaining."

He shot a glance at his son that confused Fee as she shook his hand and let go.

"I'm not sure it was the weather, sir, as much as your son basically kidnapping me."

Kellan chuckled. "Let's not say that too loud, shall we. Someone will believe it."

"Oh, it's true. I would have been perfectly fine at the hotel."

"You'd be stuck without electricity or food, freezing your ass off," Asher said, a hint of frustration sneaking back into his bland voice—passion that Fiadh found herself craving.

Kellan's eyebrows shot up at his son's reply, but he turned his smile back at Fee as he said, "Regardless, I'm glad you're here. Asher and I have been going rounds about our investment in the record labels, and I'd appreciate an inside take on the situation. You, young lady, are dropping in at the perfect time."

"Dad," Asher's voice held a warning Kellan waved off.

"I'm in back-to-back meetings today, but we'll spend some time tonight discussing it. You can tell me what you think it takes to make a label a success, and what an artist like you is looking for in one. Sound good?" His dad smiled at Fee, and it was thoroughly charming just like Asher's would be if he ever let himself smile.

"I'm not sure I have a choice, sir. You'll be here. I'll be here. It's either discuss whatever you want or the range of pill bugs."

Kellan laughed again. "Record labels are much more fascinating than pill bugs. And it's Kellan, please. None of this *sir* stuff."

Fee had just given him a smile in return when a scream rent the air. It was violent, ferocious, and terrifying in a way that sent chills over her body and triggered a flight instinct that had her jumping. What was almost more frightening than the scream itself was the complete lack of reaction from either of the men. They stood there, as if nothing was amiss, instead of tearing from the room to see who was filling the house with murderous rage. If anything, they both looked resigned.

Her breath caught, but her heart hammered fiercely, and the combination made the room spin. She put a hand out to the side table to keep from falling over.

Kellan turned toward the door. "Well, that's my cue to leave. I'm assuming you have things to explain," he said to Asher and then glanced over at Fee again. "See you tonight, Fiadh."

And the door shut calmly behind him.

Fee's mind was telling her feet to run, but she couldn't. She was locked to the floor in socks and clothes that didn't belong to her. Stuck in a storm that raged outside the huge windows, miles from town. She wasn't even sure where she was at. Her phone was nearly dead, and the last she'd checked, she'd had no signal. Would the police even be able to get to her if she called 9-1-1?

Asher rubbed a hand through his hair, messing up the perfect cut in a way not even the snow and wind had been able to do.

"You don't need to call the police," he said, reading her thoughts.

"What the feck?" she breathed out.

Asher moved toward her, and she backed up, eyes darting to the door as yet another tormented, angry scream filled the air.

He stopped at the table, picking up a frame. This one had just him and the same woman from the picture with Ronan.

"That's Nova," he said, waving the frame up at the ceiling. "She's Wren's mother."

Fee's heart skittered, thinking of the antipsychotic meds and the missing ex.

"Y-your wife?"

His gaze found hers, and instead of icy reserve, she saw something in them that made her stomach twist. As if he was begging her to understand. To see a truth he hadn't explained.

"No. We were never married, but we were engaged for a while," he said, putting the frame down and stepping closer until he'd all but removed the space left between them.

She backed up, hitting a bookcase, eyes shifting toward the door.

"It isn't what it looks like," he said calmly.

"You're not Edward Rochester hiding your insane wife in the attic of a dark mansion with a child you're raising on your own amongst a host of servants?" Fee asked, trying to tease, trying to hide the fear stirring through her as his body shifted until they were almost touching.

His lips quirked ever so slightly. "It is very Gothic, isn't it?" But the partial smile slipped away almost as soon as it started. "Rochester and I have many things in common. Let's hope I'll keep my eyes, my hand, and the house."

Fee tried to step around him toward the door, but he caught her wrist. It was a loose hold, one she could have easily broken, but it stopped her anyway. The warmth of his grip coasted over her skin, and like every time he touched her, it rippled through her nerve endings, slamming them open and shooting desire through her. If it felt this way with a simple touch that had not an ounce of sensuality to it, she wondered what it would feel like if he actually kissed her.

Her eyes fell to his lips. When she looked back up, his gaze had landed on her mouth as well. It didn't help, knowing the desire went both ways. Instead, it made her core throb in a way it never had, frightening her almost as much as the scream.

"You don't have to be afraid of me," he said. The words were soft, layered with lust.

She swallowed hard. "But I am." He flinched, the gentle hold on her wrist flexing. "For more than just this." She glanced around the room, really taking in the entire house. "I'm afraid because of the way my blood pounds when you're this close. I'm afraid of your secrets. I'm afraid if I don't keep my head and my distance, you'll be my...the band's undoing."

Using the hand not gripping her wrist, he snagged a wild curl that had fallen over her cheek, twirling it around his finger. "So soft, but so full of fire."

It was hypnotic—the low timbre of his voice, the way he tugged and twined her hair, and how he leaned his mouth until it was almost upon hers. Even though their bodies were separated by inches, it felt like there was a static electric field zapping back and forth between them. Lights you'd be able to see in the dark.

"If anyone should be afraid, Fiadh, it's me," he continued, the low, haunting growl swirling deep inside her again. "You'll burn me. Scar me. Fly away on dancing feet just like every other woman in my life."

Her heart thudded. If she moved even half an inch, she'd be able to taste him. But then, as if he finally realized what he'd said, where he was at, and how he was holding her, Asher's demeanor changed completely. He dropped her wrist, as if she'd bitten him, and stepped away.

Another scream filled the air.

It did nothing for Fee's shattered nerves or the wild pace of her heart.

Asher sighed, his broad straight shoulders hunching ever so slightly, like a kid who knew they were going to be scolded for doing something wrong. It made her ache for him when she didn't want to feel anything but hatred and distrust.

"I have to go. I'll be back."

And he left the room.

Her gaze fell to the fat flakes still falling outside the floor-to-ceiling windows taking up two walls of his office. Normally, it got quiet when it snowed. At least, that had always been her experience. But this storm was loud and fast and tossing the sea and the trees.

She pulled her phone from the sweatshirt's pocket and spied the charger on Asher's desk. She plugged it in and found she had the barest of signals.

She tried Paisley first, but there was no answer. She called Leya next, who picked up with a, "Thank Vishnu. We've been so worried. Where are you?"

"I'm at Asher's place, somewhere outside Boston."

"They say the whole city is without power and that the storm could last days," Leya said, concern dripping from every syllable.

Fiadh tried not to panic at the thought of being in this dark mansion for multiple days with screams filling the air and tension growing between her and Asher as her beliefs about him were stabbed and torn apart.

"He has a generator and food and a staff that seems to live on site. I'm not alone with him. Where are you?" Fee finally replied.

"We're in Springfield on the plane. We're just about to take off," Leya said, and a pang of longing and regret filled Fiadh. She wanted to be with them. It was where she belonged—the only place she ever did anymore. She thought of Asher's words minutes before about trying to find a role in his family. She'd thought she'd found hers with the Daisies.

"Look out, Chicago. The Painted Daisies are coming," she teased.

"Don't do that, Fee," Leya said, her voice dropping. "Don't turn this into something light. Where the hell were you?"

"I can't talk about it, Ley," she said.

"Fee—"

"No, really. I can't. Not yet."

"Does this have something to do with Asher and RMI? You've been on the road to vengeance since they came on board," Leya said. Her voice was still quiet, as if she was trying not to alert the others.

"It has to do with keeping us safe," Fiadh responded and then grimaced, wishing she hadn't said that much.

"That's why we have Reinard and, hell, even Captain Annoying himself. We don't need to risk ourselves when we're paying people to protect us."

She wasn't sure how Leya could trust any of them.

She glanced upward at the plaster strapwork to where the screams had come from. Was this the only secret Asher was keeping? An ex-fiancée who filled the mansion with tortured sounds? She couldn't get the, "It's done," he'd spoken the night of Landry's death out of her head. She had to know what it meant. The desire to know burned in her veins just like his touch. An excruciating tangle of fear and desire pulsed through her.

"Fee, I have to go. We're taking off. Are you really going to be okay?" Leya asked, uncertainty in her voice.

"I'm fine. Maybe Asher and I will actually find a middle ground while I'm here."

"Don't sleep with him!"

It brought a smile to her lips. "I'll try not to, but my dry spell has been mighty long, and have you seen his ass?"

Leya chuckled, which had been Fee's intent.

"The concert isn't until the weekend, but we're jam packed with interviews because of the album releasing this week. When are you going to be able to get out of there?" Leya asked.

"If it's more than a day, I'll find some snowshoes and walk out."

Leya laughed again. "I can imagine you doing just that."

Silence fell between them.

"Please take care of yourself," Leya said.

"Watch out for everyone there. I feel…" What she felt was irrational and based on the words of a private investigator she was starting to believe she never should have hired. "Just...he's still out there, Ley."

Leya's voice was choked with emotions when she spoke. "I know. We all know. We'll be okay. Just come back to us."

"Love you," Fee said. The words weren't spoken often enough, but she felt them to the bottom of her soul. She loved every single member of the band as much as her own family. She couldn't be with her siblings or her parents any longer, but she could be with her friends. They may have fallen apart after Landry, gone their separate ways, but she wasn't going to let that happen again.

"Love you back," Leya said.

Then, they hung up.

She wished she was with them. She kicked herself for going to meet Angel instead of making him come to her...or simply insisting he told her whatever he had to say over the phone. It had been entirely too clandestine. Ridiculous.

Fee looked at the desk she was standing behind. Asher's desk. There was a laptop closed on the top and several drawers without locks. Just as she started to open the top one, the door of the office opened, and Wren entered with a book in one hand, her thumb in the middle of it. It was a hardback with a yellow spine Fee vaguely recalled from her mother's library. Some girl-detective her ma had wanted her to read, but Fee had never acquired a taste for it.

"You have red hair," Wren said. "Under the purple."

The girl seemed like a little adult even though, from the reports she'd read from Angel, Fee knew she was only nine. There was a quiet calm to her, a graceful air that seemed like she should have been Fee's age instead of in primary school.

"I do," Fee said, coming around the desk.

"Nancy has Titian-blonde hair." She held up the book, showing the cover and a red-haired girl with a bob. "When Jay and I looked it up, it is similar to strawberry-blonde or very light red, like on the cover. Yours looks like it would be very dark." Wren had settled down in one of the wingbacks.

Fee sat in the chair next to her. "Yes, my whole family has very dark-red hair except my younger brother. He has hair most people say is carrot-colored."

Wren tilted her head as if she was considering this. "I do not think I would want carrot-colored hair."

"You look very good with your black. I wouldn't change it at all."

Wren offered her a small smile. "Would you like to read with me? Jay has to finish a paper and has left me to my own devices. He winked and told me to stay out of trouble, which I actually think meant he wanted me to get in trouble."

"Is Jay your nanny?" Fee asked.

Wren nodded. "Yes, but he hates the word. Jozef says he is family. Like an uncle or friend, and I think friend fits Jay much better than the word nanny."

"What's wrong with the word nanny?"

Wren tilted her head to the other side now. "It sounds like I am a baby in need of watching. I am in fourth grade, so I am not a baby."

Fee wondered if this miniature adult with her very formal speech pattern had ever been a baby. She wondered if Asher's cold demeanor and strict structure had taken the child out of her. It seemed so wrong. Another thing to add to Asher's list of bad qualities. Maybe if she amassed enough of them, her brain would convince her body that she didn't want to kiss him.

"If you were going to get into trouble, what would you do?" Fee asked.

Wren's eyes widened, and Fee thought she looked very much like the tiny, fragile bird she was named after.

"I do not get into trouble."

Fee's lips twitched, and she looked out at the snow, wondering if the girl had ever done something wild like throw a snowball at anyone, especially her father. But the storm was too fierce to even consider going out in it, and Fee was still shaking off the ice in her veins from that morning and had no desire to feel it again so soon.

"Hmm. How about you show me the stack of clothes in the attic?" Fee asked.

Wren went perfectly still, and then a visible shiver went over her before she shook her head. "Not right now. It is too loud up there."

Fee's heart lunged. The screams. The little girl was used to the screams and avoiding them. What must it be like to grow up in a place where that kind of sound ripped you from your sleep, your books, your peace?

"Well then, how about you just show me around this monolith so I know my way around while I'm here?"

Wren slid out of her chair with the book still gripped in her hand and headed toward the door on feet so light it was almost as if she was gliding above the floor. "What does monolith mean?"

"Like a large monument."

Wren considered this, head sideways. "But no one famous has ever lived here."

Fee joined her, matching the girl's steps as they walked down a long hallway. "Your family is famous."

Wren's feet stalled as she looked up at Fee with furrowed brows. "They are?"

"Well, in the business world, they are quite famous. And now they're making a name for themselves with movies and music. That's how I know your dad. I'm a musician in a band called The Painted Daisies."

Wren nodded and kept moving. "Jay told me after breakfast. He said you are a celebrity, so if you lived here, maybe then the house could be a monument or a monolith, but right now, it is just a home."

Fee's heart skipped a beat at that singular word—home. She lived alone in a condo she barely considered a place to keep her belongings and lay her head. These days, she preferred being on tour with the band or at the Kims' with people who sort of accepted her and at least understood her grief. The only home she'd truly known didn't welcome her anymore. The one she'd grown up in, she'd almost destroyed by merely being herself. And suddenly, she ached to have it all back. Not just acceptance, but a place where she could walk in the door, throw off all her troubles, let her guard down, and be loved regardless of what she looked like inside.

When Landry had been alive, she'd visited Fee's condo often. But even with her, Fee had held back. She didn't want her friend to feel responsible for what had happened—for her being alone in an apartment with no one. Then, there'd been Lars, who, for a brief moment, she'd thought she might actually have found something deeper with because he knew what it was like to be estranged from your family.

His band, RALE, had been the opening act for the Daisies on their Red Guitar tour, and what had started as a random hookup one night after a show had turned into texts and calls and weekly sex that had almost felt like a relationship. When the tour was over, and Fee had wanted to see him again, he'd laughed.

"Did you think we were dating, Fee? We were fucking. Screwing. Having fun. But I'm not a one-woman man, and I wouldn't think you'd want to stick with just a man at all, would you, sugar?"

She'd hated so many things about his little speech. The fact that everyone assumed being bisexual meant you'd never be happy in a monogamous relationship. The fact that she'd thought they'd grown closer than just fucking and screwing. But what she hated most was the ache inside her longing for just that…one person to claim her forever.

Lars had taken her tiny hopes and flung them away with his cold taunt.

And then she'd lost Landry. And almost the band.

Now, she was in this monolith, being shown around by a girl who could almost be a ghost, stuck with a man who clearly desired her but didn't trust her. A man she'd considered cold and heartless but now had her doubting every single thought that had led her to his door.

Chapter Thirteen

Asher

THIS IS NOT YOUR LOVE SONG
Performed by Scars on 45

When Asher made it up to the attic, Diego was shoved up against a wall while Nova swiped at him with the handle of a spoon. It looked like she'd already hit him once as there was blood on his cheek. She was moving wildly, savagely with her long black hair and floor-length white nightgown sticking to her from the exertion. Her face looked like Wren's, except it was distorted with hatred and fear.

It was always worse when she hit a pocket of clarity out of the sea of fog. She woke to find she didn't know where she was or why she was being held. It drove her to strike out—to try and escape.

"Nova," Asher forced himself to stay calm and use the most soothing voice he could manage.

As if she hadn't heard him, she ignored his presence and thrust again at Diego, who tried valiantly to grab one of her erratically swinging wrists. He was a short man with a barrel-like chest, dark hair, brown eyes, and brown skin, and his lack of height made it almost impossible for him to reach Nova, whose limbs were all longer than his.

Asher approached her from behind, treading quietly, noticing her breakfast tray had been thrown down, the yogurt and toast splayed across the floor and wall.

"Nova," he repeated softly, knowing if he showed even

a hint of emotion, she'd latch on to it and escalate even worse. His veins thudded with adrenaline as he watched her move, calculating how to counter it without hurting her. A match they'd done many times since she'd lost her hold on reality. "Nova, I'm going to put my arms around you."

Even with the warning, she still struggled once he'd pulled her against his chest, his arms surrounding her like a band. She kicked furiously. It always amazed him how someone with so little activity could be so viciously strong when she wanted to be. His knee screamed when she made contact, but he ignored it, using his body and his muscles to overpower her. It gave Diego a chance to snatch the spoon from her fingers, and then the two of them wrestled her to the bed where Diego strapped her hands and feet. It made Asher's stomach twist nastily. Binding her. Holding her. He hated it.

He hated it almost as much as the tranquilizer Diego fixed and shot into her thigh.

She squirmed and murmured while, in the background, the noise from her favorite show, *The Price is Right,* filled the room. A contestant shrieked with a joy that felt completely inappropriate for what had just played out in real life.

Diego stepped into the adjoining room, leaving Asher alone, as he always did after they'd had to sedate her. Asher wouldn't leave until she'd started to fall asleep. He sat down at the foot of the bed, watching as Nova's muscles started to loosen. Her ugly expression turning serene. Almost sweet. Like the first time he'd seen her.

She'd been sitting, legs crisscross, on the grass in the quad at Columbia, face tilted to the sun, the embodiment of peace, which had certainly been misleading after he got to know her but, at the time, had slowed his steps. When she'd opened her stormy gray eyes and picked him out in a sea of people on the crowded path, it had been as if fate had led her to him. A smile had lit her up, changing her energy from peaceful meditation to crackling life, and it had stalled his movements completely. Ronan, who'd been walking two steps behind him, had nearly run into him. His friend had laughed while sidestepping Asher. And from that moment, it had been the three of them, instead of just two.

Looking back, he could see all the signs of her drug use. The mood swings. The lack of appetite followed by gorging. The way she'd completely forget things they'd discussed or call him to come and get her from parts of town that weren't safe. But at the time, she'd always had good excuses or flighty stories about how she'd ended up there. He'd thought she was delightfully whimsical and not just an addict in hiding. He'd thought she needed his protection.

Those moments felt so long ago it was as if they had happened to someone else. As if he was just reading about it or watching a reel someone had posted on social media. A clip of a life that didn't exist anymore.

"A dollar. A dollar… A dollar…" Nova's slurred voice echoed through the room, talking to the television and the contestant who couldn't hear her.

The heavy weight of decisions needing to be made hit him. She'd hurt Diego today. Had slashed him with a goddamn spoon. It shouldn't have been able to be used as a weapon, and yet it had. Diego would have a bruise to go along with the cut.

Asher brushed aside the thick hair sticking to Nova's cheeks and forehead. Her body stilled, eyes closed, dark lashes standing out against pale skin. Her breathing turned rhythmic and slow instead of wild and thrashing.

"Sleep, Nov. Hopefully, you'll feel better when you wake."

He always said it after days like this. He always said it, and in some deep part of him, he knew he truly wished for it. To see her back to the Nova who knew what she was doing, even if it was manipulating and flirting and cheating and stealing. At least then, he could hold her accountable for her actions, for the trauma she'd put him and Wren and his family through. But this way—without true capacity for thought—all of the guilt and regret landed on him.

He stepped out of the bedroom, which was little more than a barren closet, and into the sitting room, which was almost as empty. Diego sat on the pull-out couch where he slept six nights a week. On his one day off, Asher, his father, Jozef, or Reggie stayed there. Nova couldn't be left alone. Even with locked doors, if you turned your back for even two seconds, she'd find a way out.

The entire thing was very much a fucking Gothic novel, just like Fiadh had said. And he was stuck, just like Rochester had been. Maybe less so because he'd never officially married Nova. She'd broken it off just before she'd found out she was pregnant with Wren, and in today's age, no one would have ostracized him for divorcing her anyway. But like Rochester, he was ravaged with the same torturous conscience. It was his decisions that had finally caused her to lose her grip.

Nova wasn't always violent. More often, she was docile and absentminded, staring at the television, jumping up and down in excitement when any of the contestants on her show won, as if she were with them, living their experiences.

But lately, the anger had been rearing its ugly head more often.

"What happened?" he asked Diego.

"There was a sound in the hall. I went to check, thinking it was you or one of the others, and when I came back, she'd thrown her tray at the wall. When I tried to clean it up, she lost it."

Nothing. Nothing had happened. Just Nova in her own world. He sighed and said, "If you want to leave, I'll understand."

Diego dabbed a tissue at his cut. "Nah, it's all good. But have you thought more about what we discussed? The alternative placement?"

Almost as much as he hated binding and tranquilizing her, he hated the relief that coasted through him whenever the idea of not having Nova under his roof was brought up. And once the relief hit, the guilt always followed, eating at him for feeling the relief to begin with. It was a never-ending cycle.

"I'll take a look at the list of facilities you and Torrance came up with," Asher said quietly.

"It's probably your best choice at this point," Diego said. "She's really been escalating, and I don't think that's going to change."

Asher nodded and headed for the door. With his hand on the knob, he turned back and said, "We appreciate what you do for us, Diego."

"You've done more for her than anyone I know would have. I'd like to say don't beat yourself up, but I think you will anyway."

Asher didn't respond. He left, wishing he could actually get away from Taran Ridge altogether for the day, get the smell of Nova's sweat and the stench of tranquilizers out of his bones. He headed back downstairs, stopping on the last landing to look out the window at the storm still in full swing. There would be no escaping the house or the weight of his life today. It was going to settle on him just like the inches of snow.

As he stood there, a strange sound finally penetrated his morose mood and thoughts. Music. Specifically, a piano, but it wasn't the notes that held his attention. It was the laughter tangled amongst it. Wren's laughter. So beautiful and rare it stopped Asher's heart in a very different way than it had in her mother's presence moments ago.

Before he really registered it, his feet were following the noise down to the main floor and along the back hallway to a room with a grand piano that had gone unused since Asher's mother had lived here.

He stopped at the door, breath catching once more, chest being torn open at the sight in front of him. The piano was angled so he could see Fiadh and Wren together, hands racing along the keys, the sounds crashing through the room. Wren smiled and giggled the entire time until she burst into full-on laughter as her fingers tangled up with Fiadh's in the middle.

"You still won," Wren said, grinning.

"But you were much better this time. Want to try again?" Fiadh asked, looking down at his daughter with the softest, sweetest, happiest expression he'd ever seen on her face. The real Fee on display. Joyful and full of life, just like he'd always wished Wren could be. Just like he'd been longing to see from Fiadh since he'd seen it in Korea months ago. And now his daughter had gotten it twice in mere hours.

Wren nodded, and they moved so their fingers were on opposite ends of the piano. A slow ping of the keys began as Fee named notes at an increasingly rapid pace. Then, there was nothing but a blur of action until another huge belly laugh erupted from Wren as their hands collided in the middle.

Asher's jaw ticked, and he bit the inside of his cheek when tears pricked his eyes.

Damn. It was just too much.

He was about to turn away, leave them to their joy and their laughter, when Fiadh happened to glance up and see him at the door.

Every real, easy, delighted expression disappeared from her face. The fake smile she showed the world took over instead. She flicked her hair behind her shoulder, tilted her head in his direction, and said to Wren, "Maybe not the trouble Jay wanted, but at least we've caused a disturbance."

Wren's smile remained as she looked in his direction. "Father, Fiadh is teaching me to play the piano with the most delightful game. Do you wish to see it?"

Asher crossed the thickly waxed floor of the ballroom, wondering when the last time anyone but the cleaning crew had set foot in it. Perhaps two decades...since his mother had been here... He pushed away those memories as he arrived at Wren's side, letting the smile growing on her face and the sparkle in her cobalt-blue eyes wash some of his guilt and regrets away. No matter what happened with Nova, it would always be worth it because he had Wren.

His daughter turned to Fiadh. "Ready?"

Fiadh glanced at Asher, her body stiffening as if she was not going to be able to be as free now that he was here. He wished, instead, she'd feel even more so. That she'd feel safe enough to be her real self *because* he was here. He was caught between warring thoughts and emotions with her. Wanting her and hating that he did. Hoping to keep her and needing to force her away. Self-preservation fading in the heat of her gaze.

He made no comment as he watched them place their hands on the opposite sides of the board. Fiadh counted down and then started calling out notes once more. Slower and then faster, until it was a dizzy collection of skin and pounding chords. Wren laughed, light and soft, not quite the belly laugh of before, but still pure enjoyment.

"Would you like to try, Father?" she asked.

No. He wanted to stand and watch them for ages. He wanted to hear their laughter and see their smiles, and just let the joy of it soak into his veins until there was nothing left but the purest of delights.

"I have no idea how to play," he said softly, like he had with Nova, as if he was afraid his voice might disturb the bliss wafting through the room.

"It is very easy." Wren slid off and patted the bench where she'd just been. "Fiadh can show you."

He couldn't deny Wren anything when she looked so alive, even though he saw Fiadh shift uncomfortably at the idea. When he joined her on the tiny seat, their hips and thighs were smashed together, causing awareness to flash through him. Desire he couldn't afford but also wasn't sure he could deny much longer.

Fee pointed to the sticky notes plastered just above the keys with the name of each one written on them. Then, she explained they would start on opposite ends with the same note in the opposite octave and continue toward the middle. The first one to reach the C note at the center would win.

"It is quicker if you do not look at the sticky notes," Wren said.

Fiadh counted down, and they started, with him concentrating on the papers much more than their hands or the fact he was entirely too enchanted by her being there at all. As she started calling the notes faster, he didn't even bother trying to keep up, just hitting random keys.

Wren laughed, and Fiadh did too, until she stopped right in the middle. "You lose," she said, lips twisting upward.

"That was truly awful, Father. Truly awful," Wren said, shaking her head in despair.

Asher laughed at her disgusted look, the sound booming around the echoey space, as startling and rare as his daughter's. It filled him with more regret. Regret that they didn't laugh like this more. That he ran from the house more than he stayed. That Wren was living a childhood that would leave marks on her regardless of the love everyone at Taran Ridge showered her with.

When his eyes found Fiadh's, they were concentrated on his mouth and the grin that had remained on his lips even after the laughter had died. The air tightened between them, twisting and turning the attraction, daring him…daring them both.

"There you are," Jay said from the doorway, and everyone's smiles slipped a little as they turned in his direction. "Your book report is due on Monday. Shall we get started?"

Wren sighed, disgusted. "They did not even let us read the full story. Just a silly excerpt. If we could use the entire story, I would have much more to say."

Jay swiped back his hair with a hand. "Well, you have to follow the rules."

Wren looked at Asher and asked, "Father, do you think we can consider homeschooling again?"

Asher shook his head. "No, Birdie. Remember, school is about more than academics."

She nodded sagely and then headed toward Jay before stopping and turning to look at the two of them on the bench. "I would like to play again later, Fiadh. If you have time before you go?"

"Of course. I have absolutely nothing to do while I'm here."

Wren glided the rest of the way to Jay. As they disappeared, the tension in the room swirled and grew.

"Thank you," Asher said gently, looking down and watching the deep black edge of Fiadh's brown eyes shift and change as her pupils dilated.

"It was nothing. Just a game my ma used with us kids when she taught us," she said, moving on the bench as if she was going to get up, but he didn't want her to. He wanted her to stay. He wanted her to bring the joy she brought to Wren to him as well, so he slid a hand over her thigh and squeezed.

"Stay." It sounded like a command, and he kicked himself as he saw her chin raise and her spine stiffen. "I have some work to do to catch up with Wren's level of skill. She'll demand I play for days. Shall we go again?"

He tipped his head toward the piano at the same time he let go of her leg. Her breath was uneven, and she shifted again, trying to escape him when there was nowhere to go on the tiny bench.

He grabbed her hand, thumb sliding over the pulse point at her wrist, feeling the flutter there that matched the wild beat inside him. He placed her hand on the keys before putting his on the other end.

She rolled her eyes. "It's silly for two adults. It's a child's game."

"Humor me so I'll know how to play with her."

Her throat bobbed as if his asking how to play a game with his daughter had somehow affected her.

Fiadh started the countdown, and as the pace picked up, he lost his place again long before she got to the middle. He was too absorbed in her long fingers, the way her voice sounded out of breath, and how her arm kept bumping into his. It was ridiculous to feel so much from so little.

Eventually, his hands collided with hers. The smooth

skin sent spikes of desire through him until he was tightening uncomfortably in the jeans he'd thrown on hours ago while scrambling to get the band out of Boston.

"Wren's right. You're truly awful," Fiadh said, a taunt in her voice.

"Are teachers allowed to tell their students they're awful?" he teased back.

"I bet no one has ever said you were bad at anything." Her gaze flicked to his mouth and then away. It did nothing to ease the hunger building inside him. A hunger that pushed aside every alarm bell, every warning, every ripped scar that would bleed if he let another woman have a piece of him.

"It's happened on a rare occasion or two," he said, trying to be flippant but also stating the truth. As heir apparent to the RMI billions, no one had ever wanted to displease his dad enough to fail him. He'd earned grades he never should have, but it hadn't kept him from trying to do so. Only at Columbia and then in law school had he found himself being judged for what he actually did instead of who he was.

For the second time, Fiadh went to move away, and for the second time, he stopped her, grabbing her hands and repositioning them over the keys.

"One more time?" he asked. "And the winner is allowed to ask one question that has to be answered."

He knew he had her when he suggested the bet. She had questions for him. Thousands of them. Just like he had plenty for her. But there would be only one he'd ask her today.

She rolled her eyes. "You might as well just let me ask the question now."

He arched a brow at her and tapped a key, the note trilling loudly through the nearly empty room. Another taunt.

"The winner is the person who gets to the middle C note first, correct?" he asked one more time even though she'd already explained the rules. He barely kept the smirk from his face as he did so.

She didn't answer. She just rolled her eyes a second

time.

She counted down and started calling out letters. He moved slowly at first, just like before, and then just slid his fingers along the entire board. The sound clashed around them until he stopped on the winning key well before her.

"I win," he said.

And she laughed. "You cheated. That isn't a win."

She was up off the bench in a flash, and he followed, catching her arm before she'd gotten much farther than the end of the piano and pulling her back until their chests collided. Her breath was choppier, breasts rising and falling underneath his sweatshirt, pulse fluttering beneath his fingertips.

"Next time, set better rules, Fiadh. The only condition was to reach the C note first. I did. I won."

"Is this the role model you set for Wren? A cheater?" She lifted her chin again, eyes flashing as she glared up at him, and he swore he could see actual flames beneath the brown. Flickers of fire and brimstone.

"Wren isn't here. Only you. Don't get pissed because I saw through your loopholes. I'm a lawyer. It's what I do."

"Fine, cheater, you win. What question do you have for me?"

She wasn't fighting his hold. In fact, he was certain her weight was now leaning into him ever so slightly, and her gaze had fallen to his mouth several times. He released her arm only to slide one hand to her lower back, pushing her closer while the other circled her neck, a finger caressing her jaw, his thumb sliding over her lower lip. She exhaled, a shaky breath that he needed to be his.

"Can I kiss you?" he asked.

One of her hands rested on his chest, fingers gripping his shirt. The other was on his bicep, as if debating pushing his arm away.

"You said I had to reply," her voice hitched as she said the words.

"An answer. It doesn't have to be yes. I've never taken what wasn't freely given, and I don't plan to start now." His heart was pounding almost as furiously as hers. If she said no, he'd let her go, but then he'd dream for weeks of what it would have been like if she'd said yes.

Her eyes flickered with heat, and then she nodded.

That was all it took. His mouth was on hers before she could change her mind. Before she could even take another breath. It was a light touch meant to familiarize themselves with the feel of the other. But as soon as he tasted her, the rich, heady scent combined with her sweetness ignited his body, snapping his control until he was devouring her, pushing his way past her pretty pink lips and gorging himself with long, slow licks that barely hid the wild frenzy building in him as he attempted to uncover every single secret place inside her. It was wet and raw and left him hungry for more even while he was still indulging.

She moaned a melodious little sound that tightened his chest and his balls all at the same time. He spread his fingers along her back, pressing her to him, fusing them together. His other hand tangled in her thick hair, forcing her head backward so he had better access to her mouth, her jaw, and her neck. He took it all, licking and nipping and marking before landing again on her lips and taking the air she'd just inhaled and making it his.

The harsh, desperate truth burned through him. A truth that couldn't be denied. He didn't just desire her. He wanted every last piece of Fiadh Kane to belong to him, even if it left him cracked and bleeding in the end.

Chapter Fourteen

Fiadh

TRAIN WRECK
Performed by Sarah McLachlan

Asher kissed her like he did everything else. As if he was the only one in command. As if Fee was the prey he'd hunted and caught. As if he wouldn't stop until he'd taken every breath from her lungs and every beat of her heart. She'd never been kissed so thoroughly. Never been kissed as if there was nothing else to do but continue this one action for the rest of eternity.

His body was hard in every single place that touched her, etching a mark into her skin and bones, and fanning a fire that was growing by torrential leaps and bounds. Fee wrapped one leg around his thigh, shifting their hips closer, moving until the thick heat of him lodged itself against her core and made her gasp. A gasp he swallowed as he continued the beautiful assault on her mouth.

She was afraid she might come just from his kiss. As if just his mouth could completely sate her. His fingers dug into her skin at her lower back as he tried to blend their bodies even closer. There was going to be nothing left of her—simply a puddle of melted skin and bone that had once been Fiadh Kane and no longer had a name because it belonged to him.

That thought shoved cold water over her. Ice hitting her veins. She froze before dropping her leg and hands, pulling away, and taking a shaky step backward. Her legs wobbled as if they might send her crumbling to the floor.

Their gazes remained locked, lust shooting from them like a flame that couldn't be doused. Her hand went to her heart, trying to slow the wild beat, trying to figure out what the hell had just happened, because she wasn't sure she'd ever be able to repeat a first kiss like that—any kiss like that.

"Fee—" It was the first time he'd called her by the nickname, and it came out as a growl. A complaint. A demand to return to what they'd started. But she shook her head, taking another step and increasing the distance between them.

She'd thought she'd wanted to seduce him to get his secrets, but she'd made a huge miscalculation. She hadn't added in Asher's raw sensuality to the mix. Now, she was afraid the opposite would be true. He'd seduce her, and all her secrets would leak from her. If she stayed in his arms, let him kiss her and touch her and make her come apart, she wouldn't be able to hide from him. She'd be an open book.

"That…" She stopped at the sound of her voice, raspy and full of longing. She cleared her throat and started again. "That was a mistake. A one-time deal. No more bets about kissing. No more kissing at all."

His stare was hooded as he watched every move she made with his eyes locked on her shaky hand pushing her hair behind her ear. His pupils dilated as she unconsciously licked her lips, and she retreated even farther.

"It wasn't a mistake," he said, his voice a dangerous purr. "We didn't accidentally kiss each other. You wanted it. I wanted it. And there's no damn way I want it to be a one-time thing. That one taste wasn't enough for either of us."

Her body was screaming to throw herself back into his arms, but she did the opposite, moving closer to the door and escape. "You told me I was selfish, only thinking of myself. This"—she pointed between the two of them—"this would be the most selfish thing I could do because it would be me taking what I wanted no matter what it could do to the

Daisies. I won't let sex cloud my judgment. You can't fuck me into signing a new contract."

He made a guttural protest again. Almost a roar. As if he really was the lion she'd imagined. His eyes were stormy as he grunted out, "I don't screw my way into deals."

Her gaze flew to the piano. "Isn't that exactly what you just did?"

"No," he said.

She didn't respond. She just fled, and she half expected him to give chase, but his footsteps didn't echo through the maze of corridors. She stopped briefly, getting her bearings and realizing she didn't have anywhere to go. She didn't belong here. She had no room to hide in. She had no space that was just hers. She didn't know how to truly escape as snow piled up against the windows and doors of the gloomy mansion.

Then, she realized it wasn't as if she was alone with him. There were others at the mansion, which made her think of the kitchen with its splashes of color and life. At least there she'd find other people. Bodies who might prohibit him from pursuing her and making her his.

Jozef glanced up as she entered, hands in a bowl of sticky dough.

"You need a cuppa after that?" His eyes drifted toward the ceiling.

She didn't want more coffee. Her nerves were too shattered and rattled as it was, so she shook her head and sank onto one of the wrought-iron stools along the kitchen's island.

"I can imagine it's unsettling, especially if you weren't warned, and knowing Asher, he hasn't told you anything." Jozef moved the dough to a lightly floured board to shape it.

"It scared the hell out of me," Fee said. It wasn't the only thing that scared her. She'd told Asher the truth in his office. It wasn't just being here. It wasn't just Nova or the screams or his secrets. It was the way he made her feel, and after that kiss... She shook her head. She couldn't even think about it.

But her body was still singing. Still wet and hungry and wanting more.

"He's paying penance for sins that aren't his," Jozef sighed. "No one can change his mind because he's damn stubborn if you hadn't noticed."

His words brought a small smile and a low chuckle from her. Yes, Asher Riggs was definitely stubborn. Jozef winked and then cut a cross along the top of the bread. The motion triggered memories of her mother's hands doing the same. She swallowed hard, a different well of emotion bursting in her than the desire she'd felt moments before.

"Is that soda bread?" she asked.

His grin grew. "Yes. Let's say I got some inspiration from an unexpected source today. I thought you might require some comfort food."

"I haven't had it in…" When was the last time? She never ordered it anywhere it was on the menu because she knew it wouldn't be like her ma's. Plus, she was never sure if she could handle the nostalgia—the longing. A lump grew in her throat, making it hard to finish. "It's been several years."

"How long has it been since you've been home?" he asked.

The slice to her chest his simple question caused was brutal and fierce.

"I haven't seen my family in nine years," she said quietly, unsure of why everyone in this damn mansion seemed good at pulling truths from her. His grin was wiped away, as if he'd heard in her tone the loss and agony, even though she'd attempted to keep her voice even.

"Can I ask why not? Especially after the murd—well, you had a couple of years before the band got back together, right?" Then, as if realizing what he'd asked, he shook his head as he started to clean up. "You don't have to answer that. Reggie and Asher will be the first to tell you I'm too nosy for my own good."

"You and Reggie…you're…" she trailed off.

"Happily married and grateful we get to work together every day."

"And your families? Did they accept your marriage?" she asked, chest aching with a longing for something that would never come true.

"Yes," he said. "We've been very fortunate."

"My pa..." Fee stopped herself before she'd let the whole sordid story out. What the hell was wrong with her? She needed space and time to collect herself. To pull her barriers back up and block out all the men who were assaulting her senses today.

But Jozef had already gotten the gist of it from those two words. His eyes softened, understanding and caring in them she shouldn't expect from a complete stranger.

"I'm sorry," he said.

She shook her head. "I have...the band and Paisley's parents. I have people in my corner."

Even though, since Landry had died, it felt like a terribly small corner. As if she'd been left in the back of a damp, dark cellar with a single bulb everyone forgot to turn on.

Jozef dried his hands, looked over her outfit, and then said, "Let's go up and find you some clothes. Then, I'll show you to your room so you have a place to settle in."

She nodded, grateful. Getting out of Asher's clothes would be a good thing. She needed to escape the smell of him wafting over her like a brand she couldn't remove. So, she followed Jozef out of the kitchen and up a back staircase.

They wound up, up, up until a small landing opened at the very tip of the house. The roof sloped down on either side of two doors opposite each other. The door on the left opened, and a square, muscled man in scrubs emerged, shadowed in the dimly lit corridor.

"Thought I heard someone. Everything okay?" The man's eyes slipped from Jozef to Fiadh, widening slightly as he took her in.

Jozef chuckled. "I see you recognize our guest. Fiadh

127

Kane, this is Diego Gutierrez. He's Nova's nurse." He didn't wait for either of them to respond to the introductions but just barreled along. "She's settled down then?"

Diego grimaced, touching a cut on his cheek surrounded by a fresh bruise. "Asleep for now."

Jozef and Diego shared a knowing look Fiadh wasn't privy to, but she recognized Nova's name as Wren's mom and the woman from the picture in Asher's office. Fee wanted to shout out a thousand questions. How had she ended up this way? Was Nova being kept against her will? Why was she hidden away like a dirty secret? But she bit her lip because asking the staff wasn't fair. She was sure they'd signed a non-disclosure agreement just like those who worked for The Painted Daisies.

Jozef turned away from the nurse to the opposite door. "Well, let's see what we can find you."

Diego gave a chin nod to her and then ducked back into the room behind him while Fiadh followed Jozef. He flicked a switch, and light glimmered across an attic full of trunks, boxes, and old furniture. It was the perfect place for a ghostly encounter to add to the mystery of Asher's home. It made Fee's lips curl upward again.

"I think our best bet at finding clothes to fit you is by looking through what Zelda left behind," he said. He went to a pair of artfully engraved wardrobes along the back wall of the attic.

As Fee joined him, the side of the house, under the pitch of the roof, came into view. An enormous, oval, stained-glass window shed a mosaic of colors over the space even though the day was dark and gray. She could only imagine the dazzling display it would be if it was sunny. The scene on the glass was of Adam looking from behind a tree at Eve, who was caught in the thrall of the serpent. It was a dark scene, just like the rest of the house, and Fee wondered for the first time which of the Riggs family had developed the gloomy atmosphere of the estate.

When she turned from her study of the window, Jozef

had already opened the wardrobes and was pulling clothes out of garment bags. When she joined him, she could see there were boot cut, low-waisted pants with ribbed lines down the front, cropped peasant tops, chunky belts, and a sea of pink business suits and dresses. The stunning collection of early 2000s fashion brought a low chuckle from Fee.

Jozef grinned. "Zelda loved *Legally Blonde* so much she stalked and made friends with Reese Witherspoon. She went through a whole phase of trying to be the real-life Elle. She even tried to get into law school, which may have been what gave Asher the idea to get his degree. If she'd gotten in maybe…"

He trailed off, grin disappearing.

The reports Angel had sent Fee on Asher's mom had said Zelda left when Asher was ten. She'd spent the next decade in Southeast Asia and died of AIDS when Asher was barely twenty. The women surrounding the Riggs family didn't have the same longevity as their peers. Even Asher's grandmother had died at barely forty-five.

"Well, pink is not usually my color," Fee said, forcing a smile. "But let's see what I might be able to manage."

She flipped through the clothes, suddenly feeling awkward. It wasn't filtering through another person's belongings that caused it. For several years, before the band had actually taken off, secondhand stores had been pretty much all she could afford. With a good wash, it was fine, but this…this felt like picking through Asher's childhood.

Jozef opened a drawer in one of the wardrobes, and there was a pile of lingerie tucked in satin bags smelling of sage and lavender. Fee had rarely succumbed to wearing someone else's undergarments, but at the moment, beggars couldn't be choosers. The underwear would work, but Zelda Riggs had obviously had a rack Fee did not.

It hit her how odd it was that everything was here, including underwear. As if the woman had literally just walked out the door and not returned when everyone had expected her to.

"She didn't take any of this?" Fee found herself asking.

Jozef nodded. "I'd been here…must have been two years by the time she left. Didn't say goodbye, didn't take one thing with her except her money. They were panicked for a few days, thinking something bad had happened to her, and then presto, she started charging things in Thailand."

Fee tried to imagine what it must have been like for Asher in those first days. To be worried and afraid and then to realize his mom had just left without saying a word. Without even a kiss and a hug for her only child. When Fee had left her family at seventeen, there'd been hugs and tears, and it still had been brutally hard. But at least she'd had closure with them all…except for Pa. He'd…

She shook her head. No, she wasn't going there today. Just like she wouldn't allow herself to feel sorry for Asher. It wouldn't serve her purpose to have not only desire but empathy welling through her. She might start actually liking the damn man.

Jozef headed for another area of the attic and came back with a scuffed and scraped suitcase that they piled the clothes Fee chose into.

"I'll take them down to the laundry after I get you settled into a room," he said.

"I can do it. Just point me to the washing machine," Fee said, and Jozef shook his head with a wry smile.

"Can't allow you to do that, Fiadh. It would mean you touching George and Martha, and I'm as particular about them as I am about Bartholomew."

She raised her brow, trying to pick up his meaning.

"George and Martha are my washer and dryer. Bartholomew is my espresso machine. No one touches any of them without passing the appropriate Jozef Leder test."

She grinned. "I didn't realize I'd need driving instructions for a washing machine."

He leaned in with a wink and said, "Which is exactly why you can't use my man George."

She laughed as he led her out the door and back down a flight of stairs to the floor Asher's room was on. Instead of heading in the direction of his suite, Jozef turned the opposite way. He opened a door and turned on the light. Fee grimaced, thinking about how many generators had to have been running to keep the house aglow in the middle of the power outage.

But as she stepped inside the room, all thought left her. It was stunning. Full of shades of green and cream with hints of gold and bronze, it was like stepping through jade glass into a secret lair. Thick velvets mixed with sheer organza, blending in with the gold-gilded furniture. It was a room made for a princess and as different from the black-and-white starkness of the main rooms of the house as Asher's private quarters. An unease settled over Fee's shoulders.

"Whose room is this?"

"Asher had it redecorated for Nova, but she wouldn't step foot inside it because she said green made her nauseated. In truth, as you might already know, it's a calming color, but I think Nova never wanted to be calmed. She liked living in a wound-up state." He paused as if he'd said too much. "No one has stayed here. You'll be the room's first guest. It's been a shame to see such a delightful space go unused, and as stereotypical as the Irish soda bread I made was today, I'd like to see you surrounded by the green of your homeland."

She hadn't thought she could get emotional over a color and a room, but Jozef's words made her feel that way. She suddenly longed for Ireland and her family as she hadn't in years. She wanted to run once more in the fields beyond Gran's house and dance in the wildflowers growing there.

"It's lovely," she managed to get out over the lump that had found its way back to her throat.

He patted her arm. "Why don't you have a bit of a rest? Maybe take a bath and try and shake your day. The en suite should be already stocked, but if you need anything, just pick up the phone and dial two." He pointed to an old-fashioned candlestick phone on the side table.

Then, he left, taking the beat-up suitcase with him while Fee tried to shake the walls of emotions barreling through her. It was hard to imagine Asher designing such a bright, hopeful place, and yet he had. Both his room and this one were soothing and full of colors you'd find in nature—seas and meadows. Two opposites sharing a space.

She wandered into the bathroom, unsure what she was doing, just knowing she felt unsettled and needed to move, or she'd lose herself in emotions. The en suite wasn't overly large but beautifully laid out with both a sunken tub and a rainfall shower made perfect for two. She wondered if Asher had thought of Nova and him tangled in them when he'd designed the layout. The thought caused a strange pain to emerge in her stomach. She didn't normally waste time on jealousy. Someone either wanted you or they didn't. You couldn't change the way they felt, and if they wanted someone else more than you, it was better to part ways and move on.

Which was exactly what had happened with Lars. He'd moved on just as she'd thought he'd stay. She shivered, the cold creeping back through her bones. But then again, she hadn't really been warm since the walk back from the park in the blizzard. The only time heat had touched her had been when she'd been tucked up against Asher's body. Then, flames had scorched her, leaving a different kind of burn than the one the icy snow had left behind.

She suddenly needed to be rid of it all. The cold. Asher's scent, the emotions, and an entire day's worth of mistakes, worries, and fears. She wanted to wash it away, just like Jozef had suggested.

She shed Asher's clothes and filled the tub, adding some of the bath bombs from a nearby basket. She immersed herself in the scents and heat, pressing her head into the padded curve purposefully designed for it. The room was full of so many thoughtful, little gestures it brought Asher back to her in vivid detail.

What would it be like to be the center of all his attention?

She shivered even in the almost-scalding water.

It had been dangerously thrilling to have all his focus, even briefly. The way his mouth had controlled hers had been too enticing. And for the first time, she'd wanted to be controlled. To pretend, for once, that she didn't have to be the one looking out for herself. That he'd do it for her…

It was getting harder and harder to believe that the Asher she knew now—laughing with his daughter, kissing like he couldn't get enough, eating with his employees as if they were family—could possibly have been behind Landry's death. It seemed so ridiculous she wanted to laugh and cry at the same time.

It had been so much simpler to believe he was involved. She'd needed a target for her anger and hatred, and he'd easily given it to her. He'd been such an asshole after Landry's death, seemingly uncaring, only interested in money and the delay to the album. It had added fuel to her fire.

I think you're wrong about him. You've turned this into a witch hunt, Angel's words came back to her. A twinge of guilt but also a sense of overwhelming loss. Because if it wasn't Asher…if she'd wasted all this time…

"What do I do now, Lan?" Fiadh whispered into the steamy air.

Find out the truth.

The thought hit her hard, almost as if it was really Landry speaking to her over the great divide. Finding Landry's killer was what she truly wanted. Finding them and making them pay. But she also wanted to make sure the rest of the band was safe. That they could put this behind them forever.

Fee picked at the theories the authorities had come up with for the attack. It could have been a hate crime because Landry and Fee were both openly bisexual. But the skill it had taken to murder Lan and her bodyguard didn't scream hate.

They'd also considered the possibility of it being a case of mistaken identity. Maybe Leya had been the real target because of her father's politics or Adria because of the people coming after her father's business who'd kidnapped her sister and threatened to take Adria as well. Both of her friends were, unfortunately, more logical targets and easily confused with Landry if seen from behind. Similar heights, builds, and hair coloring.

Twenty months later, they still knew as little as they had the day it happened. A senseless crime. If she let herself, she still felt exactly the same way she had walking into the house in Grand Orchard and seeing Paisley and Nikki sobbing. The way her stomach had felt as Jonas confirmed her worst thoughts. The horror. The silent tears. And the anger. She'd funneled it all into Asher, not understanding his words or the disgust in his eyes as he'd said them. It had haunted her for nearly two years.

He still looked at her the same way now and again...with disgust. It had certainly been there in the car on the ride from the hotel to his house this morning. She couldn't forget those looks. She couldn't let the loneliness and heartache she'd sensed in him, or the sweet glances to his daughter, or one heated kiss—one fecking incredible kiss—wipe away the truth. Because even if Asher wasn't guilty of Landry's death, he still had secrets. He still didn't respect her. And she'd never again let someone close who didn't. She was fecking Fiadh Kane. Rock star. Bisexual badass. That was going to have to be enough for whoever decided to step into her life.

Chapter Fifteen

Asher

FADING BRIGHT EYES DARK
Performed by Scars on 45

When Fiadh had sauntered out of the ballroom, Asher wanted to give chase. His body longed to finish what one damn kiss had started. But with every step she took farther away, the more reality sunk in.

He forced himself to remember the things that were more important than the lust beating through his veins or even the admiration he felt for her strength. Or the tenderness he'd felt watching her with Wren.

Fiadh Kane was a flight risk.

She had secrets.

She drank too much.

She found her way into others' beds too easily.

She was selfish and impulsive.

She essentially worked for him.

She was a she…and he knew how foolish it would be to trust a woman again.

With every single transgression he silently aimed, there was a soft voice at the back of his head, countering it. A voice saying she was really stubborn, protective, determined, brave, and candidly open. Her nature was to look after the people she loved even at the expense of herself.

What he *wanted* to think battled fiercely with what his

soul seemed to know. It was the debate—the war going inside him—that led him to his office instead of following her down the hall. He needed to lose himself in facts. In problems he could absolutely solve. In structure he could enforce. He needed black and white for at least a few moments.

His lips quirked at that thought as he walked through the very black-and-white walls of the estate. His great-great grandfather had a thing for the Gothic classics. He'd also been the first in a long line of Riggs men to be abandoned by a wife. She'd run off with the cook, or was it the gardener? Asher couldn't remember. It had driven the design of the mansion—brooding anger and deep mourning all thrown together.

He sat down at his desk, hand automatically reaching for his mouse and turning, puzzled when it wasn't there. He found it at the far corner on the left side instead of the right. He eased back in his chair, eyeing the entire desktop. He was almost obsessive about how he kept it. Whenever he left any of his offices, here or at the RMI headquarters, it was clean, precise, and ready for him to dive back in.

Earlier, he'd been distracted by Fiadh and Nova, but he could have sworn he hadn't touched anything on the desk. He pulled the mouse from the far edge, bringing it closer, waking his computer, and bringing up the house security system. He didn't have personal bodyguards because he rarely needed them. When the media storm had hit in Germany over Ziggy, the attack, and the lawsuit, he'd used some of Reinard Security's men. But here, the house was just monitored by a custom-built system Reinard had designed. When they weren't in the middle of a snowstorm, the team could get to him within ten minutes if he needed them. It had always felt like more than enough.

He flipped through the videos from today. There were cameras installed outside the house in strategic locations all over the estate, and then a multitude inside the house along the hallways and main living areas. He backed up several of the outside angles, playing them from the time they'd arrived at Taran Ridge. A grayish smudge on a couple of the feeds had him pausing and taking a screenshot. He sent the pictures with a message to Reinard's team asking them what the hell it was.

As he continued to fiddle with the videos, he noticed that when the power had gone out, the security system had rebooted itself after the generator had come online. He'd have to find a way to change that. He didn't want the cameras to go down at all. They needed to run off a separate, independent system not tied to the power grid.

After spending another few minutes, he couldn't find anything else out of place. The only people who'd appeared in the hallway outside his office were him, Fiadh, Wren, and his father. He was being paranoid.

But something still itched at the back of his neck, as if he was being watched. He turned to the windows all but covered in layers of snow with more flakes still pouring from the sky.

After everything that had happened recently, he felt a sudden need for a complete overhaul of the security measures here at the estate and the RMI offices. He'd speak to his father, Reinard, and the corporation's internal security to make it happen.

His mind went back to the trace Torrance had found on the money he sent each month. His jaw clenched. He couldn't afford for anyone to find her. He'd promised to protect her after he hadn't the first time.

He sent a message to Torrance in the encrypted app they used for times like these.

> *ASHER: What did Eduardo find on the trace?*

Torrance came back immediately.

> *TORRANCE: I'll have an update for you this afternoon.*

He turned his mind back to the problem he'd been putting off for too long—Nova. He opened a folder with a list of mental health care facilities Torrance and Diego had put together for him. He went through it, noting the pros and cons of each location with a tight chest and a twisting stomach. It felt wrong…too easy…to just send her away. He didn't run from his mistakes. He took responsibility. Which was the reason he had one hundred thousand dollars of his inheritance going out every year in untraceable funds.

But this was different. He couldn't just throw money at the Nova situation. Although both his father and Jay—with his child psychology degree—had told him repeatedly that having Nova at the house, listening to her cries, and seeing how they had to restrain her was not good for Wren. Asher was certain living in the gloom of the mansion with a screaming woman had impacted his daughter in ways he'd never be able to fix. More than the alcohol and drugs Nova had consumed while pregnant, the somberness of Wren's life was likely the reason for her seriousness. Doctors and teachers had said she was probably on the autism spectrum somewhere, but he'd refused to have her labeled. Refused to let her think she was anything but perfect—because she was. She connected just fine with the people here. With the people vested in her.

This entire line of thought only served to make him feel guilty again. This time for wishing earlier that Wren would laugh and joke and gallop about like a normal nine-year-old. After all, what was normal? He'd never been considered normal, especially after his mom had left and he'd retreated into himself. A shell that had only grown in high school after realizing his girlfriends were much more interested in the Riggs name than what was inside him. A shell he'd let his friendship with Nova and Ronan bring him out of for a brief period in college, only to be slammed back into with Nova's betrayals. The cheating and stealing.

It was her addiction that had been behind it. He knew that. He even knew, somewhere inside her, she'd likely loved him. Just like his mom had loved him…just not enough to stay.

His jaw tightened at the unwanted emotions and regrets

clinging to him like a noose at his neck. So, he did what he always did when his personal life felt uncontrollable—he doubled down on his work with RMI. He pulled up several acquisitions he was considering, reading reports, making notes, and giving the go-ahead to approach a production studio that would fit nicely in with the streaming services.

Maybe his dad was right, and he should cut his losses in the music industry. Drop the labels. Drop the Daisies. His chest tightened up all over again, and he cursed just as a soft knock brought his eyes to the door.

He suddenly realized the room had darkened around him. Only the dim light of the desk lamp pushed at the gloom. He'd missed lunch, forgotten the raging storm outside his windows, and shoved aside the women in his life who, unsurprisingly, caused him one headache after the other.

Another soft knock was followed by the door slowly easing open. He groaned internally when Fiadh's face peeked around the edge.

"Oh…I—" She started to back out.

"I won't bite," he growled. "What do you need?"

Her eyes darted around the room as if trying to come up with an excuse for being in his office, and it raised all his alarm bells again. He thought back to the moved mouse. Had she looked through his things when he'd left her there to go help with Nova?

Her eyes landed on the phone charger sitting on the corner of his desk.

"I don't have a charger," she said, waving her phone.

He pulled open a drawer, shuffled through some office supplies, and found an extra one. He held it out to her.

She slipped fully into the room, and he went completely still, lungs catching on the breath he'd taken and heart all but stopping. Memories of that outfit and another day he wanted to forget were seared into his brain.

"What the fuck are you wearing?"

She glanced down at the bootleg black pants and the

purple peasant top cropped to show her skin barely a shade darker than the pure snow outside. A dusting of those damn freckles trailed over the flesh there.

But it wasn't the skin she was showing that had him freaking out—and he knew it was a freak-out even though he'd sounded pissed. She looked almost like Zelda had that day. His mother had lighter hair, more strawberry blonde than the mahogany of Fiadh's natural color, and she had bright-blue eyes instead of brown as well as a fuller figure than the woman in front of him, but there was a similarity he couldn't deny.

Fiadh managed a light laugh. "I know. I look like some 2000s TV show threw up on me, right? But the clothes fit better than yours."

He wanted to rip the clothes off and stuff her back into his sweats. And not just because he'd gotten a perverse pleasure out of seeing her in his things.

She made her way over to the desk and grabbed the charger from him. Their hands skimmed across one another, and his entire body filled with the desire to bring her down onto his lap even in his mother's clothes.

He was sick.

He needed help.

His laptop and phone both rang at the same time, Torrance's face with his hipster beard appearing on the screen. Asher accepted the video call automatically, a way to escape Fee and his thoughts and the torturous feelings filling him.

"So, about the trace," Torrance said, and instantly, Asher regretted answering.

"You're on speaker," he cut Torrance off, and his assistant's eyes went wide, understanding it meant Asher wasn't alone.

"I can send you the information by email, but just so you know, it's a dead end. Wound up at some bookshop on an island most people have never heard of before."

"Which island?"

"San Fiore?"

The name prickled at the back of Asher's brain for some reason, but he couldn't place it.

"Where's that?" he asked, and Torrance grinned.

"The all-knowing Asher Riggs doesn't know something his lowly assistant does. Let me savor the moment."

"Torrance," Asher grunted, refusing to look in Fiadh's direction even though he felt the weight of her gaze.

"It's off the coast of Monaco. A dinky thing with a parliamentary monarchy and more money than even RMI."

"Any ties to Ziggy?" he asked, and he could practically hear the questions rattling away in Fiadh's brain.

"None that Eduardo could find. And we stopped the trace before it got anywhere near Krista, so we're all good on that end."

"Let me know if anything changes." And Asher hung up.

Fiadh hadn't moved, and the scent of her wafted over him. It was the scent he always associated with her, but it was also hidden beneath sage and lavender. What he didn't smell was him, his clothes, and the sandalwood in his closet, and it bothered him more than he could afford.

"What happened to Shari?" Fiadh asked, stepping away from him to plug the charger into an outlet near the side table lined with pictures and the crystal decanters of alcohol he suddenly felt the need to pour from.

He frowned at her question. "Who?"

"The assistant you had with you that day…in Grand Orchard, the first time we met," she said, her voice hitching as she said, "that day," as if even saying that much was too painful.

He was filled with his own memories of that goddamn day. The way he'd hated his immediate attraction to Fee as soon as she'd turned her brown eyes to him. The way he'd wanted to see her real smile instead of the fake one she'd worn. The way she'd burned and ignited when she'd found out Nick had sold Lost Heart Records to him.

And then the way she'd swooped her friends into her arms as if she could shield them from the brutal murder of a sister and friend. She'd glared at him that night as she'd held them tight up against her, and he'd wondered how much it had cost her to hold herself together when she'd just lost her best friend.

What he didn't remember was Shari.

When he continued to look puzzled, she laughed. "Perfectly blonde, perfectly sculpted, and perfectly sucking up to you. Called me Fee-ah-duh instead of Fee-uh."

A flash of a memory returned. An irritating woman who'd disgusted him so much he'd fired the temp agency who'd sent her. "She was a temp. Torrance was out with mono, and the agency hadn't been able to find anyone who met my specifications on such short notice."

"Specifications?" Fee asked as if she was trying to hold back a laugh, and it shot memories through him of his mother, in the same damn outfit, and a spontaneous picnic down at the shore. His mom had gotten a call while they'd been there, and she'd wandered off, laughing and flirting—although, at the time, he hadn't known it was flirting. She'd forgotten all about him, and it had been his father who'd come to find him as the tide had rolled in and the sky had darkened.

When he didn't answer, Fee didn't let it go. Instead, she dug in with lips that curved upward. "What exactly are your specifications?"

"Not a woman," he snapped, looking down at the paperwork on his desk, wondering if he should remain in the office through dinner just so he could avoid the outfit and the memories.

Fee's laugh brought his eyes up to her face. It was her real laugh, like it had been when she'd been sitting with Wren. It made every bit of guilt, anger, and doubt float away, filling his heart with something he'd sworn never to feel again.

"Wow, you really don't like women, do you?" she said, all taunt and tease.

He liked her entirely too much—or at least his body did. He sighed, rubbed his temple, and wondered how to go back ten minutes and start over. How to go back to the beginning of the day and have a redo. Make sure she got in the damn SUV with her friends so she wouldn't be there, causing him to feel and react and see things he didn't want.

"My family—the men in my family—we don't exactly make wise choices when it comes to the women we let into our lives." He waved his hand to the ceiling, stomach twisting because Nova was just one in the long line of Riggs relationships that had ended poorly.

When he looked back at her, she had an expectant look on her face. And he knew what she wanted. More truths he didn't know how to share. Things he'd chosen not to talk about with anyone. After what felt like an eternity had passed without him responding, she finally prompted, "She isn't your wife, but you're taking care of her?"

Acid burned through the lining of his stomach. God, he didn't want to do this with Fiadh. Not today, not ever, and especially not with her dressed like yet another woman—the first—who'd abandoned him, not once but multiple times.

"Nova and I were engaged, but she broke it off before she found out she was pregnant with Wren." Each syllable cost him something. A tiny piece of the solid shield he'd lived with for nine years.

She didn't say anything, and as if sensing he needed a minute to gather himself back together, she gave him a respite, which he used to try and resurrect the bricks around his soul she'd just pulled down.

"Wren's a pretty cool name for a kid," she said.

"She'll hate me for it someday, but I thought letting Nova name the baby would bring them closer, bring out some sort of maternal instinct."

"She didn't want the baby?" Fiadh asked.

He didn't say anything. He'd begged Nova...the thought of not keeping the little spark of life they'd brought into existence had tormented him. And he'd been young enough, naïve enough, to think having the baby would somehow fix everything wrong with her and him and their crumbling relationship.

"How'd she end up here at Taran Ridge with a full-time nurse?" Fee finally pressed.

"The delivery wasn't easy. She was torn up, and the doctors prescribed some pretty heavy pain pills, not knowing her history with addiction. She was never diagnosed, but her mental state...it was all over the place from childhood. And after Wren, I think she had postpartum depression too. She hated being a mother. Hated what it had done to her body. Hated me for convincing her to go through with it. She was staying here"—he waved his hand around the room—"and she hated that too. She overdosed on opioids, and the lack of oxygen...it messed with her already struggling mind."

He took a deep breath, trying to remember the last time he'd talked with anyone about what had happened. He wasn't sure he ever had.

"She doesn't have any family," he continued. "A mother who washed her hands of her years ago...which should have been my first sign."

"Sign?" Fee asked, prickling again.

"That she wasn't to be trusted."

"Sometimes, a parent walking away has nothing to do with the child," Fee said, defensiveness in her tone, and when his eyes met hers, he could see the hurt before she carefully hid it.

As a child, Asher had wanted to believe the same thing. That it wasn't the child's fault when a parent abandoned them. His father had told him over and over again his mother leaving had nothing to do with him and everything to do with her. She'd been bored and stuck in a marriage with a workaholic who was ten years her senior. She'd been alone in a gloomy mansion with a child who was almost as solemn as Wren…or was that after she'd left that he'd become so quiet? He didn't know for sure.

"More often than not, it has nothing to do with the child," he agreed, wishing his heart believed it as much as his mind. "Unfortunately, with Nova, it was her own actions that pushed her mother away. I found out much later she'd stolen money from her mom on multiple occasions and had even stolen from the Columbia bookstore where she worked, just like she'd stolen from me. When we first met, I took her flightiness for being whimsical and fun. Free-spirited in a way I wasn't. I laughed off all the things she'd forget or the way she randomly took things that weren't hers. I'd find her lying in the sun by the waterfall on campus when I was supposed to be picking her up for a date at the dorms, and she'd act like I was the one who'd gotten the date or time wrong. Or she'd tell me she couldn't be expected to keep a date she'd agreed to before the flowers had burst out in pink blooms."

He could see Nova, lying in the grass with her dark hair fanning out around her. She'd been covered in the petals she'd picked, a huge smile on her face, and gray eyes full of laughter at his somberness. She'd pulled him down, draped him with flowers, and kissed him until he'd forgotten to be upset. How could he be when she was so happy?

"I'd never had to chase after a woman before. I'd never had a woman who could forget me and who I was so easily. Instead, I'd had people sucking up because of my family for so long the entire notion of her forgetting me was enthralling. The idea that she didn't give a rat's ass who my father was, or the size of my trust fund, or the company I'd someday inherit was even more so. I thought she saw the real me and liked who I was."

After, when it was far too late, his father had told him about how much Nova had reminded him of his mother. Of the scattered laughter and the random, impulsive things his mother had done when he was little, like pulling him from school to go swim with the turtles because she'd seen a documentary about them on TV. But then, she'd forget he was at the hotel while she spent the night at a bar, picking up men.

"The wounds our parents make...they're hard to escape," Fee said, as if he'd said everything aloud when he hadn't said even half of it. He suddenly realized she wasn't talking about him. She was talking about herself, and he couldn't stop himself from asking.

"Is that why you never see your family? Because of something that happened with your parents?"

She looked a little startled he'd asked, and her shell returned, hiding all the emotions, just like he was so good at doing. They were quite the pair, putting on false faces every time anyone tried to get close.

But he suddenly wanted...no, needed...to know exactly why she was the way she was. What made her run and yet fight all at the same time? What made her hide and show the world an exuberant, easygoing party girl when she was so much more?

He had a report somewhere on each of The Painted Daisies. He'd been determined to do more diligence when he'd bought Lost Heart Records after he'd been sold a line of shit about Ziggy and the Serpents with Wide Underground. So, he'd had every ugly rumor he could find on each artist under the Lost Heart label run down. The only things he remembered about Fiadh were the ones that had raised all his flags. The party girl image. The people she had in and out of her bed. The lack of connection to anyone but the band that made her a flight risk.

Now, he suspected it was all pretend. A cover for abandonment and loss. And he wondered if there was anything he could do to take away the pain, the echo of rejection that flickered through them both. A way to drop the shields and be truly whole with at least one person.

Chapter Sixteen

Fiadh

BROKEN

Performed by Seether w/ Amy Lee

She wasn't sure why she suddenly wanted to tell Asher the things she'd never told anyone else—how a piece of her soul had closed down the day she'd left her parents' house. Maybe, in truth, she just wanted him to see she wasn't spontaneous and selfish. Maybe the memory of the kiss he'd given her made her ache for him to see her as something better. Something more.

"I was an oops baby," she said with a small smile. "My parents were seventeen, and their families were very Catholic. It was a big deal in the village where we lived, like some '50s throwback scandal. They were forced to get married, which they didn't mind. They would have gotten married at some point anyway because they loved each other madly." Fee swallowed hard, thinking about the way her parents looked at one another. How they couldn't pass by the other without touching. How they seemed to be the same parts of one whole and yet still distinctly unique and independent. "You've seen the way Paisley and Jonas look at each other, right?"

Asher nodded, shifting as if he was uncomfortable with thinking about it, and she gave him a wide grin he squinted at.

"Well, that's nothing compared to how my parents love

each other," Fee said. "It's…remarkable. Stunning. But being so young, they fought as much as they loved. It took them a long time to grow up, find their careers, and become adults. I think that's why they waited so long to have more children. I was nine by the time Toby came along, followed by Poppy four years later, and then Oscar two years after that. The only version of my parents and our home my siblings had ever seen was one full of love, laughter, and music. The passionate fights I remembered from my childhood were a thing of the past. They were almost sickeningly happy together. Dad enjoyed his job at a tech company. Ma was thrilled to be teaching music lessons out of the house to all the neighborhood kids."

"Seems like your mom, at the very least, should be proudly following you around to all the venues, watching from the sidelines instead of avoiding you like the plague."

She grimaced at his word choice. She had been a plague—at least that was how her father had seen her—and it could still tear fresh cuts in her soul whenever she thought about it. Instead of stopping, instead of walking away and leaving Asher with just those pieces of her childhood, she continued, as if suddenly there was no way to stop her past from pouring out of her.

"My dad's company moved him to California on a temporary assignment. My parents were excited about the opportunity, and even more excited when they paid for me to go to a private high school they wouldn't have been able to afford otherwise. I wasn't as happy. I missed Ireland a lot. My grandparents and friends. But then, I found Landry, and we started the band. Pa wasn't thrilled about it, but Ma was overjoyed, and he gave in because he could see she was living vicariously through me. Until one day, Pa came home early and caught Lan and me kissing…"

Her breath caught, remembering the way he'd slammed the front door. The look of disgust and anger that had washed over the face of the father she'd adored. The one who'd adored her back. They'd been so happy…and she'd ruined it by doing nothing more than being herself.

She swallowed hard. "Landry and I didn't even like each other that way. We were best friends, and the absolute lack of chemistry when we kissed proved it, but we were also two bisexual women in an extremely conservative school…so we didn't really have anyone else to experiment with. That was all it had been. An experiment that went awry."

When she risked a glance at Asher, his face was blank, hooded, and she wondered if this was just one more person she'd show her true self to and who wouldn't be able to handle it. Who'd walk away as if she was exactly the disease he'd mentioned.

"Pa lost it. It was like some switch had flipped. He all but pushed Landry out the door to wait for her parents on the street…and he slapped me…" Fee swallowed, hand going to her cheek as she remembered the sting. She could still feel it today. The way her head had swung back. The way it had felt like a blister from hanging on the monkey bars too long. "He'd never, ever raised a hand to me before. To any of us. But it was like he was possessed. He ranted about the Bible and God and asked how I could do this to him. As if it had anything to do with him…"

Fee scrambled out of the chair, needing something to occupy her hands while it all spilled out. She returned to the table with the pictures, and even though she'd looked at them all earlier, she pretended to examine them again. But she wasn't really seeing them. She was reliving the first of her worst days. She was suddenly tired of the story and just wanted it to be done, so she sped it up, skipping to the highlight reel.

"They fought over me like they hadn't fought in years—angrily and passionately. Ma kicked him out of the house for a few days. They almost got a divorce." Fee looked back at Asher, and she saw a flicker of anger in his eyes. But she wasn't sure if it was directed at her or her dad or life. Suddenly, he rose and strode across the room to join her. He pulled her hand to his chest, covering it with his own as if he could protect it…protect her. And that hurt almost as bad as the story itself.

"I'm sorry," he said, low and guttural.

She shrugged and forced a smile she didn't feel. "The rest is almost predictable, right? Pa said he didn't want me around the babes…said if Ma kept me with them, he'd fight to take them all away. I'd never seen him be so unreasonable. All because I'd kissed my friend…because I happened to be attracted to more than one gender."

"So, you left?" he asked, tucking a curl behind her ear, and the tenderness tugged at the deep corners of her soul. It made her feel cherished, and she'd never felt that way before. Not since the look in her father's eyes had turned to disgust.

"So, I left," she said softly.

"You tore yourself from them…to keep them together," he stated.

She couldn't afford for him to see her so clearly.

Not when she still had a job to do. Secrets to uncover. A killer to catch.

She pulled away and missed the crackling energy and heat that sparked between them as soon as she backed away. She reassembled her shell, pulling her smile back on as she said, "I left to live the life I was meant to, leaving them in their small world."

It was meant to sound confident. Like she didn't miss them every single day. As if they were the ones who were missing out on being a part of her life. But she wasn't sure Asher bought it.

"You haven't seen them since? Not even once? Not even your siblings?" he asked.

Her jaw flexed, her smile frozen, as she fought back tears she'd sworn to herself years ago she wouldn't cry for them again. But then, as if he couldn't help himself, Asher pulled her back into him, gathering her against his chest in a hug that felt like comfort. That felt like the home she'd left long ago. And the tears hit her lashes.

"Thank you for telling me." His voice was gruff, as if he was fighting for control over the anger and regret that she instinctively knew wasn't being sent her way. He was mad at her family, and she didn't know what to do with that. Not even the Kims had reacted this way. His next words caused an enormous knot to form in her throat, making it almost impossible to breathe. "You're a better person than most. Not many teens would have the courage or strength to do what you did."

They stood that way for a long time. No words. Just arms around each other as if it would be enough to seal up the cracks and scars. A new coating of gauze that would allow them both to breathe after the losses they'd encountered.

When the door opened behind them, it startled her back to reality. To the fact that she'd let Asher Riggs in on one of her darkest moments. She simultaneously wanted to take it all back and didn't at the same time. She pulled away, wiping at her face as Wren drifted into the room in her gliding-like manner with the same mystery book in her hand as earlier.

"Father, Jozef says dinner is ready, and if you are late again, he will not save any for you," Wren said. "Good evening, Fiadh. I see you have found the clothes in the attic. They look much better on you than Father's."

Then, the little girl drifted back out.

Fee shot a look at Asher, and his jaw was tight as he glanced down over the shirt baring part of her stomach and the low-hung black pants. She didn't think he agreed, especially after the *What the fuck are you wearing?* that had broken from him when she'd walked into the room. She'd hoped his study would be empty so she could investigate and uncover his secrets. And now she had more than she could have ever discovered by nosing through his files.

Asher's asshole persona was as false as the smile she pasted on. He really was the Gothic hero he'd appeared as she'd stepped into the office and seen him cast in the shadows of a single table lamp. A hero overcoming loss to live in a world that did everything it could to mark you.

An awkwardness returned between Fee and him that

hadn't been there moments before. The reality of the truths they'd shared mixing with the desire that flickered back and forth.

His lips quirked ever so slightly. "The dictator has laid down the law. If I ever want to eat a hot meal at home again, we'd better comply."

She couldn't help the snort that left her. He moved, holding the door open for her and then leading the way back to the kitchen instead of the cold and formal dining room Wren had shown her. The same group of people sat around the table as had at breakfast, but this time, his father had joined them, sitting at the opposite end from Asher.

Kellan did a double-take when he saw Fee, not unlike the look Asher had given, and suddenly, she understood. It wasn't the type of clothes she was wearing that was bothering the men. It was whose clothes they were. Zelda's. The woman who'd left them. The woman Kellan had never divorced, even when she'd gone to live her own life on the other side of the world.

Fee's chest knotted, thinking about how Asher had been left by not only Nova but his mother. What was it he'd said in the study? The men in his family had a bad habit of picking the wrong women. No wonder he didn't trust her gender. No wonder he didn't trust her. He'd seen what she'd let the world see—someone looking for only a good time, full of smiles, running away from her band and her bodyguards, wanting to do nothing more than dance on the same day her friend had almost died.

To him, she'd just been one more woman who'd put themselves first.

One day. She'd been in his home for one day, and all she could see now were the reasons he wouldn't have been involved with Landry's death instead of all the reasons he would.

She sat down at the table, feeling like a scolded child. Like a child who'd just realized the monsters under her bed were nothing more than a figment of her overly active imagination.

Worse…or maybe better…it meant she didn't have to seduce him to find his secrets. Maybe, instead, she could end her drought by just giving in to their attraction. Enjoy the vibration that sped through them like she was the harp and he was the strings. They could get it out of their systems right here and now, and then move on once the storm passed and they went back to the tour.

The idea shot liquid heat through her, and when she raised her eyes to Asher's, she knew he saw it, because his hand stalled in the midst of scooping from a dish. His eyes fell to her mouth, and his eyebrow arched. She smiled, not holding back one ounce, and the serving spoon he held hit the bowl with a loud crash that drew everyone's eyes.

She looked away, her smile becoming almost a smirk, pleased with the reaction she'd caused, for so many reasons, until the doubts filled in behind it. She wasn't sure she could treat him like she had so many others. Pleasure that ended with the break of a new day.

Would she end up feeling like she had with Lars? Wanting more only to be tossed aside? Was it selfish, like she'd told him earlier in the ballroom? Would it put the band…her friends…at risk?

Kellan pulled her from Asher's locked gaze with a question. "Was it your music I heard today?"

"And me, Grandfather. Fiadh is teaching me how to play the piano," Wren said before Fee could respond.

Kellan's smile drifted to his granddaughter. "I didn't know you wanted to learn. We could have hired a tutor for you."

The dinner conversation turned from there, focusing a lot on Wren, but Jay and Jozef also asked Fee questions about the band and the new album, making her feel an equal part of the natural rhythm that existed between the family, making her feel at home in a way that pulled harder on her heart strings.

What she loved most, what made her smile come easily

and readily, was the way everyone at the table, including his daughter, teased Asher. His somberness was an easy target, but he surprised her by responding to their taunts with a dry humor and quick wit.

The atmosphere was light and warm and full of an acceptance Fee hadn't felt anywhere but with the band in a really long time. The images of the coldhearted Asher and the life she'd thought he must have lived filtered through until she felt completely chagrinned all over again. Embarrassed. Angel's words about her focus on Asher being a witch hunt resounded through her brain. He'd been right.

After dinner, Kellan apologized to Fee, saying he wasn't going to be able to ask her about the band and the label because he and Asher had business to discuss. The two men took off down the hall, heading in the opposite direction of Asher's office. Wren had pointed to a set of double doors earlier in the day, saying they led to the library, but that it was off-limits when her grandfather was working there. Fiadh guessed that was where the men had gone.

Reggie and Jozef braved the snow still falling to retire to their cottage away from the main house, and Jay and Wren settled in the drawing room to play dominoes and watch television. They asked Fee to join them, but the exhaustion that had been hovering over her for days, along with the emotions wafting through her, made her eyes feel heavy. So, she excused herself to go to the room Jozef had given her.

She opened the door and was hit with a smell that didn't fit. Cigarette smoke. Like a stale ashtray had been left in the room. She looked around, and everything seemed just as she'd left it, but she couldn't quite shake the feeling that someone had been there.

Maybe it had been Jozef. She wasn't sure who kept all the rooms in the mansion clean and put together, but he was in charge, so maybe, without the staff there, he'd come in to check on things. But she hadn't smelled cigarette smoke on him any of the times she'd been around him. She hadn't smelled it on any of the people in the house. Of course, that didn't mean they didn't smoke. But it would be strange to come here—to her room—smelling like they did.

She slipped out of Zelda's clothes, and instead of pulling on one of the silky nightgowns Jozef had taken from the wardrobe in the attic, she pulled Asher's sweats back on. She dipped her nose into the sweatshirt, inhaling the heady scent of him, knowing it was folly, knowing if she opened her heart up too much, it was going to get slammed to the ground. And yet, she felt it blooming anyway, a slow uncurling of petals that would reveal the soft center of her.

She climbed into bed, realizing too late that she'd left her phone plugged in on the table in Asher's office. She was too tired to go get it. Too tired to even move. As soon as her head hit the pillow, she fell asleep with her whole being feeling lighter than it had in days…maybe months…or years.

Chapter Seventeen

Asher

FEVER
Performed by Peggy Lee

ONE DAY BEFORE

Asher's dream had started with heated kisses and Fiadh wrapped in his bed in nothing but her curves and freckles, but then it shifted. Someone was watching them, and when he turned, there was a flash of white, like an old-fashioned nightgown disappearing down the hall.

He woke with his heart racing.

The entire day had filled his subconscious with just enough fodder to change the heated kiss into a Gothic nightmare. The temptation of Fiadh he knew he shouldn't give in to, mixed with the gray blob on the security cameras, and the sense of someone having been in his office.

A soft click resonated through the room as if his door had just been shut. He bolted upright, scanning the room. A hint of moonlight through the open curtains showed nothing but empty space before the storm clouds shrouded the room in darkness again. He reached for his phone, turned on the flashlight app, and shined it around, confirming again that no one was there.

He rubbed his face. He was losing it.

He needed rest.

He needed sex.

He needed to get the hell back on tour so he didn't have sex with a woman he shouldn't. A woman who'd peeled back her layers to expose her inner self to him after he'd done the same. Memories and wounds he'd kept hidden for a reason and yet didn't regret telling her.

A sound in the hall had him heading toward the door, pausing only long enough to tug on a pair of sweatpants. He quietly turned the knob and slipped out. A vase near the stairs was still vibrating ever so slightly, as if someone had bumped the table it sat on. Asher strode toward it, irritation already rearing its ugly head.

If Nova had left her room again, he might have to fire Diego. He didn't want to. The man had done a lot for them, kept their secrets and spent more of his life at the house than anyone should have to for a job, no matter how well Asher was paying him. But if she kept escaping, then there was something wrong with how he was securing her.

The smell of cigarette smoke hit him. Just a hint, as if someone had smoked hours ago and then walked through the space with the taint of it lingering on their clothes. Asher frowned. No one in the house smoked. His father had given up his cigars at least a decade ago.

He headed up the stairs to the attic. The left door led to Nova's space. It had felt wrong to put her up here, but the doctors had told him to keep her space small and remove any objects that weren't absolutely necessary. They'd said a large room was more likely to cause her stress, so he'd designed this room specifically for her and a nurse to care for her. He opened her suite to find Diego asleep on the pull-out couch. He woke as soon as he heard the door open, bounding out of bed as if to stop whomever it was.

"Just checking on her," Asher said, and Diego nodded groggily.

Asher unlocked the door to Nova's bedroom and stepped inside. Diego had removed the straps as he always did after she'd calmed down, and she was curled in a tight ball that made him think of the way Wren slept. As if to shield themselves from anything that might come for them in the night.

He turned back, throat stuck with a sudden wrench of emotion. He'd stopped thinking about the "if onlys" a long time ago, but the weight of his decisions still hung like an anchor on him. He shook his head. If he'd made a different choice, it would mean he wouldn't have Wren, and he couldn't imagine a life without her. She was a quiet, flickering light—one he didn't let surround him enough.

"Everything good?" Diego asked, voice so low Asher could hardly hear it as he relocked Nova's door.

Asher nodded, unable to talk, and left the room again.

The door to the storage area was slightly ajar. Jozef must have forgotten to shut it when he'd been up there gathering his mother's things for Fee to wear. His jaw ticked at the memory of her in his mom's clothes, but he pushed it aside as he entered the attic.

He flicked on the light, casting the room in shadows from a single bulb that swung high in the rafters. Nothing moved. It was almost too still and quiet. It was only his memories that ran loud and wild. His mother's laugh. Nova's dancing feet. Wren's quiet glide across the floor. And Fee…all fire and flame, so different from the other women in his life, and yet also, the same. Still marching to the beat of her own drum and forging a life without her family.

For good reasons. Her family had basically tossed her aside like trash. That had his jaw clenching all over again, just like when she'd told him the truth earlier. He'd wanted to find her father and ruin him as he'd almost ruined her. If she hadn't had Landry and the Kims, what would have happened to her?

After Asher and his father had discussed the acquisition of the production company in LA, he'd reread the report on the Daisies his investigators had compiled. The Kims had paid for Fee's apartment until she'd started making money on her own. They'd taken care of her, but they hadn't brought her into their home and made her theirs. He wasn't sure if that was because Fiadh had pushed them away like she did everyone with a smiling shield declaring she was fine, or if they hadn't wanted to bring her in the house because of a kiss two friends had shared that might lead to something more if they lived together.

He shook his head, turned off the light, and had almost shut the door again when a click drew him back into the room. This time, he didn't turn on the light, he just stood there, listening.

Another click. Over by the stained-glass window.

He made his way through the trunks and boxes and covered furniture, trying to stay silent, heart pounding as his mind went through a list of things that could have caused the noise. When he got close, he saw it immediately. A small piece of the mosaic had fallen out of the stained glass, and the wind was howling through it, causing the pull chain on an old lamp nearby to sway and hit the lamp's metal base.

He pocketed the glass and headed back the way he'd come.

In his room, he eyed the crumpled sheets of his bed and knew there was no way he was going to find sleep again. He simply hauled a long-sleeve T-shirt over his head, dragged on a pair of socks, and headed to the kitchen. He fixed a cup of tea by using the microwave and a tea bag that would have had Jozef scowling, and then started back to his office. Halfway there, he changed direction once again, feet leading him down the long hall to the ballroom and the grand piano.

The sticky notes were still there. Only one had slid off the backboard to land on the keys. He replaced it, sitting and causing the sharp edge of the glass he'd put in his pocket to dig into his thigh. He drew it out and placed the green crystal next to the letter *F*.

They both were reminders of the woman upstairs. Somehow having Fiadh tucked into the green room he'd once created for Nova seemed more appropriate than if Nova had ever slept there. It wasn't just because the world knew her as the "Green Jewel" because of the damn daisy littered all over her instruments and clothes. It was because she embodied the life, renewal, and energy associated with the color. Originally, he'd chosen green for the suite because he'd been told it had healing powers. That it would be restful to those whose minds were troubled. But now, the way it represented rebirth, the coming back to life, seemed poignant and important.

As if Fiadh could bring life to him…to the mansion…to all of them…if he let her.

He scoffed at himself. Such a perfectly Gothic, maudlin thought. It was the early hour, the sleep deprivation, and the scent of her lingering in the air that was bringing it out in him.

"Couldn't sleep?" Her voice drifted over the space soft and slow, and it didn't startle him. It was as if he'd expected it. As if his thoughts had conjured her. The ghost he'd chased down the hallways of his mind instead of his house.

As she made her way over to him, he saw she was back in his sweats, and it gave him the same perverse pleasure as it had earlier. She was covered in him again. He went hard thinking of the dream he'd had, thinking of the way he really wanted to cover her body.

She didn't sit with him on the bench. Instead, she leaned against the side of the piano.

She wasn't in a black dress or a white robe, but she had the deep-mahogany hair of Julia Roberts, and he'd watched the piano scene in *Pretty Woman* a time or two. His mother had loved the movie. She'd said she'd fallen in love with his father because of it. That he'd swept into her middle-class life working at a suit shop just like Richard Gere had swept into Julia's, pulling her into a fairy tale. Later, after his mother had left, he'd watch the movie to remind him…to torment himself. And as a tween, experiencing his first sexual urges, the scene with them at the piano had become a part of his fantasies—ones Fiadh could definitely satisfy.

As if she could read his mind, her eyes fell to his lips, down over the T-shirt he'd thrown on, and lingered on his lap. He didn't hide what his thoughts had done to his body. How painfully he wanted her. When she looked back up, there was heat in her eyes that echoed in the flush of her cheeks.

He pushed with his heels so the bench moved backward, putting more space between the keys and his lap. Then, he grabbed her hand and tugged her toward him.

She came willingly, standing between his legs with the piano behind her and her hands resting on his shoulders. He watched her expression as he slid his palms over her ass, up her hips, and then under the sweatshirt where he finally connected with her skin. She let out a breathy sigh. His fingers skated along her stomach and sides in slow circles, inching upward until they brushed along the bottom of her breasts. He barely skimmed over them, but they pebbled at the light touch. He ignored them, for now, continuing his upward movement until the sweatshirt raised completely, and she was forced to pull it over her head. It landed behind her on the keys, the twang echoing through the room.

She was beautiful. Soft and creamy with those trails of barely-there freckles tempting him to taste them. He moved until he could do just that. Lick a trail up along her abdomen in a path similar to the one his hands had taken, until he had one taut tip in his mouth. She whimpered, a delightful little sound that made him even harder as she crashed backward onto the keys and sent notes singing through the air. He devoured one breast while he twisted and pulled on the other, and her breath got harsher, more uneven, and another garbled sound escaped her throat. Her hands found his hair, nails biting into his scalp, attempting to lock him in place so he would continue to savor her. But the simple taste of breasts wasn't enough. He needed to taste more, and he slipped out of her hold, hands journeying down, tugging at the rolled-up waistband of his sweats, pulling at them until they slid over her hips, revealing a pair of black sheer panties.

He bent and kissed her through them, sucking the fabric and causing her delightful moan to repeat. The hum encouraged him to slide his fingers beneath the fabric and stroke the soft, wet folds below. Her hips moved on the keys, sending more notes through the air.

When he looked up, she was watching him, lashes flickering, lips parted, and it was the most perfect image he'd ever seen. Fiadh Kane lost in desire for him. Wanting him. Wanting him to continue to bring her over the edge.

"Tell me what you want, Fee," he growled.

"You. Your fingers. Your tongue," she breathed out. "All of it. Every piece."

A slow smile hit his lips. "How about we start with one body part at a time."

Her eyes closed as his fingers flicked inside her.

God, he was going to enjoy watching her unravel, watching her say his name in a way that had nothing to do with hate or disgust, and everything to do with the insatiable lust that lived between them.

A scream rent the air.

Unlike the one earlier that only filled him with dread and guilt, this one terrified him.

He'd dropped his hands from Fee and leaped toward the door before she'd even realized he'd moved.

Wren!

Panicked, horrific memories returned. Nova's hands around Wren's tiny neck. Nova's lips curled up in a snarl. The shaking. The gasping sounds.

He took the stairs two and three at a time, heart trying to escape his chest, only one thought left in his head.

Please, let me be on time.

Chapter Eighteen

Fiadh

CHANGE MY NEEDS
Performed by Scars on 45

The scream had taken her slow-building desire and tossed it into the night, but it was Asher's reaction to it that made Fiadh's heart pound wildly. Unlike the resigned calm of Nova's scream earlier, Asher had truly looked panicked this time. Terrified. And he'd scrambled from the room a desperate man.

Fee pulled up the sweats, grabbed the sweatshirt, and yanked it over her head as she ran after him. She had no idea what she was going to do, had no idea what she'd find, but she knew that, whatever this was, it wasn't anything he'd expected.

He'd taken the second-floor hallway instead of the third, had a door flung open, and had rushed inside before Fee had barely stepped off the landing. They weren't the only ones who'd been disturbed by the scream. Jay and Kellan were emerging from doors, tugging on clothes and sending startled, worried eyes in their direction.

Fee reached the room just behind the two men and entered an unexpected fairy tale. Castles and fairies and dragons littered the walls, the ceilings, and the bed. And there, wrapped in the arms of her father was Wren, shaking and crying.

"There was someone here, Father. Someone in the

room."

"Shh, Birdie. No one is here. Just me," Asher said as he rocked her, placing soft kisses along her temple, soothing her back with hands that had just been on Fee.

Asher's eyes went to his father's and then toward the foot of the bed. It took everything she had for Fiadh not to gasp. There was a pile of stuffed animals there that had been cut open, stuffing bursting from their insides.

She couldn't move. Her hand went to her stomach, fear spiraling through her.

Jay and Kellan moved into action. They swept the animals from the bed into a laundry basket, and Jay left with it in his hands, a grim expression on his face.

The little girl was still sniffling and crying, but it was slowing.

Fee, on the other hand, felt like she was falling apart.

Someone had been in Wren's room and had sent a message. A message that they could and would hurt her. Who would do that? Who?

Her eyes journeyed upward to where Nova's room was at. Was she violent? Fee had a million questions, and when her eyes landed on Asher's face, he shook his head ever so slightly. There was rage in his eyes. Rage she wasn't sure she'd ever seen, regardless of how many times he'd been angry with her.

This was a man who could and would kill to defend his daughter.

It tore at her in so many ways. That he might have to defend her. That he would do anything to do so…especially when her own father had tossed her aside to fend for herself. To keep the wolves at bay alone. The ones Angel had said were coming for them.

For the first time, Fee wondered if Asher really was responsible for everything that had happened to Landry, but in a very different way than she'd thought before. Maybe he'd made an enemy or two. Maybe killing Landry had been a strike against Asher. A way to make his business fall apart. Had it been a pure coincidence that the day they'd found out RMI had bought their label that Landry died? Or had it been perfectly planned?

Asher rose with Wren still wrapped in his arms, carrying her out of the room. Kellan and Fee followed. The little girl finally noticed the others who'd gathered around her. "Oh, Grandfather, it was awful. The most terrible dream. A man in black with so many eyes and chins and mouths it was impossible to even count them."

Kellan grabbed her hand and squeezed it. "Just a dream, Birdie, just a dream." His voice was gruff with emotion, and he and Asher were still talking with their eyes, anger rolling off them.

The tiny, silent group went down the main staircase and into the drawing room. Reggie and Jozef rushed into the room behind them with their pajamas stuffed under their coats and snow boots. Melting flakes trailed water behind them. Fee watched as Reggie tucked a handgun underneath his clothes, and she shivered.

She wasn't sure how they'd all known to come, but they were there, grim-faced and silent. The things not being said were loud in the room. A huge cloud no one would talk about in front of Wren.

"Hot chocolate. Who needs hot chocolate?" Jozef asked with a soft clap of his hands.

Wren lifted her head from Asher's shoulder and looked around the room at all the people who'd come running when she'd called, and it tore at Fee again. She was desperately happy this solemn little girl had an entire clan of people ready to sweep her up and make her world right, but it put Fee's life in stark contrast.

There was no one to wake if she screamed.

She had the band, and she had the Kims, but when she went home each night, she was alone with her dreams and her nightmares. She'd been alone since she was seventeen. A mere child herself. At twenty-six, she barely felt more than one now.

Jozef bustled out of the room.

"Birdie, I'm going to leave you here with Fee for just a moment. Just a few minutes while Granddad and I help Jozef. Is that okay?"

Wren didn't look like she wanted to let go of her father. Fee didn't blame her. Who would want to let go of something so lovely? So safe. So strong and brave.

Her eyes pricked, but she made her way over to the couch where Asher was sitting with his daughter and sat down next to them. "Shall I share with you a song my ma used to sing to me when I had bad dreams?"

Wren looked at her father and then Fee before scooting away from him to settle into Fiadh's embrace, causing more tugs to her heart.

"Yes. I think I would like that. Father does not sing," Wren said quietly.

She would have laughed if the room hadn't been so full of tension.

Asher stood, and then all the men left the room. Fee wasn't sure if they were going to search the house, check the security cameras, or confront Nova. She shivered again, wishing suddenly they weren't alone, which was ridiculous.

She smiled at Wren and broke out into Rodgers and Hammerstein's "My Favorite Things." After singing through to the chorus the first time, she stopped.

"Now, you have to tell me some of your favorite things so we can put them into the song."

Wren looked thoughtful. "Nancy Drew, Jozef's hot chocolate, Father's laugh, and swimming with Grandfather."

Fee sang the lyrics again, adding Wren's items into the song, and the little girl smiled softly.

"What are some of your favorite things, Fiadh?"

Fee caught her breath. When was the last time she'd even thought about what made her happy? "Playing music and dancing with my friends, sunshine on the water, and bright, full moons."

Wren nodded. "Those are lovely."

Fee's lips twitched. The nine-year-old acted as if she was nineteen.

Jozef returned with a tray in his hands that he set down on the coffee table. He handed Wren and Fee each a cup just as Jay came back into the room. Wren still made no effort to leave Fee's side, and it warmed her heart more than the chocolate. It sent flashes of memories through her. Cuddling with her siblings on the couch as they watched television while their parents were out and about. Toby would tuck himself into Fee's side just like this, and Poppy would climb on her lap with the thumb she wasn't supposed to suck in her mouth. Sometimes, Oscar was asleep, but if he was awake, she'd have Poppy on one side and Oscar on the other. Toby had only been eight when Fee had left, and Poppy had only been four. Little Oscar wouldn't even remember her now because he'd only been two.

Her throat closed.

"You okay?" Jozef asked, frown on his face.

Fee swallowed her emotions and pasted on a huge smile. "Of course."

"We are singing about favorite things," Wren told him. "You must each make a list so Fiadh can add them to the song."

"Reggie and you are my favorite things," Jozef said, and Wren smiled.

"Hot dogs and perfect farts," Jay said, and Fee laughed while Wren wrinkled up her nose.

"Do be serious, Jay," the little girl said, and her obvious disgust made Fee laugh even more. She was still laughing as Asher, Kellan, and Reggie came back into the room. She ached to know what they'd found, but the frustration written on Asher's normally unreadable face said more than enough. They'd found nothing.

Her laughter died away.

This is what had happened with Landry. They'd found nothing. Over and over and over again until she'd wound up dead.

And that thought filled her with cold dread.

This had nothing to do with Landry and the Daisies. No one even knew she was here, but she still couldn't shake the fear that crawled up her spine.

She didn't let it out. Instead, she continued to make up lyrics to the song as Wren dragged more favorites from all the men, and the sky lightened beyond the windows.

It was a relief to actually see the sun through the clouds. The storm was passing. Maybe they'd be able to leave. Maybe she'd be able to escape this dream she'd found herself wandering into much like Alice down the rabbit hole.

♫ ♫ ♫

As the sun continued to break through the gray, sending the storm hurtling farther north, it somehow changed the mansion. In the dark, it was hard to understand just how many windows the house actually had, but now as the light bounced off the diamond-paned wallpaper, shifting through the millions of panels of cut and stained glass, it was filled with vivid colors. It was as if Taran Ridge was two very different places—distorted, alternate-universe versions of each other. But even with the rainbows of light spreading through the mansion, a heavy, dark feel remained behind in the men's faces and tones.

They sat around the kitchen table for breakfast, quiet and subdued. Fee kept glancing to Wren, who seemed to have bounced back from the nightmare because she didn't know it was anything more. Fiadh was sure the little girl could still sense the gloomy atmosphere, but maybe she was accustomed to it. That thought made Fee inexplicably sad for all of them.

Her eyes drifted to the light pouring through the windows and glistening across the snow piled up against them. She turned her gaze to Asher. "Are we leaving?"

He shook his head, a frown on his face and a caginess to his answer. He wanted to leave. She could read it in every tiny twitch of his jaw, but it was Reggie who actually answered.

"It's going to take a day or two for us and the rest of Boston to unbury itself. You might be able to get out tomorrow if you're lucky."

Fee's heart snagged. She looked from the serious faces to the gleaming white outside once again.

"Dang. Stuck another day. But, you know, the sun is shining, and the snow is soft and fresh. I think I'm going to build a snowwoman," she said.

Wren's eyes darted up, glanced at the window, and then back to Fee.

"It will be very cold."

Fee shrugged. "And then I'll just beg Jozef to make me more hot chocolate."

Jay clapped his hands almost giddily. "Yes! Snowman building is a must. An experience every child must have. As your nanny—and more importantly, as your friend—I demand you build one."

"May I build a snowwoman instead, like Fiadh?"

"Of course. Or a completely gender-neutral snowperson. Whatever you wish," Jay answered back.

Wren looked over at her father, glowering as he swiped through something on his phone. A wistful expression appeared on her face, tugging again at something deep inside Fee. Asher was missing it—this time with his daughter that he'd never get back. Didn't he see it?

"I'll have to find something warmer to wear. While your father and these hearty fellows finish up their meal, why don't you come and help me, Wren? Then, we can show your dad and Jay how real snowpeople are built."

Asher's head jerked up, looking from her to the wide smile on Wren's face.

Fee raised a brow in his direction. "What do you think,

Asher? Snowperson competition?"

Wren sighed dramatically. "If I have to get cold and wet in the snow, Father, it only seems fair you must as well."

"I have a meeting with Reinard Security," Asher said.

"I'll take it," Kellan said, trying to hold back his twitching lips.

"You'll be too nice," Asher growled.

"I've been running this business and this household a few decades longer than you, Ash. I think I know when to pull on the big pants and light a fire under someone. What happened…" His eyes darted to Wren and then back to Asher. "It won't happen again."

"I want action. Today," Asher said.

Kellan looked at the windows and the damage the storm had left behind. "Not sure what they'll be able to swing, but we'll figure it out."

Fee pushed back her chair and held out a hand to Wren. "Shall we adjourn to the coat closet? Or wherever you think I may find suitable snow apparel?"

Wren giggled, and the sound lit up the room in a way that seemed to surprise the men. Fee felt sad again. It was as if they all needed a dose of joy delivered to their house on a daily basis. She could do that for them, give them laughter— at least while she was here. She gave it to her bandmates easily and readily to lighten their moods. In fact, it was almost expected of her. A role she willingly played in the band.

Barely fifteen minutes later, she and Wren were bundled head to toe in thick jackets, layers of thermals, jeans, sweaters, mittens, and scarves as they headed out the front door with a secret stash of items in a bag Fiadh had thrown together at the last minute. Fiadh's clothes were large and bulky, making her think they belonged to one of the men of the house, but they worked.

With their very first step outside, they fell into the deep bank of snow—Fee to her knees and Wren to her waist. They laughed before plowing their way through until they got to more solid ground near a large oak tree that might give them protection but also a fair shot at the front door.

"Do we make a ball first?" Wren asked, looking up at Fee with her father's cobalt-colored eyes and a bit of childlike wonder.

"We have to be quick before the men arrive. Make as many balls as you can," Fee said, quickly scooping and patting together a tight round shape as big as her fist and then repeating it.

Wren watched with a small frown on her face. "Are we not building a snowperson?"

"Later. First, we need a sneak attack on the men. Show them what us women can do with a pile of snow."

Wren finally caught on. "We are starting a snowball fight?"

Fee nodded, a soft smile taking over her face. She couldn't remember the last time she'd done this. Toby must have been only five or so. They'd engaged with the neighbor kids, but their dad had joined them. They'd laughed and played until every finger and toe had been completely numb. Her dad's face had been one large grin that day with his dark-red beard covered in snow and hair dripping. It twisted inside her chest, but she pushed it away like she always did thoughts of her father.

Wren dove in, making snowballs she'd hardly be able to throw without them coming apart, but hopefully, some would hit their mark.

"I believe this should count as making a little trouble," Wren said with a giggle.

Fee nodded, lips twitching until she almost felt like laughing just for the pure joy of it.

They had only made a dozen or so when the front door opened. Asher emerged from underneath the portico with a dark beanie on his head, a puffy jacket on his body, and scruff on his jaw he hadn't bothered to shave in the chaos. He looked completely opposite of the perfectly tailored businessman she thought she hated. This man…the one giving up his important meeting to play in the snow with his daughter…he was someone she could completely fall for.

She looked down at Wren with a smile and whispered, "On three."

She counted down, picking up two snowballs and watching as Wren did the same. Asher searched for them, eyes trailing through their footprints in the snow with a frown just as Jay stepped out of the house behind him.

The snowballs were lobbed. Wren's ball went wild, hitting Jay on his shoulder, but Fee's hit her mark perfectly, snow dripping from Asher's face.

His shocked expression had her laughing, a full-bellied laugh she couldn't keep back and that gave away their hiding spot.

"Hurry, hit them again before they can retaliate," Fee said through her laughter.

Wren launched more, sometimes hitting the men softly, sometimes missing altogether. Fiadh, on the other hand, hit her mark every single time. Chest. Face. Pants. Back to his chest. All on Asher. An onslaught. She didn't even give a thought to Jay.

Both men were plowing through the snow toward them. There was a smile on Jay's face and determination on Asher's, but his firm lips were tilted upward.

"Retreat!" Fee screamed as they got closer.

She grabbed Wren's hand, and they tried to move through the snow to another block of trees, but it was so deep and Wren's legs were so small it made them too slow.

A snowball hit her in the back of the head—hard. It splashed over her shoulders and back, and she laughed. She bent at her knees. "Hop on," she told Wren.

"Using my daughter as a shield, Fiadh? That's hardly fair. And don't think I won't get even just because she's my little girl," Asher's voice rang out.

A snowball hit her shoulder and burst over Wren's legs.

Fee took off again, leaping and trudging, but Wren's little body was heavier than it looked. Packed balls of snow kept hitting them. Wren was giggling and wiggling, making it hard to carry her.

"Take that, you fair ice maidens," Jay hollered at them as more snow came their way.

They finally reached the next bank of trees, and Fee ducked behind them. Wren slid off, and they grabbed more snow, trying desperately to throw it back at the approaching men.

"You are not very good at this," Wren laughed.

Fee looked down with an enormous smile. "No?"

"Absolutely not. We do not have enough snowballs or shelter, and they are both bigger and faster than us."

"It's still fun though."

"Seeing Father's face when you hit him with the first one was delightful." Wren continued to laugh. Her smile was as stunning as her father's, and it banged away inside Fee's chest, building her ache to an almost overwhelming wave, but she wouldn't give in to it. Not amid the fun and havoc they were having that she was sure Wren rarely experienced.

And then, the men were there. Jay swung Wren up in the air. "A snow barrel as punishment for you, dear girl." He buried them both in the snow, gently twirling under the soft powder as Wren continued to giggle.

Asher was not gentle at all. He took Fee down with a shoulder to her stomach. Before she could even breathe, he was on top of her, shoving snow in her face. She blustered and laughed as the full weight of him pushed her farther into the icy piles.

"Give?" Asher's deep voice demanded, a rumble of laughter there, but also stubborn resolve.

Her gaze met his, and their eyes locked. The look they shared could melt every inch of the snow from their bodies. Burning, flaming, combusting. His wet, gloved hand landed on her smiling lips with a look of awe Fee couldn't remember anyone ever sending her way.

"Give," he repeated, and this time, it was deep with a tone that was all command.

She laughed again, shook her head, and cried out, "Wren, save yourself!"

To her and Asher's surprise, Wren's little body landed on his back, tugging at his shoulders. Her giggles sounded like jingle bells in the frigid air.

"I will save you, Fiadh!"

"Save her! Why you little traitor, Birdie." Asher's body left Fee's, and she felt the loss deep in her soul. Asher easily climbed to his feet even with his daughter hanging on his back. He swung Wren around so he had her in his arms, and then he landed on the ground with her next to Jay. He flung loose snow at her, nothing that would hurt her. His face was a glorious smile, large and full and showing teeth the same color as the powder around them. Seeing them like that, side by side, emphasized just how much Wren had his smile. His smile and his eyes.

Jay looked over at Fee from where he still lay on the snow, a grin on his face as well, and he mouthed, "Thank you."

She didn't quite understand everything he meant by it, but she had a feeling neither father nor daughter engaged in much roughhousing.

She slowly stood up, already cold and wet, knowing they wouldn't last long like this in the freezing air.

"Didn't someone say something about a snowperson competition? I can't believe you two juvenile delinquents started a snowball fight, trying to distract us women from winning," Fee tossed out.

Jay laughed. Asher growled, reaching out and grabbing her pant leg as she went by. She lost her balance, tumbling down next to him and Wren on the ground. Her eyes met Asher's again. His were crinkled up at the corners, true joy busting through. He pushed another handful of snow in her face, and she couldn't help the carefree chortle that burst free.

Chapter Nineteen

Asher

WITHOUT YOU HERE
Performed by The Goo Goo Dolls

Fee's smile was her real one, and while it didn't take over her face like her fake one, it was glorious, lighting her up from the inside out until she shone almost more than the sunlight reflecting off the snow. Her laugh was free and unencumbered. Pure enjoyment. It knocked the wind out of him way more than the snowball she'd tossed in his face.

Fee was so fiery and bright, he expected the snow around her to just melt, give in, offer itself up as a sacrifice to the deity who was Fiadh Kane. Jay dragged himself out of the snow, looking down at the three of them, and his grin said it all. The pleasure of the day was written on all of them.

When was the last time he'd felt like this? Light? Happy? Loved…

God, that last thought hit him hard, dimming his smile, and Fee saw it.

She pulled herself away from him, looking over at Jay.

"Want to switch teams before you get your butt kicked again, Jay ol' boy?"

Jay and Asher both chuckled, but it was Jay who said, "I'd hardly call your pathetic snowball fight a win."

Asher got up, helping Wren to her feet. They trudged back closer to the house and made their snowpeople in front of the drawing-room windows where his dad, Jozef, and Reggie would be the contest judges from safe inside the warmth of the mansion.

Wren helped Fee enthusiastically. Asher was so enthralled by them that he wasn't much help to Jay who was valiantly trying to make some sort of snowmonster with a dog at his side.

As they worked, Jay looked from the two women back to Asher, and a small, knowing grin stayed on his face. "She's good with Wren. I wouldn't have expected it."

Asher nodded, thinking about what she'd told him. She'd been thrown out of her house when her siblings were young, but she'd been old enough to babysit, and he was sure she had. It pissed him off all over again that her father had cut her off like that. Made her choose between being herself and having her family. What kind of dick did that? What kind of father did that?

Then, he thought of his mother and the mistakes she'd made. How little she'd cared if he was happy. She'd only cared about pleasing herself. It had been selfish.

He'd called Fee selfish too, and now, watching as she danced and wiggled her butt around with his daughter and the five snowwomen they'd made, he knew the truth. She wasn't selfish. Maybe lonely. Maybe looking for company. But whatever had made her leave the hotel yesterday morning hadn't been for herself. Just like she'd said, she'd been doing something for her band. It stabbed at his insides. She'd said something similar the night he'd taken her home from the bar in Albany. Was she using herself as bait? Did she know more about Landry's killer than she'd let on?

Was that who'd attacked his daughter's room last night?

That thought completely wiped his smile away.

At first, he'd thought it was Nova going off the deep end again, but when he'd gone up to the room and seen her carefully locked away, asleep, his mind had immediately gone to Ziggy. The asshole was in the States and pissed as hell at Asher.

"Ta-da!" Fee exclaimed, drawing his eyes back to their handiwork.

Jay burst into another round of laughter, and even Asher's lips curled upward again.

Each snowwoman had a red daisy from one of the vases inside the house embedded in their chest, and instead of forming buttons with the rocks they'd gathered, they'd spelled out the first initial for each of the bandmembers' names. The snowwomen had black scarves draped over their head like hair, except for the one for Fee, which had a red scarf.

Asher looked at their monster snowperson and his weirdly shaped dog and almost admitted defeat.

"Asher," his dad's voice called from the front door, and when he looked over, his stomach fell at the grave look on his father's face.

"I'm coming," he hollered back. "Sorry, you're on your own, Jay-Man."

Jay groaned, and Asher headed back toward the house. He stopped to tug at Wren's knit cap, saying, "Don't stay too much longer. I don't want a popsicle for a daughter."

She giggled and pushed his hand away. So much better than the terror from just hours before. His eyes landed on Fee again, and he felt his heart contract in a way he didn't like— the way he'd promised himself he'd never allow it to do again. But damn, if she hadn't forced her way past his shield, first by her fierceness and the chemistry between them, then by the loneliness that was an echo of his own, and now by the tenderness on her face as she'd lightened Wren's day with horseplay.

He owed her.

He wondered, like he often wondered with his daughter, what it would take to make Fee happy like this all the time. To keep her real, small, crooked smile instead of the larger fake one.

His dad had taken the call with Reinard in his library, and that was where he led them as Asher stripped off his wet clothing. He was dripping and hardly presentable, but the worry in his dad's eyes told him it didn't matter.

"Tell me," he said to his father.

"You won't believe it until you see it," Kellan's voice was grim, and it only added to the tension traveling up his spine, replacing the brief joy he'd experienced outside.

He sat down in his father's chair behind the huge oak desk stained black in a library that reflected the rest of the house. Black and white with hints of red.

His father stood behind him as Asher turned his attention to Reinard on the computer screen. The man was ancient with white hair, gray eyes, and an attitude that matched his background in French special forces.

"Show me," Asher said.

The man gave him a curt nod. "When you sent us the smudge from the video feeds, we ran it through some experimental programs. This is what we believe the cameras were seeing."

The smudge re-pixelated into a figure dressed all in black, but the face…it wasn't just one. It was multiple faces. Noses, eyes, and mouths were all mixed together in the wrong places. A contortionist image of half a dozen facial parts.

"What the fuck?" Asher's mind went immediately to Wren's nightmare. She'd said he'd had multiple eyes and mouths. She'd been right. Even though he'd known there'd been someone in her room—the pile of destroyed stuffed animals had been proof enough—it still made his stomach sink and his chest tighten. Rage filled him.

"There's been some chatter on the internet," Reinard said. "About how individuals can make themselves invisible to cameras and facial-recognition software. The idea is, you confuse the cameras into essentially thinking it's seeing nothing because it can't understand it, so it skips over it, thinking it's a glitch."

"He's been here for days," Asher barked, anger rippling through him as well as fear for the people in his home. Nova and Wren were particularly vulnerable, unable to defend themselves.

"It's pretty sophisticated for your average burglar. Someone knew what they were doing. The attack in your daughter's room…it was a message."

"No," Asher's voice was full of sarcasm. "Your men fell down on the job with Paisley Kim, the company before you fell down on the job with Landry. Now, you and your so-called security allowed someone in my house. Give me one damn reason not to fire you."

Reinard's mouth tightened, his eyes narrowing. "I can absolutely understand your lack of confidence. I can understand The Painted Daisies' lack of faith in the people around them as well, but I'll remind you, the FBI, Secret Service, and local police departments were all on hand for both those horrific instances."

"But it wasn't one of their own who locked Paisley Kim in a bathroom."

Reinard looked like he wanted to kill someone, but Asher knew it wasn't directed at him.

"I'd like you to bring back Garner Security," Reinard said. "I'd like my team and his to overlap."

Asher's jaw clenched. Garner Security had been the Daisies' detail when Landry had been murdered. Both the security companies had a lot to prove. They were hungry to show the world and their clients they could keep them safe.

When he didn't respond, Reinard continued, "Garner has a team being trained as we speak at Fort Drum. We're making plans to get them to you by morning, using some all-terrain vehicles. Until then, I have eyes on every camera in your house twenty-four-seven."

"You think he's still here? After that bold display? Even after we searched every corner?" They'd gone systematically, room to room, from top to bottom, in opposite directions, meeting in the middle, and still hadn't seen or heard even a peep. Asher's mind filled with the wobbling vase and the scent of cigarette he'd had the night before. The click of his bedroom door. Goosebumps traveled up his spine.

"I think, given the weather, it would be almost impossible for him to leave. He could have hoofed it out today, but you have twenty-five acres with multiple outbuildings, I'd say he'd stay close until he had a better chance of getting away without freezing."

"I'm more concerned about how he got in and out without tripping your alarms," Asher grunted.

"He hacked the system. We're doing a complete diagnostic, and we'll have the loop closed within the next couple of hours."

"Ziggy Klein was a serious computer nerd before he founded his punk band. His entire family is embedded in the seedy, dark side of Berlin. And...he's in the U.S.," Asher told them, recalling the facts from the file he had on the musician.

His dad inhaled sharply, sending Asher a look that said he wasn't happy he hadn't known the man was in the States.

Reinard nodded, which was somewhat reassuring. "We followed him through New York City to a run-down apartment in the Bronx. I'll have some men swing by and see if he's still there."

"What's it going to cost me to bring Garner's men here?" Asher asked.

"Nothing. This is all on Garner and me. I know it doesn't seem like it, Asher, but we're the best in the business, and we damn well want you to know you can trust us."

"If you're the best, the entire business needs an overhaul," Asher growled back.

Reinard's lips thinned even more, but he didn't disagree. "I'll let you know when to expect the team."

Asher nodded and disconnected. He got out of his dad's chair and turned to face him.

"You think this is Ziggy?" his dad asked. "Why didn't you tell me he was here?"

"Torrance just told me yesterday. Someone was trying

to trace the money going to Krista. While following up on it, we realized he'd shown up in the States."

"Is Krista safe?"

Asher nodded, guilt tearing into him like it did every time he thought about her. He'd failed once where Krista was concerned. He couldn't fail again. He'd left the after-party, knowing Ziggy was being a dick. Knowing he was eyeing her. Asher hadn't found out about the man's sick-ass reputation until after he'd already bought Wide Underground. He'd dived into the deal because he'd been hungry to get his feet wet in the industry. He'd been impulsive in a way he rarely was.

That night in Berlin, he'd been disgusted by the entire scene and left early, and it had almost cost Krista her life. It was why he was giving her the money from his private inheritance. He wasn't going to let RMI pay for his personal mistakes. It was Asher who'd walked out of that hotel room. It was Asher who'd known Ziggy was high and known there were groupies still in the room. But there was no way he could have expected Ziggy to drug, rape, and beat Krista almost to death and then dump her near a German police station.

When Asher had refused to continue working with Ziggy's band, even after his criminal case had been dropped, the man had gone berserk. He'd trashed an entire hotel suite, costing hundreds of thousands of euros of damage, and threatened to get his money come hell or high water. He'd sued Asher and RMI, and they'd been a breath away from losing if Ziggy hadn't shown up on speed with a knife in his pocket to the courtroom the last day.

Asher should have known the man wasn't just going to tuck his slimy tail and hide under a rock even when that was what it seemed like he'd done.

"I fired him right before Landry…" Asher's voice bottomed out as his chest squeezed tight. Had he caused all of this?

His dad caught his meaning and was already shaking his

head. "I don't think he would have come after another band. He wanted back in, or at least wanted his money, and making you lose a bunch of it by plummeting Lost Heart into chaos wasn't going to be a way to make sure you had it to give. And he hadn't lost his lawsuit at that point."

While everything his father said made sense, the truth was, Ziggy's hatred of Asher had started from the moment he hadn't given the man the alibi he'd wanted. He hated Asher more than Fee ever had. His breath disappeared. Had she disliked him enough to ruin him? When she'd ducked out of the hotel yesterday morning, was it to meet up with Ziggy? Had they teamed up? It slashed cruelly through his soul even as it rebelled at the thought, as if lamely insisting it knew Fee wouldn't do something like that to him. But what if she hadn't known it was Ziggy she was working with? What if he'd sent someone else in his place? No matter what, he had to find out what she *had* been doing and *who* she'd been doing it with. He had to know the truth, or it would eat away at him.

Laughter broke through the house—Wren's and Fee's lighter female tones and Jay's deeper chuckle. It felt like another lifetime ago since he'd been outside, joining in the revelry. He wanted that for Wren. Joy. Spontaneity. And yet, he feared it for himself because it had always ended with a broken heart. A heart he thought he'd locked up and only given the key to his daughter and his dad. But Fiadh was chipping at the hard shell, cracking it, sliding inside with her smiles and her heart and her courage. He wasn't sure what would happen to those tender, exposed pieces if he learned she'd teamed up with the sick bastard.

"She's a good one," his father said, causing Asher's head to whip back to meet his dad's stare.

"What?"

"I like this one. Smart. Sexy. Determined. She's good with Wren," his dad continued.

"It isn't like that with us. She's an employee." He heard the falseness in his tone and was pretty sure his father could hear it too. The heated kisses he'd shared with Fee were the exact opposite of her just being an employee. The taste of her he'd gotten the night before on the piano hadn't been nearly enough. If Wren's screams hadn't torn through the night, he would have been inside her, in multiple ways and multiple times. He would have claimed her and allowed her to claim him back.

His dad chuckled. "Keep telling yourself that, but every single one of us can feel the tension between the two of you."

Asher rubbed a hand through his damp hair, causing it to stick up in places. His next words were tortured, almost begging his dad to agree with them, to help him step back from the abyss he felt himself approaching. "She's a musician, Dad. They're notoriously flighty and unstable."

"And the Riggs men are notoriously unfeeling assholes. Doesn't mean either is the truth when it comes to you or her."

Damn, it hurt because he wanted to believe it. That he and Fee could both be more than what the world saw. But at what risk?

His dad's hand landed on his shoulder. "Being alone isn't the answer either, Asher. Don't follow in my footsteps in this way. It's the one thing in my life I wish I could change."

"It wasn't your fault Mom left." Asher's voice was gruff with emotions. They hadn't talked about his mother in a long time. Maybe since her death. It still hurt them both too much. "It's in our DNA. Maybe we're broken. Damned."

His dad's lips squeezed tight, throat bobbing. "I didn't put her first. That's the real curse. It's not in our blood but in how we're raised. We were taught to put our ambition above everything else, including love. I call bullshit on it right now. Right here. I refuse to let your life be marked with the same mistakes."

They stared at each other for a long time.

"I don't know if I can do it. Take this kind of risk," Asher said somberly. "She's keeping secrets...holding back."

"And you aren't?" His dad raised a brow. "No matter

how much research we do on each acquisition we make, in the end, it's still a leap of faith. You know how to take the risk, Ash."

Asher let out a self-deprecating scoff. "Weren't you the one telling me the labels were a mistake?"

Instead of responding right away, his dad stared out the window a moment before turning back, meeting his gaze, and saying, "I'd lose the hundred million if it meant I could bring love into your life. Hell, I'd give the entire business away."

Asher didn't know how to respond to that stunning admission. He'd always known his father loved him. Known it and felt it even when they were not a demonstrative family. But to hear him offer up everything with such fierceness and certainty, it grabbed Asher's breath and stole it away. His heart flipped and twisted and raced. He wasn't sure what would be left of it when it stilled again.

As he watched his dad stroll out of the room, Asher acknowledged his father was right about one thing. Researching a merger was always the smart move. So, instead of concentrating on the emotions he was so uncomfortable with, before he took any more leaps, he had to get to the bottom of the secrets Fiadh was keeping. After…well, he wouldn't think about that yet. He couldn't. It would take every ounce of self-control he owned just to have the conversation without touching her. He'd almost lost it in the snow with his daughter and Jay looking on, the spell she wound tightening spiral by spiral. It might already be too late. He might already be lost.

Chapter Twenty

Fiadh

CRAZY FOR YOU
Performed by Scars on 45

Fiadh, Wren, and Jay were dripping wet as they burst back into the house. Kellan came down the hall as they were stripping off their wet outerwear, a smile on his face.

"Ready for the contest to be judged?" he asked.

Jay groaned. "I concede. It's all over but the writing." Once Asher had left, he'd given up on whatever mangled formation of a snowperson they'd been making and come over to help Fee and Wren add instruments to The Painted Daisies snowband.

Fee put a hand on his shoulder, patting it, a small smirk taking over her face. "Don't let Asher hear you. There's not a bone in his body that would admit defeat."

"Shows how little you know me," Asher's deep voice boomed through the entry, and Fee whipped her head around to see his glance fall to where she still had a hand on Jay's shoulder, a scowl taking over his face.

Her heartbeat pulsed as she took in his disheveled appearance. He hadn't had time to fix himself from their frolic outside, and she liked him this way. Unkempt. Mussed. A hint that there was more to him than the arrogant, stiff man he presented to the world.

"Everybody, get cleaned up. Lunch is almost ready,"

Jozef hollered from the end of the long hallway.

"You'd think he was in charge," Kellan said with a small chuckle.

"I heard that," Jozef said as he disappeared back toward the kitchen.

They all headed for the stairs except Asher's dad. Fee's foot was on the second step before Asher's command halted her. "I'd prefer no one go anywhere alone today."

She turned, a protest on her lips, but the look he was sending her way dried the words up. It wasn't just worry that creased his brow. It was fear and anger, but also a glimmer of the mistrust she thought they'd moved past. He seriously couldn't think she had anything to do with this? With Wren's room? But whatever he'd discussed with his father had brought the shadow back over him. The darkness that seemed to follow him wherever he went.

She swallowed hard, barely holding back her questions—a demand to be told the truth. His jaw clenched as if he could read her thoughts.

"Is everything all right, Father?" Wren asked.

He looked down at his daughter, face softening, and it did something to Fee's insides, melting them, making her ache for something she'd never thought she'd have again. A family of her own.

"The storm wreaked havoc on the house, Birdie. Just want to make sure no one is stuck in the dark somewhere."

Wren's head tilted as if she could tell he was lying as much as Fee could, but she didn't argue. Instead, her little hand slid into his, and Asher's throat bobbed. They made their way up the stairs with her and Jay trailing behind. At the second-floor landing, Asher looked over his shoulder at Jay and ordered, "Stay with Fiadh until I can join you."

Jay clearly knew there was more going on as well and just nodded as the father and daughter continued down the hallway. Fee forced her feet to move again, continuing up one more flight to her room. She grabbed some of Zelda's clothes from the wardrobe and headed toward the bathroom while Jay fidgeted as if suddenly realizing he'd be in her room while she changed.

Normally, she would have teased him. She would have dropped something about joining her in the bathroom just to see him blush, but the thought of doing that today made her stomach shift uncomfortably. It was exactly what Asher would expect of her. The flighty, selfish musician. Images of Asher's face when he'd told the reporter at the hotel to take off and his quiet anger when he thought she'd left yesterday morning for a quick screw returned to her.

He wanted her and hated it, just like she wanted him and had thought she hated it. Now, she was just confused. Being here with him, seeing a few of the layers behind his mask, kissing him, and wanting him with every fiber of her being had shifted her thoughts. It made her ache for not just one night with him, but something more. Something impossible. But it would be selfish to indulge, wouldn't it?

So, instead of flirting with Jay, she just locked the bathroom door behind her, showered away the cold, and dressed in a pair of bootleg jeans and a cropped sweater that had once belonged to Asher's mother.

Fee wondered why Zelda had run. Kellan Riggs seemed the epitome of a gentleman, as if he'd give everything he had for the woman he loved. But then again, Fiadh knew better than anyone how looks could be deceiving. It was easy to put on a show for a few hours, even a few days, but it was impossible to keep it going for months and years. If you had someone at your side for that long, they would see the worst of you, no matter how much you tried to hide it.

When she came out of the bathroom, it wasn't Jay who was there, but Asher himself, and it caused her stomach to flutter and her pulse to quicken. He had changed into another pair of jeans and a slim-fitting sweater that shifted over his wide shoulders when he adjusted in the chair where he had an ankle of one long leg hooked over the knee of the other.

He was sinfully gorgeous, and just the sight of him in her room made liquid heat pool deep inside her. A feeling she was baffled by. She'd experienced lust. The depths of passion. But this feeling with Asher…it was different. Like comparing the heat of a volcano to the surface of the sun.

His hooded eyes scrolled up her body, hesitating on the strip of skin showing at her waist once again and then lingering on her breasts before finding their way to her lips and finally her eyes. She recognized the desire in his gaze. It was the way he'd looked before he'd dragged her across the piano keys and started to consume her as if he was a fire-eater and she was the flame.

"Where's Jay?" she asked.

"Sent him to drop Wren in the kitchen with Jozef before he got changed."

"Who's making sure he isn't alone?"

"Jay will be fine."

Fee couldn't help the irritation that flared. "So, you said everyone should double up, but you really just meant the helpless women?"

He stood and took a step toward her. She backed up, running into the wall.

"Tell me where you were yesterday morning, Fiadh."

"Why do you want to know?"

He closed the space between them. He didn't touch her, but their sock-clad feet were mere inches from each other, and the warmth of him drifted over her, the current between them flickering and shimmering.

"Did they follow us to my home? To my daughter?"

Fee's eyes widened, disbelief and hurt settling in her chest that took the desire she was feeling and tossed it away. "Of course not."

Then, she thought about Angel disappearing in the snow. His dark clothes. The danger lingering around him. And she wavered. And like the lion he was, Asher read it and pounced. His hands went to her shoulders and shook her, not viciously, not angrily, but in frustration.

"Tell me, damn it. Was it Ziggy?"

She frowned. "Ziggy? As in Ziggy and the Serpents? What does he have to do with any of this?"

He stared for a long time, as if assessing how honest she was being, before letting her go and backing off with exasperation blooming over his face. "You're a good actress. Just like the woman whose clothes you're wearing."

She was irritated at being compared to his mother whose abandonment had clearly left an unhealed wound. She had two choices. She could retreat or push back. And so, she pushed, knowing exactly what reaction it would cause—almost desperate for it. "Acting? You're one to talk."

"Excuse me?" he demanded.

"That whole seduction scene last night with the piano?" she taunted, hoping she was doing the right thing. His body was rigid as he held himself back, but she didn't want him carefully guarded and leashed. She wanted the man who'd consumed her last night. She needed him to drop his shell so she could see the entire man behind the mask and not just the pieces she was trying to fit together. "That was an act, right? You pretending you wanted me? But really, you were just using it to get information."

He pounced, arms caging her against the wall, hips pushing into her. "I wish this was an act, Fiadh." The hard length of him pressed into her stomach proved his desire was true if nothing else. "I wished to God I didn't want to rip your damn clothes off, throw you on that bed, and fuck you until you screamed my name and forgot there was any other man or woman on this planet for you but me."

Her pulse raced, and he moved a hand to surround her neck, thumb flickering over the pulse point.

"I wish I hadn't wanted you since the moment I saw you send the softest, most real, most open smile to your goddamn phone backstage in Korea."

Her mind tried to keep up with his words, but his touch was sending her thoughts spiraling away, leaving only the natural instinct to blend their bodies together.

"Do you always deny yourself any sort of pleasure?

What are you punishing yourself for?" she demanded, fingers embedding into the soft knit of his sweater, pulling him closer instead of pushing him away. Their mouths were barely a breath apart. With a mere whisper, they'd be touching. She wanted it. She wanted him. She wanted to feel every scorching flame, and then, hopefully, she could douse it out. She could leave it behind.

But her question had hit home, because his eyes narrowed.

"Not punishment. Protection. Because you'll ruin me. You'll ruin me and leave me just like every damn woman before you." His ripped confession was guttural and pained. "Like every woman has left every Riggs for centuries. We're cursed. We're cursed, and you have the ability to cast that same damn spell over me again."

Her breath caught at the trauma those words revealed. The heartache. But it matched the ones written on her veins. Her family. Lars. Landry. They'd all loved her and left her.

"Maybe we'll break it together. The curse. The heartache," she said, and she pushed her lips against his so softly it was agonizing because it wasn't enough. She murmured against them, "Or maybe we'll ruin each other a little bit more. Just watching the flames will be worth it."

He growled, pressing his lips fully into hers, forcing her mouth open with his tongue and taking command of the kiss as if he'd always done so. As if he knew her body better than she did. In two seconds, she was whimpering from his mouth on hers, from the finger that was teasing the row of earrings down her lobe, from the hand that cupped her breast, tugging and twisting in the most delightful way.

"Rochester," he murmured. "I'm fucking Rochester, and instead of burning my house, you'll burn me, and I'll still be left a partial man."

Then, he was devouring her again. Full of rage and frustration and want.

She met him lick for lick. Every nip and taste and kiss she landed on him made his body tighter, the length of him harder, and his eyes a deeper blue. His hands fell away, and she moaned her displeasure before they found her ass, lifting her off the floor so their cores aligned even more. Her legs went around his waist automatically, drawing him to her.

They continued their bash of teeth and tongues, nails biting into skin.

She ached and burned everywhere they connected.

She needed more. She needed it all.

Chapter Twenty-one

Asher

BELIEVE IN LOVE
Performed by Scorpions

It was her legs wrapping around him, squeezing him tight, that brought him back to reality, to him, screwing Fee against a wall while his family waited downstairs, a man may be sneaking around his house, and additional security was on the way.

Every time he touched her, he was pulled further under that damn spell she cast.

The talk with his father in the library had only chipped away at his resolve even more until it was hanging by a mere thread. He'd never felt this close to losing control before. Not even with Nova. Then, he'd given in to a mirage. Some glorified version of what he thought they should have been as a couple. He'd wanted *them* more than he'd wanted *her*, if only to prove he wasn't cursed.

But with Fee, he just needed the woman. Her fire. Her smiles. Her secrets. Her.

It would be the easiest thing to simply lower her to the bed and get lost in the uncontrollable flame surrounding them. Instead, he grabbed tight to the last thread of control he had left, determined to get the truth out of her before he gave everything away. He turned the torrent of kisses and touches into simpler, softer caresses, and he knew she realized what he was doing, because she let her legs fall to the carpet and let go of the fierce hold she'd had on his clothing.

"Tell me the truth," he said, hating the plea in his voice. "Who were you meeting with?"

"A private investigator," she said without hesitating.

Surprise filtered through the desire still pounding through his veins followed quickly by a pained understanding. "You're trying to find her killer."

Fee nodded but looked away. Her cheeks flushed, not from their heated kisses but from an embarrassment she rarely exhibited.

"I thought...I thought you were behind it."

Something tore inside him. He wasn't sure what. His soul. His heart. His pride. The Riggs family was known for their honor. For decades, doing business with them was like doing business with goddamn saints. But he'd ruined their image with the Ziggy debacle. His name and the RMI brand had been dragged through the mud, not once but twice, because of the bastard. He'd had to sit on the witness stand while attorneys did their best to make Asher look like a low-life, conniving snake. A mob boss in a tailored suit.

"You had me investigated?" he asked over the lump in his throat.

She nodded, crossing her arms over her chest and rubbing a hand up and down her arm. "A man...he approached me. Said he could find who had murdered Landry. I directed him to you because of what you said that night."

"What I said?" Asher frowned, wanting to be pissed and yet only feeling regret.

"At the farmhouse...you got a call, and you looked straight at me as you said, 'It's done' with disgust and anger in your voice." Fee got quieter and quieter with each word she spoke.

Asher dragged a hand through the hair he'd barely straightened and sank onto the bed. What a fucking mess. His teeth ground together as he tried to determine how much to tell her…how much to pull back the layers of chain mail that protected his heart. But his father was right. He was keeping secrets as much as she was. She'd given him one of hers. Didn't he owe her one back?

"If I was disgusted with anyone, it was myself." His voice was raw, broken, like the strings were snapping around him with the admission.

She still didn't understand. Her eyes were crinkled with confusion.

He cleared his throat, grabbed hold of his balls, and took the leap. "I don't have the best track record with women I desire." He waved his hand toward the ceiling in the direction of Nova's room. "She's only one in a line of them scattered behind me from high school on, but she was the worst. The one to fully break me. She cheated and lied and nearly killed Wren…" His jaw clenched as another round of emotions hit him. He just had to stick to the facts. Facts he could do easily. He lived and breathed them in his job. "With you…every time I saw you, you called to me like some damn siren. I hated myself for feeling anything. For being weak all over. I'd swore I'd never open myself up to that kind of heartache again. I swore I'd model myself after my father and remain focused on the business and my child and nothing else."

She eased over to the bed, leaving space between them as if knowing he needed it in order to have this pained conversation.

"You said, 'every time'…but Grand Orchard was the first time we met. I definitely would have remembered meeting you before then." She arched an eyebrow at him, an attempt to lighten the mood, and he wanted to kiss her for it, but he also needed her to understand just how deeply she'd impacted him.

"You're the reason I decided to expand RMI into music." Her eyes grew wide, and he chuckled softly. "I was closing a deal in Seoul, and they wanted to celebrate by going to The Red Guitar concert. They'd finagled backstage passes, and there you were."

Asher reached out and touched the corner of her mouth before letting it slip away again. "With your half-smile that's actually your real one."

She inhaled sharply, and he wondered if it was at his touch or because he was the only one to have seen the truth of her.

"I wanted to know who you were texting," he continued. "Who could bring that stunning smile to your lips. I wanted to know everything about you, which made you dangerous. Exactly the opposite of what I needed. So, I pushed you out of my mind and did everything to avoid you. Bought Wide Underground in a rush. And still...I craved seeing you again."

The truth that normally made him feel like he was drowning suddenly felt freeing instead. "So, I bought a second label when the first one was already going to hell."

Her eyes filled with tears, and she closed them, hiding her emotions like he normally did. "You bought...you bought the label...for me?" It was choked.

He couldn't help himself. He ran a finger along her cheek, and she shivered. "I never admitted it, even to myself, before yesterday, but yes. I think I pursued Nick until he caved and sold Lost Heart Records because it meant having you. Then, I set out to convince myself you were exactly like Nova and my mother. Flighty. Risky. Selfish."

"And I did everything to prove it to you," she said softly, shaking her head, opening her eyes to meet his again. She briefly leaned into his hand more before reaching up to pull it away. "But that doesn't explain your words at the farmhouse. They...haunted me."

His brows creased as he tried to remember what he'd said that night. He remembered Fee's grief vividly, as if it was still there, her pain hanging in the air like its own dark entity. It had sunk like a barb inside him, bringing emotions he hated to the surface, pulling him from the glacial depths he chose to live in until all he'd wanted to do was take away her hurt, find a way to give her Landry back. Only, the call he'd gotten had stopped him from stupidly pulling her to him. The call that had led them to this. To now. To the threats that had landed at his daughter's feet.

"That was the day I let Ziggy go after the courts had tossed his criminal case out. I was telling my dad it was done."

Fee's eyes widened, a rush of emotions—relief, disgust, and frustration—coating her face. "I've spent almost two years hating you not only for those words but for threatening to take the band from me."

His heart throbbed, more raw and painful movements from the newly uncovered organ. It was unguarded, easily stabbed and destroyed. Did she see it? Did she know how much he was offering her with these words?

"I hated what you did to me," he said. "It might have made me an ass."

"Might have?" Her eyebrow arched, and her lips quirked, the half-smile he so craved hitting him in the gut.

He would have pulled her to him and gone back to devouring her, everyone and everything else in their life be damned, but the candlestick phone on her bedside table rang.

Asher sighed. "I suspect it's Jozef the Dictator, demanding we join them for lunch."

He stood and held out his hand to her, hoping she saw it for exactly what it was—much more than a simple gentlemanly gesture, much more than a truce. A joining. He waited patiently while she stared at it, glad she was considering it long and hard before accepting it. He needed it to be weighed and measured carefully, the least-impulsive thing she did this day…this month…ever.

When she finally took it, relief flew through him as strong as the desire that flamed at the touch. Her palm glided against his, the soft skin scattered with callouses from playing her instruments. It was a dichotomy, just like Fee herself. She'd earned the tough layers. She'd had to wear them just as he'd had to wear his to protect themselves against the heartache of their lives.

He tugged her a little closer, until he could inhale the scent of her again. His voice was deep with the well of emotions gathering inside him as he said, "Lunch, Fee, and then you need to tell me about the man you hired."

Her throat bobbed, but she didn't argue. Instead, she nodded, and more relief flooded him. He'd taken the leap and landed, but the ground still felt shaky. A ledge that could drop him easily into a chasm. But at least she'd taken the same leap. If it crumbled beneath them, maybe they'd simply fall together.

♪ ♪ ♪

After lunch, he made sure Wren and Jay were tucked with his father in the library while he took Fee back to his study so she could tell him everything she knew about the investigator. She held nothing back, and it only made the enormous feelings in his chest grow right along with his apprehension about the man she'd hired. Angel Carter had approached her, which, in and of itself, was suspicious, but even more so was how he'd found out everything about Asher. Not only things about Nova and his mother the world didn't know, but also about the money he was sending Krista, which was layered in witness-protection-level security.

Asher's body grew tighter and tighter the more Fiadh unveiled. When she mentioned Angel's warnings about cutting ties with RMI and the wolves who were still circling the band, he wanted to find Angel and take apart his entire world.

He gritted his teeth, holding back as much of his anger as he could, because it wasn't directed at her. "Describe Angel to me," Asher demanded.

Fee ran her finger along her row of earrings as she verbally drew an image of Angel. Something niggled at the back of his brain while she talked. Something from the files he'd commandeered from when the FBI had talked with Arthur Mason back in Albany. Asher brought up his laptop and flipped until he found the sketch-artist rendering of the man Artie had seen arriving in the orchards next to the farmhouse shortly before Landry had been killed.

"Is this him?" he asked, turning the computer toward her.

The drawing showed mostly the back of a man with a hint of a profile. Angular nose, harsh jaw, muscles bigger than most professional boxers.

Fee eased forward, eyeing the drawing. "Maybe…probably. Who is this?"

"This is the man Artie identified as being in the orchard that day."

Her eyes went wide, and the fingers twisting her earrings stilled.

"You think he killed Landry…" Her voice cracked. "Oh my God. He was using me. To find out what we knew?" Her hand pushed against her heart, pain filling in every ounce of her features. He was around the desk in two steps, doing what he'd wanted to do that awful night by tugging her into his arms.

"I don't know. I think he's worth following up on."

Her entire body slumped into him before stiffening again. She pounded a fist against his chest. "Damn him. Damn me. I had him this whole time. I…I…"

"You don't know it's him, Fee."

She looked up at him with haunted eyes. "Why else would he be there?"

Asher didn't know. He only knew Leya's and Adria's families were hot targets. The band as a whole was a soft target because of their mixed ethnicities, religions, and sexual preferences. They had bags of hate mail he was pretty sure none of them even knew about, but he was privy to it because he *had* done his due diligence the second time around.

"If you give me the okay," he said softly, "I'll have Reinard track down all your text and phone communications with him and see what they turn up."

"He told me he wanted to find her killer. That it was

important to him as well. And it sounded like the truth. Like it was almost...painful. Whenever I asked why, he'd close down, but I never once thought..." She convulsed and slammed his chest again with a balled fist. "Damn him."

"While my mind is relieved your hatred is now focused in a different direction, my body isn't sure it believes it," he teased, a failed attempt to try and stop her from beating herself up.

She wrenched herself away, and he let her go with reluctance.

There was remorse and fear on her face as she looked around his office. "The reason you didn't want us going anywhere alone in the house today...it's because you believe he's still here? That he's the one who was in Wren's room...that I...I allowed him..."

She sagged at the waist, and he was there again, dragging her back to him for the third or fourth or millionth time. But it was the only way he knew how to comfort her— with his body—because he knew, from experience, how ineffectual words could be. No one could ever tell you not to feel guilty. You had to choose to give it up. And he hadn't. He couldn't. Not yet. Maybe never.

Even still, he tried to dissuade her from feeling it by focusing on the facts.

"I think the person who has the most to gain by coming after me right now is Ziggy. I know he's looking for the hundred-million-dollar payday he didn't get. I don't know if he would go so far as to target Landry and the Daisies as a way to get to me, but I do believe he'd target my family. I don't know if Carter is working for Ziggy or if it's all unrelated."

His frustration grew. He'd brought this to his family's door regardless of the cause. He'd bought the Daisies' record label. He'd provoked Ziggy, dismantling the psychopath's world. He ground his teeth together, rage simmering. If he was the reason for all of this, he would make it right. He'd fix it once and for all.

Chapter Twenty-two

Fiadh

DON'T LET ME STAND ON MY OWN
Performed by Imelda May and Niall McNamee

TWELVE HOURS BEFORE

Fee wanted to slam her fist into a wall. She wanted to lose herself in her instruments. She wanted to put on her jacket and hunt down Angel Carter, zap him with a stun gun, and demand he tell her the truth.

The thought she might have been interacting with Landry's killer for months on end…God, it made her want to throw up. It made her skin itch and burn and made her want to run and fight and hide all at the same time.

He'd found and targeted her so easily. Singled out the one who was removed from everyone and lost in grief.

Asher's hand ran over her back, and his lips pressed softly into her hair.

It felt wrong and right. Just like everything with Asher did. Perfect and yet so fucked up. The revelations he'd shared with her in the room before lunch and again now were almost too much to bear. She didn't know what to do with all the pieces he'd handed over or how to meld them with the vision she'd had of him from before. The one that had slowly been crumbling and rebuilding itself the longer she was with him.

He'd bought the label…for her…

Because he couldn't get her out of his mind.

He said he hadn't known it at the time. But…feck…

And now she could be responsible for bringing this to their door. To his somber, delightful daughter. To the small family he'd assembled here. She couldn't let him lose any of them because she knew all too well what it was like to lose one—or all—of the people you had at your back.

"We need to leave," she breathed out, turning her face so her chin was resting on his chest and she could look up at him.

His gaze met hers, and the grimness that had shrouded him as they'd talked about Angel seemed to deepen even more. "We do. Unfortunately, there is no way out today. We have additional security coming to us in all-terrain vehicles, but they won't be here until morning."

She inhaled a shaky breath and said, "Once we're away from here…I can contact Angel. See if I can set up a meeting."

Asher's eyes narrowed. "No."

"We can get answers."

"We're not using you as bait. No way in hell. So get that thought right out of your head. Let the men investigating this take the risks they're supposed to take."

"But Asher…they haven't done their job. Not once. Not at all. We lost Lan…" Her throat bobbed. "We almost lost Little Bit."

She closed her eyes.

"You won't lose anyone else, baby. I promise you." The deep, guttural claiming tied with the sweetest of nicknames and intense promise sent a shiver through her.

She never would have thought she'd like being called baby. Had always thought it was a bit condescending. But uttered in that tone, from a man known only for his reserve, she found herself more than just liking it. It sent an almost savage longing through her.

She only wished he could keep the promise he'd uttered

with it. If only it was that simple. To put your trust in one man and have it all come true. Fairy tales weren't even that perfect. They were darker. Closer to her reality and closer to the Gothic stories the mansion had originally brought to mind.

Asher's hand tangled in her hair, tugging softly but insistently until she opened her eyes. Then, he leaned down and gently took her lips. Even though it was a tender kiss, it was also fierce and deep, filled with a reverence that sealed the cracks of Fiadh's heart like hot metal welding together. She kissed him back, slowly and steadily, the hunger in her to consume and be consumed growing stronger, offering her body to him openly and without reserve, but also offering him something she'd never given anyone else…every ounce of her soul.

When his lips moved away, she almost reclaimed them, but then the look he gave her tugged at every ounce of her inner being.

"You're not alone anymore." His voice was deep, gravelly, and thick.

Her eyes filled.

"I'm not letting you risk yourself again," he continued. "You're needed. Not just by the band, but me. You've been in Wren's world mere hours, and you've already brought her to life in the same way you dragged me back to the surface. You're the piece my family has been missing. I've been missing. I'm not letting you go."

A sob broke free.

"You're mine now. And I protect what's mine," he said before his mouth covered hers once again, sealing his promise with a sweet kiss that turned savage, as if he was telling her he'd accept no arguments.

And she had none to give, because the truth was, she'd been aching to belong…to be accepted…to be cherished for too long. Forever. Since the door had shut on her parents' house with the lock sliding in place and her on the outside.

She would have lost herself completely to him there and

then, except they were interrupted once more by the screams that had chilled her to the bone just yesterday.

Asher sighed, eyes closing, and she felt the weariness in him leaching from his bones.

"Even Mr. Rochester was freed from his prison at some point." She met his gaze and wondered how she'd ever considered it icy and cold. There certainly was a fierceness to it, but it was alive with emotions sparking through the depths. Or maybe it was just because he was no longer hiding them from her.

"Diego, Torrance, and I have narrowed down some facilities for her, but it feels… like taking the easy way out."

She squeezed him. "Can I ask you a question?"

His jaw tightened, but he nodded.

"Was she an addict before you got together?"

He didn't like this line of questioning. She could feel it in the way his body grew taut in her embrace, but he still answered her, when even a day ago he wouldn't have.

"I didn't think so when we met, but looking back, yes. It's why her mother washed her hands of her."

"Did you try to get her help once you realized she had a problem and before she overdosed?"

He nodded.

"Then, stop paying penance for her choices."

"I all but begged her to have Wren, and then I was so entranced with my new daughter I didn't notice how bad she was falling until it was too late."

"She could have said no to having the baby. She could have asked for help. None of this is on you."

She didn't think he believed her, or maybe he did, but he was still masochistic enough to continue to beat himself up for things out of his control. She and Asher weren't as opposite as appearances would lead them to believe.

"I'm going to go check on Diego and her," he said. "Let me walk you to the kitchen so you won't be alone."

"Who's going to keep you safe?"

"Diego will be with Nova."

She stepped back reluctantly, feeling the loss of his warmth but not his promises because those were still there in his steady gaze.

He guided her with a hand on her back into the kitchen where Jozef was chopping vegetables, and Reggie sat at the counter, watching. Another scream rippled through the air, and Asher sighed, squeezing her hand before leaving her there.

She didn't miss the look Reggie and Jozef exchanged at the tender move. It was an oxymoron—Asher Riggs being anything but hard and prickly—but before either of them had a chance to say anything, her phone rang with Leya's text tone.

> *LEYA: Just your friendly afternoon check-in to make sure you haven't killed Asher. Do I need to send bail money? Are things okay?*

She hadn't told the band about anything that had happened here—Nova's screams or Wren's nightmare visitor. Just like she'd held on to the knowledge Angel had uncovered about Asher. At first, it was because she hadn't wanted them to think she'd gone off the deep end chasing her theories. Now, she didn't want to share because they weren't her stories to tell. They were Asher's, and he had to decide when and who he opened up to.

How quickly things could change, she thought to herself.

> *FIADH: Ha, ha. No bail needed…maybe a very different kind of protection though.*

> *LEYA: …*

> *FIADH: Before you respond, I already know it's an epically bad idea.*

LEYA: But?

FIADH: I don't know. At first, I hated how attracted to him I was after all he put us through. But now that we're here, he's just, well, different. I understand him more.

LEYA: Okay, but what happens when the snow melts? Does he know you'll move on?

FIADH: Who says I will?

LEYA: You always do.

Fee bristled a little, but she knew this was her own fault. It was the image she'd carefully cultivated.

FIADH: Lars and I were together for a long time.

LEYA: Not exclusively.

Lars may not have been exclusive, but Fee had been. Once The Red Guitar tour had started, she'd only been with him. The band didn't know because she'd concealed her real feelings from them like she did so many other things. The persona she showed the world was almost a way of holding up double fingers at all of them. Some of it to hide from those who assaulted her bisexuality. Some of it to hide the loneliness that welled through her. Some of it because it wasn't fair that only male rock stars got to revel in their sexuality without ending up with a not-nice euphemism tagged onto their name.

It took her too long to reply, and it was Leya who came back first.

LEYA: I didn't mean to upset you.

FIADH: You didn't.

LEYA: Just...be careful. I don't want you to get hurt.

FIADH: You don't want me to screw this up with our label.

Fee regretted it as soon as she said it.

LEYA: You're right, but we can replace a label, Fee. We can't replace you.

It tugged again at all those wells of loneliness she'd let herself wallow in for a long time—since Landry's death...maybe even before that. She'd held herself back from all of them, even these friends—these sisters—because if your own family abandoned you for being yourself, what were mere acquaintances likely to do?

FIADH: No one is going anywhere. I won't feck it up for us.

LEYA: I trust you. Just be careful. Lust is notorious for misleading us. Be honest, both of you, and that's the best you can do.

Was that all she felt for Asher? Lust? It seemed impossible to think otherwise, but it felt like so much more than that. Deeper. Fuller. Those promises she'd felt in her soul at his touch. Maybe she was just setting herself up for another heartache. More slices to an already scarred heart that really didn't have room for more.

LEYA: Any idea when we'll see you?

FIADH: We're hoping to leave tomorrow. They're sending all-terrain vehicles.

LEYA: Okay, well then, have a good time tonight. ***tongue out emoji*** ***jalapeño

emoji***   ***peach   emoji***   ***flame
emoji***

She chuckled.

> *FIADH: I feel like I need to give you a book on how to use those emojis in real life.*

> *LEYA: How about this one? Am I using this one right? ***one-fingered emoji****

> *FIADH: I don't know. Do you know where you can put that finger?*

With no immediate response, Fee sent another text.

> *FIADH: You're blushing, right? I made you blush.*

> *LEYA: I hate you.*

Fee laughed softly. But then, worry for Leya funneled through the humor. The thought of Leya giving herself to some buttoned-up man her family picked made her want to bust something. Leya needed someone who was going to honor her and her gifts but also push her out from behind her glittering, fairy-like shell.

> *FIADH: While I, on the other hand, love you to the end of the universe and back.*

> *LEYA: You know I really love you too, right? Now stop chatting with me and go light his fire.*

Fee chuckled out loud.

> *FIADH: We seriously need to work on your sexual innuendos.*

Leya sent back an eye-roll emoji, and that was it.

Chapter Twenty-three

Asher

LULLABYE (GOODNIGHT, MY ANGEL)
Performed by Billy Joel

When Asher came out of Nova's room, Diego was pacing by the couch.

"I don't have any more tranquilizer left," he said.

Asher's stomach flipped, a dizzying mix of feelings returning to him as it always did when it came to Nova. He hated having to give her the sedative but feared not having it. Ever since she'd attacked Wren, they'd never been without it. He wouldn't survive a repeat of that night. Just thinking about it caused his stomach to burn, acid roiling through him.

If he hadn't dragged his feet about putting her in a facility, they wouldn't have been in this situation. As uncomfortable as it still made him, the truth settled over him. He needed to do this, not just for his own peace of mind and Wren's safety but also for Nova herself.

"I looked at the sites you and Torrance came up with. I'll place a call and see which of them has openings," he said, fighting back the wave of emotions those words generated. "Would you be willing to stay with her at one until she got settled? Until we're sure we can trust the facility to take good care of her?"

Diego nodded. "If they'll let me."

"They will," Asher said.

"How do you know?"

Asher cast him a sardonic look. "I know what money does."

The nurse just stared at him for a moment. "Right."

He didn't wait for another response, simply left, calling Torrance as he headed back down to his office. There, the two of them spent the next few hours talking to administrators to see who had room for Nova. Only two facilities could take her immediately. Neither of them was thrilled about having Diego there. One adamantly refused, even when Asher threw money at them. The other did so with some hesitation. He wasn't sure if that made him feel better or worse. But knowing Diego would be around would help him sleep at night.

His phone buzzed.

> *DAD: Where are you?*

> *ASHER: My study. You?*

> *DAD: In the kitchen. Fiadh and I are having a nice little chat about the band and record labels.*

Asher's heart stumbled, the cold, broken muscle rebelling at being used after being shut down for so long.

> *ASHER: I'm on my way.*

> *DAD: You've got it bad, son. I was just teasing. She and Jozef are having a hearty discussion about coffee.*

His lips curled upward in a half-smile. While his family and staff regularly gave Asher a hard time, it had been a long time since his dad had joked with him in private. They'd both been somber and serious for too long. Yet, in less than the two days Fiadh had been with them, she'd already shattered the glass dome they'd been living under, laughter and light leaking out like water and crystals from a broken snow globe.

DAD: What I really want to know is why you're alone when I thought the rule was no one was to be alone?

ASHER: I was with Diego and Nova, then on the phone with Torrance. If someone attacked me, you would have gotten a call, but I'm on my way.

Asher shoved his phone into his pocket and stepped into the hallway. As he turned the corner, he found Jay and Wren in deep discussion. Her shoulders were slumped, and her head was down. While his daughter was never bubbling over with vivacity like Fee, she was never really depressed either. So, finding her this way made his heart sink all the way down to the pit of his stomach. Dark images flashed through his mind. The torn stuffed animals. That man in the weird-ass mask. Nova with her fingers around Wren's neck.

"What's wrong?" he demanded, joining them.

Jay tucked his too long hair back out of his face with a sigh, and then looked down at Wren, waiting for her to answer.

Wren wouldn't meet his gaze. She just shrugged a shoulder.

He sank down on his haunches and gently pulled her chin so she was looking him in the eye.

"Birdie? What's up?"

"I do not want to go to school tomorrow," she said softly.

Asher looked from his daughter to Jay and then back.

"I'm pretty sure no one is going to school tomorrow. Maybe not even for a few days with the snow and the blackout."

She perked up a bit. "Truly?"

"Yes. But tell me why you don't want to go."

Her eyes welled. "It is awful there."

Anger, guilt, and frustration welled through him. Was someone being mean to her? Asher's chest and stomach felt like they'd been worked out more in the last few days than they had in months…years. All the women in his life were pulling and tugging and twisting him up in the ways he hated. He'd thought it didn't include his daughter, but maybe he'd just lived so long with his shield in place that he hadn't allowed her to affect him.

"Are they mean to you?" he asked, and when Wren looked up at Jay, Asher turned to glare at the nanny. "Is there an issue you haven't made me aware of?"

The school cost a small fortune, and that was before he and his father had agreed to fund their new library. If there were people being nasty to her—staff, kids, otherwise—he was going to talk with the administration. And if that didn't work, he'd pull their donations.

"No one is mean, Father," she said softly. "My teacher does get upset when I correct her facts, but she is never mean. I tried reading while she is teaching things I already know, but this also upsets her. I just have to sit there, and it is very boring."

The tight stranglehold on his heart eased slightly. Bored he could handle.

"There's more to school than just the lessons," he repeated, like he had hundreds of times to her.

"Yes, you have said this. I do not seem to be learning any of the things you expect." She looked regretful, as if she was letting him down, when he knew it was very much the other way around. He wasn't doing his job as her dad.

"Social skills are just as important. Learning to get along with others. Playing with others. Making friends. Dealing with problems Jay, Grandpa, or I aren't there to solve for you. That's just the tip of the iceberg," he told her.

"I have tried to make friends, but it is very difficult. I do not seem to like the same things as the other students."

Asher sat down on the floor, back against the wall, and she joined him with her knees pulled to her chest, toes hidden under her long skirt.

"Sometimes, you have to compromise," he told her. "Play things the other kids want to play."

She looked incredibly disgusted. "But Father, they only play tag and chase the boys."

This comment made Asher's stomach spasm in a different way. Wren was only nine. Boys should not have been a part of the picture. Not yet. Not for at least another half dozen years—or twenty, if he had any say in the matter.

"And what do you want to play?"

"I want to solve a mystery. Or write about solving a mystery."

Asher looked down at the Nancy Drew book in Wren's hands. She was fixated on the stories at the moment. A few years ago, it had been a series about puppies that she'd read constantly. She'd asked for a dog over and over again, and he hadn't wanted to put the responsibility on Jozef and Jay, knowing he'd never be around to help train it.

He'd been focused on his own needs for too long—the things he needed to do and accomplish with RMI—all the while keeping himself hidden behind his armor. His throat bobbed, and he pulled her into him, hugging her while he tried to figure out what to say. How to apologize. How to let her see beneath his shell so maybe she'd do the same. Just like Fee. God, he'd screwed up. When her little arms went around him, hugging him back, his throat closed, and he had to squeeze his eyes shut momentarily while he got hold of his emotions.

"I don't have a good answer for you on this problem today, Birdie, but I promise Jay and I are going to think about it," he said.

She sighed as if she doubted the resolution going in her favor, and it tore at his heart as much as Fee's story about her father had. Worse was the thought that he might be as big of an ass as Fiadh's dad had been. He'd never kick Wren out for kissing a girl, but here, he was forcing her to be someone she wasn't by going to a school where she didn't fit. Where she was smarter than the teachers, and the students seemed apathetic.

He stood, pulling her up with him, and the three of them made their way down the hall to the kitchen. He heard Fee laugh and his father's deep chuckle in return, and he ached to join in the joy. To lose himself in laughter. To not feel the heavy burdens of life weighing him down.

"Go on in. I'm going to chat with Jay for a second," he told Wren, squeezing her hand just as he had Fee's several hours ago.

He watched her float into the kitchen before turning to Jay.

"Why didn't you tell me it was this bad?" he demanded.

Jay's eyes narrowed. "I have been telling you. She's struggling. She doesn't fit."

"Is homeschool really the answer though? Won't her social skills regress even more?"

"I can search around for some charter schools. My friend, Stacy, in Grand Orchard runs an amazing one. It's a pretty tightknit community, so maybe she'll have some connections to ones in the Boston area. Some specialize in kids with different needs."

Asher bristled. "She's not abnormal, Jay."

"No. Abnormal isn't a word I'd ever use. But she clearly faces challenges that are different than the average student."

Asher ran a hand through his hair. This was the last thing he had time to deal with, and yet, it was something—like Nova—he'd put off dealing with for way too long. Now, everything was sliding down the hill to land on top of him at the same moment, colliding together.

When he hadn't responded, Jay filled in more painful words.

"What she really needs…is you."

Jay looked like he was uncertain what would happen

once he'd laid the truth down, and maybe Asher should have been pissed on being called out, but it wasn't anything he didn't already know. The knot around his heart grew tighter. He'd protected the stupid organ for so long, attempting not to feel—not to get hurt—that he'd kept it hidden from even his child. It hadn't completely ruined his relationship with his daughter, but it certainly hadn't helped it.

"What am I supposed to do? Take her on the road with me? I travel more than I'm home. What kind of life is that for a child?"

"What kind of life is it if she never has her father around?"

Even as he'd known he was failing Wren, he'd justified it by using his father and him as an example. They loved each other. They had a good relationship even though his dad had been gone as much as Asher was now. It wasn't Kellan Riggs who'd left the wound on Asher's psyche. It had been his mom.

Jay read his silence as anger, and it was, but it was all internally directed.

"If you didn't want the truth," Jay added on, "then you shouldn't have asked. I've never bullshitted you, and I never will. I care about you and Wren both too much." After he let that settle down between them, he walked away to join the others.

Asher stood in the hallway, weighed down with the responsibilities and choices swirling around him. He'd worn blinders, pretending his life was in order—perfectly lined-up pegs—and now it seemed completely askew. Dots he couldn't connect. Decisions needing to be made that he had no desire to make and had put off for too long. He never would have sat this long on a decision for RMI, but he'd let his personal life crumble around him.

He'd find the right solutions for all of them.

Nova was in process, and he'd find the right answer for Wren as well.

Laughter pierced the air again, Fee's and Wren's lighter

ones and the deeper ones of the men in the kitchen. It made him hungry for Fiadh. It brought back every aching need he'd had earlier to blend their bodies together until it felt like they were one. To devour the joy she brought to others so it became embedded in him permanently, easing away the grim solitude he'd built around himself. And maybe in the process, he'd be able to ensure her joy was no longer a charade she painted on with a false smile, but the truth.

Chapter Twenty-four

Fiadh

DON'T LET GO
Performed by Bryan Adams w/ Sarah McLachlan

When Asher joined them in the kitchen for dinner, Fee could tell the weight of the world had landed on his shoulders. She wondered what had happened with Nova that had him even more serious than normal. Wondered if he ever felt the weight lift for even a few hours, or if he was always responsible for everyone around him. What Jozef had said was utterly true—he was paying penance for sins that weren't his. She suddenly felt chagrinned that she'd ever thought he was responsible for Landry. If anything, he was so honor bound to do the right thing that it was tying him up in knots.

After dinner, they all retired to the drawing room where Jay challenged them to team up for a game of Scrabble. Jay picked Wren, Reggie obviously was with Jozef, and Kellan asked Fee to be his partner before Asher could get a word out. This made Asher scowl so beautifully she wanted to laugh and kiss him all at the same time. It also meant he had to play by himself. He pouted and groused about it while everyone made fun of him. Fiadh saw it for what it was—an unspoken effort by the people who cared about Asher to help lighten his load.

They were well into the game when the house alarm blared, jerking them all out of their laughter. Asher pulled out his phone and was growling to Reinard as he stormed out of the room, demanding his father stay with Wren and Fee while the rest of the men searched the house.

Fiadh's stomach twisted and turned, unhappy that Asher's lighthearted moment was ruined. Worried about what the men would find…or worse, what they wouldn't. She felt as if all their nerves that had begun to unwind were pulled taut once more.

Kellan patted her hand, bringing her mind and her attention back to the room as he shot a look from her to Wren, as if trying to tell her to keep it together for the little girl. She did her best, tempting her to sneak a peek at her father's letters.

"I will not cheat," Wren said, shaking her head sadly.

When the men came back, they had the same frustrated looks on their faces as when they'd searched the house for Wren's visitor during the night. This time, Wren finally caught on there was something amiss, and her normally somber face turned downright frightened.

"Father…I am scared," she said, running to him.

He squatted down and pulled her into a warm embrace. "I know, Birdie. I'm sure it's just the storm messing with the system, but I'm going to have you spend the night with Jozef and Reggie until we can have the security company check it out."

Asher exchanged a meaningful look with Reggie, and the man gave a curt nod. Jozef reached for Wren's hand, and she took it without question.

"Let's go out to the cottage, and I'll whip you up a treat before bed," Jozef told her.

Wren kissed her father's cheek goodnight, hugged her grandfather, and then left with Reggie and Jozef distracting her with their chatter about what would be the perfect late-night snack.

Once they were out of hearing range, Asher turned his eyes to the rest of them. "We think he left. Reinard's men saw the anomaly they've been tracking at the front door and then again outside."

No one said anything, but Fiadh's heart was still racing, galloping at a speed that felt like it would go off track at any moment.

"Reggie is ex-special forces, armed, and can protect Wren and Jozef in the small confines of the cottage. Dad, I'd like you to bunk with Jay tonight. This way, you won't be where he'd expect you to be if he already knows the layout of the house. Diego will lock Nova and him in. I'll stay with Fiadh."

Fee didn't miss the small smirk Jay and Kellan exchanged, and it helped lighten the heaviness in her heart, but Asher didn't notice. He was still wound up too tight.

"Let's give Fiadh a choice, shall we, Asher?" Kellan said, his grin emerging. "I promise I'll give up my bed for you, Fiadh, whereas Asher is quite obnoxious in claiming a mattress. I know this for a fact as I've had many chances over the years to share a bed with my son. When he was a kid, I used to wear a cup at night if he ended up with me."

"Dad." The warning was softened by Asher's lips quirking upward, and Fee's heart swelled again at how much these people cared for each other. In the midst of danger, Kellan was still trying to loosen the death grip Asher's emotions had on him.

"What's Jay's offer?" Fee asked with an Adria-worthy wink, wanting nothing more than to make Asher's tipped lips turn into a full smile. But when all amusement left his face instead, she knew it had been the wrong taunt. "I'm just teasing. Staying with Asher works for me."

"If you change your mind, use the inter-house phone and press three." Jay grinned, and then he and Kellan headed out with Kellan mumbling about needing his silk pajamas or he wouldn't be able to sleep.

Fee's natural instinct was to try to lighten the mood. It had always been her role. Even as a small child while her parents had been fighting, she'd somehow been the one to break the argument. It may not have been a conscious choice back then, but it had become one. But for some reason, after the one attempt that had backfired, she couldn't put on the false bravado required to try again. Maybe because the idea of sharing a room with him—a bed—made the desire spike through her veins until that was all she could feel. A heady craving that seemed out of place given the situation. The danger.

Or maybe that was why it curled through her even stronger—a need to feel passion instead of fear. To feel like, even if they couldn't solve the problem of the intruder, they could answer the question of how their bodies would fit together. They could forget, for a few hours, everything but lips and tongues and hands as they slid over sweaty skin.

As she headed for the stairs without saying a word, she felt his eyes on every inch of her. By the time they reached her room with him two steps behind, her body was burning. Yearning. Aching. And he hadn't even touched her.

Asher stalked through the room, checking under the bed, opening the wardrobe, and searching the closet and bathroom. Once he'd made sure it was clear, he walked back to the door. "Lock it behind me. I'll be back in just a moment."

She swallowed down the desire in order to finally get out a Fee-worthy tease, "Getting your silk pajamas like your father?"

"I don't sleep in pajamas. I'm not two or sixty, but I do have some silk ties we can use, if that's your thing." His response only increased the throbbing in her core, a desperate need for friction. For him.

"Are you going to claim my mattress, Asher?" The sultry question was way more breathless than she wanted it to be.

His gaze slid down her so slowly, so intensely it felt like his hands had caressed her.

"Not the bed, baby," he said huskily, making her veins thrum and a pink bloom cover her cheeks both from his meaning and the sweet endearment he'd now uttered a second time.

In two strides, he'd come back to her, stroking the flush on her cheeks. "The great Fiadh Kane, blushing. I'll enjoy discovering what else I can do to make this sweet color appear."

His fingers trailed down her jaw and her neck, past her collarbone and the swell of her breast.

"But there is something I need from you," he said, and at that moment, she thought she might agree to anything he asked. It was perilous to her heart and soul, and yet she somehow knew she could trust him with both. She'd already given him pieces of herself over and over, and he'd accepted each one with an unexpected tenderness. When she didn't respond because her emotions were too raw, he continued, "If we do this, I need us to be all in. Exclusive. No other partners on either of our dance cards."

"So, the wallflower promises a dance after all."

"Fee." The single syllable was both a demand and a beg, and below it, she heard the boy who'd been abandoned. The lover who'd been used. The man who'd been alone for too long. Her heart bounced out an erratic rhythm that wasn't just because of his fingers or his lust-filled gaze. It was more than a physical reaction. This was her soul pattering and panting and frantic to know what it would feel like when they were joined.

"No one else, Asher. Just us."

She wasn't sure how it was possible for his look to turn even more heated, but her response had fanned his flames to a whole other level. He stepped back, dropping his hands, and she let out a little whimper that made a smile tug at his lips.

"Lock the door, Fee. I'll be right back."

He strode to the door, opened it, and then looked back to where she was still stuck in the middle of the room. "Fee," he growled.

And it did nothing but curl the lust deeper into her.

She finally dragged herself to the door, shut it in his face, and locked it.

As soon as he was gone, the blood pounding through her eased enough for her to capture a coherent thought. But it was only the same thought her body was already chanting. She wanted Asher. Damn any consequences. Damn the nightmare surrounding them. They deserved this moment—needed it, even.

She slipped out of his mother's clothes, eyed the nightgowns Jozef had taken from the attic, and then decided against them. It would be too weird to be sleeping in his mother's things while they lost themselves in each other. Instead, she threw on the T-shirt she'd worn under his sweatshirt the day before. She paused as she drew it over her head. Had it really only been a day?

It seemed like an entire chapter of her life had gone by. An eternity.

She'd barely settled the shirt around her hips when he knocked.

"Fee," he said through the door.

"What's the magic password?" she asked, another taunt she could barely muster over the heady sensations filling her veins.

"Baby, if you don't let me back in, we'll have to find a new room when I break down the door."

She chuckled and opened it. He slammed the door shut behind him, locked his gaze on her, and took one enormous step to engulf her. His hands went to her waist, lifting her up and settling her about his hips. She curled her legs around him, hooking her ankles and squeezing.

His mouth was almost punishing in its ferocity when it found hers, forcing her lips open and taking command. She reveled in the taste of him as his tongue stroked and dived and seduced. She let him lead for longer than she'd ever let anyone, and then she countered with a twist of her tongue, finding his deepest recesses, plunging into him the way she wanted him to dip into her.

He dropped her on the bed, practically tore his shirt over his head, and then joined her, lying on his side, pressed up against her. He watched her face as his hand slid under her T-shirt, eyes widening when the realization hit him that she'd lost her underwear with the rest of her clothes. His palm stilled briefly on her inner thigh before moving to barely skim her curls. An agonizing whisper. A delightful torture that sent shivers over her skin.

With slow, teasing fingertips, he dragged the T-shirt up until she had to raise her arms and remove it. When she turned to face him, he was consuming her nakedness with a hunger she was sure would obliterate her. A look his fingers followed, etching a line over the freckles on her stomach and chest, as if he was memorizing them. The flame leaped inside his eyes when they landed on the barely visible dots on her breasts, leading him to her pink tips like an arrow.

"You're beautiful, Fee." His voice was gravelly and tortured. "So beautiful it makes me forget everything. The curse. My family. My responsibilities. Just looking at you fills me with an insatiable hunger."

Her body convulsed, an orgasm threatening just from his light touch, anguished words, and passion-filled gaze. She dragged his head down, devouring his mouth while her hands explored, blindly memorizing the lean muscles that shaped his broad shoulders and wide chest before moving downward. His stomach rippled as she moved across it, searching for the perfect indents on either side just above his hip bones, and when she found them, she dug into them with her fingertips before rocking them together. He made an inexplicable sound as their cores collided, deep and guttural.

Then, he was incinerating her with his lips again, leaving a blazing trail over her jaw and neck and chest, continuing down until he was all but swallowing a breast, swirling the tip with his tongue. The wet heat forced another moan from her that was followed by a whimper when he lifted his head. His eyes pinned her with his as he dragged his palm between taut tips, circling lower and lower in a tantalizing movement that felt very much like a dance.

"I didn't get to finish what I started last night, and the brief taste has haunted me ever since."

She fisted the blankets as his mouth landed right where she was aching the most. A cry escaped from the depths of her that she'd never heard before. Visceral. Pained. Exquisite. She shivered and shook, the need for relief blooming and growing until it might have been the only thing she'd ever feel again. He'd hardly begun before she'd exploded, quivering and shaking around his tongue and his fingers as she chanted out his name like a song. All passion and fire in the syllables instead of the anger and hate that had been there just days ago.

He kissed his way up her body until his eyes greeted hers with a cocky smirk—an assured twist of his lips—that somehow pissed her off and turned her on even more.

"I liked the sound of my name that way," he said with his smug smile still in place. "How many times do you think I can make you chant it before the night's over?"

Fee cupped him through his jeans and squeezed. "Take these off, and let's find out."

His grin was sensual and playful—an Asher no one else got to see—as he moved away to unbutton his jeans and slowly let them fall. She stared openly at his carved beauty. It wasn't just his chest that was lean and muscular. It was all of him. Abs, thighs, ass. His entire body screamed how hard he must exercise to keep it looking this way. She imagined he pushed himself in the gym just as much as he did at his job. At anything. And right now, she wanted that extreme nature to work itself out all over her.

He dropped the foil wrappers he'd pulled from his pocket onto the comforter, and then returned to sit next to her. His eyes were hooded as he caressed a breast. She sat up and slid her hands down over his shoulders and sides, swirling lower and lower just like he had until she was gripping his length. He hissed, a tangled release of pleasure and pain, and she rejoiced in her ability to give him the same delightful agony he'd given her. Fee grabbed one of the wrappers, tore it open, and then rolled it over his length all while he watched, and his eyes grew darker.

When she finished, he pushed her back on the bed,

settling between her hips, his elbows holding his weight off her. He played with a long spiral of her hair, lust filling every ounce of his expression, but she also felt him pull back ever so slightly, guarding himself. She hated that more than anything she'd ever hated with him, because she didn't want him restrained. She wanted him to share every pound, every weight, every problem, and every scar.

"Don't hold back, Asher. I can take it. I can take every inch and every secret. Every dark wish and every forgotten promise. Don't hide any of it. Don't keep even one piece, and I promise I won't either. We'll trust each other with all of it."

His eyes closed, dark lush lashes briefly resting against sharp cheekbones before he opened them again, and she saw the boy who'd been abandoned. The one she wanted to hold close and show that there were people who stuck by you, even though she'd never found many in her life. But they only needed one or two. They only needed each other.

Chapter Twenty-five

Asher

HELP ME MAKE IT THROUGH THE NIGHT
Performed by Bryan Adams

His heart flipped harshly at her little speech. At her plea to just let go. To give her all of himself—even his darkest parts. And God did he want to. He wanted her to have everything because she deserved it, but also because he did too. It didn't matter that he hadn't wanted to take this kind of risk again. It was too late. He'd already done it, and now he wouldn't deny her. Not when her gaze was so open. So trusting. So full of hope that he'd reciprocate by giving her exactly what she'd asked for—every last piece.

It was exactly what he'd wanted to give her before he'd walked into the kitchen this evening. Before the alarm. Before more worry about his family and the darkness looming around them had broken through.

He'd wanted to devour her and have her devour him back.

And that was what he did. His mouth found hers in a crushing kiss that gave as much as it demanded while he slid home, loving the gasp she made as he bottomed out. Loving how her nails dug into his shoulders in a way that would leave marks. Loving how her hips arched up to meet his and the way their heartbeats echoed each other's, as if screaming, *You go. I'll follow.*

Then, all lucid thought left his brain. There was only the

sweet scent of Fee. The blood rushing through his veins, the soft taste and feel of her. The long, wet slide out before he was back inside. The beautiful, slow way they moved seamlessly together until the ache grew too much and it became raw and ravaged, slamming into each other. Minutes rolled into what felt like hours…days… just two bodies called to one another.

Her eyes fluttered closed, and she gasped out, "God, I'm so close…"

"Open your eyes, baby."

When she did, he got lost in the blaze there, feeling it burn him from the inside out. Desire. Longing. Home.

He dragged his hand down between them, encouraging her rush. And she was gone, convulsing and shivering and quaking around him, and he let go and followed her over the edge, slowing their movements, rocking it out, enjoying every last pulse of pleasure.

He rolled to his side so he wouldn't crush her, although Fee was hardly some tiny thing he could easily break. And he loved that about her. Loved that she was strong and fit and tall. Loved he could do what she asked and not hold back. Give her everything.

And he realized how many times he'd thought that single word in the last few minutes.

Loved.

He loved her.

Fuck.

When had that happened?

When hadn't it happened? his brain countered.

They were still tangled, legs and hips and arms, but he drew her even closer, kissing her temple. His fingers traced a sweet trail over the marks on her skin, both the ones nature had placed and the ones she'd had inked on.

Words in Gaelic.

Words in English.

The green jewel daisy that represented her in the band stood out. Long, lean petals with a green tinted faintly yellow. The middle was a ball of soft spikes that were an even deeper green, hiding the core of the flower just like Fiadh hid herself. It was perfect for her, just as this room he'd once designed for Nova was really more suited to Fee. But he actually didn't want her in this room. He wanted her in his. He wanted her where they could open the windows and hear the ocean battering against the shore. Where they could feel the timeless rhythm of the sea in each beat of their hearts and each pound of their bodies against one another.

"Does it upset you?" she asked quietly, watching his fingers trace over her.

He frowned. "What?"

"The way I've decorated my body. The piercings, the tattoos," she said, scrutinizing his face.

"No. Why would you think that?"

"You don't have any." She shrugged. "Some people think it's a violation."

Suddenly, he understood. "Your father?"

She ran a hand through his mussed hair. "In some ways, you're like him."

He grunted with displeasure at the thought of being anything like her asshole dad, frustration brewing because he'd already made the analogy himself, and all he could do was promise himself he'd fix it. Do nothing but honor the people in his life the way they were.

"He was always perfectly dressed and perfectly put together. He issued commands, and they were followed," she said.

He heard the sorrow in her voice, and he hated it.

"I can see how this would be a problem for you since you've not listened to a single one of my demands," Asher grumbled, forcing the tease into his voice and trying to pull her away from the pain and loss of her family. He knew that loss. Knew what it felt like to be left behind—or, in her case, pushed out.

Her lips twitched. "I've listened to a few."

"Only the ones ending up with one of my body parts inside yours."

"The very best kind to listen to," she said, lips curving upward again, and he liked the hint of laughter much better than the pain.

"Then, listen to this one. Don't move," he said. He went into the bathroom, lost the condom, cleaned up, and came back. And of course, she'd moved. But it was only to slip under the covers and turn off the lights.

When he joined her, he was pleased to see she hadn't covered her body back up. She was bare and beautiful. He dragged her to him, tangling his feet with hers and feathering fingers over her hips to a round cheek and back up.

"Can I ask you something?" She seemed hesitant.

"Open, honest, no secrets. That's what you said. That's what I gave."

"Why didn't you come to Landry's funeral?"

His insides churned, his mind returning to the dangers that faced them tonight, the masked man hovering around the estate. To Ziggy. To the ugly truths he hated holding on to but also didn't know how to let go of. "I wanted to, but I was in the middle of moving Krista into protective custody."

"Krista?" He felt the way her breath hitched over the name, and some asinine part of him was pleased it might have been because she was jealous.

"Krista is the woman Ziggy attacked in Berlin. After the prosecution lost its criminal case against him, and he was released from jail, she started receiving increasingly disturbing messages. The authorities couldn't prove it was Ziggy, but we all knew it was. So, I helped her disappear."

"She's the one you're sending money to," Fee breathed out softly.

He nodded. Krista had said he'd already sent more than enough, and his father agreed. But Asher's conscience didn't.

How could you ever give enough money to repay permanent injuries to eyes and limbs? The loss of being able to have children? The nightmares that would forever haunt her?

"Asher." She cupped his cheeks, thumbs resting on the edges of his mouth. "Do you even know how beautiful you are? So few people would even see the need…never even consider…and here you are taking on every wrong and trying to make it right. You're not Rochester. You're Tony Stark."

"An egotistical billionaire?"

"Willing to sacrifice yourself."

He scoffed, but her sweet words released one of the pieces weighing him down. A darkness that he'd been holding on to since that day in Berlin. He kissed her temple, inhaling her sweet scent and reveling in the soothing balm she'd brought to his life now that he'd stopped struggling against his desire for her. Instead of fighting the tides and the waves, he'd let her current sweep him to shore.

His fingers circled along her sides, a slow waltz that inched upward ever so slightly with each round until he was touching the curve of her breasts. Her breath turned shallow until it was a little pant that made his body burn and his dick jump.

He wound his hand into her long waves, pulling her head back so he could fully take in the black-and-white image she appeared in the moonlight pouring through the open curtains. Like the prints in his office. Timeless. Classic. Sexy as hell.

His lips found her pulse point, and he sucked. It fluttered underneath his touch.

He'd intended to proceed in another slow dance. Measured, tempered beats that would drive her wild. But as soon as she gasped, he was hard as a rock and yearning to be inside her.

"You're ready to go? Again? Really?" she breathed out as she felt him against her thigh and stomach.

"Why so surprised?"

"Just…most men I've been with…they take hours…"

He laughed, a slow chuckle from somewhere deep inside, loosening even more of the anchors that had been holding him down. "I can see how this would give women an unfair advantage in your book. But I don't think I've ever looked at you and not gotten hard. And that was with your clothes on."

Fee smiled, and it was her crooked, delightfully small one he craved.

She kissed him, savoring him, sipping him, and drawing his tongue into her mouth. He took everything she gave him and returned it, the flame growing. The heat consumed them until he had to slide on another condom, plant her on top of him, and let her drive them home while he watched. Her hair glimmered in the light of the moon, dark lashes rested against her cheeks, and her face shifted as the tension built. He watched as pure joy and surrender took over. Utter perfection as she shuddered around him, clenching tightly. Then, he flipped them over and picked up the pace until she had to grip the headboard and hold steady. Until she was gently, quietly saying his name in that songlike way again. Until they'd both hit the peak and tumbled back over it.

Until he'd lost all sense of anything but Fee.

As he stared at her, carefully cataloging every single expression moving over her face, the truth he'd acknowledged earlier was still there. She had the power to destroy him. To be the final nail in the coffin that buried his soul once and for all. But after only hours of having her this close, there was no way he could let her go. Not even in self-preservation. If she left, he'd never again experience this feeling of absolute surrender, absolute trust, and absolute care. This was his only chance at breaking a century-long curse and finally keeping a woman he loved.

Chapter Twenty-six

Fiadh

AIN'T NO GRAVE
Performed by Crooked Still w/ Aoife O'Donovan

THAT DAY

They hadn't shut the curtains the night before, and the slow creep of dawn into the room greeted Fee when she woke up. She found herself tangled in Asher with his arms and limbs folded around her and him holding on sweetly but possessively, as if he couldn't bear to let her go.

They'd had earth-shattering sex four times, and it still hadn't felt like it was enough. It hadn't assuaged one ounce of the desire and longing that surrounded her, the ache to have him embedded in her. The need to feel connected. To feel like she finally belonged somewhere.

Her heart skipped several beats.

She'd asked him to give her everything, and he had. She'd felt it in every caress. She'd given him the same in return, and that was what scared her. Because what would be left of her when he decided he no longer needed her in his life? He couldn't possibly intend to keep her forever, could he? The sweet promises…the intense sex…they'd alluded to something bigger, longer, stronger. But she only had experience with things ending. How could they possibly turn the hate of two years into something lasting?

Did it matter how? She'd told Leya the truth. She didn't

want this to be one night. She wanted more. More than she'd ever wanted with Lars. She'd jumped off the ledge, damn the consequences, and now she'd have to live with them.

Suddenly, the weight of her emotions, the weight of him, the weight of what she'd done made her feel claustrophobic. As if she couldn't breathe. As if she might be dragged down to the bottom of the sea.

She carefully and slowly extracted herself from the knot they'd made.

He stirred, and she stilled.

But he didn't wake.

At the side of the bed, she looked down at him, and her heart beat out a tune she couldn't deny. It whispered of love. His dark hair was mussed, a small curl dropping over his forehead. The sharpness of his features was softer in sleep, as if he didn't have to guard himself. As if he was at peace. His firm lips, so often set in a straight line, were curled ever so slightly upward. Lost in the sweetest dreams. She hoped they were of her. Of them.

She pulled herself away. Needing space. Needing caffeine.

She searched the floor, sliding into the T-shirt and sweats he'd given her the first day. They felt better than his mother's clothes even though they were so much larger. They were his. She was his…

A sob hit the back of her throat that she barely held back.

She wanted to be his. She wanted him to be hers.

It was too late to go back. She was desperately in love.

How had that happened?

She opened the door quietly, the need for air and space still filling her. The need to escape the emotions threatening to overcome her. She needed to get them all back in hand before he woke and read every single one of them as he was so good at doing. The doubts. The love. The fear.

She found her way down to the kitchen, searching for tea, not daring to use Jozef's espresso machine without the correct tutelage. Just that thought brought a curve to her lips. All the men here took care of each other. Took care of Wren…and Nova. Would they add her to their collection? The rare woman allowed inside their gates.

It wasn't until there was a hint of noise behind her as she stepped out of the pantry that she realized her mistake. A twist of trepidation spread through her as she remembered Asher's request for no one to go anywhere alone.

An arm wrapped around her middle and pulled her back against a male chest, much leaner than Asher's but still strong. A hand covered her mouth, thick and wide. A switchblade appeared before her eyes.

Pure terror flooded her veins as images of Landry's slit throat swam before her, and her body turned into solid ice. She was a frozen block as he dragged her backward, farther from the pantry, and then the wild beat of her heart freed her from the glacier as anger sliced its way through the terror. She reacted on instinct, fiercely kicking, hitting, and biting.

"Bitch!" he cursed. She knew that voice, and it made her struggle more.

Her bare foot collided with his kneecap, and he grunted out in pain. She escaped for a mere second, a bare whisper of a scream escaping her before clawlike fingers grabbed her arm and yanked her back, spinning her into the counter. Her lower spine collided with the edge, and then he was in front of her. A heavy hand tattooed with a serpent tail landed over her mouth as he pinned her to the cabinets with his body. His hips and legs held hers in place. She thrashed against him, but it did nothing to move him. The switchblade rose, piercing her skin as he dragged the tip along her collarbone just visible above Asher's shirt. She cried out against his palm as pain tore through her. Tears filled her eyes.

"Shut up!" he snarled. He was wearing a cloth mask with dozens of eyes and lips and mouths sewed in all the wrong places, but it didn't hide him. She already knew who he was.

She attempted to push him away, and he jammed his

knee into her pelvic bone. She gasped as more pain wracked her body. Then, his hands were around her throat, the tip of the knife perilously close to her mouth. His thumbs cut into her esophagus. Her lungs shrieked, and tears flew down her cheeks, the salt dropping into the bloody cuts on her chest. She tried to gasp. She tried to breathe.

Regret filled her.

The band. Her family. Asher…

God, he'd never forgive himself.

That thought brought the fight back to her, but she could barely bat weakly at the arms holding her as all the air turned to acid inside her. The pressure on her hyoid was all consuming, knowing it was going to give at any moment. Break. Shatter. Crumble.

He leaned his face into hers, the mask brushing her cheek as his fingers let up ever so slightly. Enough for her to take a gasp of sweet oxygen but not enough to release her completely.

"I could kill you right now. Do you feel it?" he asked. "Does it excite you? Bet you get off on it more than you got off on him last night."

The sick desire in his voice sent chills over her.

She started to say something, but he pushed again, cutting off her air, forcing her lungs to convulse and black spots to appear before her eyes.

"I want to kill you. I'd love to play with you a little first. Fuck you up some. Mark you. Then, he wouldn't want you, would he?"

He squeezed tighter. The black grew. She forced herself to stay awake. Forced her hips to push at him in a futile attempt to shove him away, but it only made him laugh.

"Unfortunately, I don't have time for games. Someone will be here soon."

As if he'd predicted it, she heard a door slam, feet pounding. Hope and dread filled her. He pushed his mask where the mouth should have been up against her lips, and she tried to avoid it by twisting her head, but the hands on her neck only squeezed tighter.

"Tell Asher I want my fucking money."

He eased up, and air hit her screaming lungs just as he let out a pained snarl.

At first, he leaned into her in surprise, but then he was twisting and turning, grasping at his back until Fee could see a long-bladed knife stuck in his shoulder. It was a huge carving knife from Jozef's collection. As he wrestled to remove it, his elbow came up, knocking Fee in the chin, slamming her head back into the cabinet. Sparks of light hit the black that had been closing in on her vision. Her head swam, and her body tilted.

Her attacker moved, cursing as he ran for the archway leading to a hallway and the back door.

Fiadh barely had time to register Asher's voice calling her name as a black-haired woman in a long cotton nightgown came into view.

Fee couldn't hold on to the images and sounds.

She couldn't hold herself up.

She went down, and the darkness absorbed her.

Chapter Twenty-seven

Asher

BLOOD ON MY NAME
Performed by The Brothers Bright

The ringing of his phone brought him out of a deep sleep. The most restful one he'd had in what felt like a lifetime. Then, he realized Fee wasn't with him, and that had him sitting straight up, searching the room with a scowl, and reaching for his phone at the same time. He'd plugged it in and left it on the nightstand somewhere between the third and fourth time they'd made love. The last time was the sweetest, slowest seduction, as if they were speaking of forever promises with each tender move.

And yet, she wasn't even here. The bathroom door was open, the entire space empty.

Fuck.

"Riggs," he glowered into the phone.

"The kitchen, Asher. It's Fiadh. She doesn't have long." His heart spasmed painfully as Reinard's growl registered. He dropped the phone, leaped for the door, and sprinted down the hallway. Adrenaline pounded through him, barely registering the cold marble under his feet.

Silence filled the house. Nothing.

"Fiadh!" he shouted, the agony of that single name tearing through him.

Hold on, baby.

He heard another door slam somewhere on the first floor. Fear and panic rushed through him. As he burst into the kitchen, what he saw made chills run up his spine. Fee was on the floor, blood staining his T-shirt she'd worn to bed. Nova was kneeling next to her, hands on her neck, her white nightgown billowing around her.

Every breath left his body.

Memories assaulted him. Waking to strange gurgling sounds over the baby monitor. Going to Wren's room and seeing Nova with her hands around their daughter's neck. Shaking the one-year-old as if she was nothing but a doll.

Fuck no!

He tore around the counter, jerking Nova away, and all but tossing her backward toward the island as he reached for Fee.

Her dark lashes were closed against sweetly dusted skin, the freckles standing out against a face so pale he thought she might already be gone.

Pure agony tore through him. A wild cry burst from his chest.

His fingers searched her neck for a pulse. Ugly bruises were already appearing. Fingermarks. He wanted to rail against Nova. Scream and shout and shake her. But Fee…Fee was his focus.

Her chest rose ever so slightly, and he almost cried with relief.

"Fee, baby. Come back to me." His voice was choked, anger and fear and sadness ripping through him. He pulled her body into his lap, blood coating his hands. Where was she bleeding? Where was she hurt?

The T-shirt shifted, and a gash along her collarbone became visible.

Asher was responsible for this.

He'd done this to her.

Fuck!

He slid one hand under Fee's knees and another under

her neck and stood up with her, realizing he was still naked.

He tossed a glare in Nova's direction. She was curled up, knees to her chest, and nightgown pulled over her toes. She was rocking back and forth, head hitting the cabinets, eyeing him and Fee with fear.

"What the fuck did you do?" he snarled.

Then, Reggie was there, stepping between them, darting eyes at Nova and back to Fee, glancing down at Asher's nakedness.

"Take her to your room, Ash."

"We need a doctor," he demanded.

"Reinard already called it in. He said Garner's men are fifteen minutes out."

As Reggie started to follow him, Asher jerked his head back toward Nova. "Stay with her. Make sure she doesn't hurt anyone else."

He stormed up the stairs, and instead of going toward the room they'd made love in, he took her to his. He laid her down, and her lashes fluttered. Relief and anguish poured through him in equal measure. He pulled gently at the T-shirt, slipping her arms out so he could see her wounds better.

"Asher." Her voice was hoarse, torn, pained. Her eyes kept fluttering open and shutting again.

His jaw clenched, tears threatening. He grabbed her hand.

"I'm here, baby. I'm here."

His dad burst into the room with wild eyes and his silken robe askew. Asher pulled the sheet up to cover Fee's body, pushing his T-shirt into the bloody cut that had sliced through one of her tattoos. It didn't look deep. God, he hoped it wasn't. The dark colors on her neck were much more worrisome. Her voice. Her band…

His stomach lurched. A lump formed in his throat.

A hand landed on his shoulder, his father looking from her to him.

"Get some clothes on, Son."

He shook his head. He wasn't leaving her.

Jay stumbled into the room at a run. "What happened?"

"Fucking, Nova," Asher barked.

Fee's fingers squeezed weakly around his. "No…"

She tried to shake her head, and she grimaced at the movement.

"Don't move, Fee," he said softly. "We've got someone coming to check you out."

"She…" Her voice was so raw it physically hurt Asher when she tried to talk. Her eyes opened, trying to tell him something, worry and fear and relief all in that gaze. It almost broke him. Almost made him run down the stairs and shake Nova until her brains rattled around. This was his fault. He should have sent Nova away years ago.

The anchors on his soul he'd thought had released last night came sliding back around his ankles, latching on, clicking into place.

"Don't talk," he said softly as he brushed her hair away from her face and blood hit his fingers from where the strands had gotten caught in her wound. His stomach churned, bile rising into his throat.

His dad's phone rang, the sound sharp and loud in the tense silence.

"Talk to me," his dad demanded. Silence as he listened. "They're searching the grounds?" Pause. "Have one of them come back. We need to get Fiadh to a hospital."

He hung up. "Garner's and Reinard's men are here with the all-terrain vehicles. They're searching the grounds as we speak. He escaped through the back entrance. We'll use one of the vehicles to get Fiadh to the hospital."

Asher's eyes narrowed. "What are you talking about? Nova…I found her…she had her hands…"

Asher couldn't even say the words. Fury and regret choked him.

His dad rested his hand on his shoulder again. "It wasn't Nova, Ash. She actually saved Fiadh. He was wearing the damn mask again, but they still caught pieces of him and saw what was happening. Nova grabbed a knife from the block and stabbed him in the back with it."

Asher's eyes widened, shock traveling through him.

"Go get dressed. I'll sit with her until you get back."

Asher's eyes turned to Fee. He pressed a kiss to her forehead. "I'll be right back, baby. Just two seconds."

She squeezed his hand, brown eyes meeting his briefly before they closed again. "Tired…" she croaked out.

"Don't sleep, Fee. Stay awake until they can look you over. Stay awake for me."

He didn't want to let her go. Not even to get dressed. His dad pushed his shoulder, and he let her hand slip from his as he stood. His father immediately slid into his place.

Asher looked over at Jay fidgeting by the door. "Where's Wren?"

"Still with Jozef in the cottage."

Asher turned back to his dad. "Make sure some of the team goes to them."

His father nodded, picking up his phone to relay the order.

Asher's chest hurt. His jaw hurt. His entire body hurt from how tightly he was wound. He took two steps away from the bed, then three, and then four. Finally, he turned and stalked first to the bathroom to wash his hands and then into his closet.

He was pissed, rage burning through him. At himself for bringing this to his family's door. At Fee for leaving his side when he'd told her not to go anywhere without him. At the man who'd hurt her. At his instant belief that Nova had been the villain here.

He jerked a shirt off the hanger, pulling it on and buttoning it up, sliding on a pair of black slacks. He was stepping into his uniform. The outfit where he wielded the most control in his life. Not quite a suit and tie, but professional. All business. He needed it to regain some semblance of restraint.

He glanced at himself in the mirror hanging from the back of the door.

His skin looked pale. Sallow. His eyes were haunted.

He shut them. Seeing Fee on the floor with Nova huddled over her.

Had he always expected the worst of both women?

Had the wounds his mother left behind and the curse haunting his family made him believe they'd only hurt him? Had he gone into his relationship with Nova waiting for it to break? Waiting for her to break him? Had she known that? Had her mind, already struggling, given him exactly what he'd expected?

Noise on the other side of the door had him pulling himself back into the room.

Trevor was there, standing on the opposite side of the bed from his dad. Relief filled Asher. At least this was someone they knew. Someone who'd already saved one of the band members.

"Trevor," Asher acknowledged.

"We have a stretcher out in the hall for Fee. Do you want an update on the attacker now or later?" Trevor asked.

"Fee is the priority, along with getting my family the hell out of here," Asher said, trying to control the tremble of anger and remorse barely below the surface. "But I expect you to find him."

Trevor stared at him for a beat before giving a curt nod.

"Son, find some clothes for Fiadh," his dad said, and he knew what his father was doing. Giving him a job. Focusing him on the black and white so he wouldn't go over the edge.

Asher's eyes landed back on Fiadh. Her bare arms and the top of her chest were sticking out over his sheet. God. He wanted to cover her from head to toe in more than clothes. He wanted to hide her and his daughter in a protective bubble.

Keep them both safe. Away from everything and anything that would harm them. And right now, that meant getting them away from Taran Ridge.

They were leaving. Now.

And then he'd help his team find the man who'd done this—Ziggy or Angel or whoever the hell else it was—and dismantle their world inch by fucking inch. There'd be nothing left but an empty shell, a soulless life that would simply blow away in the breeze.

Chapter Twenty-eight

Fiadh

LOVE BESIDE ME
Performed by Sarah McLachlan

Fiadh's hold on reality was slipping. She was so tired, and it seemed like every single part of her hurt, pain radiating from the inside out. Her body was demanding rest, but every time she heard Asher's voice, the remorse in it pulled her back to the surface. This wasn't his fault, and yet, she knew it was another thing he'd add to his list of transgressions—the sins he felt the need to pay for when they weren't his.

"Fee, I'm going to slip a robe around you. Can you sit up?" His voice was so gentle it made her want to cry.

She tried to move, tried to get her heavy limbs to respond, but it felt like she was underwater with the tides pulling at her.

"I—" The single syllable sounded as if her throat was cracked and bleeding.

"Shh. Don't talk. I got you," he said, lifting her body and sliding the satin material over her. He pulled it closed in front, tying it, all the while holding something to her sliced skin that was burning and screaming.

Then, he lifted her in his arms, cradling her to him like he had as they'd left the kitchen.

"So tired…" she croaked out again.

"Stay awake, baby. Try, at least." His tone was pained.

"You're not going to use the stretcher?" another male voice called out to him. Fee knew it but couldn't place it at the moment. Her mind was too muddled.

"I got her. Just get us out of here."

That was the last thing she remembered until she was being jostled along on a gurney with bright lights overhead and pale-tan walls zipping past. Her heart raced, and fear leaped along her veins. "Asher!"

"I'm here. You're at the hospital, but I'm not going anywhere." His large, warm hand grabbed hers and then slipped away again as the gurney parted them.

The world spun every time she tried to keep her eyes open, making her stomach lurch. She was conscious enough to be aware of hospital staff coming in and out of the room, examining her, but it was through a thick haze, as if she was watching someone else move on the other side of a sheer curtain. Through it all, Asher remained at her side.

They asked where she was hurting, someone stitched the wound along her chest, and they rolled her to the radiation lab for X-rays. When she was back in the room, the doctor came, talking about her throat and her head and what she needed to do to recover. She only heard parts of the words. Maybe it was denial. Maybe it was a self-defense mechanism, but when he said only time would tell how well her voice healed, she gave up on reality. She let herself slide into oblivion.

She wasn't sure how long she slept, but pain was spiraling through her body again when she woke. The room was quiet, and a moan escaped her before she could hold it back. She tried to bring her hand to her throat but realized it was captured in Asher's large one. He sprang from the chair next to the bed, pushing her hair from her face, concern washing over it as he took her in.

"You're hurting. Let me get a nurse."

She watched him step out of the room and almost called him back as fear traveled through her veins. Her mind was the clearest it had been since she'd passed out in the kitchen, and the memories assaulted her, making her feel every moment of the attack all over again. She felt the arms holding her...the thumbs pressing into her neck. She shivered and barely stopped herself from crying.

Asher came back with a nurse on his heels. She took Fee's vitals while he watched, gaze hooded. The nurse glanced between them before saying softly, "I'd give you some more pain meds, but they'd make you sleepy, and the police would like to talk to you first. Is that okay?"

"They can wait," Asher commanded.

But Fee shook her head. It caused her ears to ring and the room to sway. She tried not to grimace because she didn't want Asher to worry more than he already was, but she was afraid he saw it anyway. He'd been good at reading her before they'd fallen into bed together. Before they'd promised to let down their guards and give each other everything. Now that they had, it made it almost impossible to hide even the littlest thing.

"Let them come," she finally said. It took so much effort to talk. Not only did it cause agony to her throat, but it also required double the air it normally did.

Asher pulled her phone from his pocket and handed it to her.

"Don't talk, Fee. The doctor said complete rest to your voice. Just type whatever you need to say for now."

> FIADH: *I want to talk to them. I want to get it over.*

His jaw clenched, and his eyes narrowed. As unhappy as he was about it, it wasn't his decision to make.

> FIADH: *The sooner I talk to them, the more likely they'll catch him.*

"Fine," he groused and left the room again for a few moments.

When he came back, he was followed by two plainclothes detectives and two men in the black uniform of their old security team. A sense of relief filled Fiadh when she recognized Trevor and Marco. Marco was a dark-haired, dark-eyed man who happened to be Jonas's adopted brother. He was usually the lead on country-rock legend Brady O'Neil's detail, but he'd helped out on The Daisies' detail in the past. If there was anyone in the security field Fee felt like she might be able to trust again, it was these two. Not only because of how Trevor had already protected Paisley but because they were both vested in the Daisies. They had personal ties to the band and wanted them safe—for Jonas's sake, if nothing else.

She spent the next hour typing up her responses to their questions and telling them as much about the attack as she could, all the while trying to detach herself from the memory. From the feel of his hands on her. The disgusting tone of his voice and the ugly things he'd said. It would be so much easier if she could just speak the words. It would be quicker, and they'd disappear in the air, but writing the words felt so much more permanent...harsher. Black-and-white letters that wouldn't go away until she deleted them.

"Are you sure it was Ziggy?" one of the detectives asked.

> *FIADH: I saw his tattoo. And I know his voice.*
> *It's all over the damn radio. It was him.*

"It was him," Asher growled, his voice dripping with disgust, and she knew it was directed at himself as much as Ziggy. It tore at her insides in a different way than her physical pain. "Like he said, he wants his damn money."

She watched as he told the two detectives about Berlin, firing Ziggy, and the lawsuit he'd lost. Everyone's face turned grimmer.

"You followed him out of the estate?" the detective asked the two bodyguards. Marco explained that the team had followed the blood drops from the kitchen to the far side of

Taran Ridge where they'd found the kitchen knife Nova had stabbed him with in the snow.

"There was an outline from a vehicle he'd obviously had parked there before the eye of the storm hit. The heavy snow must have hidden it from the road and the cameras, but we followed the tire tracks until they hit the streets the road crews were clearing. We lost his tracks in the slush and tread of other vehicles," Trevor told them.

"We've got notices out to all the hospitals, doctors' offices, and vet clinics. He'll need someone to patch that shoulder," one of the detectives said.

It didn't really matter if they found him or not because Fee knew the truth. The truth that sent a wave of nausea through her and had her skin breaking out in goosebumps. Ziggy would find them. He wasn't done. He'd used Fee to deliver another message to Asher, and until he got his money, he wasn't giving up.

She didn't dare say it. Didn't dare cause the agony and anger she saw in Asher's eyes to spike even more. The throbbing in her throat burned, and the cut along her collarbone felt like it was splitting every time she shifted even the slightest. Even though she hadn't been able to examine them, she could feel the bruises along her back and hips from being slammed into the counter. There was a knot on her head from the cabinet. She'd never in her life had so much physical pain all at once.

The longer she talked with them, the more the pain took over as whatever painkillers they'd given her before completely disappeared. She closed her eyes and bit her lip, trying to pull herself together. When she opened them again, Asher's eyes were dark and furious, but she could also see the worry and frustration there.

"We're done here," Asher told the others. The two detectives didn't look so certain, but he just cut them off. "If you have more questions, you can come back tomorrow. Just go find him."

All the men except Trevor left the room. His light brows

were creased together. "What have you told the band?"

Fiadh's heart pounded, regret washing over her. They didn't need this. Her friends had already been through so much. God... Fee picked up her phone from her chest. There was no way she could do this in text. She had to call them.

She hit dial, and Asher took the phone from her grasp. She would have tossed out a snarky complaint if it didn't hurt too much to talk. Instead, she just grunted out one word, "Speaker."

He acquiesced, hitting the button so she could hear Paisley's soft voice as it came through. "Hey, Fee. How are you?"

"It's Asher and Fee," Asher responded.

"Oh, hey. What's up?"

His jaw was tight, and Fee could see the guilt eating at him as he explained to Paisley what happened, but you'd never know it in his tone. It was all ice as he laid out the bare minimum required to get his point across. After just a moment, Paisley halted him to go and get the others, and Fee's heart leaped in a mix of joy and sorrow when she heard all of their voices demanding to know what was going on.

Asher was required to repeat the story, and Fee could see just how much it cost him to do so, but he did.

"Why does this keep happening? What does it say about the people guarding us?" Paisley demanded, and Asher flinched at her question.

"This wasn't about the Daisies. This was about me. Fee just happened to be in the wrong place when it all came tumbling down. I didn't have the security I should've had at the estate."

"There's no such thing as perfect security," Adria's voice wafted over the speaker. Her words were bitter, the pain of her own losses dragged through every word.

"Maybe not, but I promise you, yours will be as damn close as possible," Asher's voice deepened with emotions, and silence took over on the other end. When it continued for too long, he drew the call to a close. "If you need to talk to Fee today, text her. Otherwise, we'll keep you posted."

He had barely hung up and handed the phone back to her as a flurry of texts hit the band's group chat.

> *LEYA: You really slept with him.*

> *NIKKI: Was that Asshole-Asher or some alternate-universe version of him where he's madly in love?*

> *PAISLEY: Does this mean we're signing again with RMI?*

> *ADRIA: You broke Asshole-Asher, didn't you? Good job, Fee.*

The humor in their texts normally would have had her smiling, but she was too exhausted. Before she could reply, the nurse came in and took her vitals again before shooting her IV full of painkillers. Once she'd left, Fee raised her phone to see she had a text from Paisley outside of the group chat.

> *PAISLEY: I'm trying to find a way back to Boston, but the weather is still screwing everything up.*

> *FIADH: Don't come. I'll be with you soon.*

> *PAISLEY: Tell me you're okay, but mean it. I just can't…I can't lose you too.*

She hadn't realized how close Asher had come again, sitting in the chair, leaning close, and he growled as he read the text.

"Do any of them ever stop to think about you? What you've lost? I'm not saying it isn't awful that Paisley's sister died, but you lost your entire family."

It twisted her chest with pain and joy all at the same time and prompted her to answer Paisley with the most truthful answer she'd given in over two years.

FIADH: I'm alive. I'm not sure if I'm okay. I'm nervous about my voice. But Asher's here, so you don't need to worry.

PAISLEY: Just because you know I have Jonas at my side doesn't mean you don't worry about me. It's the same. I will always worry. You're more than a bandmate and a friend, Fee. You're my sister. The only one I have left.

Asher was right. She'd lost her blood family, but she had this one—the band. She had a visceral need to be with them again. Not only because it would comfort them to see she was wounded but recovering, but because she would be comforted too. She hadn't had that after Landry died. They'd slipped apart, and she'd let them, holding them at arm's length. Maybe it had been a self-defense mechanism, as if knowing that if she lost one more person she loved, then the cracks already splintering across her soul would completely shatter her. But somehow, now that Asher was here, sliding his way in and sealing up the breaks, she could handle the risks that came with loving them.

FIADH: You have all of us, Paise. Not just me. You have Adria, Leya, and Nikki too.

PAISLEY: It's different with us, Fee. I love them, no doubt, but you were the one who helped my parents and me pick up the pieces. You were there every day, making sure we were okay. That we ate. That we put one foot in front of another until we could walk on our own. I never said thank you for what you did. I never told you how much it meant to me. To them. We saw it and loved you for it even when we

couldn't say the words. Never doubt the truth.
You are our family.

She shut her eyes as tears leaked out. Asher brushed at them with gentle fingers. He pulled the phone from her grasp.

"Enough, baby. Rest." His tone was deep and guttural, a tortured command mixed with a beg, as if he couldn't handle one more minute of her pain.

She should have been upset with him for reading her texts, for invading her privacy, for the demand, but she was just too exhausted to do anything but listen. Besides, the medicine was taking hold, adding a protective barrier between her and the throbbing, holding it back enough for sleep to tug at her again.

She felt featherlight kisses on her forehead, her cheek, her lips. The warmth of Asher seeped into her, soothing her. She heard his voice, soft and low, telling her something important, but she couldn't quite get her mind to comprehend it before she lost any chance at response, and the dark took her again.

Chapter Twenty-nine

Angel Carter

BARTHOLOMEW
Performed by The Silent Company

FOUR HOURS AFTER

1-555-777-2120: *He's coming for you, and if that doesn't make you fear for your life, this should—I'm coming for you.*

ZIGGY: *Who the hell is this?*

1-555-777-2120: *Question. Did you kill Landry Kim?*

ZIGGY: *Fuck off.*

1-555-777-2120: *Did you know it was Landry? Or did you think it was one of the other Daisies? Was it a mistake?*

ZIGGY: *I don't answer to fucking unknown freakazoids.*

1-555-777-2120: *You'll tell me. You'll tell me because if you don't, I'll hand you to him without any skin left.*

SIX HOURS AFTER

> *1-555-778-3130: Did you really think blocking me would help?*

> *ZIGGY: Fuck. You.*

> *1-555-778-3130: Fiadh Kane was under my protection. Every wound you inflicted on her will be marked on you before I'm done. Then, I'll gift wrap you and give you to Riggs.*

> *ZIGGY: Listen, shithead, you don't scare me. Tell Asher he can easily end this. ALL I WANT IS MY FUCKING MONEY.*

> *1-555-778-3130: Money can't save you now.*

Chapter Thirty

Asher

BEAUTY'S RUNNING WILD
Performed by Scars on 45

TEN HOURS AFTER

Asher watched as Fiadh fell asleep. He ached to take both her emotional and physical pain away. It should have been his. This was his fault. All of it spreading back as far as Berlin. He'd made instant assumptions in the hotel room in Berlin, just as he'd made them in the kitchen when he'd seen Nova bent over Fee's body. His stomach turned, bile rising into his throat, coating it with an acid that burned and left a disgusting taste in his mouth.

He could try and justify his reaction in the kitchen because of what Nova had done to Wren. God, the noises Wren had made…he still heard the gurgling in his nightmares. But the truth was, he hadn't tried to understand anything that night either. Had something gone wrong with Wren before he'd stormed into the room? Had Nova been trying—badly—to save her just as she'd saved Fee?

While Fee slept earlier, he'd demanded to see the video of the attack. Anger and hatred had swelled through him, fingers aching to reach through the screen and do much more than strangle Ziggy. When Nova had floated in, grabbed a knife, and stabbed Ziggy in the back, he'd been overcome with a mix of emotions. Gratitude. Fear. Regret.

Asher leaned forward in the chair, elbows resting on the mattress, face in his hands.

He'd let the scars of his childhood and the pain inflicted by Nova cloud his judgment. Just like he'd allowed it to interfere with his job, his relationship with his child, and his interactions with any woman who'd come into his life. The bloody trail left around the Daisies was proof that both genders could harm with equal impunity.

He sat up, pulled his phone from his pocket, and punched out a text to his assistant.

> *ASHER: I want it made clear to every single person who's ever had even a one-word conversation with Ziggy Klein that if they help him, I will make it my mission to end them.*

> *TORRANCE: If it helps, he's already burnt most of his bridges.*

> *ASHER: Then, we incinerate the rest of them. I want him dangling off a cliff with no one to save him.*

> *TORRANCE: What exactly do you want me to do?*

> *ASHER: Offer every single contact he has left money, business connections, goddamn houses in paradise. Whatever they're interested in. They can have anything as long as they stay the hell away from him.*

> *TORRANCE: I'm not letting anyone take advantage of you in this state, but Eduardo and I will spend some time digging up dirt on all his remaining "friends." We'll have a plan for you by the end of the day.*

He put his phone away, turning back to Fee. His heart

felt strange—enlarged and beating off-key—full of love that terrified him. She didn't look right, lying in a hospital, frail and broken. It was like looking at a wounded tigress—the exact opposite of the woman he'd first met—and he would do anything to bring her back to full strength, to see the fire blazing in her eyes as she taunted him.

His gaze landed on the bruising on her throat, and his stomach churned again. God...if she couldn't sing...if he was responsible for taking away the family she'd found in the band, he'd never forgive himself.

He suddenly realized his cheeks were wet. He wiped at them, staring at the water on his fingers as if it were an alien. When was the last time he'd cried? Decades ago. After his mother had left?

A hand landed on his shoulder, jerking him from his reverie. He spun around, fists up, to find his father taking a step back.

"Sorry, I didn't mean to startle you."

His dad eyed him, gaze slowing at the wetness still on Asher's face.

"Where's Wren?" Asher demanded.

"With the others at the Mayberry Hotel," he responded, tugging at the cuffs of his suit. "Surrounded by an entire platoon of men. Reinard might have gone a little overboard."

Asher drew a hand through his hair, turning back to Fee. "Not soon enough." The words were harsh and bitter, but they weren't directed at just their security company. He'd been too late to the party. Too late to the realizations that could have saved more than one person.

His dad moved to stand next to him, also looking down at Fiadh. He reached over and squeezed Asher's shoulder. "This isn't on you, Ash."

Both the words and the touch made him flinch. It was the exact opposite of the comfort his father had intended.

"I brought the snake into the henhouse," he snapped.

"You bought a record label who didn't disclose the

snake was already there."

Did it really matter? He hadn't done his fucking job, and people had gotten hurt.

"Goddamn it, Ash, you are not responsible for the actions of others. Ziggy, Nova, your mom. Why do you keep raking yourself over the coals?"

It had been so much easier to blame everyone else for so long, to retreat behind his wall of disdain. But he'd told Fee he wouldn't do that with her, and his father deserved the same.

His jaw tightened, making it difficult to get the words out. "That night, in Berlin… Even though I was disgusted by Ziggy's behavior, I didn't consider him the villain. When I looked at Krista flirting with him…" He swallowed hard. "I didn't see some innocent college kid swept away by a musician she idolized. I saw a woman who could inflict pain. I left her there, Dad. I left, letting my screwed-up relationship with Mom and Nova and every girl I'd ever dated blind me. I believed in a damn curse that has no place in reality. And because I did…"

He left the rest unsaid. It didn't need to be explained. His dad had been there every step of the way since Berlin. His father's brows scrunched together, sorrow in his eyes.

"You aren't the only one who blamed an entire gender for our misfortunes. I let my hurt and anger for Zelda influence you. I knew it. I saw it, especially after Nova, and I didn't do anything to step in. We can't change the past, but we can make amends and give ourselves a little mercy along the way." His dad looked down at Fee, and his face softened. "You can make a life with her, Asher. Don't lose this chance because you can't forgive yourself for being human."

Penance. Fee had said he was paying penance. And he was, all part of the making amends his dad had mentioned. But it had never felt like enough. Maybe it was because, like his father had said, he'd never been able to absolve himself of his sins. Weren't there some you should never escape? The truth was, he'd never wanted to before. He'd wanted to bury himself under the weight of them. When he'd felt the shackle lift last night with Fee for even a second, it had been a relief.

But it was back again, dragging him down.

His fingers tangled with Fee's. She didn't even move, lost to the drugs that were shielding her from the pain. Drugs that scared him almost as much as his love for her did, because he'd seen them destroy lives…his life. Would he be able to break this cycle of doubts and hate and remorse? Could his love for her overcome his past? Was it enough? If it wasn't, he had to set her free right now, for both their sakes, because he already loved her with an intensity that was incomprehensible after so little time. What would he feel after a month…a year…ten years?

His jaw ticked. His stomach heaved once more.

He needed a moment to gather himself.

He needed a breath that wasn't surrounded by her and everything he'd done that had ended with her here. A wounded tigress.

He looked at his dad. "Will you stay with Fiadh? I have something I need to do."

His dad scrutinized him, a look Asher himself was good at giving that said he knew there was more to it than those simple words expressed. To his surprise, his father wrapped him in a hug. One that wasn't a man-pat, but a full-strength, holding-on-for-dear-life hug. It took a minute before he could return it as emotions and memories he'd thought were long buried washed over him. Visions of his dad coming down the stone steps to the beach to find Asher alone as the dark settled over the sea. His mom had wandered away, forgetting him there, and his dad had pulled him in for a hug, lifted him up, and taken him home.

"You deserve to be happy, Son. You deserve love and joy. This woman, she deserves it too. Make sure you come back and claim her before someone else beats you to it."

He stepped back and then gave Asher a smile. "Hell, it might even be me."

It brought a tortured laugh from deep inside Asher's

chest.

"Don't let her talk. If she wants her voice back, she has to stay silent."

His dad smiled. "Challenge accepted."

Before he changed his mind and simply lay down next to Fee, waiting for her to wake and offer him the grace she'd repeatedly given, Asher turned and walked out.

He'd barely taken two steps toward the elevator when Trevor arrived at his side. "Where are you headed?"

He hadn't really thought about a location. He'd just needed air. Space. A place to figure out his shit. His chest ached, seeking a relief he wasn't sure he'd ever find except inside Fee's arms. Forgiveness. Redemption.

And suddenly, he knew where he needed to go.

When he told Trevor, the man didn't even blink, just spoke into the two-way mic he had in his ear while Asher shot off a text to Diego. When the elevator opened, Trevor led the way through the emergency department's lobby and out the doors to where one of the tank-like armored SUVs they'd used to leave Taran Ridge awaited them.

Most of the streets were still covered in snow piles taller than most men, but a few of them had been plowed. The vehicle they were in drove through the slush and snow as if it wasn't there. Asher wished he could plow through the chaos of his life as easily. What had happened to the contained order he'd always surrounded himself in?

His phone buzzed, and he read the text twice before it actually settled into his brain.

> *1-555-222-7200: Did I ruin your pretty little bitch? She ever going to be able to sing again? I'd heard from Lars Ritter how good she tasted. I wished I'd had more time with her to see for myself. But there's always next time.*

Fury flew through him. Rage he'd never felt for another human being. Not even Nova.

ASHER: Your life is over, Klein. You won't find a single rock to crawl your slimy self under that I can't overturn. I'm coming for you.

1-555-222-7200: Big man. Big talk. Did your little girl cry when she saw all her favorite toys cut up? She sure was pretty, lying there all tucked in. You're lucky I'm not into kids. You know how to end this all. It's simple. I WANT MY FUCKING MONEY.

Asher turned to Trevor, barely controlled anger audible in each syllable he uttered. "How quickly can you set up a trap if I meet with the bastard?"

Trevor's eyes narrowed. "What?"

Asher handed him the phone, watching the man's hands tighten around the plastic as he read the disgusting messages.

"Don't reply yet. Let me talk to Marco and the team," Trevor said.

"I want this over with. Any way possible," Asher growled.

"We're not a hit squad. We don't do business that way. But I promise he'll be behind bars for good."

Asher's entire body was roiling with fury. Dead was too good for Ziggy. "What he did to Fee…it's fucking devastating. Her voice…" His throat bobbed, emotions filling him. "That wasn't even a tenth of what he did to Krista in Berlin. She lost an eye and the use of her right hand. She'll never have children…"

Asher's voice cracked and he stopped, choked with that damn remorse his father wanted him to give himself mercy for.

"There's only one way to deal with a rabid animal. You put it down," Asher asserted.

"I'm not saying we wouldn't take the kill shot if we had to, but believe me when I tell you, that won't relieve any of the guilt you're feeling right now. If we put him behind bars and take away his power, you'll get to see the scumbag rot away for the next hundred years."

Asher didn't respond because they'd pulled up in front of a simple box building that screamed healthcare. He needed to be calm before he went in there, or it would do the exact opposite of what he'd intended. It would rile her up instead of giving her peace. Maybe she'd never have it. Maybe he was there only to selfishly take it for himself, but neither one of them would get it if he stormed into the facility with fury emanating from him in waves.

He stepped out of the vehicle, breathed in the frigid air, and tilted his face to the sun. Its warmth was weak, fighting to take a chunk out of the cold. Just like Fee had broken through his ice with her fire. He needed that in his life. His father was right. He could have it…if he could just figure out a way past this moment. This horror. This last enormous mistake. He'd do his best to never make another one again, not when it came to her or any of the women in his life. Wren. The Daisies. They'd get his full support, not some reserved tolerance.

He stepped toward the entrance, and the bodyguards shuffled around him. Inside, Diego was waiting for him in the lobby. They didn't say anything as the nurse led him down quiet, sterile hallways. It was supposed to be soothing, but it made the back of Asher's neck itch. If he had to stay here, it would push him over the edge. Was it different for those who'd already gone over it?

Outside Nova's room, he did what he'd always done at home and was now protocol. He took off his watch, his shoes, his belt, and his phone, leaving them on a shelf before going inside. She was in another white nightgown, much like she'd spent her days in at the estate. Her black hair was brushed long and straight, and her eyes seemed clearer than he'd seen them in a long time. She was watching *The Price is Right* on a television she could only see and hear through a clear window. Her bed was on the floor, and there was nothing else in the room. No metal or wood at her disposal, but everything was clean and soothing in tones you'd find in nature and not the stark white Asher had expected from the hallway.

He dropped down on the mattress next to where she sat cross-legged. His stomach churned, thinking about the first time he'd seen her at Columbia. The way she'd stunned him with her beauty and vibrancy. She'd brought unbridled joy to his life whenever she wasn't high. But now, looking back, he could see there'd been an almost manic energy to her. He hadn't understood it then. He could forgive himself for that, couldn't he?

"A dollar," Nova said to the television. She hadn't even registered he was there. "A dollar. A dollar. A dollar."

The woman on the TV bid a dollar, and Nova's face lit up. It was a smile that, once upon a time, had made his entire day better when she'd directed it at him. It was *those* pieces of her he needed to remember.

"I wanted to say thank you, Nova," he said softly.

She jerked at her name, eyes slithering sideways to him and then back to the screen.

"And say I'm sorry. Sorry for thinking you hurt her. Sorry if I hurt *you*." Asher's throat bobbed. Had he?

Nova frowned. "Baby cry. Baby cry. Stop it, baby. Stop it. Stop it. Stop it."

She started to wring her hands, rocking gently.

Asher covered them with his. "No baby here today, Nov. Just you and me."

She continued moving back and forth, but she turned her eyes back to the television.

"I'm sorry I couldn't be what you needed. I'm sorry I didn't get you help sooner. I'm sorry I hated you for so long…" His voice disappeared into a choke of emotions that would only disturb her, but he couldn't help himself.

She twisted her hands from his, searching his gaze with wild ones.

"Pretty girl. Pretty girl hurt. You save."

"No, Nova, you saved her."

She shook her head. "You save. You save. You save."

She was wringing her hands again, agitation growing.

He closed his eyes, wishing he could fix it. Fix her. Give her something besides these blank walls and a fucking television show. But Fiadh had been right when she'd said he hadn't forced Nova to make any of her choices. Wren was the only thing he'd ever pushed on, and in the end, she could have made another decision. What was left of Nova's life was of her own making.

But God, did he wish it hadn't ended this way for her.

He stood, stepping away as she continued to rock and twist her hands.

He looked back at the television screen. Maybe this was the only peace he could give her.

"What do you think she should bid for the car?" he asked softly.

Nova's eyes flew to the screen.

"Twenty-nine thousand. Twenty-nine thousand. Twenty-nine thousand."

As they watched, the car's price was flipped over, and it showed thirty thousand five hundred dollars. Asher smiled softly at the joy that littered Nova's face.

"Take care, Nov. I'll be back to see you soon."

Then he knocked on the door, and Diego let him out.

He watched Nova inside the room as he reassembled the items he'd taken off. Maybe being away from him, the mansion, and the daughter she'd never wanted would be exactly what she needed. Maybe it was all she'd ever needed—a safe space and *The Price is Right*.

His heart wasn't light, far from it, and he would always feel responsible for her in some way. But there was a much larger piece of him that knew this was better, not only for her but for Wren. His daughter would no longer hear her mother's screams breaking through the night. She wouldn't have to grow up with that shadow constantly lurking over her head.

His dad and Fee were both right. He had to stop burying his head under the blanket of penance forever. He'd done his time. He'd done what he could for each screwed-up situation that had come his way. Nova. Krista. The Daisies. He had to look forward to the people, the joy, and the love that were waiting for him.

He just had one last thing to fix. One last asshole to bury—figuratively or literally—whichever came first.

After that, he could look forward again to a future where he might not have to be alone. Where Fee didn't have to be alone either. A future where he could actually spend time with his daughter without the guilt eating him alive. He didn't know exactly how all those pieces would come together yet, but he'd figure it out.

The Riggs men hadn't been cursed by the women in their lives. The curse had been the time and focus they'd spent on their business while they'd left their personal lives to wither, turn to dust, and blow away. He didn't know if his father could have saved his marriage by being around more, but he wouldn't repeat the mistake with Fiadh.

He couldn't. She was too damn important.

Chapter Thirty-one

Fiadh

LOVE IS ALIVE
Performed by Lea Michele

ONE DAY AFTER

Fiadh's eyes were heavy and encrusted, and her throat was dry and achy, like the morning after the very worst hangover. Except, it wasn't just the inside of her throat aching. Her body and even her skin felt raw and sensitive. Her head pounded as if Adria was playing her drumsticks on it.

That was when it hit her. The hands on her throat. The knife.

Her eyes flew open. She gasped, trying to sit up and getting tangled in wires and sheets.

"Baby, take it easy. I'm here. You're safe." Asher's warm hand settled around her waist and dragged her body against his wide chest. They were lying in a hospital bed. He was fully dressed, in slacks and a pale-blue dress shirt with shiny black shoes. She was in a hospital gown under a blanket with an IV in her hand and monitors beeping a bit wildly now that she'd woken with a start.

He'd left yesterday, but he'd come back. He hadn't said much other than he'd gone to make sure Nova was settled in. But she could feel the heaviness clinging to him because he felt responsible for Fee being in the hospital.

Tears pricked her eyes.

The same feeling that had hit her and caused her to scramble from the bed with Asher the day before crashed over her. Emotions that were overwhelming. Claustrophobic. As if she couldn't breathe. She needed away from the wires and machines that were holding her down.

"I want out of here," she said slowly, wincing at the sound of a stranger's voice coming out of her. It was raspy and harsh, and she hated it because it was one more reminder of what had happened. That she could have died. Worse, it was a reminder of what the doctors had said…she may not have the same voice she'd had before.

Her singing…the band…

She couldn't think of it yet, but it didn't prevent more tears from filling her eyes. Ones she couldn't hold back this time. Asher's hand slid up and down her arm. A gentle caress. A reassurance. But she could also feel the worry drifting from him.

"The doctors said they want to watch you for a couple of days. Other effects can present themselves up to thirty-six hours after. I can't…"

She felt his body shudder against her, and it made her heart soar but also the tears to flow more at the thought of him caring so much. This strong, beautiful man had put behind a world of hurt to somehow open himself up to her.

"I'm fine," she said, whispering, because when she did, she sounded more like herself.

He gently turned her chin so her eyes met his. "You're not fine. You're far from fine. Don't try and pull that shit with me. Open. Honest. All the pieces of us on the table. That's what you asked. That's what I gave, and I demand you give it back."

She cried, softly, silently, and he swiped at each tear as if he could stop them. Asher's face was so pained it hurt her heart worse than the bandaged slash across her chest.

"What if…" It was all Fee could get out. So many what-ifs. What if Ziggy came back? What if no one stopped him?

What if she couldn't sing? What if she lost the band? What if she lost Asher?

A harsh sob broke from her chest.

He wrapped her closer, as if he could make it all better. And even though he couldn't, she wouldn't trade having him there for anything. Not even a hundred percent reassurance that she'd heal completely, that she'd have her voice back. It felt like a decade since she'd had this…someone focused completely and utterly on her, making sure she was okay. Even with her parents, once her siblings came along, their love and attention had been divided. She'd never once minded. She loved her brothers and sister with all her heart. But to have this—all of him, for even a few moments—it was almost too much.

Asher kissed her temple.

"I want to go to Chicago," she said into his chest. "The Daisies…we need each other…" He nodded, but she felt him stiffen, and she knew he thought it meant she didn't need him. "I need all of you," she whispered, and he relaxed slightly.

"Let's see what the doctors say," he said quietly.

Her phone buzzed—Paisley's text tone.

> *PAISLEY: How are you this morning?*

Fee thought about what Asher had said about her being honest with him. It was time she was honest with all of them, wasn't it?

> *FIADH: I feel like I got stabbed and choked almost to death.*

> *PAISLEY: Not funny.*

> *FIADH: Honestly, I wasn't being funny. I feel like shit.*

> *PAISLEY: I hate that I'm this far away from*

you.

FIADH: I'm working on it.

PAISLEY: Work on healing yourself first.

Fee turned to Asher and insisted again, "I want to go to Chicago."

They stared at each other, a silent war of wills. She closed her eyes, resting her forehead on his chest.

"Please."

She felt him give in at the plea, his entire body softening. He kissed the top of her head.

"We'll figure it out."

Marco and Trevor stepped quietly into the room, faces solemn and almost ominous. Asher untangled himself from Fee, and she felt the loss deep in her soul. A momentary flash of panic filled her that she brushed away. He wasn't leaving. He was here. She could stand on her own for mere minutes. She'd done it for days…months…years…after every single hit that had come her way. Only Landry had ever been at her side, and since she'd lost her best friend, she'd been on her own more than ever.

"Do you have everything set up?" Asher asked.

"We have men in place. You've got an hour to get there," Marco said.

Worry spread through Fee, a strange tingling coming over her as she looked from Asher's set face to the grimness of the other two men.

"What's going on?" she croaked out.

He turned back at her. "Stop talking, Fee. Rest your voice."

She pounded the mattress in frustration, whipped out her phone, tapped out a message, and shoved it in his direction.

He came back to her, taking the phone and reading what she'd written.

FIADH: Tell me you aren't meeting with Ziggy.

His jaw ticked as he handed it back to her.

"It's the only way."

"No!" Fee's voice was vehement, and she shook her head, making it ring and her vision go blurry. She latched on to his hand, looking into his face as pure panic bled through her. The thought of losing him after she'd just found him…it made her gasp for breath almost as if Ziggy had his hands on her neck again.

"You wouldn't let me use myself as bait when I suggested contacting Angel. I won't let you either," she said. Each word she spoke caused pain, not only physically but with stabs to her heart.

"Damnit. Stop talking. Rest," he commanded.

She glared at him. "I won't. I can't. Not if I think—"

"Can you give me a minute with Fiadh?" Asher asked the men.

Her entire insides clenched until they were almost as painful as the marks Ziggy had left on her body. Except, this pain wasn't for her. This was for Asher. For the new penance he felt he owed. Because of what Ziggy had done to her.

When Trevor and Marco had left, he sat down on the bed and pulled her into his lap.

"He sent me a text, Fee. Threatened you again. Wren…" She felt the tightness in his body, every muscle and sinew on alert. Fear of losing him spiraled through her again, making it hard to breathe. They'd just found their way to each other. She'd barely gotten a taste of a place…a person…who made her feel like she belonged. A home. A family.

But she also knew the truth.

Asher wouldn't rest. He wouldn't truly let his guard down again until this was over.

"Why does it have to be you? Send someone else. He can't expect you to show up." She hated her voice like this. Hated that Ziggy had done this to both of them.

"It's exactly what he expects. Me at his mercy."

She shuddered, thinking about how she'd been completely at his mercy the day before. Unable to stop any of it from happening. But Asher was bigger. He'd have protection, people watching his back.

"I hate this." She buried her head into his chest and tangled their fingers together.

"You keep talking, and I'm going to find a way to muffle you." It was half snarl, half tease, and she knew he'd done it on purpose, to lighten the mood, to try and distract her. The way she normally did. And God help her, it worked a little because now all she could think about was him and her twined together, his mouth pressed against her, swallowing her cries.

Her eyes dropped to his lips before issuing her own challenge. "Promise?"

A hum of protest erupted from deep within his chest, and then he was kissing her with a passion fueled by shared fear and frustration but also something more. She wasn't sure if it was hope or love or a combination of them both.

She shifted closer, and the movement sent a spiral of pain through her muscles. She groaned, and he instantly released her, worry coating his gaze. "I hurt you."

FIADH: The only thing that can really hurt me now is losing you.

The blue of his eyes darkened into a deep midnight as he issued a quiet promise, "You won't."

She swallowed hard, wanting to believe him but knowing just how life could screw you over. He tucked a curl behind her ear before allowing his thumb to caress her cheek.

"For as long as you want me, you've got me," he uttered, and in those words, she heard the echoes of the abandoned boy again, and it twisted and turned her heart.

FIADH: I'm not very good with relationships.

"You've been hurt. Repeatedly."

She nodded. "Like you."

"Can I ask what happened with Lars Ritter?" His voice was gravelly and deep. She wanted to laugh at the twinge of jealousy she heard there but didn't because she knew how hard this was for him, trusting a woman after years of not. She could only be as open and honest as she'd demanded he be.

> FIADH: *I thought we were more than he did. We got together during The Red Guitar tour, and when it was over, he went back to his life and expected me to do the same.*

The press had swarmed all over the supposed breakup, wanting the juicy scoop on the dynamic lead singer of RALE and the "bisexual playgirl" from The Painted Daisies. The entire thing had hurt way more than it should have. She'd berated herself for thinking it was more than it was. But now, sitting tucked into Asher, feeling the emotions they'd had every time they'd connected, made what she felt for Lars seem ridiculous. Asher was tied intrinsically to her being. A part of her that had lain hidden until the moment they'd touched. An age-old fairy tale bursting into real life.

"Do you want me to buy RALE's label and end his career?" Asher asked. There was a tease to his tone that caused her heart to do cartwheels of joy. But there was also a note of steel underneath it that had her gaze flying to meet his. He'd do it, buy the label and destroy Lars if she even gave the barest of nods. Her eyes filled with more damn tears, not because of Lars but because of how much Asher would do for her.

"You loved him. And he cut open your heart. I'll end him for it."

Her fingers settled at the corners of his mouth that were drawn in a straight line, smoothing them out, wanting to reassure him.

"Thank you, but I don't want you to do anything. It

271

wasn't his fault. My feelings changed, and his didn't. I should have cleared the air as soon as I realized it. And looking back...I can't even say it was love. It was just this childish hope that..." She faded away, not sure if she could say the words aloud.

"That someone would keep you," he finished for her, his voice deep and guttural.

Their eyes locked, emotions pouring from them.

"Let's clear the air, baby," Asher said. "When I said you had me for as long as you wanted, what I should have said was, I want to keep you forever. End of discussion."

She smiled, and his lips curved upward in response.

"I need to see you actually dance first, Wallflower, then we can talk about forever."

"Stop talking," he growled.

She laughed, and it hurt, tearing through the wounds in her throat, but she didn't care. She'd do it repeatedly if it brought the same look to his face as it did now. Joy. Happiness. A lightness Asher needed before the dark settled in again.

His phone vibrated, and his face turned serious.

"Dad says Wren wants to come and see you. Is that okay?"

Fiadh thought about how bad she must look, the bruising and stitches hiding behind gauze. She was sure her hair was wild, and her skin would be pale and shadowed. But her heart also flipped over at the idea of the little girl wanting to see her. The idea of maybe not just having Asher to love, but his daughter. His father. His family. It hurt terribly and yet filled in missing pieces of her life, topping it off.

FIADH: Wouldn't it frighten her to see me this way?

He looked her over as if really seeing her. His jaw clenched.

"Maybe, but I think not seeing you might frighten her more. This way, she knows you're going to be okay."

He said it so firmly, so naturally, as if he knew everything was going to work out, which only brought back all the ways it might not be okay if he went to meet up with Ziggy.

FIADH: She needs her father. She needs you. We both do.

He knew she was talking about Ziggy, but he didn't acknowledge it. Instead, he gave her a different piece of himself. "I'm not exactly sure how to bring together all the incongruous parts of my life that need me. Wren. RMI. You. But I promise right now, I'm going to figure it out." She heard the promise there just as he'd promised forever. Just as he'd promised to open himself up and not hold back. The sweetest of pledges.

When she'd first arrived at Taran Ridge, she'd thought Asher was missing all the little moments with his daughter, but now she realized his absence from her life was just another one of the things he was paying for.

FIADH: She loves you.

He ran a hand over his hair. "It's more than just wanting to be around more for her. I didn't understand how much she was struggling at school with the teachers and the students. Now, I realize she needs something else. Just like Nova needed more than I was giving her."

His voice cracked almost as bad as Fee's had been all morning. She wrapped her arms around his waist, squeezing even though the entire action caused her body to scream. His hand moved slowly in circles over her back.

She leaned back and typed out a new message.

FIADH: Bring her with you.

"With me?" He frowned.

> *FIADH: Plenty of musicians and actors bring their children with them. They're homeschooled and go wherever their parents do. You already have a nanny. Just have her and Jay tag along.*

His eyes narrowed, as if considering it.

The door to the room swung open, and Trevor stepped back in. "We need to get going."

Asher's face turned hard again, all joy and gentleness disappearing beneath the icy front he showed the rest of the world. It was that look almost as much as the knowledge of where he was going that had panic settling in her veins again.

She leaned up and kissed him.

"Come back to me, Wallflower. Come back and finish what you started."

"Damn it, stop talking."

Then, his mouth was on hers, another silent oath.

When he let go, he set her gently on the bed and walked to the door with only a momentary look back before his shoulders steeled and he left. She wanted to cry. Instead, she bit her lip and thrust prayers out into the universe before sending a flurry of texts to her friends, updating them. She needed them to reassure her. To distract her.

> *ADRIA: Who would have thought that Asshole-Asher had a noble bone in his body?*

> *FIADH: I was wrong about him. We were all wrong.*

> *NIKKI: I never understood why you hated him so much. It's like Adria's hatred of Ronan? Why? What happened?*

Fee snorted, wondering if Adria would actually respond to the dig and finally open up about it.

PAISLEY: I'm sorry, Fee. I hate not being there with you right now.

It squeezed into all the lonely cracks inside her.

LEYA: I think Adria should tell us about Ronan just to keep Fee's mind off Asher.

ADRIA: Turn on a K-drama or a telenovela if you need juicy gossip and stories. Don't use me for it.

LEYA: Ah-ha! You admit there's a story there.

ADRIA: I like it better when we're harassing Fee about Asher.

PAISLEY: I won't feel better until we're all together again.

The band continued to text her, trying to distract her like she needed them to do, but her veins pulsed with worry for Asher. She knew he had backup. Trevor. Marco. But her fear still twisted and pulsed like a shadow growing larger on the wall. Images she couldn't hold back of the knife Ziggy had used on her ending up in Asher.

She shuddered, looking at the clock, wishing she could make time go faster.

The door opened, and Wren and Kellan walked in. The little girl was in another flowery dress that ended at her ankles even though it was still bitterly cold outside. Kellan held a bright-pink, downy coat in his hands that had obviously been on his granddaughter. As soon as Wren got close to Fee, her eyes grew wide.

"I'll be okay," Fee said softly.

And it would be true. But only if Asher came back to them in one piece. Otherwise, she wasn't sure she'd ever recover.

Chapter Thirty-two

Asher

ME AND MINE
Performed by The Brothers Bright

Walking out of Fee's room physically hurt. But he'd known if he didn't walk out right then, he might let her convince him not to. So instead, he'd turned on his heels and forced himself from the room with Trevor following him. They had two uniformed police officers and four of Garner's men at the door.

Asher wasn't sure if even those six men were enough. He felt the need to have GPS devices embedded in everyone he loved, in everyone under his protection. GPS devices and cameras hanging from their jewelry, their phones, and their clothes. Constant surveillance. Not quite literal bubble wrap, but a wrap of technology that could be monitored from anywhere in the world.

Instead, all he could do was meet with the bastard who'd come for them and hope he could end this. It had felt like ripping his own skin off the night before to text Ziggy, pretend to be contrite, and ask to set up a meeting. As if he'd already known Asher would comply, he'd told Asher to meet him at Bayview Park at nine in the morning. The fact that the park was so near the hospital made Asher itchy.

With only minutes left until the meet, he stepped into the vehicle Marco and Trevor had waiting outside the hospital. His phone vibrated, and his stomach clenched so tight he thought it might never loosen again when he saw it was Ziggy.

> *SLIME BUCKET: Don't get cute, dickwad. I'll know if it isn't just you.*

He ignored it, turning to Marco. "Walk me through the plan."

"The park is still buried in snow, and with everything pretty much shut down because of the storm, we won't be able to blend in with a nonexistent crowd, so we've placed two men under snow blankets inside the park. One at the entrance and another by a garbage can near the closed coffee stand. That's your target location. My man there will be the one to do the takedown once you get Klein in place. We have a sniper set up on a barge in the bay as well, but you'd have to be right on top of the railing for him to be of any use to us."

Marco waved at a rifle he had sitting across his lap.

"I'll be in a vacant storefront across the way with my eyes on you. Trevor is going to be at the east-side exit in a car that's hip-deep in snow. If things go hairy, make your way to him. Questions?"

Asher's response was a raised brow.

Marco scanned him from head to toe.

"You're not dressed for the weather, but if you look like you are, Klein might think something is up. I did manage to get you a ski jacket to hide the vest."

Marco handed him a bulletproof vest that said S.W.A.T. on it. Asher slid it on, wondering why he didn't feel more anxiety. Instead, he was filled with an anticipatory rush, like he felt when a big deal finally came together at RMI. He wondered if this was the type of adrenaline high that drove military and law enforcement people to do their jobs. He had no desire to rush into a firefight, but he did want to end this with Ziggy.

After he'd gotten the vest strapped on, Trevor handed

him a bright-red-and-orange parka. It was ridiculous. Nothing he'd ever wear. And when he shot a look at the bodyguard, Asher could see he was trying not to smile.

"We can see you this way," Trevor said, barely holding back a laugh.

Asher simply glared and zipped the jacket up over the vest. "You think that bastard isn't going to think something is fishy with me in this?"

"If he says anything, just tell him it was the only thing available at the hospital," Marco said.

The SUV stopped at a streetlight, and Trevor slid out.

It left Asher alone with Marco and the driver as they headed for the park entrance, and an awkward silence settled down between them. Asher could feel the weight of the other man's thoughts hovering around them.

"Just spit it out," Asher barked.

"My brother is in love with Paisley. Going to marry her someday. So, she's basically my sister-in-law. Fiadh's a sister to her, so I guess that makes her family too."

"And?"

"They've had a rough couple of years, and I'm wondering if you're going to make it better or worse."

"Worse?" Asher snorted. "You're joking, right? Let's just get this slimeball, and then you can turn your energy back to where it should have been for two years—on finding Landry Kim's murderer. Chase down Angel Carter, and get some damn answers."

"There is no one by the name Angel Carter who meets his description. A blond-haired ten-year-old in Kansas, but we'll keep digging."

"Don't just dig, Marco. Get them answers. They deserve it."

Marco nodded and then listened to something on his headset.

"Trevor's in place. You're up. Once Ziggy's there, and you're ready for my man to grab him, the code word is coffee."

"Coffee?"

Marco shrugged. "It's fucking freezing out, and you'll be near a closed coffee cart. I figured you could work it into the conversation."

They pulled up to the entrance, and Asher opened the door and slid out. Marco's voice followed him. "Stay safe, Riggs. I have a feeling none of the women in my family will ever forgive me if something happens to you on my watch."

He didn't bother replying.

As the vehicle took off, he headed down the sidewalk. The sun had been out in bits for two days, and the snow had melted and then frozen all over again at night. Everything was slick and icy, and his dress shoes were not made for it. He almost slipped and fell more than once as he made his way into the park.

The large trees along the path were still weighed down by the snow. Even though the calendar said spring had already come, it felt as if winter had never left. He eyed the closed coffee shack, not letting his gaze linger on the garbage can or anyone who might be near it, and made his way to the wrought-iron railing along the brick path near the water. Normally, the park was full of joggers and people walking their dogs, but today, it was almost deathly still. Even the water in the bay was surprisingly calm, as if not even the biting breeze could stir it up.

Asher's cheeks and nose were numb after only a few minutes. The sun may have been shining, but it was still only in the teens. His hands and feet would soon be as frozen as his face if he had to stay out here long. He kept swinging his eyes along the different avenues Ziggy could take to the shore. But there was no sign of the man's shaved head even after five minutes.

He paced the railing, snow gathering on his black slacks and shiny shoes. Cold seeped into every inch of his body, and anxiety started to crawl up his back as another ten minutes ticked by.

Something wasn't right.

He knew it. Deep down.

His body was almost solid ice by the time his phone vibrated thirty minutes past their scheduled meeting time.

SLIME BUCKET: I guess you really are stupid.

Asher's heart banged, searching the park. The snow was sparkling, reflecting the sunshine and making the shadows appear even darker.

ASHER: If you want your money, you need to meet me in person.

Ziggy's response was slow, but as soon as Asher saw it, his chest squeezed tight, and bile hit his throat.

SLIME BUCKET: Private room. That's nice. Fewer witnesses. Extra security, but I know how to make them look the other way. They'll never see me, just like your lame-ass alarm system didn't.

Fuck. He was at the hospital. Asher sprinted toward the exit, slipping and sliding on the slick surfaces. He had been stupid. He'd led half the goddamn detail on a wild-goose chase while Ziggy slithered in.

By the time Asher got to the east entrance of the park, Trevor was already emerging from a tiny sedan. One look at Asher's face, and Trevor's turned grim. Asher didn't slow down. He flew past him as adrenaline, fear, and anger grew.

"Talk to me," Trevor demanded, matching Asher's frantic pace.

"He's there. At the hospital," Asher growled. Blood pumped through his ears, closing out the sounds around them. Desperation and regret made the stretch to the hospital seem like a hundred miles.

Trevor barked into his two-way mic an alert that Ziggy

might be on the premises.

Asher's breath came out in pants, frantic white gusts that echoed the panic inside his chest as they neared the hospital. The long set of steps leading to the Roman-columned façade of the entrance finally came into view, and he cursed himself for poking the goddamn wild animal. He'd known the risk. He'd just expected it to come at him instead of Fee.

Asher's phone buzzed again. He didn't want to slow down to look at it, but he ripped it out of the coat's pocket when it was the tone he'd given to the shithead.

> *SLIME BUCKET: Do you think Daddy will pay? To keep the grandbaby safe?*

Wren was with Fee. His dad. His goddamn family. If Ziggy touched any of them, he'd fucking kill him with his own hands. The cold and the wind brought water to his eyes as he took the steps two and three at a time, blood pumping at a rate that was near deadly. They were almost at the top when his phone vibrated again.

> *SLIME BUCKET: It's going to be fun watching your whole world crumble like you made mine. Too bad you won't be around to watch it all go down. But I'll pay a visit to your bitch after I finish you off. Just for fun. Just to make sure everyone is clear on the consequences of messing with a Klein.*

Asher's feet slowed as they approached the entrance, stepping past the enormous pillars. His heart banged, and his lungs screamed as he gasped, "He's not after Fee. He's coming for—"

A long blade landed in the chest of his ski jacket, slicing into the bulletproof vest, but before it could pierce his skin, Trevor was there, twisting the asshole's arm and jerking it away. Trevor ripped the sick multi-faced mask that had allowed Ziggy to go unseen by the cameras from the bastard's head.

Asher barely had time to register Ziggy's real face, and the contorted expression there, before the snake had tossed the knife from one hand to the other and thrust it into Trevor's unprotected chest. Trevor grunted but didn't go down. He punched Ziggy in the face and then took a staggering step sideways, reaching up for the blade stuck in his body that was already dripping blood.

Ziggy attempted to sweep-kick the bodyguard, and Asher finally moved, throwing his shoulder into the sleazebag's chest. The force threw them both to the ground. Red-hot anger welled through Asher. He landed a punch that caused Ziggy's head to bounce off the stone floor. "That's for Krista."

He landed a second one that busted the man's nose, blood spraying out. "That's for my daughter." Ziggy howled and threw a wild punch that barely grazed his jaw. The sick bastard jerked and bucked, starting to slip from Asher's hold.

He sent a series of fierce jabs to the man's kidney and spleen. "And that's for Fee."

"I'm going to fucking kill everyone in your family!" the bastard gasped as he wrenched out of Asher's grasp enough to send a wild kick that collided with Asher's knee. He ignored the pain, raising his fists, ready to land another punch, just as three men swarmed them, pulling them apart with guns raised.

One wore the black outfit of Garner's security team, and the others were Boston police officers.

Ziggy snarled and wrestled like a wild animal, lunging toward Asher, and it took every ounce of self-control Asher had ever had to not throw off the arms of the bodyguard holding him back and land another punch—this one to the bastard's esophagus. He wanted to harm him permanently. End him.

"Get him out of here," the bodyguard snapped.

"Ziggy Klein, you're under arrest for the attempted murder of Fiadh Kane," one of the officers said, going through the Miranda rights as they handcuffed him.

"Fuck you, pig. Fuck her. Fuck Asher Riggs." Cold, black eyes landed on Asher. "I won't rest until you're dead."

Asher's heart was cold with fury. "You've written your own death certificate, shithead. Not a single person is going to come and bail you out this time. I've made certain of it."

Ziggy fought against the officer's hold until another one aimed a gun at his face. "Keep resisting, asshole. Give me just one more reason to pull the trigger."

Ziggy went still, but his gaze was pure evil as the officers dragged him off.

A loud clatter of metal hitting cement had Asher jerking around to see the knife that had been in Trevor's chest laying on the ground. Impossibly, the blade looked even longer covered in blood. His gaze flew to Trevor's chest where blood pumped out of the open wound, and it felt like time slowed down as the enormous man sagged. He hit his knees. A muttered, "Fuck," escaped his lips, and then Trevor's eyes closed as he landed facedown.

Asher lunged, flipping the man over. He tore the ridiculous orange jacket off and shoved it at the deep gash in Trevor's chest, applying pressure. The unforgivable truth hit him. Trevor had taken a goddamn knife for him. Asher's pulse banged as if he was still at a flat-out run. Another fucking person who'd been hurt because of him. His decisions. His mistakes. He wasn't sure he could afford to have the list grow. He'd finally thought he was narrowing it down…letting go of some of the guilt.

"Man down. Man down. Outside the main entrance. Send a medical unit ASAP," the Reinard guard barked into his headset, dropping down next to Asher and reaching for Trevor's pulse.

Nurses and doctors poured from the hospital. They forced Asher aside, loading Trevor onto a gurney. They were just cutting off Trevor's jacket and shirt when Marco appeared with the detail from the park. Their faces were grim as they watched the hospital staff work on their teammate.

Marco's eyes narrowed, his nostrils flared, and his hands clenched tightly at his side.

The emergency team moved, rolling the gurney into the hospital at a run while calling out orders for an operating room. Asher and Marco followed with the other bodyguards trailing behind them, like the very worst kind of parade.

At the operating room doors, they were told to wait outside.

The doors whizzed shut, and Asher locked his hands behind his head and paced, the last few minutes swirling through his mind on repeat. A reel you couldn't look away from even when you desperately needed to. Trevor was in there, bleeding, fighting for his life because of him. Asher wouldn't have liked it any more if the man had taken the hit for one of the Daisies, or Fiadh, or any of his family, but it would have at least felt like he'd offered himself up for a worthy cause. Asher had been the one to set this chain of events off to begin with. The consequences should have been his.

Marco stood, stance wide, arms across his chest, eyeing Asher, coolly assessing him in the way Asher normally did others. Asher was far from composed. He was completely unable to find that icy reserve he was known for. Instead, he was full of rage and agony and disgust. For Ziggy. For himself.

Marco's eyes lingered on the slashed vest on Asher's body and the blood on his hands and clothes. It was all from Ziggy and Trevor. None of it was his. He'd survived unscathed. Again.

"You hurt?" Marco finally grunted out.

Asher clenched his jaw and shook his head. His fist was throbbing from the punches he'd thrown, but it was his heart that felt as if it was going to explode.

He needed to calm the fuck down.

He needed to lose himself in something good. Fee. Wren.

"I want to hear as soon as he's out of surgery," he

snarled and then turned on his heels and headed for the stairs.

Fury was still rippling from him after he'd climbed a flight of stairs with one of the security team following him. The more he climbed, the faster he went, suddenly desperate to hold Fiadh. Desperate to feel something other than regret.

When he got to her hospital room, he almost ripped the door from its hinges before the sight inside had him stopping with his hand on the handle. Wren was on the bed next to Fiadh, and their heads were pressed together as his daughter read from one of her Nancy Drew books. Her long black hair was tangled with Fiadh's mahogany and lavender strands. Beautiful shades on beautiful people. Emotions clogged his throat until he felt like he might not be able to breathe. The ache in him grew from somewhere it had been hiding for decades. The longing for a family merging with the desperate hope that he'd found one. The possibility of keeping Fee just as he'd pledged earlier. Forever. He'd keep her and the music labels, no matter if it cost him a million dollars or a billion. She was his to protect, just like Wren.

Before he'd really thought about what he looked like, he'd already opened the door and taken two steps in. When two sets of eyes went wide in shock and horror, he instantly regretted it. Wren froze, her hand with the book falling, and it clattered to the ground.

Fee was out of the bed, rushing to his side in an instant, fear covering every inch of her face. "You're bleeding. God, Asher, you're bleeding. Where are you hurt?"

"It isn't mine."

Then, he yanked her into his arms and held on to her. Relief poured through him knowing she was safe and Ziggy was in custody. But hell…why did someone else have to be hurt because of it? His eyes darted across the room to where Wren stood stock-still.

"I'm okay, Birdie. I promise," he said, but she still didn't move. He felt like the very worst father, lover, friend, coming to them looking like this—covered in blood with rage still flowing through him.

"What happened? Whose blood is on you?" Fee was struggling against him, her raspy voice squeaking and squawking. It was muffled, with her face still buried in his chest because he couldn't let go. He couldn't ease up, not even an ounce.

Wren came out of her trance, floating over the distance, joining them, and tentatively putting her arms around him and Fee. His heart lodged in his throat, and he tugged her tighter into their joined embrace.

"Asher!" Fee demanded again.

"Just let me hold you both a minute," he growled.

Beneath the antiseptic scent of the hospital clinging to Fee, he caught a hint of her sweet essence tangled with the flowery scent he'd always associated with his daughter. It pulled at all the broken strings inside him. His jaw ticked, fighting back tears of relief and remorse and grief.

His body shook, and Fee must have felt it because she finally wrapped her arms around them both and squeezed back. The three of them stood that way, joined together, until his heart rate slowed from a perilous stampede to a simple jog.

The door swung open, and his dad stepped in. Wren immediately released them to go to her grandfather, and Asher tried not to let it tear into his sliced-up soul. He'd fix it. Soon, she'd be as comfortable with him as she was with Jay and his dad.

"Is it done?" his father demanded.

"He's in custody," he replied. His gaze landed on Wren and the wide eyes she kept darting to the blood coating him. "Take Wren back to the hotel, Dad."

His father looked like he might argue, but then looking down at Wren and seeing her pale face, he just nodded. He drew Wren's hand into his and led her out of the room.

Asher released Fee just enough to look down, and as soon as she turned her face up, his mouth crashed onto hers. An agonized claiming full of everything he was feeling. Love. Fury. Frustration. He couldn't devour her in the hospital as he wanted—needed—to do at the moment. Couldn't lose himself in her until he forgot everything. But he could leave this mark. A memory she wouldn't forget. One he wouldn't forget either.

She let him take it out on her, keeping her word that she could handle all of him. The worst. The best. The secrets. The weight. The truth finally settled into him. She wasn't alone, but neither was he.

Chapter Thirty-three

Fiadh

TWICE
Performed by Christina Aguilera

It was hours before they heard Trevor had pulled through surgery. He was in ICU and was going to have a hell of a recovery, but he'd be okay. The relief Fee felt was enormous…the one man who'd been there through all of this for the Daisies was going to be okay. But as she turned to Asher, lying next to her in the hospital bed, she could see that even this news hadn't taken the weight off his shoulders.

She ran a hand through his hair, disheveled in a way that was so unlike him—except, maybe it wasn't. She'd seen him this way when he was inside her, moving beautifully, tormenting her with fingers and lips and pistoning hips. And she'd also seen him this way, worried about Wren and her and every damn thing that had gone wrong in the last few days. The mussed Asher was the real one. Her hand slid to his jaw, stroking the scruff and wondering how she'd ever looked at him and seen an asshole when all she could see now was a man determined to protect everyone he cared about through sheer force of will.

"He was doing his job, Asher. This isn't on you," she said. Her voice was still scratchy and raw, but she thought it sounded just a little better than it had a day ago. It gave her hope that she tried not to dwell on.

"Stop talking, damnit," he growled, his thumb coasting

over her lips.

She smiled against his hand, and his eyes heated.

Her phone buzzed, and she pulled it out, expecting a text from the band. They'd been as relieved as she'd been when they'd heard Ziggy was in custody and Trevor had made it through surgery.

Her heartbeat increased when she saw it was from Angel, and when she opened the message, a horrified gasp escaped her that had Asher twisting it so he could see as well.

The image was of Ziggy Klein in what looked like a police interrogation room with a two-way mirror and a sign for the police department on the wall. The man was strapped down to a table with a gag in his mouth, and he'd been worked over. There was a large slash along his collarbone that resembled the one on Fiadh's and black bruising from a hand being wrapped around his throat. His right eye was closed, a long cut going from his eyebrow down into his cheek, his nose was broken, and his lips were bloodied and swollen. His head lolled to the side, and it was impossible to tell if he was alive or dead.

"What the hell is this?" Asher growled.

Her phone buzzed again, and they both looked down to read the text together.

> *ANGEL: Klein wasn't responsible for Landry.*
> *Tell Riggs he owes me.*

"Who is this man, Fee?"

She shook her head, doubts and confusion welling through her as chills littered her body. Was Angel admitting he was responsible for Landry or just that Ziggy hadn't done it? Had Angel killed Ziggy for Asher? For her? Nausea wafted over her.

Asher rose, taking her phone and stepping out into the hall to show Phillip, a brown-haired, brown-skinned man brought on board by Garner at Reinard's blessing. She hadn't seen the man leave her door once since he'd shown up. It was like he was a robot without bodily needs.

While they talked, Fee's emotions zigzagged all over the place. Alarm. Terror. Dismay. And maybe even a tiny bit of joy because Ziggy had gotten the payback he deserved. Did that make her an awful human being? To be glad someone else had been hurt? Might even be dead?

Asher strode back into the room, face somber. "He's not dead. An officer at the precinct just found him."

"How the hell does this happen at a police station without anyone hearing or seeing it?" Fee asked.

Asher's jaw ticked as he shook his head slightly. "I don't know if I should be impressed, pissed, or worried."

Fee's hand went to her throat and the wounds there. "Angel did this...for me?"

Asher's gaze narrowed. "The cut on his eye...that's what Ziggy did to Krista. There was more... Lots more, down her body... Angel, or whoever the hell this man is...he didn't just duplicate what Ziggy had done to you. He also duplicated what he'd done to Krista. This was a message for me, Fiadh. He said it in the text. He feels like I owe him now."

Fee shivered, and Asher noticed. He pulled her into him.

Even a week ago, she would have resisted this, would have forced him away and ignored the comfort of his embrace to toss out a saucy reply. But now, all she could do was soak it up. To revel in the knowledge that neither of them was alone. That no matter what came at them, they'd handle it together.

♫ ♫ ♫

When Fiadh came awake the next morning, the noise of pencil scratching on paper made her eyes flutter. No one used paper and pencil anymore. When she opened her eyes, she saw Wren sitting in a chair next to the bed, feet curled up under her, writing in a notebook. Asher sat in the chair next to her with his computer on his lap, but his eyes had been drawn to whatever Wren was doing.

He leaned over and asked quietly, as if not to wake Fiadh, "What are you working on there, Birdie?"

"What happened to Fee would make a very interesting Nancy Drew story. I am writing one," she replied even quieter than him as she lifted her head to meet his gaze. "I am thinking of calling it *The Night of the Rock Star*. Is that a good name?"

He rubbed his jaw. "I think it's a very good name."

She smiled at him, and Fee saw Asher's jaw tick, as if his daughter's smile was something that moved him.

"Writing a novel is hard work. Have you made an outline?" he asked.

Her brows furrowed together. "An outline? No."

"Some writers use one to help them guide the story. In film, they use storyboards to lay out the critical scenes. It's the same idea."

"I am not sure I know how to do this."

"Would you like me to help?" he asked.

"Do you have time?" she asked, eyes dropping to the laptop he had open in front of him. Her words made Fee's heart convulse, and she saw Asher's throat bob.

He shut the computer and then patted his leg, and Wren didn't hesitate. She simply joined him, snuggling into his chest. A strange warmth filled Fee at the image of them together—father and daughter. A rush of tears filled her eyes that she had to blink back.

"Birdie," he said quietly, and his daughter looked up at him expectantly. "I will always have time for you. You come first. The work will be there whenever I get back to it."

His daughter grinned and then launched into the details of her story. Fee watched with the love she felt for him—for them—blooming and growing until it seemed to fill every single spot in her body and soul, even those places her dad had left bleeding. It seemed impossible that she hadn't known Wren even a few days ago…and now it felt like they both had always belonged to her.

They'd been working together for several minutes when Asher announced, "I don't think this should be a Nancy Drew book." Wren looked momentarily crestfallen before he continued, "I think you should create an all-new girl detective. Birdie LaRue or something like that. Create your own world."

She giggled. "Birdie LaRue, Father?"

He smiled and ruffled her hair, and she laughed more. Jesus, Mary, and Joseph it was too much. Too much for her wounded heart. She felt like she was going to explode.

Asher looked over and saw Fee was awake, and his smile grew even wider, warmth hitting those blue eyes as if the sun was shining on them. The hard statue she'd once thought he was melted away into a creation of love and joy.

"Look who's finally awake," he said to Wren.

His daughter jumped off his lap and came over to Fee's side, grabbing her hand. "Guess what, Fiadh?"

"What's that?" Fee croaked, and Asher frowned, but Wren just smiled.

"Father is letting me come with you. Jay and I both. I am going to be homeschooled for the rest of the year."

Fiadh's eyes went from the huge smile on the little girl's face to the thoughtful look on Asher's. "Yeah?"

"You're not supposed to be talking," he said, standing and coming over to lean down and place a gentle kiss on her forehead. Then, he tweaked one of Wren's braids. "And just remember, it may not be permanent. Jay's looking into new schools for you for the fall."

The hospital door opened, and Kellan entered with a bag followed by a man in scrubs. The doctor approached the bed and asked, "How do you feel about being discharged?"

Fee gave him a thumbs-up sign.

"Well, that's good because the plane will be ready in an hour," Kellan announced.

Fee's eyes met Asher's, hope sparking as his hand tangled with hers. "You ready to go to Chicago?"

God…did it hurt. The sweetness in his gaze as much as the idea of being with all of them…The Daisies and Asher and Wren… It was almost too much for her. The tears that she'd barely tucked away came back, and this time, she couldn't hold them in.

Asher swiped at one as it fell, brows furrowing in concern.

"What is it?"

She shook her head, unable to express it. She remembered leaving Albany, feeling like a door had shut. A chapter had closed. But she'd never imagined the new page would look like this. Full of love and hope and family. There may have been some horrible, awful moments in there, but this…these feelings inside her, inside them…they were beautiful. The very best kind of emotions.

Kellan and Wren left to gather the little girl's things from the house while Asher stayed with Fee. The bag his dad had brought was full of her clothes Jozef had washed and sent back for her. When she came out of the hospital bathroom in them, Asher's eyes narrowed.

She made a "what" motion with her arms.

He came over, sliding his hands around her waist and drawing her close. "I like you better in my things."

He kissed her, and even though it was gentle, it hid none of the fire that raged between them and would need very little to be stoked to full blaze. The mix of it, the tenderness and heat added to the other emotions she'd already been feeling since she'd woken up, left her feeling raw, and she found tears slipping down her face again.

"Baby, you're worrying me," he said as he cupped her face and brushed at them with his thumbs. "Are you in pain? Should we stay here longer?"

She shook her head, and the motion didn't hurt as much as it did the day before. It was an ache that would be with her for days, but not quite the sharp agony it had been.

"Your family…" She couldn't even get out the rest as a surprised sob escaped her chest. He hugged her to him tightly.

"Did you want me to call yours?" he asked.

She snorted, head buried in his chest as she squeezed him tighter. "Why?"

"You almost died, Fee."

She shrugged, wondering bitterly what their reaction to that call would have been. As far as her father was concerned, she'd been dead a long time. Almost a decade.

He grunted out a protest and then lifted her chin so he could kiss her again, fiercely and passionately, as if making more promises to her. His gaze held all the intensity of when she'd first met him but also a promise as he said softly, "You can have mine."

Her heart contracted, fluttering and pulsing and feeling again like it was going to be too large for her chest soon.

"I love you," she breathed out. The day before, he'd said he was keeping her. Today, he was offering her his family. The "I love you" seemed almost…redundant. But she'd learned through loss and heartache that you needed to say the words. You needed them to be said out loud so the entire universe heard them spoken. Then, if the worst happened, you could remember the way they sounded. The way they beat a rhythm in your veins.

His face grew serious. "As much as I love those words, as much as I love you, I'm seriously going to wrap one of my silk ties around that pretty little mouth if you keep talking."

She pointed to him as she mouthed silently, "You"—she drew a heart on his chest and then pointed to herself—"me?"

He pulled the finger she'd been using to his mouth, kissing it.

"Baby, I love you so damn much I don't know where I end and you begin." He drew her hand to his chest. "It's a big mess in here. Chaotic. Fiery. Just like you."

His voice was gruff, full of the truth of his words. She stared for a long moment, amazed, thrilled, scared, but mostly feeling sure she needed this in her life. Needed him.

Needed the love in her heart to be returned. She stroked his face, letting the words settle into the space between each heartbeat, filling in the last spaces of loneliness.

"It feels...too much...too soon...like we skipped a hundred steps. I'm terrified it will crumble away," she said softly.

His palm landed fully on her mouth, pressing slightly into her lips. "I wish I could keep this here permanently to stop you from talking. You need to heal, damnit. I need you to sing again..."

He choked on the words, throat bobbing, and she heard beneath it what he couldn't say. The regret he felt. The new penance he'd add to the list of others if she didn't get her voice back completely, and it tortured her almost more than it did him. She wanted him to feel freer, to let go of the things that weighed him down, not add more to the pile.

"We're not ending, baby," he said after a long moment. "I promise I'll do everything and anything to keep you."

"Anything?" she said against his hand.

His eyes narrowed in warning, and it did nothing but coil desire through her bruised and battered body. An adrenaline rush that pushed the pain behind her, leaving her achy in a very different way.

"Anything," he repeated with a fierceness she believed.

She tugged his hand from her mouth and smiled. "Even dance? The wallflower will take the floor?" She kept her voice low so she sounded as much like herself as possible.

He growled, "Stop talking. Any dance we do won't be for public consumption."

"One dance in exchange for forever. It seems a fair trade. We'll start with a slow dance and work up to the fast ones."

Then, she leaned in and kissed him, slow and steady, but he took command of it with ease, as if already proving his point. She was already his. The physical pain on the outside was worth it as desire curled through her, the flame burning stronger with each languid lick and flick of a tongue. Growing stronger with each nip and slide of his warm hands. Glowing so bright it felt like they could light up the room with the love that poured from them.

Chapter Thirty-four

Asher

WHEN YOU LOVE SOMEONE
Performed by Bryan Adams

TWO DAYS AFTER

Even though she'd barely gotten up, Fiadh had fallen asleep on the plane. It gave Asher one more thing to worry about. He knew she'd be determined to go onstage Saturday, and he was damn sure her voice couldn't handle it. He wasn't even sure her body could. They'd have to figure something out. Something that would let her do her thing without putting him in a cardiac unit.

He watched her sleep for a long time, hating the marks on her body, some of which were hidden behind her clothes. It was a little sick that he wanted to strip her of them and put her back in his sweats, as if, in doing so, he could keep them tucked into the little bubble they'd lived in for a few days, forging a family out of tragedy.

He frowned, thinking of the family who'd walked away from her. The one she hadn't even wanted to tell about her attack. Before Asher could question the idea, he sent a text to Torrance.

> *ASHER: Get me contact information on Remy and Bitsy Kane.*

As always, Torrance responded immediately. Asher needed to give the man another all-expense-paid vacation to a sunlit island soon.

TORRANCE: Who?

ASHER: Fiadh's parents.

TORRANCE: Got it. We might have it in the reports we did on the Daisies, but if we don't, I'll get them.

ASHER: Thank you.

When the plane landed, their little entourage made their way to the hotel where the Daisies were staying. Fee was tucked up next to him, her head on his shoulder, and Wren and Jay sat opposite them in the limousine, chatting about the book she was writing, that he'd spent the morning helping her outline, and his chest contracted again. He felt lucky. So damn lucky. How could he have ever imagined loving people like this was a curse? The brittle, cracked parts of his soul had softened in a handful of days. Between Wren and Fee, he felt like he no longer had petrified wood for a heart. Like the Tin Man, he'd been given a new one. Fleshy and beating fiercely. It was soft and easily wounded, and trusting it wouldn't be stabbed wasn't easy for him, but he'd do it. Because both the women with him deserved it.

They'd barely checked in and found their way to their two-room suite when the rest of the band burst into it.

"*Dios*," Adria said as her gaze landed on Fiadh's bruises and bandages.

Then, the women surrounded her in a group hug, just like they did every time they came offstage. A tangle of limbs and hearts and souls. Asher's eyes met Jonas's across the top of the band's heads. Jonas stood with his feet wide and arms across his chest, looking very much like his brother. Marco had stayed in Boston to be with Trevor but also to ensure nothing else prevented Ziggy from making it to his cell in a maximum-security prison.

As the women drew Fee out onto the balcony, likely to discuss not only the attack but her relationship with Asher, his stomach grew taut. He hated when she wasn't within reach, but even more, he hated the thought of them reminding her of the asshole he'd been.

Jonas joined him, and they both watched the band through the curtains. Jonas's voice was low as he grumbled, "You haven't done a very good job of protecting them."

Asher's jaw clenched, but he didn't respond. What did you say to the truth?

"You've been a prick to these women...all of them," Jonas continued. "What assurances do I have that things will be different now just because something's going on between you and Fee? How do I know you aren't going to hurt her worse than she's already been hurt? Any of them?"

Asher didn't need or want to justify himself to some twenty-year-old kid in his employ. His eyes narrowed. "I've always had their best interest at heart."

Jonas scoffed.

"By telling them they had to finish the album and the tour or you'd sue them? That was what you thought was the best for them?"

"They are one of the most unique bands of this decade...maybe this century. I wasn't going to let them give up and fade away into has-beens. They needed to know they could do this without Landry. As much as her loss has been felt, the absence of The Painted Daisies on the music scene would have been worse. They needed the push in order to remember that, and it was my job to give it to them."

Jonas's eyes narrowed, and he started to say something, but Asher cut him off. "As for what's happening between Fiadh and me, that is between us. Off the table for discussion. You don't get to pretend to look after her now when none of you have done right by her."

Jonas's eyes narrowed. "Excuse me?"

"She's been alone. For way too long. When Landry died, everyone scuttled back to their respective lives and individual troubles, and she had no one. They all had their families—people who hugged them and loved on them—while she sat in that apartment in LA all alone except for an occasional drop-in from a drunken manager. So, you tell me, Jonas, who really has done right by Fiadh?"

Jonas's face turned into a blank slate.

"No one," Asher said, scowling. "But she isn't alone anymore. And she won't ever be again. Do we understand each other?"

To his utter surprise, Jonas started chuckling. "You've got it bad." Jonas stuck out a hand and said, "Welcome aboard the Daisies Ultimate Fan Club." When Asher didn't shake it, Jonas continued, "Don't be a dick. Shake my hand. We can commiserate over beers about how fucked up it is to find the woman you love being attacked by some sleazy bastard. Or how you'll never, ever feel like you can keep them safe when they're in the public's eye all the damn time."

"You're not old enough to drink a beer." But Asher shook his hand.

Jonas smiled. "At least it isn't a one-man club anymore. I wasn't sure I could hold it together on my own much longer."

Asher just raised an eyebrow in response. He knew Jonas would tell Paisley what he'd said, and she'd tell the rest of the band. But maybe that was what they all needed—for him to have expressed his frustration with them for leaving Fee so isolated and for them to have said their piece about what an asshole he'd been. He'd done it with a purpose, but it had still been cold. Calculated. The man Asher had been when he'd done it was already gone. A memory from his past.

This new man, the one Fee had put her trust in, would have handled things differently. Would handle the new bumps in the Daisies' path with more grace and gentleness than hard love, but he'd still push. He had more reason to now than ever because Fiadh needed the band. Needed the family they were on and offstage, and he was going to make sure they kept it together…for her.

SEVEN DAYS AFTER

Chicago was a mess. He hadn't wanted her onstage at all, but just like he'd known she would, she'd insisted. So, they'd arranged for Fee to lip-synch her parts, even when it was something the band had sworn they'd never do. She'd worn a sleeveless turtleneck that covered her wounds, and she'd hardly moved around onstage. The audience and the critics picked up on something being off with her, and rumors swirled. He had the band's PR folks release a statement saying she was sick, and somehow, that satisfied the wolves enough. The last thing the band needed was the world to find out that yet another Daisy had been injured. It would turn their lives into a soap opera, and Asher wanted everyone to focus on the stunning beauty of their music and not the drama surrounding their personal lives.

Once they arrived in Toronto, he felt her impatience to be back to her normal self growing, both when he refused to make love to her until she'd healed more and with her inability to perform. Being with the band, playing her instruments…it was soothing, but not enough. She needed to be onstage, filling an arena with her fire, and the longer she went without it, the edgier she got.

It meant he barely left her side, making sure she didn't push too hard too soon, but the day after they'd landed in Canada, as he got ready to go with her to practice, she stopped him.

"What's wrong?" he asked, stroking her cheek down over the line of her jaw, resting a finger on the row of earrings sitting barely above yet another black turtleneck she was hiding behind. He hated it. Not only because of the reason she needed it, but because it hid the true Fee with her tattoos and freckles.

Looking over his shoulder at Wren, she whispered, "You brought her with you to spend time with her, yet all you do is follow me. Take her to the zoo or the aquarium. Do something together."

God, she was right. He was still struggling to find balance, finding it hard to let either of them out of his sight for long. His jaw tightened as he debated how to be in two places at once, and then he exhaled slowly. "Be safe," he demanded.

She smiled—her real smile—kissed him, and then walked out with a swarm of security following her that he'd never think was enough.

His phone buzzed.

MARCO: We might have picked up a lead.

ASHER: On Carter or Landry?

MARCO: Carter. Working with Eduardo, we were able to backdoor the trace he placed on the funds to Krista. He was using a computer in a library in Boston.

ASHER: That's not much of a lead.

MARCO: We'll show the sketch Fee helped us make around and find where he was staying. It's a step.

It was frustrating how slow it was going, how invisible the man had become, but he also wondered if Carter was as big of a threat as they'd originally thought. He could have harmed Fiadh many times over the last two years and hadn't. There was something else the man wanted. Not knowing was what kept Asher awake at night more than fear that the man would come after them.

He put his phone away and looked at his daughter, scribbling away in her little notebook. She'd worked nonstop on the story she was making since they'd outlined it together at the hospital.

"How do you feel about going to the zoo, Birdie?"

Her face lit up, and Asher had one more thing to thank Fiadh for because she'd known exactly what he and Wren both needed. He'd thought Fee would wreck his world...and she had, but in the very best way possible.

He and Wren spent the morning at the zoo, had lunch at a renowned restaurant, and then spent hours in a bookstore. As they left the shop, with Asher carrying a heavy bag of mystery novels and nonfiction writing books, his feet stalled in front of a jewelry store.

In the window was a stunning choker. Thin lines of leather, black stones, and emeralds twined together with a long chain of black pearls dripping down the center. It was sexy as hell and stunning in a way that was entirely Fee. The necklace might not cover up all her bruises, but it would hide the majority, and makeup could do the rest.

He tugged Wren inside and asked the salesman to see it. Looking at the choker as it lay on the black velvet, he almost lost his breath. Asher could imagine Fee in the lace halter she'd worn at the bar in Albany with the long strand of pearls settling down between her breasts. It was her in so many different ways. Dark and sparkling. Fiery and dramatic. He asked if the jeweler could add a small set of emeralds and diamonds to the edge of the collar in the form of a daisy.

As the salesman went into the back to talk to the jeweler, he joined Wren where she was staring at a case of engagement rings.

"Are you going to marry Fiadh, Father?"

Yes. The thought came immediately, unprovoked, and without even the slightest hesitation. He inhaled deeply and then considered the question more slowly, but the answer didn't change. They'd already branded each other. Marked themselves on each other's souls in ways that were permanent. Unyielding. If, God forbid, something happened to pull them apart, he'd never recover. He'd return to the icy man he'd been before and hope his daughter could melt the corners enough for him to give her what she needed.

"I'd like to think so," he answered softly.

Wren pointed at a ring made of black gold. Ornate and Gothic looking. A dozen or so small emeralds of stunning clarity twisted into black stones that reminded him of the trefoil arches at Taran Ridge. Petals grew up from the sides to hold a large, square-cut diamond.

"This one would be perfect for her," Wren said, and she was right. The ring was as perfect for Fee as the choker.

"We'll take this as well," he said when the salesman returned.

Wren's face turned into a full-wattage smile, and she spun around in a circle, her floral dress spinning. She looked like Nova, dancing in the grassy quad, but she was nothing like her mother. She was completely and utterly different. Grounded in a way that he had his dad and his staff to thank for. It certainly hadn't been anything he'd done.

"I love you, Birdie," he said softly.

She stilled, her smile growing even wider, and then she stepped close enough to hug him, head to his stomach, arms tight around his waist. "I love you also."

♫ ♫ ♫

TWELVE DAYS AFTER

Fee's voice had returned to normal, and Asher was more grateful for it than almost anything in his life, but she hadn't attempted singing yet. Not until today. It was their last practice before the concert, and she had to try now or get stuck lip-synching again. He wasn't entirely sure she shouldn't do just that and give herself another week to heal. But she wanted this, and he was doing his best not to be Asshole-Asher. In compromise, the band had moved the set list around again, so there would only be a few songs near the end of the concert that were completely dependent on her.

The closer it got to the time for her to sing, the stiller Fee seemed to get, retreating into a shell instead of prancing around in her normal, fiery way until she now stood onstage, mic in hand, completely motionless, with nervousness bleeding from her.

Asher couldn't stand seeing her this way. The opposite of the confident Fiadh Kane he'd fallen head over heels for. He stalked over to her, surrounded her with his arms regardless of who was watching, tucked his chin onto her shoulder, and whispered in her ear, "Close your eyes."

She did, automatically following his command, trusting him in a way that tightened his chest, his gut, and his groin. She placed her hand not holding the mic on top of his arms locked around her waist.

"Sing to me, baby," he said softly.

She hesitated again and then started out so quiet that, even with the mic, it hardly registered in the space.

"Surrounded with people, moving fast through the crowd, not a single person seeing me. Not an idea of how to be found." Her voice quivered with emotions, and it almost brought Asher to his knees. He'd heard the song many times. It was one of Paisley's best, a chart-topper. But hearing the words now, after everything he'd learned about Fee and everything they'd been through, it was even more poignant. It was them. Just like the ending of the song, where the singer steps onto an empty ballroom floor and a man sweeps her into a silent dance.

The music filled the stage around them. The rest of the Daisies joined with their instruments, and Fee continued. Her voice got louder with each word until, at the chorus, she was blending in at full volume just as the other band members joined her.

It was beautiful.

Sensational.

Fucking rock stars at their peak. No, not their peak. They

still had mountains to show the world.

He spun her out of his arms but held her hand, moving again so they were face-to-face. He shuffled his feet, swayed his hips, and then brought her back to his chest. It was a dance. An awkward-as-fuck one, but it lit up her face. Her amber eyes sparked, flames growing in their depths. She dropped the mic, but her friends didn't stop singing, they continued as Asher and Fee slowly turned and shifted across the stage, blending together.

It went from awkward to smooth and practiced in mere steps. He'd told her once that if they danced, it would go from G- to R-rated in a heartbeat, and it did. Because once she shifted her hips against his, aligning their cores, he couldn't keep his hand from sliding along the skin at her waist and his mouth from landing on hers. Their feet came to an abrupt stop as they consumed each other.

The song ended, her friends laughed and clapped, the crew whistled, and Asher stepped back, feeling not even an ounce of embarrassment. He never did when he claimed Fee. A mutual claiming because she always marked him back. A nip. A bite. A heated look that warned anyone around them she'd likely go down fighting if they tried to put a move on him. He loved it. He loved her.

She was smiling, and it was small and crooked. Heartbreakingly perfect.

"Marry me." It sounded like a command. And fuck if it wasn't one, but he also knew commands and Fee were like oil and water, and he felt her stiffen in his embrace.

"What?"

There was movement from behind them on the stage. Her friends had started putting things away, ready to call it quits until the concert the next day. But he couldn't take his eyes off Fee. Hers were narrowed, as if wondering if he'd really asked her that enormous question in the middle of the chaos of their practice.

He grabbed her hand, pulled her to the edge of the stage, and sat down so his feet were hanging off. He tugged her onto his lap, surrounding her with his arms, and repeated the question, "Marry me, Fee."

"Asher…" Her voice was choked, a sea of emotions that, for the first time in a long time, he didn't know how to read. Was she happy? Pissed off? Regretful? His heart banged in his chest as he waited for her answer.

"Don't say no," he growled when it took her too long to respond.

"No." She reached out to touch his cheek, and his entire body went still. "I mean I'm not saying no." Relief wafted over him. "I'm just…I love you…but are you sure? This is…we haven't even been together but a handful of days."

"I could wait two weeks, or six months, or a year to ask you, but it wouldn't change the question. It wouldn't change the way I feel." He brushed her curls back, cupping her cheeks. "Could time ever deny the truth of us?"

She stared for so long panic grew inside him. She didn't know he'd already thought about this, that he had a damn ring waiting for her at the hotel. She didn't know how much he truly meant it. But then, to his utter relief, she leaned toward him, lips brushing his, and whispered, "Feck it. I've seen you dance, Wallflower, so we might as well get married now."

He chuckled, but then she was kissing him, and that was all he could think about. Her lips. Her body. Her ass as it shifted against his groin.

He slid off the stage with her in his embrace and headed across the grass for the exit.

"Fee and I are going back to the hotel," he hollered back.

Laughter accompanied them across the field.

He realized, as he strode toward home plate, that their room was too far even though the hotel was attached to the Blue Jays stadium. In the corridor, just past the dugouts, he stopped, pushing her up against a wall and devouring her lips. His hands slid under her T-shirt, fingers dancing across the smooth skin to where she was braless. God, he hated it and loved it all at the same time, and he punished her for it by tweaking her taut nipples.

She gasped, hips thrusting into him.

He removed his lips, stepping away just far enough to drag her down the corridor behind him at almost a run. It took far too many minutes for them to make it back to the suite. As he slammed the bedroom door shut behind them, he thanked his foresight in sending Jay and Wren out to the aquarium for the day because he wasn't sure if either he or Fee would be quiet. Not after days of longing to be back in each other's skin.

They shed their clothes all while they were touching, kissing, and caressing until they finally fell, naked, as a tangled mess of limbs, onto the bed. Slick with want, their bodies were already desperate for the rhythm they'd found together days ago at Taran Ridge.

He went to grab a condom, and she stopped him. "I have an IUD in. I'm clean," she said, and the meaning over her words settled into him in a way that made him impossibly harder. The thought of sliding into her bare, nothing but the real them between them…it was almost too much.

"I'm clean," he said, and he slid home with a jagged relief that had him groaning.

She arched into him, nails digging into his shoulders, a whimper of desire escaping her. He grunted and growled like some wild animal. He'd never be able to get enough of her. Never be able to get deep enough, far enough, and yet they still seemed to fit completely and perfectly. It made no logical sense. But then, nothing with Fee did. She'd wrapped him in her spell and broken the curse on the Riggs men with the truth. She was never going anywhere. He knew it to the bottom of his soul and back.

Her eyes fluttered shut, and he knew she was close. He sat up, shifting so he went even deeper, and she let out a moan of pleasure. He grabbed her hips, using her force and his to thrust harder in an effort to topple her over the edge before he lost control.

"Feck…" she breathed out, and then she was convulsing around him, the pulse pushing him over with her.

They rocked to a stop. Her cheek went to his shoulder. His arms pulled her even tighter up against him.

"I love you," he said. Then, he tossed her on the bed, and she laughed.

He cleaned up, and while she did the same, he slipped into a pair of sweats, dug through his computer bag, and returned to the bedroom with the items he'd retrieved from the jeweler. One was still in its box, the other in his pocket.

She was tugging on a pair of black lace underwear when he returned to her. The dusting of cinnamon spread over her body was one of the sexiest things he'd ever seen. Almost as sexy as the way her hair curled and twirled down over her shoulders, covering rosy tips. She was breathtaking.

He wrapped his arms around her waist from behind and flicked the box open in front of her. She stilled in his arms.

"You already have a ring?" There were tears in her voice.

He kissed her temple. "It just happened."

She laughed. "How do you just happen to get a ring?"

He didn't answer at first. Instead, he took the band out of its black velvet case and slid it on her left ring finger. It fit just as it should have, blending in with her other rings and black leather bands around her wrists. It was her...but also a reminder that there was more to her than the rock star. That she was part of what lay between them now—a family who loved each other.

"Wren picked it out," he said, and a little sob escaped her that twisted his heart with a similar emotion. "We got it when I was getting this." He pulled the choker from his pocket, leaned back, and settled it around her neck, brushing her hair aside to hook it behind her. Her hand with his ring on it went up to the necklace, feeling it, grasping the long strand of black pearls that had settled between her bare breasts, and he thought he might come all over again at the sight of her this way. Diamonds and leather and skin.

"What is this?" she asked.

He turned her ever so slightly so she could see into the mirror above the dresser. He was still behind her, hands on her shoulders, their bare skin blending from the waist up, the gems glimmering in the faint light coming in through the windows as the sky turned from blue to a fiery orange that reminded him of the flame in Fee's eyes.

"So you don't have to hide," he said, stroking her neck where a tiny bit of yellow bruising peeked out beyond the necklace.

Her eyes met his in the mirror. She swallowed hard.

"It's too much, Ash."

"It's perfect."

"It's beautiful. They're both beautiful." She turned in his arms, gaze meeting his, rising up to kiss him softly. "Thank you."

"They're nothing. Not compared to what you've already given me," he said gruffly.

"Sex?" She smiled, lips twitching.

He growled a protest at the idea of them being so little. Sex was nothing. What they were…it was indescribable. "You've given me my entire future back. My daughter. My dad. Me…"

"I don't know how you can say I did any of that. Those things already belonged to you."

"They were behind a locked door that you freed me from. You snuck in, showing me what I was missing, what I needed."

She pulled away from him, messed with her phone, and a slow, sultry song came on. She walked toward him, pulling at the long strand of pearls, and coming close enough to wrap it around his wrist, a loose knot that would come apart at the gentlest of movements, and he stilled so it wouldn't. Then, she was sliding and grinding down his body, a dance that made his already aching dick strain and jump even more.

"You danced with me. Now I get to dance for you," she said softly, eyes finding his as her mouth closed around him, sucking. A gentle pull that almost undid him.

He put his hands under her arms, dragging her back up.

"You do that with your tongue again, and I'll be out for the count, and I'm not done with you yet."

He took her to the bed, promising to show her just how much she meant to him.

How much he loved the fiery rock star, Fiadh Kane, but also how he worshipped the sweet heroine, Fee, who tried to protect everyone she loved at the expense of herself. Not anymore. Now, he would do everything and anything to make sure she didn't have to sacrifice one damn thing again. Not for anyone. Not even for him.

Epilogue

Fiadh

LOVING YOU IS EASY
Performed by Sarah McLachlan

FOUR MONTHS AFTER

𝒜sher was acting weird. He'd been withdrawn and cranky for a couple of days now. She'd called him on it several times, asking if it had something to do with the hunt for Angel or the search for Landry's killer, but he'd said no. Both of those investigations had stalled. Angel had disappeared completely, no trace of him to be found, and the number they'd used when she'd thought he was just a P.I. was no longer active. Landry's murder was still exactly where it had been before, unsolved with no further leads.

It was frustrating, and the only thing that kept Fee on an even keel when she thought about it was the fact that Marco had been tasked with searching for answers. She'd felt even better when Trevor had recovered enough to join Marco in his search. The two men were people Fiadh knew the band could trust.

When all their friends and family had started showing up that morning at Taran Ridge, Asher had gotten even quieter, retreating almost to the cold man she'd first met. It gave her an itchy feeling, as if things might be falling apart instead of coming together.

As if he was getting cold feet.

In the months they'd been together, they'd only been apart four nights for two business trips Asher had been unable to rearrange. On the first one, he'd closed a deal on a production company that was merging with RMI's streaming service, and on the second, he'd put Ronan in charge of the combined company.

While Asher insisted it had been a smart business move, it also kept the director out of their hair some, relieving Adria, who bristled and turned cold whenever Ronan was around. It made Fee think of how she used to react when Asher was around. All that hate-to-love-you attraction. She wished she could get Adria to talk about it, but her friend shut down whenever Fiadh tried, saying she was just exhausted. While she knew it wasn't a lie—they were all drained from their intense schedule—she also knew it wasn't the complete truth.

It was good they'd reached the first break in their tour. Four beautiful weeks to rest, regain their strength, and recoup before they started another string of weekly concerts. For the first time in as long as she could remember, Fiadh wasn't lamenting the break from the band. Probably because she wasn't going back to a lonely condo in LA. She actually didn't even have it anymore. Asher had carefully and methodically arranged for her items to be packed up and shipped to Taran Ridge and for the condo to be sold. In another lifetime, she would have felt steamrolled. In this lifetime, she felt cared for and loved.

After a beautiful dinner Jozef had made for all their guests, everyone retreated to the drawing room for drinks and board games led by Jay. Asher slipped away, saying he had to make a call. Kellan eyed him as if he, too, sensed something off, and he and Fee exchanged a knowing gaze. Her almost father-in-law tilted his head in the direction of the door, and she darted from the room as Kellan distracted her bandmates, Jonas, Zia, and the Taran Ridge family with a story about one of Asher's most embarrassing moments.

Fee searched the mansion for Asher, determined not to let anything come between this beautiful thing they'd started.

No barriers. That was what they'd promised each other, and if he wasn't going to be able to keep it, she needed to know now, before they got married tomorrow.

When she found him, he was on the back patio, a huge black marble expanse with ornately carved wrought-iron rails and stone steps as glossy as obsidian in a rainstorm. She'd originally thought the black of Taran Ridge made it dark and broody, but in some ways, it was the perfect neutral, allowing the colors and energy of the people living there to shine.

Beyond the patio, the garden's mass of flowers and greenery felt just a bit wild, as if it was going to escape into the trees along the estate's border. Two dozen lavender-draped chairs and a daisy-covered arch that had been set up for the ceremony brought a softness that seemed out of place. Wild and tame blending.

Asher stood at the balustrade, head tilted, listening to the waves on the shore beyond it. He loved the ocean as much as she'd once loved the fields behind Gran's. Now, she just loved wherever they were together. She wrapped her arms around his waist, pressing her cheek into his back, pulling him to her. His hands landed on her arms, squeezing.

"Why aren't you with the others?" he asked.

"I had to come and find my broody Rochester and remind him that the Gothic novel he once was living has ended now."

He chuckled, pulling her around so she was in front of him. She rested her chin on his chest, looking up at him, feeling at home, and yet also still feeling the unease in him.

"No barriers, Asher. Remember? Truth. Honesty. Openness," she told him. He looked down at her, eyes growing wide and then hesitant, and it stirred the apprehension in her even more. "Just tell me, for feck's sake. Are you thinking we shouldn't do this? Or maybe wait?" She waved her hand out at the chairs lined up.

"Absolutely not," he said with a surety that surprised her. "We are getting married tomorrow. You can't escape me that easily, Fee."

She smiled softly, squeezing him. "I don't want to escape. I want to get completely lost in you. In this family we've made. So, tell me what's wrong."

He sighed. "I did something, and now, I'm unsure if it was the right thing."

She laughed, taking a line from his assistant. "The great Asher Riggs? No way. He always knows exactly what he's doing."

His lips twisted. "Thanks for boosting my ego, and tonight, when we're finally alone again, I'll remind you of that so you let me do exactly what I want to you."

"I always let you do exactly what you want to me."

"In the bedroom."

She laughed softly. She was never going to just give in…and he knew it. And in truth, he didn't want her to. She didn't need to be something she wasn't with Asher. The push and pull that was them, the passion that had them arguing and then making up…it was beautiful.

"You're procrastinating," she said. "Just tell me."

His head shifted, catching onto a sound just as she did. Wheels on the drive out front.

"I guess I'll just show you."

He gave her a wry smile, took her hand, and led her down the steps, around to the front of the house. Reggie had pulled up in the estate's Escalade. He was talking to someone in the back with a smile on his face.

The back door opened, and the first thing Fee saw was a mass of short, carrot-red hair. The next thing she saw was a thin body of a male teen who hadn't yet hit his full height. He turned, as if he'd sensed them there, and Fee's entire stomach fell, her body froze, and her heart stopped.

It might have been eight years, but she'd know her brother anywhere.

"'Ey, Fee, howaya?" he asked with a grin that looked so much like her ma's she burst into tears.

Then, she was running toward him, and he caught her,

skinny teen arms surrounding her. She clung to him. Sobbing. The part of her heart she'd thought had been sealed up burst like a dam, cleaving her with its ferocity.

Toby patted her on the back a bit awkwardly. "I don' remember ye bein' such a crier." His accent was so thick it crumbled over her like a cookie, one she ate up with joy and love in her heart.

She pushed herself back, wiping at her face. "I'm not. You just... How are you here?"

Toby looked over her shoulder at Asher. She turned to her fiancé, arching a brow. "This? You did this?"

Asher brushed a hand through his normally perfect hair, mussing it up, proving he was still nervous. She suddenly understood the war that had been going on inside him. He hadn't known how she'd feel about seeing the family who'd abandoned her.

She turned back to Toby. "Is it just you?"

She didn't know if she was hopeful or not. She wasn't prepared for any of them, least of all her father.

"Just me," Toby said, a small, unhappy look making his brows crease together. "But Ma sent this." A small brown package came out of his backpack. He handed it to her, and she started to undo it, but he stopped her. "Open it later."

"Shall we bring him in off the drive, baby?" Asher asked.

She laughed. "Of course."

She led her brother into the mansion, and Toby's eyes bugged out a bit. Instead of taking him into the drawing room with the entire gang, Asher suggested they go to his study so they could be alone for a while and catch up. As Asher went to leave, she mouthed, "Thank you," to him, and the unease that had been wearing on him for days disappeared. He nodded with a huge, rare, Asher smile and shut the door behind him.

It was left to Toby to explain how Asher had first contacted their ma after the incident with Ziggy, and while

Ma hadn't felt right about talking with Asher or Fee behind Pa's back, she'd given Toby the number. He couldn't do anything while living at home, but he'd landed in the States last week for college and had gotten in touch with Asher.

"Where are you going to school?" she asked.

"Just down the way at Bonin University in Virginia. They have a huge acting program."

"You want to be an actor?" she breathed out.

He laughed. "Career in the arts—so ye can imagine how Pa feels abou' that."

Fee frowned. "He didn't mind the music, Toby. He just minded me."

Toby's smile was stripped away. "I missed ye. I didna' understand for so long why ye'd gone. But once he started grousin' about ye in the news, I figured it ou'."

It tore at Fee's heart a bit in places she thought were healed, but she ignored it, happy to have Toby here. He showed her pictures of the family. Poppy was thirteen and looked like Fee's doppelgänger, but Oscar, at eleven, seemed somber in a way that was all Pa. Ma looked older, more tired, sad around the corners of her eyes that had always been full of laughter.

"Ma misses ye," he said softly when Fee commented.

Fee's eyes pricked again, but she couldn't let it eat at her. They'd all made their choices—her parents and her. It was only her siblings who hadn't had a say in what had happened.

Hours later, Asher came back, a small smile on his face when he saw them tucked up together, arm and arm. "You coming to bed anytime soon? Or you planning on staying awake until the ceremony?"

Fee laughed and rose. "It's your own fault, dropping a surprise like this on me hours before we're getting married."

Toby stretched and yawned. "I'm beat, any'ow. Think the time change has finally hit me."

They showed Toby to a room on the second floor near

Jay's, and Fee wrapped him in another tight hug, unsure if he was really here or if she was dreaming. He hugged her back and then went inside.

She was quiet as Asher led her up to their room—Asher's ocean room that was now hers as well. She sat down on the bed and pulled on the strings holding the brown package together. It revealed an old-fashioned, pearl-encrusted comb. Fee was flooded with memories of sitting on her ma's lap in front of the mirror as she watched her mother get ready. She'd played with the comb dozens of times, listening to the story about it. "*My ma passed the comb to me. And her ma before her, and hers before that. It's been in our family generations, Fiadh, and someday, when you get married, I'll pass it along to you.*"

Fee's throat bobbed, and more tears filled her eyes. There was no note with the gift, but there didn't need to be. She was still family—a daughter who you handed a precious heirloom to.

Asher pulled her into him, kissing her temple.

"Fee?"

She shook her head and wiped at the tears. "I'm okay. Just a little overwhelmed. I felt so unloved for so long, and now I realize it was always there, just a little out of reach but still following me around."

She stood up, but he grabbed her hand, holding her back as he scrutinized every inch of her face. She didn't hold back. She let him see the mess of emotions going through her.

He grabbed her hips, pulling her in between his legs and kissing the scar that slashed through her tattoo along her collarbone. "You'll never have to doubt you're loved again. I'm going to cover you with it until you almost can't breathe."

She kissed the top of his head, reveling in everything she'd found at his side. The family. The future. Rare gifts she would never take for granted.

She pulled away, and he let her this time. She set the comb next to her jewelry box and headed into the bathroom to change. When she came out, Asher was already tucked under the sheet in bed. His eyes darkened as he slowly took her in from head to toe. She was in a long nightgown with a slit up the side and the barest of lace straps. She'd planned on wearing it tomorrow night, but after what he'd done, she wanted to show him how much she was grateful. How much she loved him for knowing, even more than she'd known herself, exactly what had been missing. What she'd still needed. A touch of her family. A piece to connect with again so she didn't feel adrift. She rarely did anymore with him there to moor her, but occasionally, she still felt like an orphan.

She sat down on the bed next to him, and one strap fell off her shoulder. He touched it with a long finger, tugging at it gently but not pulling it up or down.

"You look…" His voice fell away, deep and guttural, filled with emotions. "Like the embodiment of love."

Her heart, stomach, and core all spasmed at the same time.

She pulled back the sheet and was happy to see he was naked. She shifted until she was sitting on him, hips draped around his, the silk of the nightgown sliding over them both.

"For the merest of seconds, I thought you'd changed your mind…that you didn't want me," she said softly.

He looked angry, and one hand dug into her hip while the other went to the back of her neck and tugged her face closer, lips brushing across hers. "Baby, you're mine. We promised ourselves to each other, and I never go back on a promise."

"I don't want to be just a promise." His eyes narrowed as her fingers danced along his skin. "I want to be an absolute need. The oxygen you can't live without."

In one powerful move, he rolled them so he was on top.

"Accomplished. Because even knowing you're mine, even knowing we'll end every day like this, whenever you're not at my side, it feels like I can't fucking breathe until you're next to me again."

She kissed him, and he kissed her back. An exploding crescendo of love and hope and passion. A familiar rhythm they'd never had until they'd found it in each other's heartbeats. A rhythm that sang a truth their bodies had known first and their hearts and minds had discovered later—it was only when they were together that they were truly home.

♫ ♫ ♫

I hope you loved Fee and Asher's story of two broken, lonely souls finding their way to each other. Did you miss out on the ***Swan River* bonus material** showing what was going on with each of the Daisies the night Landry died? Get exclusive scenes from each of their points of views, including Landry's, with a newsletter sign-up:

https://bookhip.com/NQWSQLF

Or if you want the next clues in who murdered Landry all while finding out who is responsible for bursting Leya's belief about love and lust, keep reading the series today with ***CHERRY BRANDY***. It's an opposites-attract, forbidden romance that will keep you on your toes from beginning to end and drops a few more clues about Landry's killer.

Forbidden is another word for everything to lose.
Being on the run with only one bed is no excuse to touch her…

The Painted Daisies – Book Three

Cherry Brandy - Sample
CHAPTER ONE

Leya

STRONG ENOUGH

Performed by Sheryl Crow

EIGHT DAYS BEFORE

The text from US Secret Service Agent Holden Kent had Leya wishing she'd flung her phone down the toilet so he couldn't trace it. It also had her heart rate picking up in that irritating way it did whenever she had a conversation with the man. After more than two years of him being the lead—and often only—agent on her detail, you'd think her reaction to him would have faded. But it hadn't. Lately, she thought it was getting worse.

Even though she hadn't responded to his text, she knew she had mere minutes until he found her swaying on the tire swing in the yard of Number One Observatory Circle. Joe Biden had installed the swing during his vice presidency, leaving a note to his beloved wife engraved on the tree. *Beloved…* Loved... Wife.

Her stomach flipped, and nausea flew through it.

She wasn't ready to be any of those things.

And yet, the time had come for her to make a decision. She couldn't put it off any longer. Krish and his family needed a formal answer. Needed to move forward with an actual wedding and not the mere idea…the mere promise…of one that had been waiting in the background for a decade.

While she understood why they needed it, the idea only made her soul curl up inside her chest as if hiding from an intruder instead of blossoming as it should. Her sister-in-law, Devleena, had been so excited when she'd married Rishik that she'd strained a cheek muscle from smiling so hard. All thoughts of marriage did for Leya was make her eye twitch.

Holden appeared around the corner, and the sunlight hit his head, turning the strands a radiant gold. With his light-brown hair, blue eyes, and wide shoulders, he looked like the epitome of the stereotypical American legend. The captain of the football team. The small-town hero. Like a superhero you couldn't believe walked in your door. He had the muscles, the bulging biceps, and narrow hips that tights would show off perfectly. But it was his beautifully chiseled jawline and the aquamarine aura that surrounded him, flickering and growing whenever they were in the same space, that called to her the most. Her fingers itched to draw every curve along a clean canvas. It had been too long since she'd allowed her other artistic side free rein, and the need welled inside her almost as large as the attraction to the man storming toward her.

He was not smiling. He rarely smiled, as if doing so would be some violation of the Secret Service code, but as he drew closer, she could see there was more than just somberness surrounding him today. His dark brows were furrowed together, and his jaw was clenched tight. It felt…grim…and her heart beat wildly for a moment, thinking of the times he'd come to her with bad news. She wasn't sure she could take more.

He stopped a few feet away from her on the tire swing, watching as she swayed back and forth, assessing her as he did every single time he came into her presence. It was as if he took in every single molecule to make sure she was unharmed.

"You should have returned my text," he said, and the deep timbre of his voice settled over her like a blanket, strangely soothing while, at the same time, her entire being danced furiously, as if called to a chorus only he knew how to sing. He put his index finger to the two-way mic in his ear and said, "Firefly located on grounds. Standby."

"I'm allowed to move around the grounds without you following me," she replied, lifting her chin and arching one eyebrow in a challenge.

He was in a suit today, just like when he'd first shown up in Grand Orchard over two years ago after her father became the nominee for the vice presidency and the hate groups had come out in full force. It was perfectly tailored to hide his weapon. Perfectly tailored to sit across those broad shoulders like a second skin. It was a complete contrast to the black cargo pants, shirt, and military-grade boots he wore when on tour with her and the band so he blended in with the rest of their security team.

"Normally, you can," he groused, and she waited for him to finish his thought, and when he didn't, she prompted him.

"But?"

"For Greater Tomorrows has been ramping up."

Mention of the hate group had her dragging her bare feet into the grass and pulling the swing to a stop. Her chest tightened as it always did when they were mentioned.

"What have they done now?"

"There were pictures of the residence. They were of you and your family coming and going."

The tight feeling grew, fear and guilt twisting deeper, grabbing hold until she could barely breathe. Every time the group was mentioned, she was overcome with a terrible guilt that her family was the reason Landry had been killed. Fear that the FGT had mistaken her friend for her that awful day at Swan River Pond.

"What do the notes say?" She had to force the words out over the lump in her throat.

His jaw ticked again, and his hand went to the lapel of the suit jacket, tugging at it. "Does it matter? It's the normal spew of hatred. You don't want or need to hear it."

She didn't. And yet, she did. It was the same perverse reaction she had when there were negative posts or articles about her or any of The Painted Daisies. It was as if knowing what they'd said could somehow thicken her skin against them and take away the pain, but it never did.

Instead of responding or asking for more details, she just pushed the swing into motion again, sending the tire backward with as much force as she could. When she came forward, she almost slammed into Holden. He had to jump to the side so he wasn't knocked to the ground. She smirked. It was childish, but it felt good to get an unexpected reaction out of him. To prove he wasn't a robot.

She swung harder, and the limb on the tree groaned. Wood crackling.

Holden glanced up at the branch, assessing it.

"I'm not sure it was designed for a takeoff into space. Maybe take it easy."

As a little girl, one of her favorite things to do had been to leap from the swings, arms and legs spread wide, and then try to land perfectly on her feet. She rarely accomplished it, and she'd gotten a lot of bumps and bruises in her attempts. *You're not a little girl anymore.* Those had been her mother's exact words inside the private den of the residence with only the family present—well, the family and their lead agents. Like Holden. They'd been standing at the open door, within ear reach of the humiliating conversation.

She kicked back one more time, a big shove, and as she came forward, she let go, leaping from the swing and spreading her body wide. Unpracticed and much older, gravity took its hold fast. Her toes on her right foot barely caught the grass, and as she started to fall, she twisted, landing hard on her elbow in a way that made her wince and then burst out laughing.

Holden was there in a flash, feeling her arms, cursing under his breath. "Did you break anything?"

His face was so close to hers that if she leaned even slightly, she could kiss him. She wondered what it would feel like to have those stern-looking lines pressed against her soft ones. To have his focus on her one hundred percent but for a different reason. She was twenty-six, had been kissed multiple times, but never once had those kisses come close to making her feel like she did when *not* kissing him. In truth, she'd rarely felt any kind of sexual attraction to anyone, and certainly nothing like the heat coasting between them now so large and strong that if she reached out, it would burn her. Like touching the tip of a lit incense stick.

Instead of pulling back as she should, her body leaned forward, their lips nearly brushing. They were so close she could taste the wintergreen scent of his exhale. She swallowed it, longing and desire bubbling through her veins in an unfamiliar way even as her heart was screaming, *Danger!*

He stood up so fast it almost made her dizzy. As he stared down at her with brows drawn even more tightly together, his brilliant blue eyes flared with an emotion she wanted to think was something more than irritation before it disappeared. If she was going to be tormented by this ridiculous physical attraction to him, it only seemed fair that he be tortured as well.

Holden's face turned into an emotionless blank, and he said dryly, "Let's not do that again, shall we?"

Don't be so impulsive, Leya. Think before you act.

The words her mother had said so often it had almost become a mantra rushed over her, causing remorse to roll through her. Not only because of Krish, but because she liked Holden even when he irritated her, and kissing her would end his career. She wouldn't have him in her life at all if she pulled another stupid stunt like this.

She rolled onto her back, looking up at the blue sky littered with twirls and curls of white and hints of orange as the sun began to fade. More shapes and colors tempting her to paint but also to pick up the baby sitar *Nani* had taught her to play and add the stringed notes to the air.

She felt his gaze on her, as always, and just like normal,

she was confused by her reaction to it. When he looked at her...it was like he saw everything. Every pore, every vein, every muscle. But more importantly, every thought and wish—even the ones she thrust into the recesses of her mind, locking them away.

Wishes that went against everything that was right for her family. For her.

Desires she knew weren't logical and would lead to disaster.

The same disaster she feared awaited her friend and bandmate who'd let lust lead the way. Fiadh had gone from hating Asher to insisting she loved him in mere days. They'd gotten married only a handful of months after they'd started seeing each other, were even on their honeymoon at this moment while the band took a break from their hectic tour schedule. It was the perfect example of letting your libido rule, and she worried what would happen to Fee when it all came apart.

Leya's friends thought she didn't believe in love at all, but that wasn't true. She believed in *jeevansathi*—life partners, soulmates—but she also believed most people confused lust for love. You didn't just stumble onto your life partner and know instantaneously they were the one. It was more complicated than that.

Lust was the reason divorce rates were so high. People let it guide them, and then when it faded—as it always did—they had nothing holding them together. There was very little Leya and her mother agreed upon, but in this, they saw eye to eye perfectly. Finding your match was a process, one that often came with your family guiding the way.

Which brought her back to Krish. The man her family and the star charts had guided her to since she was a teenager. Where once the idea of him—of them—had brought her comfort and relief, these days, it brought tension...and an inexplicable feeling of loss.

Was it just the argument she'd had with Krish at the inaugural ball that still hovered between them causing these feelings? Or was it something different…something more?

Krish was close to reaching his dream—being appointed as an associate justice to a California appellate court—and he needed his wife at his side. Needed to appear grounded in family. A married man who was stable and reliable. Not a single man looking for a mate.

But she wasn't ready to give up the band. She wasn't ready for this future that had seemed to come too fast. What would she do with the endlessness of her days in California, waiting for Krish to come home? She had her art—the other half of her flighty, creative ways that *Nani* had encouraged while her mother had frowned—but she would miss the band if she gave them up. And they needed her. The band had lost too much already.

Her stomach twisted and turned. A decision that she'd made years ago, that she'd thought would always fit, now seemed like a shackle holding her back. She shouldn't feel that way about her life partner, should she?

"Are you staying at the residence this afternoon?" Holden asked.

He used the tone she hated the most. The one that made him sound like the robot she'd once accused him of being. Somewhere inside her, she knew it didn't fit him any more than the way his aura turned steely blue instead of flashing aquamarine at moments like these. She didn't understand how she knew these things about Holden when she could barely even see Krish's aura and never understood his tones.

Her thoughts were making her sick. She needed to escape them. An escape from not only the thoughts but her emotions and the weight of expectations.

With her bandmates all off in separate parts of the world during their break, she couldn't go to them, but she still had a friend in Washington D.C.

LEYA: Want to go out tonight?

LINCOLN: You feel like talking or dancing?

As the "playboy" son of the president of the United States, Lincoln Matherton understood the pressures that came from being so visibly on the political stage when all you really wanted to do was get lost in the images in your head. He understood being the only one in your family who didn't fit the mold of the rest.

LEYA: Can't we do both?

LINCOLN: Let's start at Pilot's for dinner, and if you still feel like dancing, we can hit EchoBar.

LEYA: I know you're trying to give up the bar scene.

LINCOLN: Bars, not dancing. I'll be eighty and still doing it.

LEYA: *** old man GIF ***

LINCOLN: *** nag GIF ***

LEYA: See you at 8?

LINCOLN: *** thumbs-up emoji***

She pulled herself off the grass, ignoring the tingling that went up her spine as the action brought her back into Holden's space. Ignoring the way his eyes trailed over her, leaving a mark.

"I'm going out with Lincoln."

His eyes narrowed, and she could almost hear his internal groan because he hated going to the clubs with her and Lincoln. Holden had never actually said he hated them, but it was the only time he ever trusted her to other men and women in the detail. She wondered if he'd hand her off tonight also. Wondered if, as always, she'd feel his absence. She didn't dare analyze why she missed him when he was gone. Doing so would bring her too close to that locked door in her mind. To the impulsiveness her mother accused her of and the emotions she accused her friends of—misreading lust for love.

Cherry Brandy – Sample
CHAPTER TWO

Holden

ON FIRE
Performed by Garbage

As Holden followed Leya back into the vice president's residence, only one thought was repeating through his skull—get away. He needed a break. He needed to put distance between himself and his protectee. She was driving him batty in more than one way.

She'd ignored his texts.

She'd left without him.

She'd almost kissed him.

And he wasn't sure which of those things pissed him off more.

What was worse, what had him screaming silently to himself, was the fact he hadn't pulled away immediately. The look in her eyes as she'd leaned forward, the way the natural honeysuckle essence of her had washed over him, making him hungry for everything she'd offered, had bent the last straw of his reserve. His control was fading.

He snapped himself back to the house as they approached, scanning the porch, the door, and the hedges. No movement at all. Emptiness. Her hips swayed as she mounted the steps, and his assessment fell apart. Never had he wanted to strip someone bare the way he craved doing with Leya Singh. It frustrated him and drove him right up to the edge every single day.

He should have walked away from her two years ago when the first hint of desire had slammed into him the moment he'd walked into the recording studio in Grand Orchard. Instead of turning tail, he'd seen it as just another challenge. Admitting an attraction to his protectee on his second protective assignment would have derailed his career in a heartbeat. His boss would never have trusted him again.

Rather than admit defeat, he'd simply added, *Don't look at Leya's mouth* and *Don't stare at her hips* to the mental task list he kept in his head. It was a mix of daily to-dos as well as short- and long-term goals he'd kept running for as long as he could remember. He'd already checked off thousands to be here—on one of the most coveted assignments in the Secret Service. Protecting the president, vice president, and their families was why people joined, and if they told you otherwise, they were lying. This was the job. The suit. The earpiece. You putting your life between the enemy and the leaders of the free world.

Leya reached for the handle of the back door, and he stepped in after her, casting a wide glance over the entrance, the stairs, and the hall. He didn't have to do any of it, as there were cameras all over the place, watching twenty-four-seven, but the continual assessment was a built-in habit after two years of being the only Secret Service agent on her detail. She had a private security team, one he respected even though there'd been plenty of reasons not to, but it was never the same as Holden checking the boxes himself.

When Leya had insisted on having only one agent with her, the Secret Service had balked, but she'd held firm. He never minded being a lone wolf, even preferred having the control all in his pocket. Preferred it so much that when Leya came back to D.C., and he had to revert into being a pack animal—the one who wasn't in charge—his mind and body rebelled at the idea.

As soon as they'd arrived in D.C. after Fiadh's wedding in Boston, his boss had called him in and said, "Take some time off." Most people wouldn't have balked when the special agent in charge of the vice-presidential protective division gave them a command, but Holden had insisted he didn't need a vacation.

He'd told himself it was because he didn't want to look weak, but really, the weakness was in staying. He couldn't stomach the thought of another agent watching over her, staring at the full lower lip hovering over a delightful cleft, or watching the way her hair danced around sharp cheekbones when she talked, or being mesmerized by the way her long fingers played with the rows of leather and silver bracelets dangling up and down her wrists. He didn't want another agent getting the text that begged for them to show up...

Jesus. He really needed to get a grip.

He watched her almost dance the way up the stairs, feet light and graceful. Her entire body would be tucked up against Lincoln Matherton's tonight. He'd be the one surrounded by her sweet, floral scent, and even though Holden knew her well enough to know she wasn't interested in Lincoln the way half the planet seemed to be, it would still be a challenge to stay focused. Instead of having his eyes on the room, the people, the movement of the crowd, they'd be drawn to her hips slammed against another man's.

As her lead agent, he was usually with her when she went out, regardless of the time of day. When he was the only USSS agent on tour with her, he didn't have a choice. But today, he did. Technically, his shift ended in thirty minutes, and he was suddenly, desperately in need of the space his boss had offered. He needed to get his priorities in check—his dick in check. His head back on straight.

"You'll have someone else with you tonight," he called after her.

She turned at the landing, and brown eyes ringed in deep, lush lashes looked back at him with a dash of sorrow and regret filling them. "I figured."

He frowned. She'd known he'd leave her? Why did that stab at him? "Well, now you know for sure." The snip erupted from him before he could stop it.

Her eyes flared with a hint of the anger he was stupid enough to like seeing. It happened so little. Normally, she was even-tempered, like the rest of her family. Calm in the face of the storms during the election as well as the attacks on her bandmates. But he'd been the one to see her break in her private moments. Not another agent. Not even her friends.

"You don't owe me an explanation, Special Agent Kent. Any *body* will do, right?" It was the formal use of his name instead of Holden or Captain Annoying as much as her arched brow and the emphasis on the word *body* that had him wanting to take the stairs two at a time and remove the look with his mouth pressed against hers.

He turned on his heel and exited the building.

Outside, he inhaled deeply, centering himself and attempting to clear the haze of lust and anger and frustration. He scanned the surroundings, noting the buzz of the lawnmower and the crush of steps on gravel as one of the uniformed division officers came around the house.

The first time he'd shown up at the Queen-Anne home on the grounds of the National Observatory, he'd been overwhelmed with the beauty of the place. The curved tower and pointed roof along with the wraparound porch full of lush wicker seating were graceful and elegant. But these days, he barely noticed them. Instead, he only saw what was out of place. The furniture that had been moved. The gardener who wasn't supposed to be on duty. Or the newly arrived agent, like the woman walking toward him.

Once he'd gone through the handoff checklist and stalked toward the command center, he almost changed his mind and went back. It was this reaction that pushed him finally over the edge, dialing his boss.

"I'm calling about that vacation you suggested," Holden said, cheek clenched and hating the words. Hating that he was asking to be relieved, and wanting to blame Leya for his weakness, but knowing it wouldn't be fair. This wasn't on her. This was all him.

Although, she had been the one to lean into him…to almost brush their lips together. He forced his brain to stop before it traveled further into the realm of what-ifs.

"Ardell will take over as lead while you're out. Go visit your family. Forget the job for a few days," Roy Camp tossed back.

Camp likely knew Holden wouldn't be able to forget the job. That he'd actually worry about it the entire time he was away, because they both lived and breathed the USSS. That was why Camp was forty and still single. When Holden's dad had been an agent, it had almost broken his parents' marriage. It was why his dad was watching carefully to see if Holden had reached his own tipping point. And maybe he had. But there was no item on his mental goal list beyond becoming lead agent for the president, and he was so close he could taste it. Every task he'd given himself since he was seven years old had led here. To this objective. To a life of honor and service.

As he got into the metallic-blue 1968 Pontiac Firebird he and his dad had restored when he was barely a teen, Holden debated heading home to his condo near the river. The place would smell stale after being vacant for months, and he wasn't in the mood to clean it. He needed someone to interrupt his solitude so he wouldn't wallow in thoughts of things that would never be.

So, as the engine rumbled to life, and he pulled away from the guard station at the entrance to the observatory, he headed over the Francis Scott Key Memorial Bridge to his parents' home. He let the schedule he'd had in his brain for the next two weeks—Leya's schedule and the duty roster—empty, and his stomach tightened. Uncomfortable with the blank spaces, he attempted to fill them. Maybe he'd paint the condo or redo the scuffed wooden floors.

It was with a strange sense of relief that he pulled into the brick-and-white colonial in Arlington. It had been his parents' home for the last ten years, allowing his mom to finally see her landscape designs come to fruition—a park-like masterpiece. The mix of plants in the backyard was a bird and butterfly haven, and the enormous, multi-leveled patio was perfect for the entertaining his dad so enjoyed doing.

For as long as Holden could remember, their house had been full of his father's Army, Secret Service, and then National Guard pals—men, women, and their families who served a country that seemed to be falling to its knees these days but was still trying to raise its head proudly. Just like Leya Singh was bringing him to his knees, and he was stubbornly trying to keep himself from falling over completely.

He let himself into the house with his key, and the noise of pots and pans rang down the long hall to greet him. Despite the dark-wood floors and mahogany wainscotting, the space was still light because of the number of oversized windows the house boasted.

"Hello!" he called out.

"Holden?" His mom's face appeared at the end of the hallway as she wiped her hands on a towel.

A smile burst over her face, echoing in her eyes. Only the faint lines around them and the slight sag to her jawline proved she was over fifty—little details most people wouldn't notice, assuming she was much younger. Her dark hair was still thick and full without a hint of gray, and she was fit and tall with hazel eyes that typically showed humor more than any other emotion.

"Come give me a hug!" she demanded.

"Let me put my piece away," he said.

She nodded, retreating to the kitchen.

He slipped off his dress shoes and suit jacket before going into his dad's study where he added his Glock to the stack of weapons in the gun safe. The house was filled with the smells of his childhood, and when he found his mom in the kitchen, it was to find her adding shrimp to a pot of *fideuà*.

The distinct saffron and fish stock aromas comforted him in a way nothing had all day.

He squeezed his mom's shoulders, and she draped her arm around his waist and hugged him back.

"Looks like I made it home just in time," he said. He kissed her temple and stepped away, asking, "Dad home?"

"Outside, putting together my new pizza oven."

Holden smiled for the first time in probably days, the muscles groaning from lack of use. "How long are you going to keep this one?"

She swatted him with the towel she'd had resting over her shoulder.

"I can't help it if the others were shit."

"Wow, cussing and everything. You must be serious."

She rolled her eyes.

"Go tell your dad dinner will be ready in about ten minutes." He headed for the French doors as she added, "And then you can tell us what's eating at you enough to bring you out to Arlington."

He didn't respond. He'd never understand how he could be in his mom's presence mere minutes, and she'd know exactly what he was feeling. A maternal instinct, he supposed, or just thirty-four years of living with his father who also kept his emotions buried for his job.

As Holden stepped out onto the wooden deck, the warm, heavy air hit him. It was early enough in September that summer hadn't let go yet, and the humidity was clinging to the sky even though the sun had fallen below the horizon.

His dad looked up from a large stone contraption where he was using an Allen wrench to tighten a bolt. The strings of fairy lights hanging on the latticework above the deck barely broke through the darkness, but it was enough to show the smile that hit his dad's face at the sight of him.

"Holden! This is a surprise!"

Holden rolled up his sleeves as he joined him. "How many ovens has she actually gone through?"

"I think this is the fifth one, but she swears it's the last," he said with a chuckle.

Even in jeans and a T-shirt he rarely wore, his dad still had a military aura to him. It wasn't just that he kept himself in shape, unlike some of his peers. It was a strength and power that emanated from him. Or maybe it was just the hair shaved so short you could barely notice the white that had crept into the light brown.

"Grab us a couple of beers," his dad said, waving to the mini fridge set in the outdoor kitchen.

"Mom says dinner is almost ready."

"Damn. I was almost done," his dad replied.

Holden pulled out two local IPAs as his dad rose from his work to join him. In general, Holden didn't drink, only a beer on the rare occasion, but he felt the need for one tonight. He needed to steady nerves that had been shaken by a dark-haired beauty and an almost kiss he couldn't burn from his brain.

They popped the tops and snapped the lids with identical movements into the open garbage can. They took a swig, and then his dad's eyes settled on him.

"How long will you be in D.C.?"

"Most likely till the end of the month, but I'm taking a couple of weeks off."

His dad's hand paused with the beer bottle a few inches from his mouth, taking him in, brows frowning.

"What the hell you going to do with time off?"

His dad wasn't asking because he expected Holden to be the job. He was asking because, like his mom, he knew there had to have been something wrong for him to take a vacation. Something pushing him to walk away. It wasn't like he had a girlfriend he was running home to or a pile of friends waiting to head to the beach with him.

He'd given all those things up for the dream he was living.

And he hadn't ever cared. Hadn't ever looked back.

When he didn't respond, the frown on his dad's face grew, and he demanded, "Want to tell me what's really eating at you?"

He wasn't sure he could. Wasn't sure he even knew the whole truth of it himself—not in any way he wanted to admit. But he was saved from responding by his mom popping her head out. "Dinner, gentleman. Before it gets cold."

They headed into the house where his mom had placed a colorful platter in the middle of a walnut table that had moved around with them for as long as Holden could remember. It had grooves and marks showing its age but was stained and polished as if it were brand new.

The three of them dished up in a comfortable silence. One that often settled down whenever his sister wasn't with them. It was Gia who normally kept the conversation going non-stop. And if she wasn't filling the house with her voice, there was usually a podcast or music blaring until someone finally hollered at her to turn it off.

"How's G?" he asked, deflecting from the conversation he didn't really want to have.

"Still floating around the globe like a waif," his dad said, the furrow in his brow growing.

"Just because you don't understand her job, doesn't mean it's not a real one," his mother scolded before turning to him and saying, "She's in Tennessee at the moment, but she's been all over the Midwest, doing a study on dude ranches."

Holden almost choked on the piece of shrimp he'd put in his mouth. "Dude ranches? Like in *City Slickers*?"

His father's deep laugh joined his. "You see my confusion. Before that, she was in Brazil, talking about deforestation."

"She's an agricultural journalist," his mom retorted. "She may not be saving the world with guns like you two bohunks, but she *is* trying to make sure we have one to save."

That put both Holden and his dad in their place. He hated to think about his beautiful little sister traveling around the world to some pretty unsavory locations, all in the name of journalism, so he chose not to think about it at all.

"You still on Leya Singh's detail?" his dad asked.

He nodded, shoveling food into his mouth so he didn't have to respond right away.

"I heard that sniveling weasel of a man heading up For Greater Tomorrows is about to announce his candidacy for president," his dad said.

Holden nearly choked, grabbed a swig of beer, and then looked at his father with narrowed eyes. "Where'd you hear that?"

"Meeting at the Pentagon. Smythe's been schmoozing military leaders to gain their support."

Jesus. Holden shouldn't have taken time off. He thought back to the images Camp had sent to the detail today of the Singhs coming and going from the residence and the white-supremacist, racist comments that had come with them. The USSS couldn't tie them to John Smythe and FGT directly, but Holden hadn't spent two years on the FGT case in Nevada without knowing what the man was capable of. His fingers itched to pick up the phone and call Ardell to check in on Leya.

Would he ever forgive himself if he wasn't there when something went down?

He already had a list of things he felt responsible for, including Landry Kim's death and Paisley Kim's attack.

"Anyone actually falling for his act?" Holden asked.

"Unfortunately, you'd be surprised."

It turned Holden's stomach. If that man was in charge of the country, they'd become another Nazi state. Holden was damn sure he'd never step in to take a bullet for the man. He'd lose his career. It was the only thing that would ever make him walk away from the Secret Service.

"He say anything directly against the vice president?" Holden asked, immediately going into investigator mode.

His dad raised a brow at the ridiculousness of his

question.

But there was something eating at Holden about the pictures and the timing of Smythe's latest news. Something he couldn't put his finger on. Something that made him itch to get back to work.

As if reading his mind, his father asked, "You going to re-up for her detail next month?"

Yes was the instant response that came to him, born of years of wanting this, but then he remembered what had him calling Camp and making the journey over the river to his parents' place. The almost kiss.

Could he get a different assignment if he walked away from this one? Would it be a better one or a worse one? He'd been on Leya's detail for over two years. He'd joined her right before the Democratic convention, been with her in the dark months after Landry's murder, and had trailed after her to D.C. once Matherton and her father had won the election. He'd stood by as she mourned her friend and supported her family with a grace not many had, especially not in their twenties. He'd tagged after her as she went from her art studio in Truxton Circle to the bars and clubs of D.C. It had been painful to watch her bright light as it flickered, sometimes going out when she cried, sometimes shining so radiantly it was nearly blinding when she laughed and danced and sang.

It had always been easier to watch when she was blinding, because he'd been less tempted to wrap his arms around her and provide comfort. Less tempted to kiss away the tears traveling down her heart-shaped face. She hadn't cried today. Her deep-brown eyes had been dry, but her light had still flickered. It had snagged at him as it had every time he'd seen it happen.

"Is it getting to you?" his dad asked. "The lifestyle?"

The unspoken reminder of the threats the Secret Service life had brought to his parents' marriage hung in the air. His father had once told him it was the hardest job he'd ever done, and that was no little thing. Not when his dad had spent his entire life in one form of military or the other and was now serving as vice chief of the National Guard Bureau.

"It's not the same for me as it was for you," Holden replied. "I'm not married with little kids at home."

His dad raised a brow, knowing he'd evaded the real question. But his mom just sighed, "You'll never be married with little kids at home if you continue this way. Which means no grandchildren for me to spoil."

"Vera," his dad said, the warning clear. His parents had always let Holden and his sister make their own decisions about their careers and love lives. If either he or Gia asked them for advice, they gave it, but they never forced any expectations on them. Saying she wanted grandkids was probably the closest his mom had ever gotten to saying she wanted something different for him.

He'd let Gia pick up that mantle. A wife and kids did not fit with his life goals.

Neither did an almost kiss with a certain rock star.

"I'm getting too attached," Holden finally breathed out. His eyes met his dad's, and he knew his father understood what he was saying. Living and breathing someone else's life meant you knew more about them than you did anyone else on earth. You saw every emotion. You felt every emotion. And yet, your job was to be perfectly detached, to assess only the threats, stay alert and on top of each possible scenario that could hurt your protectee, and stop the threat before it ever materialized.

"Damn hard not to after two years," his dad said.

"You were with Gore for two and Bush for one. Did you get too attached?" Holden asked.

"I wasn't the lead agent on either of those details. They knew me, and I knew them, but I rotated out with the rest of the team. I wasn't living their lives like you're living hers," his dad said, pausing. "And neither of them was as beautiful as she is."

"Howie," his mom tsked, but then she looked at Holden curiously. "Is that it? Are you attracted to her?"

There was no judgment in his mom's tone, just curiosity.

"No," he said, another automatic response, but he wondered if his parents could see through the lie. If they'd ever been in the same room with him and Leya, he was sure they'd see how every single cell in his body seemed drawn to hers. He could find her in a crowded space in mere seconds. He'd found her today on the tire swing without even looking up her phone's location. It felt wrong. And right. And the right was what bothered him the most.

KEEP READING CHERRY BRANDY RIGHT NOW ON AMAZON.

Message from the Author

Thank you for taking the time to read the second book in *The Painted Daisies* series inspired by The Brother's Bright and Valerie Miller's "Yours Alone." I hope you adored how Fee's and Asher's broken hearts healed each other, and I hope the mix of music and words in this story burns a memory into your soul you'll think about every time you hear one of the songs from now on.

Green Jewel is the second book in a connected series. While each couple will have their own suspense plot line and their own happily ever after, you'll need to read the entire series to find out just what happened that day at Swan River Pond with Landry. The good news is that the rest of the series is coming to you this year, and you can order the next book, ***Cherry Brandy***, now.

If you like talking about music, books, and just what it takes to get us through this wild ride called life as much as I do, maybe you should join my Facebook readers' group, **LJ's Music & Stories**, and join the conversations there today. Hopefully, the group can help *YOU* through your life in some small way.

Regardless if you join or not, I'd love for you to tell me what you thought of the book by reaching out to me personally. I'd be honored if you took the time to leave a review on BookBub, Amazon, and/or Goodreads, but even more than that, I hope you enjoyed it enough to tell a friend about it.

If you still can't get enough (ha!), you could also sign up for my newsletter where you'll receive music-inspired scenes weekly and be entered into a giveaway each month for a chance at a signed paperback by yours truly. Plus, you'll be able to keep tabs on all my stories, including fun facts about The Painted Daisies and more.

Finally, I just wanted to say that my wish for you is a healthy and happy journey. May you live life resiliently, with hope and love leading the way!

Acknowledgments

I'm so very grateful for every single person who has helped me on this book journey. If you're reading these words, you *ARE* one of those people. I wouldn't be an author if people like you didn't decide to read the stories I crafted, so THANK YOU!

In addition to my lovely readers, I'd be ridiculous not to thank these extra folks who've made this journey possible for me:

My husband, who means more to me than I can explain in one or a thousand sentences, and who has never, ever let me give up on this dream, doing everything he could to make it come true, and then CHEERING from the rooftops at my tiniest success. Here's to you being a "Kept Man" someday, my love.

Our child, Evyn, owner of Evans Editing, who remains my harshest and kindest critic. Thank you for helping me shape my stories and reading this one a million and one times until I got it right.

The folks at That's What She Said Publishing, who took a gamble on me, this wild idea I had for a series, and then were determined to see the best in all of it even when I chewed my lips to smithereens worrying that it would fail.

My sister, Kelly, who made sure I hit the publish button the very first time and reads my crappy first drafts and still loves my stories anyway.

My parents and my father-in-law, who are my biggest fans and bring my books to the strangest places, telling everyone they know (and don't know) about my stories.

My dear author friend, Kathryn Nolan, who stepped in to sensitivity read some scenes to ensure my badass bisexual rock star was everything she should be.

The talented Emily Wittig, who made the perfect covers for this heart-wrenching series.

Jenn at Jenn Lockwood Editing Services, who is always patient with my gazillion missing commas, my hatred of the semicolon, and scattered deadlines.

Karen Hrdlicka, who ensures the final versions of my books are beautiful and reminds me hyphens aren't always optional.

To the entire group of beautiful humans in LJ's Music & Stories who love and support me, I can't say enough how deeply grateful I am for each and every one of you.

To the host of bloggers who have shared my stories, become dear friends, and continue to make me feel like a rock star every day, thank you, thank you, thank you!

To a host of authors, including Stephanie Rose, Lucy Score, Erika Kelly, Hannah Blake, Annie Dyer, and AM Johnson, who have shown me that dear friends are more important than any paralyzing moment in this wild publishing world, MWAH!

To all my ARC readers who have become sweet friends, thanks for knowing just what to say to scare away my writer insecurities.

And I can't leave without a special thanks to Leisa C., Rachel R., and Lisa K. for being three of the biggest cheerleaders I could ever hope to have on this wild ride called life.

I love you all!

About the Author

Award winning author, LJ Evans, lives in Northern California with her husband, child, and the three terrors called cats. She's been writing, almost as a compulsion, since she was a little girl and will often pull the car over to write when a song lyric strikes her. A former first-grade teacher, she now spends her free time reading and writing, as well as binge-watching original shows like *Wednesday, Ted Lasso, Veronica Mars,* and *Stranger Things.*

If you ask her the one thing she won't do, it's pretty much anything that involves dirt—sports, gardening, or otherwise. But she loves to write about all of those things, and her first published heroine was pretty much involved with dirt on a daily basis, which is exactly why LJ loves fiction novels—the characters can be everything you're not and still make their way into your heart.

Her novel, ***CHARMING AND THE CHERRY BLOSSOM***, was *Writer's Digest* Self-Published E-book Romance of the Year in 2021. For more information about LJ, check out any of these sites:

www.ljevansbooks.com

FaceBook Group: LJ's Music & Stories

LJ Evans on Amazon, Bookbub, and Goodreads

@ljevansbooks on Facebook, Instagram, TikTok, and Pinterest

Books by LJ

Standalone

After All the Wreckage

A single-dad, small-town romantic suspense

He's a broody bar owner raising his siblings. She's a scrappy PI who's loved him since she was a teenager. When his brother disappears, she forces aside years of pining and family secrets to help him.

The Last One You Loved

A single-dad, small-town romance

He's a small-town sheriff with a secret that can unravel their worlds. She's an ER resident running from a costly mistake. Coming home will only mean heartache…unless they let forgiveness heal them both.

Charming and the Cherry Blossom

A contemporary, new adult romance

Today was a fairy tale…I inherited a fortune from a dad I never knew, and a thoroughly charming guy asked me out. But like all fairy tales, mine has a dark side...and my happily ever after may disappear with the truth.

Perfectly Fine

A Hollywood, second-chance romance

He's a charming, A-list actor at the top of his game. She's a determined, small-town screenwriter hoping for a deal. They form an unexpected connection until secrets ruin their future.

My Life as an Album Series

My Life as a Country Album — Cam's Story

A boy-next-door, small-town romance

This is tomboy Cam's diary-style, coming-of-age story about growing up loving the football hero next door. She vowed to love him forever. But when fate comes calling, will she ever find a heart to call home? Warning: Tears may fall.

My Life as a Pop Album — Mia & Derek

A rock star, road-trip romance

Bookworm Mia is trying to put years of guilt behind her when soulful musician Derek Waters strolls into her life and turns it upside down. Once he's seen her, Derek can't walk away unless Mia comes with him. But what will happen when their short time together comes to an end?

My Life as a Rock Album — Seth & PJ

A second-chance, antihero romance

Recovering addict Seth Carmen is a trash artist who knows he's better off alone. But when he finds and loses the love of his life, he can't help sending her a host of love letters to try to win her back. Can Seth prove to PJ they can make broken beautiful?

My Life as a Mixtape — Lonnie & Wynn

A single-dad, rock star romance

Lonnie's always seen relationships as a burden instead of a gift, and picking up the pieces his sister leaves behind is just one of the reasons. When Wynn enters his life just as her world is disintegrating, their mixed-up pasts give way to new beginnings neither of them saw coming.

My Life as a Holiday Album – 2nd Generation

A small-town romance

Come home for the holidays with this heartwarming, full-length standalone full of hidden secrets, true love, and the real meaning of family. Perfect for lovers of *Love Actually* and Hallmark movies, this sexy story intertwines the lives of six couples as they find their way to their happily ever afters with the help of.

My Life as an Album Series Box Set

1st four Album books plus an exclusive novella

In the exclusive novella, *This Life with Cam*, Blake Abbott writes to Cam about just what it was like to grow up in the shadow of her relationship with Jake and just when he first fell for the little girl with the popsicle-stained lips. Can he show Cam that she isn't broken?

The Anchor Novels

Guarded Dreams — Eli & Ava

A grumpy-sunshine, military romance

He's a grumpy Coast Guard focused on a life of service. She's a feisty musician searching for stardom. Nothing about them fits, and yet their attraction burns wild when fate lands them in the same house for the summer.

Forged by Sacrifice — Mac & Georgie

A roommates-to-lovers, military romance

He's a driven military man zeroed in on a new goal. She's a struggling law student running from her family's mistakes. They're entirely wrong for each other…except their bodies disagree. When they end up as roommates, how long will it take before intense attraction shatters their resistance?

Avenged by Love — Truck & Jersey

A fake-marriage, military romance

When a broody military man and a quiet bookstore clerk end up in the same house, it isn't only attraction that erupts. Now, the only way to ensure she gets the care she needs is to marry her.

Damaged Desires — Dani & Nash

A frenemy, military romance

A grumpy Navy SEAL reeling from losing his team fights an intense attraction for his best friend's fiery sister. Until a stalker put her in his sights, and then he'll do anything to protect her, even if it means exposing all his secrets.

Branded by a Song — Brady & Tristan

A single-mom, rock star romance

He's a country-rock legend searching for inspiration. She's a Navy SEAL's widow determined to honor his memory while raising their daughter. Neither believes the intense attraction tugging at them can lead to more until their futures are twined by her grandmother's will.

Tripped by Love – Cassidy & Marco

A broody-bodyguard, single-mom romance

He's her brother's broody bodyguard with secrets he can't share. She's a busy single mom with a restaurant to run. They're just friends until a little white lie changes everything.

The Anchor Novels: The Military Bros Box Set

The 1st 3 books + an exclusive novella

Heartfelt reads full of love, sacrifice, and family. The perfect book boyfriends for a binge read.

The Anchor Suspense Novels

Unmasked Dreams — Violet & Dawson

A second-chance, age-gap romance

Violet and Dawson had a heart-stopping attraction they were compelled to deny. When they're tossed together again, it proves nothing has changed—except the lab she's built in the garage and the secrets he's keeping. When she stumbles into his dark world, Dawson breaks old promises to keep her safe.

Crossed by the Stars — Jada & Dax

A second-chance, forced-proximity romance

Family secrets meant Dax and Jada's teenaged romance was an impossibility. A decade later, the scars still remain, so neither is willing to give in to their tantalizing chemistry. But when a shadow creeps out of Jada's past, seeking retribution, it's Dax who shows up to protect her. And suddenly, it's hard to see a way out without permanent damage to their bodies and souls.

Disguised as Love — Cruz & Raisa

A chemistry-filled, enemies-to-lovers romance

Surly FBI agent, Cruz Malone, is determined to bring down the Leskov clan for good. If that means he has to arrest or bed the sexy blond scientist of the family, so be it. Too bad Raisa has other ideas. There's no way she's just going to sit back and let the infuriating agent dismantle her world... or her heart.

The Painted Daisies

Interconnected series with an all-female rock band, the alpha heroes who steal their hearts, and suspense that will leave you breathless. Each story has its own HEA.

Sweet Memory

Paisley and Jonas's opposite-attract, second-chance romance.

The world's sweetest rock star falls for a troubled music producer whose past comes back to haunt them.

Green Jewel

Fiadh and Asher's enemies-to-lovers, single-dad romance.

He did it. She'll prove it. Her body's reaction to him be damned.

Cherry Brandy

Leya and Holden's opposites-attract, forbidden, bodyguard romance.

Being on the run with only one bed is no excuse to touch her... until touching is the only choice.

Blue Marguerite

Adria and Ronan's celebrity, second-chance, frenemy romance.

She vowed to never forgive him... Not even when he offers answers her family desperately seeks.

Royal Haze

Nikki and D'Angelo's bodyguard, on-the-run romance.

He was ready to torture, steal, and kill to defend the world he believed in. What he wasn't prepared for… was her.

Free Stories

FREE with newsletter signup

https://www.ljevansbooks.com/freeljbooks

Perfectly Fine – A Hollywood, second-chance romance

He's a charming, A-list actor at the top of his game. She's a determined, small-town screenwriter hoping for a deal. They form an unexpected connection until secrets ruin their future.

Rumor – A small-town, rock-star romance

There's only one thing rock star Chase Legend needs to ring in the new year, and that's to know what Reyna Rossi tastes like. After ten years, there's no way he's letting her escape the night without their souls touching. Reyna has other plans. After all, she doesn't need the entire town wagging their tongues about her any more than they already do.

Love Ain't – A friends-to-lovers, cowboy romance

Reese knows her best friend and rodeo king, Dalton Abbott, is never going to fall in love, get married, and have kids. He's left so many broken hearts behind that there's gotta be a museum full of them somewhere. So when he gives her a look from under the brim of his hat, promising both jagged relief and pain, she knows better than to give in.

The Long Con – A sexy, antihero romance

Adler is after his next big payday. Then, Brielle sways in with her own game in play, and those aquamarine-colored eyes almost make him forget his number-one rule. But she'll learn… love isn't a con he's interested in.

The Light Princess – An old-fashioned fairy tale

A princess who glows with a magical light, a kingdom at war, and a kiss that changes the world. This is an extended version of the fairy tale twined through the pages of *Charming and the Cherry Blossom.*

Made in United States
Orlando, FL
02 October 2024

52253135R00219